TIED

with

TWINE

TIED with TWINE

a novel

PAM RECORDS

Editors: Liesel Schmidt & Regina Cornell
Cover and book design: Robin Vuchnich

Printed in the United States of America

Library of Congress Control Number: 2019934545

First Edition

Chapter 1

Hegewisch, Illinois 1920

Halina shoved the dirty sheet in the tin washtub as quickly as she could. Water splashed over the side, puddling at her feet, then snaking to the drain in the middle of the basement floor. She started to scoot out of the way, but realized it was a little late for that. She was already as soggy as a dead bird in a gutter, all mud and suds, from her bloomers to her work boots. In her rush, she had been sloppy and would likely catch hell for it. Too bad. She wanted to be done. At this rate, she'd never be through with the laundry—not to mention the rest of the chores—in time for tonight's poker game at the shanty. She'd better step on it.

She kneaded at the sheet as if it were bread dough. Shove down, fold over. Again. She closed her eyes and hummed a polka. That usually kept the heebie-jeebies from crawling up her arms, but not today. She hated doing the sheets. The dribbles, smears, and stains told stories too intimate for a stranger to hear. She knew what happened in bed in the dark when no one could see—except maybe the mice in the walls or God, hovering near the ceiling as if he had nothing better to do. Sometimes she heard the giggles and the moans, then the threats and slaps, flesh on tender flesh. The sounds seemed to bubble up from the sheets. Either she was crazy—just like Ma—or she had an imagination with one or two colors too many. Didn't matter which it was; she still had sheets to scrub. There were also lamps to fill with kerosene and rugs to take out back and beat.

And where was Patcja? Halina always got stuck with the hard scrubbing. Patcja washed the dainties—the kind the women with bobbed hair and pleated skirts dropped off in their laundry baskets. Not once since Ma had started taking in laundry had Patcja done her share of the helping. Halina paused to listen for footsteps on the floor above, the joists creaking under her sister's generous curves.

Maybe she'd have to tell her sister—once again—that she wasn't too fragile, or too perfect, to help. But then again, Patcja's damned breathing spells did seem to be getting worse—just as Baba had warned them. *Patcja will gasp for air, and there will only be smoke.* Baba's creepy predictions were always hanging in the air over them, dripping dread, like birds crapping as they flew by. Too bad the predictions were as close to right as mumbo jumbo could be. That old woman's Gypsy ways were as powerful as ever—even if the rest of her earthly frame was straddling the fence between the living and St. Florian's cemetery.

Halina sighed and reached for the bar of borax and the scrub brush. Her pruney fingers, numb from the cold water, dropped the hunk of harsh-smelling soap. She fished for it, mumbling a string of blasphemies, including some new ones she was breaking in so they would just roll off her tongue, natural-like, when she needed them. Maybe at poker tonight. If—

Suddenly, she saw a hand. It was under the suds, just below the surface of the water. Not a *real* hand, just a handprint on the sheet. It was smeared, formed by something dark and reddish-brown. *Blood? Disgusting.* What trouble had Ma brought home now? Again?

She looked closer. Small blue letters ran along the frayed hem of the sheet. "HAWTHORNE HOTEL." Wasn't that the seedy place north of town, on the way to East Chicago—the one where bootleggers and their women stayed? Sure. She could see the newspaper stories in her head. Stach was always saying to stay away from there.

Everyone with any sense in their heads stayed far away.

She scooted backward, but she could still see the handprint—small, with fingers outstretched. Maybe too small to be a man's hand. It might even be too small to belong to a woman, she thought. But her ma had little hands like that. Short, stubby fingers—just like that.

Really, this sheet could belong to any of the snooty ladies—or their hired help—who dropped off their baskets of soiled clothes, she told herself as she tried to remember which of the laundry regulars might have dropped off a basket yesterday. Queenie, Ditzy, or Darling? Mama Bella or Floozy-Flora? Floozy's clothes were so pretty, with lots of lace, fringe, and fancy tassels in just the right places. Oh, how she hoped something hadn't happened to Floozy.

She'd seemed fine when she came to the house on her usual day to drop off a basket. Halina remembered Ma meeting her at the front door before the doorbell even buzzed. Ma had stood in front of the open door, as though she was blocking the view. Of course, she didn't want her favorite customer to see inside this pitiful house.

"Hello, Missy Flora. Good day! A very good day to you. A full basket, I see. Good, good," Ma had said in that sugary-sweet voice she used for customers. She probably thought it hid the nervous tremor that sometimes crawled out of her throat, but it didn't.

After Flora had left, Halina had tried to take the basket. "I'll start on these," she had said.

"No—I'll do them," Ma had snapped, pulling the basket away, trying to hide it behind her back as if it held something wicked—or horribly contagious.

Halina wondered if Ma knew about some nastiness that Flora was involved in or *with*—someone who had left a bloody handprint. This didn't look like ordinary time-of-the-month bleeding, either. Maybe there had been an accident or someone had been hurt. Perhaps some man liked to play rough with his woman—whether it was a wifely kind of woman or the kind that was bought. Maybe he got carried away or he had a temper. *Or worse*, she thought. More possibilities appeared in her imagination, each more hideous than the last. Maybe it was some sickness, a gut-eating disease eating away at a poor soul.

She looked again at the sheet but kept the handprint under the surface of the water, as if the water could keep the trapped evil from escaping. The water seemed to magnify the handprint, but it was still oddly small. Maybe a child's hand. *Holy Mother Mary*, thought Halina, *please not a child.*

Halina fumbled with the matchbox hanging from a ribbon on her neck. The worn textures were comforting. The sounds of rattling seeds and dried petals, bug wings and pebbles were muffled and sweet. She imagined an invisible protective net snaking out from the matchbox and cloaking her. The amulet, a gift from Baba, was full of prayers and conjured curses, Old Country nonsense. *How silly. What am I worried about?*

She scrubbed harder and faster, in a hurry to be done with this dadblasted sheet. She didn't want a mystery wallowing around in her head. She sure as hell didn't need to get all riled up and nervous, tugging on a spirit doctor's handiwork for protection. There was likely some innocent explanation behind this filthy sheet, but it was none of her business, anyway.

Sounds bounced around the cinder block walls. The coal furnace took up most of the basement and made so much noise that it was impossible to think. Kneeling on the cement floor was putting a crick in her back, too.

Get on with it, she thought. *Poker tonight. I need to play and win. Win big.* She wondered just how much a train ticket east would cost. She had no idea. Did she have enough yet? Maybe after tonight. Maybe this was the last sheet she would ever need to wash.

In circles, then up and down in long strokes, she scrubbed. More water splashed. This time, the trickles across the floor seemed pink, like something from a fairy story, like the kind Ma used to tell them when they were little and the world was safe, a floating island attached by a long ribbon of memories to Poland, where the souls were left. She shook her head, as if that could clear her mind of the nonsense.

"You've always got your head in the clouds or some made-up world where you can be something you're not," Ma was always lecturing. It never made much sense to Halina. She knew she could never be anything here in this God-forsaken swamp on the edge of Chicago. And that's why she was saving for a train ticket, her escape from the Polish stink that clung to her skin and clothes, her hair, and the fringe of eyelashes that hid her coal-black eyes.

She wiped her mouth on her apron hem, trying to wipe away a bitter taste, warm, salty, and metallic. She realized it was blood. She must have bitten her tongue clenching her jaw as she scrubbed.

She cringed at the thought of more blood. *Disgusting. Stupid girl.* She wanted to slap her own face. How could she even think of being a nurse when she cringed at the thought of blood? Childish. She had better get over it if she was going to be a healer, like Baba. She wasn't ready to give up on the one plan she'd had ever since she was a little girl. Those Red Cross ladies during the Great War hadn't known a thing when they'd sent her on her way, telling her that only American girls could be nurses in America. She didn't know enough English, they'd told her. They didn't want her, they'd said.

Well, neither did anyone else.

And they'd all be singing a different tune when she learned all there was to know about doctoring and medicine and fixing up the busted and bleeding. Lord knew there were enough trampled feet and severed fingers and festering sores in Hegewisch. And crazy-minded souls who—

"Halina, stop your lollygagging around! I want to be done with these last sheets before the air turns damp and they won't dry," Ma hollered as she clomped down the stairs. Her short legs wobbled under her weight. Her bib apron barely covered her generous belly and matching bosom. But her babushka was too big. It came down past her forehead, nearly hiding her face.

"This one is going to take more scrubbing," said Halina as she reached for the bleach.

"Well, get on with it. Stop your daydreaming. Your mind wanders off, gallivanting here and there like you have all the time in the world," Ma said, shaking her head. "You don't know how to put in a good day's work." Then Ma launched into the usual stories about how hard she had worked on her family's farm in the Old Country.

Halina interrupted, not wanting to hear the speech once again. "Who dropped off these sheets, the ones I have in the washtub now?"

"Those? Ah, those are, umm, mine," Ma said absently, concentrating on the bushel basket at her feet. She was sorting out the apples that were rotten from the ones almost rotten. "Why?"

Halina pulled the edge of the sheet up out of the washtub, just enough so her mother could see the faint imprint of outstretched fingers, what was left of the handprint. A pink rivulet of water ran down Halina's arm.

Ma's face fell. Her chin dropped, and her empty mouth gaped open, as though she was looking for some explanation or story to tell, something perfectly simple, innocent. She twisted her apron in a knot, and her cheeks flushed.

"Is there something you want to tell me, Ma? Did something happen? Is Pa at it again?"

Her mother took a step closer. The woman glared and snorted, her nostrils flaring. Hot air hit Halina's face, and she knew she had made a mistake. She had clumsily trodden on her mother's private pains—ones that were too perverse to be seen or mentioned out loud and certainly not meant to be witnessed by her daughter, who was old enough to understand pain but didn't know a thing about marriage. Not a dadblasted thing, Halina realized an instant too late.

Ma slapped Halina's cheek.

Halina winced, turning her face away as she grabbed her mother's wrist, firmly. She wouldn't let go.

They stared at each other, eye to eye.

"Just get the washing done—*today*," Ma said tightly. Some other emotion smoldered under her breath. Was it fury or shame? The way her eyes flicked back and forth, it seemed more like fear. Halina couldn't tell. Maybe all of those. Maybe they were all mixed up, crazy-like. She wanted to say she was sorry. She was sorry for asking about the sheet, sorry for being callous about it, sorry for the blood—and whatever had happened that had caused it. And whatever made her mother think it was something to be kept a secret, endured in silence.

But Ma was already plodding back up the stairs, carrying the bushel basket while trying to hang on to the railing at the same time. She stumbled. Maybe a knee had buckled, or maybe she had just lost her balance.

"Here, I'll help you." Halina dropped the sheet back in the water and dried her hands on her apron. She took the basket from her mother and followed her up the stairs, carrying the rotten fruit for her. She could see dozens of green worms writhing in the bottom, trying to crawl out. One landed on her hand. It was sticky with apple gore.

Halina's stomach turned. She dropped the basket and ran out the kitchen door. She needed air—*now*.

The spring day was damp and chilly, but it also felt good to her, refreshing. Wind smacked her cheeks, a brisk wake-up slap. She took a few deep breaths and tried to wipe the invisible creepy-crawlies and goosebumps off her arms. Those green wiggly—

Halina's thoughts were interrupted. She smelled smoke. A fire? She looked around, worried, hoping it wasn't close by, something burning out of control. The shacks of flimsy old wood went up quickly once they caught a spark, and the burnt-out Patchiecki place down the street was testament to that. The whole family had gone up with the house, too. *May they rest in peace.*

No, it was just a trash fire in a steel drum, she saw. At the back of the yard, by the alley, there he was, the man himself. Her father was burning a week's worth of trash in a steel drum. Flames shot out of the top, sending sparks floating off into the air. He had his shovel over his shoulder and used it to tap the trash down into the flames. Why was he standing so close to the fire? Was he proud that he could take the heat or just stupid? *Maybe he's just drunk. Or he had been chewing those toothache pills with their magic ingredients.*

His back was to Halina. He was a big man, with broad shoulders and a barrel chest. He took his shirt off and hung it over the fence gate. The sleeves of his long johns didn't reach to his wrists. Halina wasn't close, but she could see the scars on his arms from the time he got caught in a thrasher when he was a boy. She knew the story well. Another Old Country yarn that got bigger and more important with each telling. All made-up horse shit, probably.

But remembering the thrasher story kindled a pang of sympathy for her father. He'd been a young boy in a small village when it had supposedly happened. There had been a traveling doctor who had patched him up. The old coot had ridden around in a carriage, with a carpetbag of simple instruments, homemade bandages, and medicines. That was how they got their doctoring in the Old Country. Amazing anyone lived to be thirty.

She was sorry for the little boy—but not the man he grew up to be. He was a bully, mean, gruff, and cold. She could see through his forlorn act. She should tell him that, too. Or maybe she should ask him, *Why is there a bloody handprint on the sheet in the basement, the one Ma says is hers? Did you hurt her?*

But she could never ask that. What could he say? And there would always be that question hanging from her mouth, like a cobweb she couldn't brush away, no matter how hard she tried. No, she decided, she'd better stay quiet.

Halina couldn't see his face, but she knew what his expression would be: a grimace, the same scowl that was frozen in place, day and night. When she was young, a few other expressions had popped up now and then: surprise, sadness, longing—his mouth hanging open as if he were starving and could almost taste a dollop of honey about to drop on his tongue. But it had been a long time since she had seen any expression other than the familiar scowl.

Halina crept closer, the ground squishing under her boots. The grass was littered with old twigs and mud puddles she tried to step around, trying to be quiet; she wasn't sure why. Maybe she wanted to sneak up on him and scare him, or hit him. Or maybe tap him on the shoulder so that, when he turned around, she could slap his face hard enough to make his store-bought teeth go flying out of his mouth. *That's for Ma. For treating her like trash,* she would say. *Could say*—or not.

She didn't know what she wanted to do. She glanced toward the house and saw some old tools that had been left out on a bench: a hammer, a screwdriver, a big wrench that had been there a while, maybe all winter, judging by the rust. She went over and picked up the wrench. It was heavy in her hand, much heavier than she'd thought it would be. What was she expecting? A child's toy? Something made of cardboard and paste?

The flames in the old drum crackled, the trash popping and sizzling as it burned. Pa stirred and poked at it with the shovel. It was a coal shovel, the kind used on a steam engine to heap coal into the hopper. He'd likely stolen it from somewhere or someone while God made notes and said, "Tssk, tssk."

Halina took another step, careful to avoid the deeper mud bogs. Already, she could feel water seeping through the holes in her boots, making her feet wet. She was still yards away, but smoke burned her eyes. She cut though the garden, where the spongy ground was quieter. Her footsteps were muffled. The remains of last year's garden were brown and brittle. Stalks were empty of life, used up. Old tomato plants drooped in awkward tangles, like scattered skeletons.

In the center of the garden, a scarecrow still hung on stakes, one up his backside and one horizontal stake that ran through the sleeves of one of Pa's old shirts. It used to be red plaid, but after the winter, it had mostly faded into varying shades of gray. The burlap face was weathered away, its red yarn mouth pecked away by crows. The button eyes had fallen long ago, lost somewhere in the muck at her feet. *Or something ate them and squirted them out in the next county.*

Halina hid behind the straw-stuffed shell of a man wearing her father's clothes. She was close enough to hug this creature, smell its mold and decay. He wasn't going to scare away much in this condition—half man, half straw-monster that seemed close to returning to the earth, where he belonged. Dust to dust.

She went somewhere else. Her mind played one of its tricks—a distraction or a promise or prediction. She wasn't sure. But she saw herself dancing with the straw man, even though he had no face. She held his hand, even though his hands were empty work gloves on the end of the stake. She knew it was absurd, but a pretend dance was better than no dance. *A straw man is better than none*, she told herself. But she wasn't sure.

She ducked behind the scarecrow's shoulder, flirting, a silly smile on her face that some man would surely find charming. But then she was back in the garden, her feet wet, her wet dress plastered against her skinny legs. A warm blush crept up her face and over her scalp, tingling. She was embarrassed to catch herself in her own foolishness. *Grow up!* she wanted to yell at the idiot girl who still hid in pretend moments and drifted to nowhere.

She still clutched her wrench. It was real. And cold and made of metal that wouldn't fall apart or wither. Loosening her grasp, she hefted it back and forth from hand to hand. It wasn't so heavy anymore, or else she was stronger.

Pa threw more of the broken twigs and branches he had gathered from the ground into the fire. He leaned on his shovel, looking like a smug master of fire. But then she saw his hands shake, and it wasn't from the chill. The man had the shakes again. He was dangerous like that.

She ducked lower, behind some withered rhubarb. She should go in the house, but she was afraid to move. Anything could set him off when he had the shakes.

"I know you're there," her father said without turning to face her, not even glancing over his shoulder.

She said nothing but squatted lower, wishing she could dissolve into the ground. Rotten leaves and stems, tomatoes that had gone unpicked and then rotted on the ground and weathered all winter closed in around her. A robin hopped and pecked at the dirt, digging worms out of the mush. She startled a chipmunk, and he scampered along the fencerow, his cheeks full of seeds from the hollyhocks that had grown along the edge of the garden. He was taking them somewhere, to some nest near the alley. He chattered, running past the trash drum in circles as if he weren't sure how to get home. The funny thing was cute with his cheeks ballooned out like that, she thought.

Pa jumped at the sound of the chipmunk's chatter and growled suddenly, coming to life, finding some energy and swinging the shovel in bursts of reflexes and fight.

"Damned rat! Git, you rat!" Pa shouted.

NO.

"Hate rats. Damn dirty things," he mumbled as he chased the chipmunk, shovel swinging in wide, random arcs that were far from hitting the target.

Halina hunched over, ducking and hiding her face. "It's not a rat," she mouthed, soundless. She should stop him, she knew. She should jump out and make her father quit, but she couldn't make her legs move.

The chipmunk darted left. Pa swung to the left. The chipmunk darted to the right. Pa swung the shovel again, like swinging a bat at a baseball. He missed. The chipmunk ran up the fence, then down.

This time the shovel hit. The chipmunk fell. Maybe he was just stunned. Maybe he would get up. Maybe he would be fine. *Sure, he could be fine*, she told herself.

Pa scooped him up with his shovel and dropped the chipmunk into the smoldering fire.

"No!" This time sound came from her mouth, high-pitched and frantic. But too late.

Pa leaned the shovel against the fence and turned around. He looked straight at Halina as she cowered behind the scarecrow. She was so ashamed of her herself and her cowardice.

"I knew you didn't have the nerve. Weak. I knew you were nothing," he spat as he grabbed his shirt from the fence and walked past the garden. So nonchalant, so calm, so heartless.

Why hadn't she hit him over the head with the wrench when she had the chance?

She still had the wrench in her hand. She clutched it tighter, her muscles tensing. She raised it, then began running toward her father, her legs pumping hard and fast.

Mary had returned to the basement and the tin washtub. The sheet was still in the cold water, just where Halina had left it. She knelt, her knees making grinding sounds as she lowered herself to the cement floor. *I'm too old for this*, she thought. *Far too old.* But she didn't waste time moaning. She didn't even bother to see if the stain was gone. It was good enough, she told herself. That lousy fancy-talking hoodlum with his stinking cigar wouldn't know a clean sheet from a filthy one.

And he deserved nothing better than this blood-stained rag of a sheet to lay his bare ass on. Let him wallow in the shame, roll in it, the way Flora had rolled helpless on the floor. Such a mess . . . Just thinking of it . . .

Mary swallowed hard, forcing the sourness in her mouth back down.

She twisted the sheet into a ball, squeezing the water out. She twisted it again, like twisting the stiff dough for *kreteche* as she had done thousands of times. She draped the heavy sheet over her arm. With it slowing her down, she climbed the stairs sideways, her good leg always first. She heard a commotion, a voice—Halina's shrill scream—from somewhere outside the door.

"No, you can't just walk away from me!" Halina shouted. "You can't!"

But there he was. Fryderyk strolled away from the angry girl. The man simply waltzed through the door and shut it before Halina could come in—before Mary could get out with the wet sheet still over her arm.

Outside, Halina pounded on the door with a wrench, again and again. Mary could see her and hear the door cracking and splintering. Fryderyk was unmoving, his face frozen in his usual old-man expression.

Then Mary heard a thud—the girl had dropped the wrench on the sidewalk—and there was no more banging, no more yelling. But the sudden silence was just as jarring.

Fryderyk shook his head. Was he confused or disappointed? Mary wondered as she watched him walk past her to the kitchen, saying nothing, not even acknowledging her, just his stink filling her nose.

"What now, you oaf? Teaching her lessons again?" Mary shifted the wet sheet that was dripping water down her leg. "Eh? Preparing her for *Ameryka's* injustices again? You think you can make her fierce so no man can take her and ruin her?" Mary demanded, her voice hoarse, throat muscles taut. "Why?"

She didn't really expect an answer—or want one. She knew the truth. He did too. And they both knew the soldiers had given her no choice. In the end, it didn't matter, did it? Used was used.

"So she won't be like her mama, that's why," Mary mumbled to no one.

She watched him pour a cup of coffee and add whiskey from the bottle on the table. It had no label, must have been home-brewed moonshine he got from some alley-man selling hooch to the stupid—or the desperate. Fryderyk wasn't stupid. He wasn't all bad, either. There had been some good days.

Mary went out the door, letting it slam behind her, the splintered trim rattling. She looked around, but Halina was nowhere in sight. It was just as well, she thought.

Mary hung the sheet on the clothesline. The weight of the water made it droop, a heavy burden, unmoving despite the wind. As the sun hit it, a faint handprint was visible, just a shadow. But still, the outline of her hand was there, in Flora's blood.

I need to be more careful.

Chapter 2

Halina patted the lumpy bundle in her skirt pocket, making sure it was still there, still safe, even if it was damp, like everything she wore. She swished her skirt around as she walked, letting the wind get to it, hoping it would dry faster that way. Baba lived only three houses down the street, so the walk wasn't far—barely time for the skirt to catch a good breeze.

Halina walked around to the back, as usual. The house was dark, all closed up, as if no one lived there. She knew better, of course. Baba just didn't like nosy neighbors or visitors, unless they came on business, the doctoring kind. Everyone else could go to hell, the old woman liked to say. She didn't mean it most of the time.

Halina could see smoke curling from the chimney. She could smell it, too. Willow. She wondered what Baba was brewing with willow, a soft wood that held water so it burned at low temperatures—not good for brewing most medicines. She tried to remember what else she had learned about willow, but her mind didn't want to focus on lessons about flames and wood. She was thinking about wood creatures—chipmunks, to be exact—and fire.

She had to knock several times before Baba came to the door. The old woman didn't look happy, mumbling complaints and warnings, recipe ingredients and bits of scripture, mixed up in a ramble that seemed like dialogue from a dream—or a nightmare. Halina was used to it and just let the woman carry on, like a kettle that had to release its steam before it could be quiet.

Baba returned to the kitchen. Halina followed cautiously, not wanting to interrupt whatever Baba had been focused upon. Halina could see several pots, bowls, and baskets scattered about. Herbs and roots, powders and bottles of deep-colored liquids were strewn across every surface. Something was boiling in a pot over the fire.

Maybe it was just dinner, she thought, a good Old Country stew. Baba had a stove and an oven but seldom used them. Halina knew the woman liked to make her special concoctions directly over flame, so she used the small fireplace in the corner. That was how Baba had learned to make the recipes, taught by an old Romani woman over campfires in the evening as the brightly painted wagons made camp on the edge of some town. And so that was how Halina had learned to make the recipes, as well—in this kitchen, over flames in the brick fireplace.

Baba frowned, concentrating on the recipe in progress as if the world depended on it. Maybe it did—at least *their* world, which seemed so topsy-turvy these days. Halina could smell the sharp, acidic liquid that was bubbling in a big copper pot, and nearly gagged. Then she remembered to breathe through her mouth, as she had been taught.

She'd come without a plan, and now she regretted the impulse, feeling nervous in this kitchen that was hardly a kitchen at all. She really had no idea what she could do for this creature, but decided to go through the motions and at least try. She found a clear corner of the table and carefully pulled the rolled bundle out of her pocket. She had wrapped him in her apron when she'd rescued the fella from the trash drum. It seemed he wasn't burned at all. He had been in an old coffee can that was wet with coffee grounds and potato peels. They must have protected him a bit. He was still breathing, his furry white belly moving ever so slightly. That he'd survived being hit by the shovel was a miracle. Maybe he hadn't been hit so hard, after all, just stunned.

Baba was busy, not noticing. *Good.*

Halina spread her apron out and set the chipmunk on top, taking a moment to appreciate his intricacy of form, fur, limbs, tail, texture, and colors. And that sweet face with whiskers and bulging cheeks still full of seeds. With her pinky finger, Halina cleared his mouth, then massaged his chest, mimicking the rhythm of his shallow breaths but pushing slightly more, encouraging more air to flow in and out. At the same time, she put her mouth close to his nose and blew gentle puffs.

Puff. Push. Puff. Push.

With her eyes closed, she focused only on this rhythm and lost track of time. When she finally opened her eyes, she was startled to find Baba beside her. The old woman was watching. How long had she been there? Halina hung her head, embarrassed that Baba had witnessed her silly fumbling.

"Oh, I give up. It's no use. It's not working," Halina said.

"Nonsense, silly girl," Baba said and pushed Halina out of the way. She picked up the small animal, cupping it in her chubby fingers. She held the animal to her face, rubbing his fur against her own weathered cheek, lined with deep wrinkles, and whispered into his face, breathing words and hot air into his mouth and eyes and ears. She started to sing some old Polish song—or was it a hymn? Halina didn't recognize the tune, but it was sweet and heavenly. When it ended, Baba flipped the animal, laying him down on his belly, and made the sign of the cross over the animal and then across her own chest.

"The rest is up to him. Does he want to live?" she asked, shrugging her shoulders. "Who are we to say?"

And then she flicked his rump, hard, with her thumb and forefinger, as though she were flicking lint off her shoulder.

Halina held her breath. The chipmunk shook his head, then his legs, finally finding his footing—and was off. He scrambled down from the table and across the room, straight to the door, as if he had known the way all along and had simply been napping.

Halina gasped and ran to open the door for him, partially in disbelief. She was happy for him, yet sorry to see him go.

"He forgot to say thank you," she said to Baba as the animal ran out and disappeared.

"They never say thank you," Baba said. "Never. And why should they?"

They both stood in the open doorway looking, watching, as if they could possibly see where the creature had gone.

Halina wasn't sure how long they stood like that. Time had a way of becoming muddled when Baba was near.

Stach, making a ruckus as he came down the alley, broke the spell.

He pushed his homemade wheelbarrow over the gravel, struggling with a heavy load that seemed to repeatedly become stuck in the ruts and mud holes of the alley that ran behind the houses on Avenue O. Halina could hear him cursing and grumbling and groaning, as if he were trying to announce his arrival and get the attention of Baba or God—one or the other.

"What's he up to?" Halina asked. But Baba shook her head.

"Phfft. Stach is his own man. How should I know? I am not his keeper."

"But you're his aunt, and he lives in your shanty. Doesn't he ever tell you what he's up to?"

"No. And I don't ask."

"I just hope it doesn't interfere with poker night," Halina said as she walked through Baba's backyard, past the chicken coop, scattering a dozen noisy black-and-white chickens. She wanted to see what dadblasted big, heavy bundle was in the wheelbarrow. She hoped it was something good and that he would be willing to share.

But as she got closer, she wished she hadn't stepped off the stoop of the house.

She could make out the shape of a man, folded up in thirds, like an accordion, his arms and legs tucked in under him to fit into the wheelbarrow. His head rested against his chest at an odd angle. Halina wondered if his neck was broken, if that was his ailment. But then she saw the bloody red holes on his chest and realized he had been shot—at least three times.

Halina couldn't stop herself. She had to see more. Who was it?

"Ahh, missy, you don't need to get closer and look at this," said Stach when he saw her coming toward the alley fence. "There's nothing for you to see. Stay where you are."

She didn't listen, and walked around the wheelbarrow so she could see the man's face.

She gasped. It was Milosz, a young man her age. They had been in the same fourth-grade class at St. Florian's. His open eyes stared at her. Flies hovered at his nose, swarmed the bloody holes.

She choked and gagged and spat on the ground. "Milosz, you bum! What did you go and do?"

Baba was beside her, pulling her arm, turning Halina's face away from the wheelbarrow as if she were some child—as if turning away could erase the image now burned in her mind.

"Stach, why did you bring him here?" Baba demanded, spittle flying from her mouth as she shouted. Halina could see her eyes were wide open and sparked with fury.

"Well, he wasn't dead when I started this way," Stach answered. "When I found him, I thought there was some hope of you fixing him up." He shrugged his shoulders, possibly realizing now that his logic had been flawed.

"Are those bootlegger bullet holes?" Baba asked.

"I don't see someone's name on them, but since Milosz was acting as doorman at The Corner, deciding who got in and who didn't, seems he might have made an enemy—or two or three—out of a customer who had a thirst and didn't like being turned away," Stach said, looking at the man—not much more than a boy, really. "But who can say about whiskey men? They are a crazy lot, you know."

Halina's horror subsided, replaced by worry. "Where'd you find him? Did you see who did it?" Halina asked, looking around for any signs of the mysterious trucks that had recently started driving around Hegewisch. She thought of the white truck she saw frequently, the milk truck Nicky drove. And a rusty black one, too. "Did they follow you?"

"No, I found him behind The Corner, in the alley, bleeding like a stuck pig and asking for a priest—like a priest could fix the holes in his gut." Stach shook his head.

"So you put him in that stupid wheelbarrow and wheeled him through the streets for everyone to see?" Baba looked as if she might burst into a fireball. She was all horror and gasps of hot spit. "Do you know the Russians did that in my town? Killed the men at the roadblocks and put them in wagons and paraded the pile of corpses through the streets! No dignity!"

Stach stepped back and started to wipe his face with his hands, but saw blood on his palms. "I was more worried about getting him here fast, while there was some breath left in him, than maintaining his dignity," Stach said. "Maybe I should have left him there."

Stach looked miserable, Halina thought. He was a good man, her friend, someone who had taught her so much—including how to play poker. As she watched him squirm under Baba's glare, she couldn't help but think of the many kindnesses he had shown her. She wished she knew what to say to help. Her heart ached for Milosz. And Stach. And Baba, who seemed to have lost every ounce of compassion she once held. What was her problem? Halina wondered. *Why is she so crazy-mad at Stach?*

"Maybe you can fix him up, Baba. Maybe *we* can," said Halina, suddenly hopeful. "You fixed the half-dead chipmunk. Maybe you can fix a man with only three bullet holes. That's not many. Come on, bring him in the house, Stach." And she started to run back through the yard to the kitchen where miracles happened.

No one followed her. She froze mid-step, realizing how childish she must sound. Stach wouldn't even look her in the eye; neither would Baba.

"Wheel him to the church," Baba commanded, her voice sounding cold. "Take him to the priest, like he asked. Let Father say last rites, and let the church bury him." Baba turned away. "And hurry with it. I don't want bootlegger blood in my alley," she said.

"Are you sure he's gone, Stach?" Halina asked, still not wanting to give up. "Are you sure there's not a breath left, nothing we can do?"

"Nope, missy. Not a thing. See his eyes open like that? He isn't blinking. Means he's seeing nothing but God's parlor full of harps and angels. He's probably taking a singing lesson 'bout now."

He might have meant it to be comforting, but his tone was too close to sarcasm. Everyone knew Stach didn't think much of the church. He scorned it every chance he got. And this was one time when it wasn't funny.

Halina hit Stach's arm with her elbow. "Show respect. He was a friend of mine," she said.

"I am. I'm gonna wheel him back to the church." Stach took off his coat and laid it over Milosz, tucking a limp arm that was hanging down back into the wheelbarrow.

"Stach," Halina said, "what in God's holy name were you doing at a boarded-up saloon, closed for Prohibition, with an empty wheelbarrow?"

"I never said it was empty," he said.

And that was that. Halina was left wondering if Stach was buying from or selling crates of moonshine to Augustino, the man who ran The Corner—once a tavern, now one of those speakeasies everyone was talking about. The whole dang world had gone crazy all of a sudden—all over this stupid Prohibition nonsense. People who used to be normal were now completely nuts, stockpiling and hiding crates in garages. And some idiots were trying to brew their own concoctions—just swamp water and turpentine—and pass it off as whiskey. Then there were the fights and threats and the snooty-snotty do-good ladies calling drink sinful and acting all aghast and horrified at the sight of a beer. So strange. St. Florian's couldn't even do communion with wine anymore. Imagine that. Jesus drank wine, didn't he? He made some at that wedding, for crying out loud. This loony law, or whatever it was, couldn't possibly last long. It better not, anyway.

Stach turned the wheelbarrow around and started back the way he'd come. Baba was already hobbling toward her back door, favoring her bad leg.

Halina watched them both, Stach going one way, Baba the opposite. She stood in the middle, unsure, once again, where she belonged.

And she wondered if there would still be a poker game tonight. *I sure hope so*, she thought as she walked home to finish the laundry.

Chapter 3

Halina didn't get far from Baba's house. The white milk truck was behind her, she noticed, following her at a distance, nice and slow, as though it was carrying something fragile or dangerous—maybe explosives that could blow up at any minute. She closed her eyes as a picture of an exploding fireball came to her, then was gone in an instant. She wiped her eyes with the back of her hand.

Wish I could be done with this imagination.

With a quick glance over her shoulder, she could see the truck was still there, still slow-poking along. And she saw the driver. It was Pock-Face, just as she'd guessed. She knew him, in a way, one of those mixed-up ways that made her toes curl and her fists clench. She might hate him or love him. She wasn't sure which.

Instead of walking by the burned-out Patchiecki house as usual, she turned up the sidewalk that once led to the front door of the house. Now, there was nothing but rubble—bricks, some charred wood, a chimney and fireplace, half of a cinder block wall that used to be the foundation or a basement wall. Halina didn't remember much of the place before it burned, but she had known the children who had lived there, had played with them—a boy and girl with blond curls, like hers. They must have been around five or six when the house burned, Halina remembered. She still saw it in her nightmares.

Tossing a rock to make sure no rats or snakes were hiding in the tall grass, Halina walked through the yard and climbed on top of the waist-high block wall. It was her thinking-wall, where she went to ponder. She hummed and swung her feet, just as she had when she was a child. But this time, she wasn't thinking of silly, made-up games—or even mulling over whatever injustice Sister Beatrice had doled out during the day at school—as she had so many times in the past.

"What took you so long?" she asked, tossing the question over her shoulder as she caught a glimpse of him trying to sneak up behind her through the long grass.

"I was trying to surprise you," he said, pulling his fedora farther down on his face, as if it were a mask he was trying to hide behind. In the slanted afternoon sun dappled with specks of shade, his face didn't look so bad—just rough, like a sandy beach, pebbled.

"You can't surprise me. I see the future."

"Like hell you do."

"No, I do. Really," she said. "I'm not bragging. It's more a curse than a gift."

"Hmm." He hopped up on the wall in one show-off move that was meant to be impressive. But she didn't impress easily, and those muscles weren't enough to make her gush and swoon with adoration like some silly American girls would do. Or her sister would do, if she had the chance. Halina wanted a man who could think. So far, Pock-Face—Nicky—wasn't passing the test.

"I try to focus on here and now," he said as he looked her over, eyeing her dress, still damp from doing laundry, the thin cotton still clinging to her legs, making her cold—making her *sutki* stand upright, like soldiers. He was evaluating her Here and her Now.

"So, *that's* the way it is with you? Only have *one thing* on your mind, like most Italian men?"

He chuckled. "Sicilian. And weren't you listening? *Two* things: *Here* and *Now*."

She jabbed him in the ribs with her elbow, just as she had jabbed

Stach a few minutes ago. The image of Milosz was fresh in her mind again.

"Do you know what happened?" she asked him. It came out sounding more like an accusation than a question.

The smiles were gone from both of their faces now. Halina felt tears well up, but she wiped them away.

"Yeah, I know."

"Couldn't you stop it?"

"No. I got enough problems watching out for my own hide. It ain't easy being a driver."

"So why do you do it?"

He shrugged. His wide shoulders, busting out of the seams of his old white shirt, looked so funny as he made a little-boy kind of shrug, as if he were five and his mama had asked him why he'd broken the last china cup. And Halina wondered if his mama was still in Sicily or if she lived in Back of the 'Yards, too.

She realized she really knew very little about this young man, except that he was one of Sal's gang, a driver. And they had been friends—or something—for years, since before the Great War. He seemed so confident, even then, and she was envious, wishing she could be so sure of her footing in this world.

He must have been darling as a little boy, she thought. *All those dark curls* ... And she couldn't resist poking a few stragglers that hung over his eyes back under his fancy felt hat. Her hand lingered just a second too long.

He grabbed it and held it, right where it was, pressed against the side of his face. Maybe just a little too hard, too tight. His face was warm. His hand was hot, sweaty, smudged with dirt and red steel dust.

"Well, for one thing, I can drive around, see what's happening, watch out for you—and your sister, too—"

"My sister, too?" Halina interrupted. "You watch out for my sister, too? How *dare* you sit next to me and tell me—"

She jumped down from the wall, angry that he, too, could be

wooed by the perfect auburn—

The grass moved. She had startled a snake that twisted in the tall grass. Halina yelped, jumped, danced, trying to avoid it.

Nicky picked her up, took her back to the wall. "It was just a garden snake. He's gone."

"Don't you go thinking I'm afraid of no snake," she hissed.

"I know. You're fearless," he said.

Was that tone sarcasm or awe? She didn't know.

"And you're just another big rat," she said as she pounded on his shoulder with a fist. Just once. No, twice. And then once more, but not so hard.

"A big one, I know. With big rat teeth." And he made goofy gnashing noises that made her laugh.

"Don't watch out for my sister," she said, a petulant lip sticking out, which she instantly hated. She wasn't that kind of girl. She wasn't silly or jealous.

"But she needs more watching than you. *You* are the smart one. She's going to get you both in trouble. That's why I worry. For you. *You* only."

"Oh, you see the future now, too?" she scoffed. "I thought I explained that was *my* special calling."

"Well, anyone with half a brain could see what's ahead for Patc-ja, I think," he said, suddenly turning serious. This somber expression was so . . . so . . . responsible, wise, scholarly. Handsome, too.

She thought about her sister. Maybe he was right. Maybe she was trouble waiting to happen.

"Be careful, Halina, and don't ask more questions about Milosz. He was stupid."

"I know. I helped him with fractions in fourth grade—"

And then Pock-Face Nicky was gone, jumping down from the wall and off through the tall grass toward the stand of trees behind the Patchiecki house—where the cellar used to be. The Patchiecki vegetable cellar. She hadn't thought of that in years. She remembered being in it for some reason as a kid. Oh yes, it came back to her. They had been playing hide-and-seek.

"Come out, come out, wherever you are . . ." She could still hear herself calling for her friends. She couldn't find them, not anywhere. Then she'd stumbled on the door in the ground, which had been left open, she remembered. She'd walked down the steep stairs into the cellar, a big room with shelves lined with Mason jars of canned vegetables . . . and Irena, her friend, had jumped out at her! *"Boo!"* the little girl with curls had shouted.

All that space, and shelves, she thought. *It would be one hell of a place to store illegal whiskey, wouldn't it?*

Chapter 4

The next morning, Baba was out early on her front step, sweeping. The broom was a pitiful old thing, missing most of its bristles. It didn't matter, though, as she was sweeping just for show, an excuse to be outside, where she could watch.

The batch she had brewed yesterday was done, cooled into a waxy tar that would freeze a man in place for eternity and then some. She had a two-pound coffee can full of the stuff at her feet, just in case. She also had an empty Mason jar in her pocket, its lid ready. Now she just needed the spark, something from the target with life still in it—hair, fingernails, saliva. A burning cigar, flame at one end, spit at the other.

She had a plan. Baba was tired of these no-good thugs and their whiskey wars taking over the good town of Hegewisch, and she was going to put an end to it.

So she watched and waited and swept back and forth at the grit that had collected on the stoop overnight. Steel dust, fine red soot from the steel mills, coated every surface, from the doorknobs and windowsills to the sagging wooden stoop that was shedding its paint in long peels.

She rubbed her aching back, taking another quick glance down the street. Baba focused on the north side, toward downtown

Hegewisch. When the whiskey men came, it would be from that direction, she knew. They always came from the north, then stopped at the corner and turned down the alley to the abandoned lot. For more than three weeks now, that was their daily routine.

At least they were predictable.

A truck rumbled past, throwing gravel and dust in the air. But not *the* truck. She pulled her babushka across her face to keep the dust out. She didn't need to start in with a coughing fit now. She had no intention of letting the neighbors know she was ailing. No one wanted their town healer to be sickly. Baba sighed. She could smell her own stink.

A crow flew over, so low she could hear the whoosh of ragged wings. It landed on the wash line next to the chicken coop. A resting crow was another sign that her days were limited.

"Shoo! Shoo! Git! *Not yet!*" she shouted, waving her arms. It flew away, but she knew it would be back—*soon*. Her mind wandered to what was ahead, guessing at the weeks or days. She hoped she'd see Easter, at least Palm Sunday, but she knew chances weren't good.

She heard a hymn, moody and sweet, the way God liked them. Was it in the wind, in her mind, or was it some angel trying to lure her to the gold-paved streets in the sky? She stomped her foot. She wasn't going anywhere yet, not even heaven. And she hoped God heard her this time. She and God had fought many battles, argued many times whether a patient should live or die. God always won, didn't he?

Her knees weakened, nearly buckled. She clutched the broom, leaning on it like a crutch. The sky swirled, the ground rose up, and her mind flooded with colors and voices, all unlocked from the past, from the Old Country. She saw in front of her a memory of the first time she had realized there was no use fighting the will of God—or a father who had been disobeyed.

She could feel her young hands clutching at Mama's skirt, Papa's jacket, begging forgiveness.

She fought. She couldn't leave. Not now.
"I won't go! I won't!"
"You must. It's all arranged—money exchanged."
"Your knapsack is packed. Hurry, they're waiting."
A cigar box of treasures under her arm:
Blue ribbon, beeswax, rose-scented soap, dragonfly wings.
A bottle of rain from that day.
A piece of hay from the loft where they'd lain.

Baba's breath caught in her throat for just a second, the time it took for the vision to come and go. The flashes seemed to be coming more often now, and she wondered what that could mean. The images were always jumbled, tangles of prophesies and parables, nightmares and regrets, past and future—all out of order, sometimes with Bible verses tossed in for good measure.

Maybe the sickness was doing it, or God, or the medicine she made for herself to ease the transition from this world to the next. She didn't know. But they were wearing on her; the burden feeling heavy. She was ready to hand it to someone else. The girl, Halina, was the right one, Baba was sure.

Seeing Milosz in the wheelbarrow had been a terrible jolt—for her and for the girl. Baba regretted that she'd let her anger show—and her weakness. She couldn't have helped that boy, even if Stach had delivered him to her door sooner. She knew nothing about bullet wounds and such. Her medicine was the natural kind, for natural illnesses. There was nothing natural about bootlegger battle wounds.

Her usefulness was up, and she knew it. She thought about these things as she looked up and down the street. Maybe she could do one last good deed for the neighborhood and her people. One last curse that would make a difference.

Still, there was no sign of the white truck and the big man, Salvatore, with his cigar. She went back to sweeping.

"Look, she's going to fly off on her broom!"

It was the squeal of a fool-child. He wasn't much taller than a mule's ass. And not any smarter. Why wasn't he in school? Baba wondered. He and his four hee-hawing pals all bunched up across the street in their filthy knickers. Their virgin mouths opened and shut in slow motion as guffaws and childish chants floated out. She shut out the noise. She had heard them all before. She had been called a Gypsy witch many times. She was used to it. But still, she corrected the uneducated when she could.

"They're called Romani! They are good people—persecuted, but good. They took me in when my parents were ashamed of me," she would say. But other times, like this one, it wasn't worth the effort. She didn't mind being called a Gypsy witch. She wore the label like a badge of honor, even if it was slightly tarnished.

Baba waved her broom at the boys, flapping her arms, as if she might fly at them, a bat out of their nightmares. They ran, the little bastards.

That was fun, she thought. But it took too much air. She leaned on the front door, wheezing, panting, like a dog in August heat.

Leaning like that, she suddenly felt vibrations travel through the house. Someone was knocking on the back door, around the corner. *Who could that be?*

Two heads poked out from around the corner of her house. *Matka i jej chłopak.* Was it Borys and his mama again? It was just last week that she had patched up his hand. Had he gotten into trouble again already? *Foolish boy.* And she thought of Milosz, also lured by bootleggers.

Baba remembered the mess the stupid boy's hand had made in her kitchen. Took hours to mop up—*after* she spent hours washing out the rust and bone chunks and potato mash from the wounds. Maybe they had come to bring some sausage or cheese for payment, or the promise he'd never do it again—grind potatoes for moonshiners. Last week, the annoying boy wouldn't say exactly what had happened. He was paid a quarter, he kept blubbering. *A quarter.* For what kind of job?

Baba had her suspicions—and her worries. She had pieced the hand back together as well as she could. But her ailing eyes had blurred, and her shaky hand had dropped the needle. She'd used yards of thread, maybe too much or not enough. Then she'd bandaged it up the best she could and told him to stay out of trouble. *"Keep it dry. No more making mash in a damp cellar,"* she had told the boy.

So what do they need now? Baba wondered. Had the stitches not held? Had she failed him? She didn't want to face this stupid boy, couldn't let him see her shame. First, she'd failed Milosz. Now, this boy, too?

The mama pushed the boy forward.

"It's his hand, Baba. Something's wrong. It's worse."

"I'm busy. Go away."

"Please, can you just look at it?"

The boy tried hiding his hand behind his back as he looked down, turning his face away, but Baba could see his hair was wet, his cheeks flushed. He shivered in the sun. That meant fever and infection, she knew. That wasn't good. *The stupid boy. Rotten boy.*

"Not now. Come back."

The mama protested, holding the boy's hand up despite his wincing. The bandages Baba had applied last time were now soaked, yellow and green—and black. That was the worrisome part. Was it blood? Just mold? Potato mash? Or gangrene?

"I told you to stay away from the bootleggers, boy, didn't I? And you didn't, did you?"

He shook his head, swooning with fever and shame. He was only a few years younger than Milosz, the dead boy. This one would end up like that if he kept working for the whiskey men. *Crooks, hoods—rotten.*

"Well, now infection has set in, making it worse. I'll take care . . ."

Baba could feel her fury driving her legs as she marched through the yard to the tree stump, the chopping block where she took the heads off chickens. The hatchet stood upright, blade wedged in the wood.

"Here's how we'll have to fix that hand now," she said, reaching for the handle.

"No!" the boy screamed and ran. His mama chased after him. Baba realized she should follow them, reassure them, try to help. Maybe a poultice would suck the infection out. She told herself to go, but she didn't have the energy left in her.

Nor the time, because just then a white truck turned the corner, coming her way. Finally, *the* truck. White bottles clinked in crates stacked in the bed of the truck, tied down with rope. Brushstrokes on the truck's side showed the barely hidden black finish underneath. "MILK" was hand-painted on the truck's side in red letters.

Baba tried to see who was driving the milk truck as it came closer, bouncing over ruts in the gravel road, making the bottles clink. It was a wonder they didn't bust and leak all over the place. She recognized the boy driving. It was Krzysztof, a Polish boy. He used to be such a good youngster, an altar boy with blond curls, just like a cherub in a painting. No more. He slouched down in the seat with a smirk on his face, as if he knew a dirty secret and couldn't wait to tell it. With one hand, he fiddled with something metallic, flashy. It was a switchblade, she saw. He opened and closed it, over and over, as he drove past her house and turned down the alley. He stopped behind the Patchiecki house. Krzysztof sat in the truck, apparently waiting for something or someone. But what? Who?

Baba watched as another motorcar drove up and parked behind Krzysztof. This one was all waxed and polished; it must belong to someone important. Two men got out in slow, exaggerated ceremony, as though they knew they were being watched. The driver was a tall, skinny young man. The other was fat, with a rumpled plaid suit and a gold watch fob on his vest. That was him, the one she had waited for—*Salvatore*. He puffed on his cigar, blowing smoke toward the sky.

That was the cigar she needed. She tapped the jar in her pocket. She was ready.

Krzysztof climbed out of the truck and walked over to the boss man and his skinny-ass driver. They talked. Oh, how she wished she could hear what they were saying. She wished she could get in their faces, tell them what she thought. How she hated them and the terror they caused the good people in her little town, who deserved so much better.

Krzysztof started unloading the crates from the back of his truck, carrying them off to the stand of trees. Then he seemed to disappear. There must be a basement or root cellar, some hiding place that the bootleggers had found, she realized. The boy made several trips back and forth. Salvatore and his driver didn't lift a finger to help. They just watched. Salvatore smoked.

Baba squinted a mean stink-eye in their direction, even though she knew they were a tad too far away. Or maybe not, if the wind was on her side—and God. She took a deep breath. She breathed in air that held Salvatore's air. His stink mingled with hers. She climbed on the scent, a ribbon connecting him to her. She crawled inside his head and hunkered down. She felt for his arm. She flexed it. She moved his hand to his mouth. She made a throwing motion. As if ordered, Salvatore threw the cigar stump on the ground and got into the motorcar. His driver got in, too, and they drove off.

Perfect, she thought.

Just like that, the whiskey men were gone and the cigar she needed for the curse was on the ground, still smoldering. She sat on the bench by the chicken coop for just a minute so she could gather her strength to walk down the alley and fetch the cigar. And for just a second, she wondered if casting a curse was the right thing to do. Would God approve?

She heard the rush of wings. The crow circled three times, then landed on the hatchet sticking out of the stump. The bird settled, ruffled and resettled its wings, over and over.

"Shoo! Shoo! Git!" she yelled, waving both arms.

The lousy bird wouldn't budge.

"I'm not going anywhere, I tell you! *I'm not!* I'm not ready!" she shouted, shaking a fist at the bird. He didn't seem to notice, preening his jet-black feathers with his golden beak.

"All right, all right," she said, her head falling to her hands. "I give up. I'll finish training the girl, make her ready to take over. I can't go without a successor," she said, relieved she'd made the decision.

She watched the bird finish grooming his feathers. He looked quite smug, proud of his regal plumage, as if he were a majestic eagle rather than an omen.

"And I can't go while those whiskey men are on these streets," she mumbled to no one. Because there was no one to listen.

With the empty jar ready, she hobbled down the alley, hoping the cigar was still smoldering, still juicy with enough spit and sin for a Gypsy curse. *Ahhh, a Romani curse,* she corrected herself. *Romani.*

Chapter 5

Halina paced in the coal room, back and forth across the small patch of floor between the bed and the dresser, listening to the noises overhead. She was waiting for a lull in the footsteps, slamming, shuffling, and scraping of chair legs over floor planks. Silence—if it ever came—would mean that Pa had dozed off on the front porch, Ma had left to work in St. Florian's kitchen, and Patcja was out chasing Romeo-Joey, her current beau—the usual Saturday afternoon. But for some reason, she still heard clod-hopping, stumbling noises on the floor over her head.

What's going on?

Now that she had made up her mind, she was impatient and ready to go. The bottom of her feet itched, anticipating what the hum of the trolley car would be like, then the roll of the train heading east. How far could she go? She needed a map and mentally added that to her list of items to borrow from Stach. But then he might guess at her plan, and she didn't need *that*. She wrung her hands, once again wishing there had been a poker game last night, a chance to win a little more to add to her savings, but she would just have to go with her current funds, as meager as they were. She wondered again how far they would take her.

Far enough, she told herself. Far enough.

By the time Stach had gotten back from dumping off Milosz at the church, explaining to Father Chodniewicz why he was wheeling around a dead fella, finding Milosz's poor mama and breaking the news, he was in no mood for poker, he'd said. Maybe she should have tried harder, but the more she pestered him to round up the usual poker men and go a few rounds, the more he seemed to dig in his heels and refuse. Polish men, they were all stubborn like that—even Stach, she thought as she paced and listened. And planned.

Finally, quiet settled over the house. Time to go. She took another look around to make sure she didn't forget anything, not that there was room in her satchel for one more item. The dresser top was bare, and she bit her lip thinking, one more time, how strange it was that so many things had gone missing recently. *Stolen?* An almost-empty bottle of rose water, a barrette, a ribbon for her hair, a comb, her ladybug ring, made of wire and tiny seed beads . . .

How she had loved that ring when she was a girl! It had come from the hat that Sister Beatrice had given her after the hair incident, she remembered. Pa had had his temper even then—whiskey, a temper, and tin snips. She could still picture it vividly. She had been about twelve. Milosz had sat behind her in Sister Beatrice's class teasing and laughing at her all morning about her chopped-up hair, sticking out every which way, stubble and spikes.

How miserable she had been, she remembered. She had been hiding behind a book until the tears came, and then she had buried her face in her arms, snot and tears running everywhere. What a mess. What a mean-ass Milosz had been. And now he was dead, and she was leaving, and the damned blue hat that the sister had given her to hide her stupid hair and the ladybug that had been in the brim were gone. Someone had stolen them weeks ago—but why? Nothing made sense anymore in this lousy town.

She had never worn the ugly-as-sin blue straw hat, no matter how desperate she had been, waiting for her hair to grow, but she had turned that little hat ornament into her lucky ring, wearing it at poker games. All those years, she had thought she won at poker because she'd polished her lucky ring. Then she realized Stach was probably letting her win a few hands so she could buy licorice or an orange soda with her winnings. Then, she started winning because she had picked up the art of bluffing. She could tell a lie without a twitch and could sense a lie coming a mile away—good skills for poker.

Ahh, good times, she thought. *I'll always remember those poker games.* Her throat tightened. She coughed, wiped at her watery eyes, and picked up the satchel.

The supply of coal was down to a few bushels, but it still made a nice slope from the floor to the small windows at the top of the wall. Expertly, she climbed the coal chunks, as she and her sister had done hundreds of times as girls, sneaking out—or back in.

She climbed out the window, shutting it behind her, but leaving a stick wedged between the sill and the window frame, out of habit. Curly, the neighborhood stray dog, greeted her on the sidewalk, wagging his tail as if she were his best friend, expectant that she might be carrying food in her pocket. This time she wasn't.

"Git, dog, I don't have time for you today. Go on."

The shaggy mutt didn't listen, and followed her down the street, trotting close on her heels, tongue hanging out in one of those goofy, carefree expressions that only dumb dogs can muster. She might even miss Curly, she realized as she paused on the walk to reach down and scratch the ears of the animal she had diagnosed and treated for countless made-up maladies when she played nurse as a child. The dog always went along with it, letting her bandage him up and feed him doses of mud tonic sprinkled with dandelion juice and ground-up grasshopper wings.

"Thanks for being such a good sport, Curly. You made a good patient, boy," she said, petting his head. He was damned lucky, too, she thought. Amazing she hadn't poisoned the stupid dog with some of those recipes—before Baba had started teaching her the real thing.

She had told herself she wasn't going to think about Baba and the lessons. She gave the dog a final, firm pat.

"Off with you, now. No more following me. I've got a job to do, and I don't need you calling attention to me. It's secret," she said and stood up.

But as she did, she caught sight of a truck creeping down the road out of the corner of her eye. For a second, her heart lurched, but then she realized it wasn't Nicky driving. She didn't recognize this man. A new whiskey man?

Why isn't Nicky driving? she wondered as worry crept in.

Curly's ears stood up. He growled at the wind or some smell that arrived on the wind. What did he sense that she couldn't see?

"Shut up, dang dog! Go home, wherever home is for you. *Go!*"

Halina pushed past the dog and walked faster. She wanted to get to the peach tree before shift change, when the herds of men from the steel mill and battery plant started traipsing past, coming and going, looking for trouble along their way. She didn't need their snooping eyes. She thought of Milosz, his open eyes staring, bloodshot, vacant, unseeing. The image wouldn't go away. The truck following her wasn't going anywhere, either. It putt-putted behind her, yards back.

What does he want?

Halina thought about walking around the block or uptown, cutting through the alley to try to ditch him. There was no way she was going to let anyone see her digging up her poker money or where she had it hidden.

She wondered why Nicky wasn't driving the bootlegger truck. She had a moment of worry. Nah, he could take care of himself. Those Sicilians were all as tough as nails. And strong—those muscles . . .

Maybe he was driving the other truck today, the rusty old black thing. That was the one he'd been driving when they'd met, back during the war. He'd given her a ride—her first ride in a horseless carriage! How frightened she had been, but also excited. She was just a kid.

DearLordinheavenJesusChristMotherMaryandJoseph, have mercy on my stupid soul! But a smile crept out onto her lips, and she couldn't help but think of that glorious day. What an adventure!

She hadn't even known his name back then, always thought of him as Pock-Face because his face was all ruined from the measles or something. He was a young guy then, too, not much older than her. He might have stolen the bottle of Seagram's from the liquor store. That was back when liquor was legal. He ran in and out so fast it was hard to imagine he'd had time to pay for it. She had tried protesting. Well, a *little*.

Neither of them had talked much. He had driven all around Little Italy, by the docks, and past the shanty towns where men huddled by fires. Pock-Face had done most of the drinking. He had offered her a swig for every three or four that he had. That was plenty for her. The bottle had been half gone when they'd driven through the warehouse district. Women had been waiting on street corners for their dates, twirling their little bags and swinging their long beads, their faces all painted up and scrunched up into mad scowls because their fellas weren't showing or something. One lady, all dolled up with feathers, had pulled up the hem of her dress and taken out a silver flask tucked in her garter. How brazen!

Halina had been shocked then. She wouldn't be now. She had seen much worse. *Much* worse.

Like dead Milosz.

She paused at the picket fence that ran along the edge of Baba's house. It was well hidden by tall hedges. She glanced left and right and realized no one could see, even the driver of the truck. She nudged two loose pickets aside and slipped through, her skinny butt barely touching the sides. Curly slid through, too, before she could stop him, the pain-in-the-ass dog. He rushed ahead, scattering the chickens through Baba's yard and running in circles around the small shanty, no bigger than a tool shed, where Stach lived.

She ducked behind the coop, waiting for the noise to settle, the dog to calm down, and to see if either Baba or Stach were curious about the chickens raising a fuss. But neither came out.

The old peach tree was within sight, up ahead, near the alley and the outhouse.

The tree was mostly bare, holding on to winter, just because. It was an old cuss of a tree, with a streak of meanness. It liked tripping her with its roots or poking her in the eye with a gnarled finger. Halina wasn't sure if the tree's nasty disposition was her imagination or Baba's fault, maybe some curse gone wrong, some years back.

She had been burying her poker winnings in a Mason jar under the peach tree for years. She had picked the spot when she was a girl, because the whole town said the tree was haunted. So who would bother nosing around it?

Halina wasn't sure if she believed the stories old-timers told—how Baba had buried her mister among the roots of the peach tree, wrapped him up in a gunny sack, not even a proper coffin, his pickled soul seeping up into the tree. That's why the peaches from that tree weren't fit for stealing, they said. It was probably just a yarn to keep naughty children from bothering the grouchy woman with strange ways. And now that she was grown, Halina knew better than to listen to the tree's moans or to pay any attention to the finger-taps on her shoulders when there wasn't anyone there.

The sky suddenly seemed dirty, with clouds of exhaust from the steel mills rolling in. The ground under the tree was a bog, smelling of mold and decay. When she took a step, the spongy ground shifted, buried rocks moved, and water pooled in her footsteps. The silly dog went in circles, nipping at its butt as if something had just pinched its tail.

"Stop that, Curly. Go sit somewhere. Make yourself useful—watch for any whiskey men. Bark if you see one. Howl, nice and loud."

Halina took her digging spoon out of her pocket and hunted for the exact spot, brushing aside a thin covering of old, wet leaves. She found the small mound marked with two twigs tied with twine, like a cross on a grave. She remembered making that marker when she was just a girl, just a dumb Polish girl who hoped she'd find a place to fit in—someday.

Look at me. Still wanting the same thing.

Halina dug. And dug and dug, scooping the sandy soil away. Finally, she hit the Mason jar with her spoon. She pulled out the blue-green jar and wiped the sand off the raised letters.

"Hey, you there—"

Halina jumped up, dropping her spoon.

"Who is messing 'round my tree? Git outta here!" Baba shouted. The old woman's voice cracked, as if she had cobwebs and gravel in her throat. It sounded as though she was still up at the house.

Halina ducked lower, but she also knew the old woman couldn't focus on something so far away. Maybe she would just go back inside her house. Halina wasn't up to explaining why she was digging among the peach tree roots. And she sure as hell didn't want to hear that Baba's dead husband was buried here, under her feet.

"I said, who's there?" Baba shouted again.

Halina didn't answer. She was looking at the Mason jar in her hand, the one that was supposed to hold months' worth of savings, over twenty dollars of poker money, so she could buy a train ticket.

But it didn't.

The jar was empty, except for a piece of paper, folded into a neat square.

And some ants.

Chapter 6

The next day was rotten as hell, even though it was Sunday—usually a good day. Halina hung on to her fury, afraid if that were gone, she'd be empty—just like the Mason jar.

Someone had stolen her poker winnings. That was all she could think, over and over.

She didn't even go to Mass with her mother and sister, as she usually did. She'd told them she was sick. She *did* feel ill, her stomach churning with a jumble of emotions: anger, loss, self-pity—and then, a hunger for vengeance. And sitting squarely on top of all that was a curiously sweet-sour question: What about Nicky?

She needed a new plan, something brilliant and fool-proof, some way to discover who had taken her money—and then a way to get it back and a way to leave town. Maybe Nicky would visit her when she was set up in a new town with a proper job.

She sat on Pa's bench under the maple tree. This was where Pa liked to smoke his pipe and stare off into the distance, concocting excuses for the last job he didn't keep or the next one he wouldn't get. She could smell his pipe smoke in the worn wood grain of the bench slats. This bench hadn't seen paint for years. The seat bowed, screws were rusted, and some of the back slats were chewed up by some critter with gnawing teeth and a taste for ants and mildew.

Yet the bench stood, seemingly ever resilient. *Persevere!* she could almost hear it say.

Maybe it was just the smoke from Pa's pipe that was doing the talking, she thought. She knew the toothache pills Pa crumbled up and put in his pipe had some powerful medicine in them—the foolhardy and dangerous kind, far more potent than anything Baba brewed up.

She had seen the small tin he carried in his pocket, even though he had tried to hide it. Dr. Watson's Toothache Pills, the label said. She remembered the time he had fallen asleep with them on the table and she had read the ingredients, curious about why he was so protective of that darn little tin, as if his life counted on it. Something from cocoa or cocoa-cane was in them. She had no idea exactly what they did—or why Pa thought he needed them.

Pa and his drugstore witch-doctor miracles—just thinking about it was making her mad. Ma worked so hard to make a little money, and Pa wasted it on drugstore nonsense, she fumed, making her hands into fists and wishing she had something to punch, or *someone*—like the dang fool who had taken her money.

Halina took the note out of the jar and studied it again. Maybe she had missed a clue. The paper was heavier than newsprint, sturdy, like the cover of the Sears and Roebuck catalog. And written in tidy pencil-scrawled letters, it said:

IOU

$22.37

Its a emergencee.

Don't be mad. I will pay back soon.

—a desparite frend.

Halina couldn't imagine what kind of desperate emergency would make a friend of hers steal her money. Why not ask to borrow it or ask for help? She didn't believe it was a real emergency for one minute.

She studied the paper more closely. It reeked of smoke—cigarette smoke on top of mill stink. How disgusting. But there was something else, too. Cigarettes, mill stink, and . . . *soap*. That was it—whisker-lathering soap for shaving. The barbershop!

She thought of another clue: even though the spelling was atrocious, the note was written in English. That ruled out most of the residents of Hegewisch. Most couldn't read or write English; some couldn't write Polish, either. Most of the old-timers signed their names with a wobbly *X*—not even knowing the right way to hold a pencil. Pa couldn't read crap. Lucky Strike and Johnny Walker, maybe.

Ma could read Polish and German, too—though no one would ever admit to knowing German these days. Halina patted the drawstring purse hanging on her wrist. She felt for the familiar shapes, small and round. The buttons were still there. Just her secret. Well, *Ma's* secret. Halina had taken them—stolen them—because they were too magical and mysterious to leave in the cigar box buried in Ma's bottom drawer. They meant something! Someone had loved her mother. A soldier, brave and not afraid. So gallant. And it was a nice feeling to carry that bit of goodness around with her in her purse.

Halina remembered finding the cigar box in Ma's dresser when she and her sister had been looking for stockings to borrow. They were far too young to wear stockings, but they had been invited to a party at the shanty and wanted to look more grown up. After all, Camel and Bear were going to be there. She had found the cigar box under garters and underthings, way in the back. She could still close her eyes and picture the square cigar box with words printed in gold, words she didn't understand. In the box, she had found brass buttons, the kind from a uniform, and a letter in an envelope. The fountain pen ink had been smeared and messy.

"Fräulein . . ."

German! She had dropped the letter as if the ink had scorched her fingers.

That was so long ago, but she could still smell the trace scent of cigars, ink, brittle paper—

She heard a noise, snapping her back to the present, and she froze. "Who's there? Pa, is that you?"

No answer.

She saw it again, as brief as a wink: motion in the basement window. Had to be Patcja. No one else went into the coal room. Halina and Patcja shared a mattress on the floor. They had a small dresser, some shelves. A pile of coal lined one wall. The wall by the door had some bushel baskets of cabbages, potatoes, and apples— half-rotten apples with those creepy green worms.

Yes, there was Patcja—climbing out of the basement window. The sight was good for a laugh. Seemed the window had shrunk or Patcja was rounder. Which could it be? Her top half was out, but those voluptuous hips seemed stuck. And her round belly that seemed to get rounder every day wasn't budging, either.

"Want some help? Give me your hand, and I'll pull," Halina said.

"Help from *you*? Not on your life," Patcja answered, brushing damp curls off her face.

"Why don't you just go through the door and up the steps to the kitchen door?"

"Your contraption is in front of the door, you dimwit. I'm not going to move all that mess. *You* move it."

"Later. You can help—you helped make it."

"Just to shut you up, that's all."

Halina wasn't about to take apart the brilliant booby-trap that was just inside the door to the coal room—the room at the back of the house, opposite the furnace room. Built of empty cans, tin pie pans, and a jar of tacks and nails balanced precariously, it was supposed to keep scary things out. It worked sometimes; others times it didn't.

But she saw no reason to dismantle it now—even though someone had managed to steal so many things from her dresser. How had they done that?

"All right—here, take my hand," Patcja finally said with a sigh.

It took three tugs to get Patcja out. Her dress was miserably filthy now, covered in coal dust. She was still beautiful, though, darn her.

"I think we'd better start using the door, like normal people do," Patcja said, brushing the black dust off her hands, knees, and dress.

"Yeah. I suppose. That window isn't going to get any bigger," Halina said.

"Not hardly, bird-brain," Patcja sneered, wrinkling her nose, as if a whiff of swamp-stink had suddenly floated her way. She tossed her head back, waves bouncing and catching the light. "How stupid can you be?"

Halina looked at her sister and saw nothing but arrogance, hot air, and paper-doll-pretend nonsense. She'd had enough. She was tired of the never-ending assault of prickly jabs from her sister, who seemed to hate her, and she didn't know why. What had she ever done to deserve this hate?

"Patcja, you know why you can't fit through that window any-more? Because you are a lard ass, a fat turd with stuck-up ways." Halina took a breath. "You've got a big head, too, pumped up with some highfalutin' ideas that you're better than me. And you're *not*. You're just as stupid as me."

Patcja attacked. She went for Halina's hair, pulling, then slapped at her arms and face.

Halina stumbled back, off-kilter. She tried to catch herself, groped at the air, found branches of the lilac bush. Halina fell to the ground and rolled in the grass away from her frenzied sister. Patcja stood hunched over her. Her jaw was clenched into an ugly gorilla face, and her hands were balled into fists. She might have grunted. Or was it a groan? Maybe she realized how absurd she looked.

Halina saw that she had lilac blooms in her hand. They had come off as she grabbed at the bush. What a waste of pretty flowers. Senseless violence and temper bursts seemed to be breaking out every which way. Was nothing safe? Was it the whole town or just her crazy family?

Halina found her footing and stood up, collecting her composure. She took a deep breath. Calm. Cool. She picked up the flowers that had scattered on the grass and arranged them neatly, lining up the stems, making a tidy bouquet. Perhaps some dignity could be salvaged.

"Here, these are for you, Queen of Sheba, Your Royal Plumpness," Halina said, handing the flowers to Patcja with a formal curtsy and a childish smirk.

Patcja knocked them to the ground, snorting like an insulted hog. She spun around and stormed off, with more huffing and puffing. Halina watched her sister go. A wind shoved her along. The space where she used to be was empty; just a sucking sound was left. The lilacs on the ground looked pathetic, like flowers on a grave after the funeral-goers have left and the crying is done. Already they were scattering in the breeze. Already they looked wilted. Poor things. Halina scooped up the flowers and arranged them in the empty Mason jar. She added water from the pump. Then, some dandelions for more color.

Not so bad after all.

She wished she could say the same for her sorry dress. Grass stains from rolling on the ground, mud on the knees, and the bow was undone and dangling. Again.

Damned thing looks like a noose.

❦ ❦ ❦

Halina found the embroidery basket by the rocker in the front room, where she'd left it. That was where the light was best for sewing. She had been working on a pillowcase that morning. When it was done, it would bring another fifty cents from the lady on State Street with the shop.

Halina used the fabric shears and cut the blasted bow off her dress. She started to throw it away, then decided that was wasteful. She might as well keep it. She tied the bow from her dress around the Mason jar of lilacs. The jar sat on a small, round table, like a trophy in a place of honor. The purple flowers added majesty to the room. They looked out of place.

Ma must have heard the squeak of the embroidery basket hinge. The woman had lousy eyes, but her ears didn't miss much.

"You need to finish the ironing, girl," she said, coming into the room, wiping flour-dusted hands on her apron.

"What's gotten into you?" Ma waited, but no answer came. "You think you are too smart to have to work? I got news for you, honey: you're not that smart, or you'd be married and gone from here by now."

"Gee, thanks, Ma. Just what I needed—more words of wisdom and loving advice," Halina said. "And from the woman who has it all." Her voice cracked. Her sarcasm was like barbed words, piercing her tongue. They turned into an awful noise, a sob. She hid her face, first in her hands, then in the pillow on the rocker.

"I don't have it all," Ma answered in a shout. Then, in a softer voice, she said, "At least I have a roof, and a man, and two girls." She reached out her hand as though she wanted to touch Halina's hair. "Both, beautiful girls."

Well, that ended the pretty little moment. Halina pulled away. *Hogwash.*

"Don't make me laugh, Ma," Halina said, stepping back and

catching her breath. "Only a blind fella would call me beautiful. And I don't see many of those in Hegewisch, I'm afraid." She wiped her face, smoothed her hair.

She had so much to do: a thief to catch, a train ticket to buy. No time for this nonsense.

"I gotta go, Ma. I'll do the ironing . . . well, later."

"Where are you going? Tell me that. Where?" Ma demanded.

"I need to collect on an IOU. I need to see the barber, see what he knows about it," she answered, knowing quite well her mother wouldn't understand—or approve. But so what?

"Don't mess with such bad men, Halina. You will only be sorry. You need money? Here, take this." She reached inside the collar of her dress. From somewhere in all those billowy rolls, she pulled out a crumpled fistful of money. She took a few of the top folded bills—five or six dollars—and handed them to Halina.

Halina didn't know what to do.

Good Heavenly Lord. How much is in that wad?

Halina took the money. It was warm and damp from her mother's body heat and sweat. That could have been disgusting, but it wasn't. It was . . . well, *humbling.* That was the only word she had for the odd emotion that rolled over her—along with a good dose of shock.

"My God, Ma. Where'd you get so much money? How much is there? Fifty dollars?"

"I don't know. I work hard and save, and I hide it so it doesn't go to whiskey or those drugstore pills," Ma said. She shook her head, shrugging her shoulders, as if producing a hidden roll of cash happened every day.

"I can't take your money, Ma. You saved it. *You* keep it."

"You help me with the sewing and the laundry, so you can have a few dollars. You earned it." Ma was already tucking the rest of the wad back inside her dress. "I suppose," she added then.

She was having second thoughts, it seemed.

"No. I've got my own money I've been saving. I just misplaced it—temporarily. I'll get it back."

Halina didn't wait for an answer. She was out the front door. She took the jar of lilacs with her. She wasn't sure why.

Just like she wasn't sure why Ma's wad of money was unsettling. All the way to the barbershop, she tried to think it through. Walking and doing math in her head at the same time wasn't that easy. She knew all of the laundry money barely covered the house payment and food, so anything else came from the embroidery sold to the shop downtown. She divided and multiplied over and over, thinking she had to be wrong. Ma would have had to sell over a hundred pillowcases to make that wad of fifty dollars. Each one took a week to embroider.

Where else could Ma have gotten that kind of money?

Wonder what goes on at the Hawthorne Hotel?

Chapter 7

Stach sat on the metal stool in the newsstand, shifting every ten minutes, like clockwork. Hemorrhoids—that was the worst part about this newspaper-selling business. All the sitting was hard on a man's ass. It seemed that was all he did anymore. He came in and opened the stand's window before dawn. Then the trucks dropped off bundles of papers at the curb. Three bundles of the *Tribune,* and then the truck from the *Dziennik Związkowy*—the *Polish Daily News*—came by. It dropped off ten bundles, if he had enough money for ten. Sometimes there was only enough for seven or eight.

He set out the papers for the day; then he sat, waiting for customers. More people came by to talk than to buy. He didn't really mind. It kept him up on the news of the neighborhood—good news, bad news, gossip, wrongs that needed righting. He liked hearing those things. Sometimes he could fix them. There was no other law in the town, unless you counted the Church. And that was good for a laugh.

"Hey there, Stach!"

It was Janusz calling, walking down the street, waving one arm, then both, with big circular motions, as if he were trying to row an invisible boat with his arms. His shirt was unbuttoned and flapped as he paddled the air and called to Stach. The man had no idea how goofy he looked. Janusz had come back from the war that way. Changed, simple in the head. He limped, too, sometimes favoring his left foot, sometimes the right, as though he wasn't sure where the hurt was.

"Hello, Janusz, my man! Come, stop by my headquarters, see how the big world of publishing and commerce is doing today," Stach called to the man, standing up and waving him over.

"Nah, I'm coming to see if you are selling any newspapers today. Is there any good news?"

"Well, you know, Janusz, I haven't stopped to read the papers today. I reckon I've just been so busy tending to the crowds. It's been chaotic, all day," Stach said, joshing a little with the man.

Janusz looked around. The street was nearly empty. Waldemar, the barber, was sweeping down at the end of the block. In the shop next to him, Mr. Marchewka, the grocer, was rolling the barrel of pop out toward the sidewalk. He had probably just iced down a couple of cartons, getting ready for shift change. But besides that, the street was quiet.

"Where did they all go?" Janusz looked left, then right, then behind the back side of the stand to the alley. "I don't see no crowds," he said.

"You're right, Janusz, they all seemed to have git. *Odeszli*. Gone," said Stach, hiding his grin with a big hand. "But c'mon. Let's you and me see what's in the newspaper today. English or Polish? Which should we read?" Stach held up one of each so Janusz could pick.

"Which has the good news?"

"Well, I reckon that would have to be the *Trib*. Polish news is never good news, you know that."

"How come that is, Stach? How come?"

"Well, I don't know, Janusz. I just don't know."

Stach brought the stool out front so Janusz could sit. Stach figured he would stand for a while; might do his hemorrhoids some good. A man could hope.

Stach read the paper to the man—only the good stories, though. He skipped the ones about secret taverns being raided and government men busting up stills. He passed over the ones about the gangs, young hoodlums trying to make a name for themselves. And then there were the Families, fighting it out, too—sometimes in street brawls, sometimes with guns, sometimes just fists and accusations and promises of revenge on mothers and sisters.

Today there was another story about Death's Corner, just a few blocks north. Prohibition was turning Chicago—the whole region— into a chaos of factions battling it out over territory and distribution rights. It was getting messy. Stach skipped those articles, too.

That didn't leave much to read, so they got through the paper rather quickly. Janusz didn't seem to have some place to be, so they spent some time reading the ads, too, looking at the pictures, pretending they had a fortune to spend. For only three dollars, they could get a new derby. They decided they each needed two—one for weekdays and one just for Sundays.

"You got everything else you really need, Janusz?" Stach tried to be serious for a minute. "See this ad for men's things—skivvies, socks, undershirts, long johns—things like that? See here, this man in the ad? You got enough of those in your drawer at the boarding house, or do you need me to spot you some money?"

Janusz laughed and looked down, shuffling his feet. "Oh, Stach, it's not right to go talking about private things. You know that. Even *I* know that." Janusz tugged on the waist of his trousers, trying to see inside.

"Janusz, leave your pants alone. I'm not talking about your privates, man. I'm talking about britches to keep your Johnson all covered and tucked away when you walk down the hall in that boarding house, out to the outhouse. We don't want those women screaming anymore, you know."

"I know, I know. And that's why I can't live at the boarding house no more. The old lady, Aunt Beula, kicked me out last week,

Stach. Said I had to get my things and move on. Tony, that tall fella, drove me over to the Hawthorne. Said I could stay there. He'd put me up if'n I behave and help him with chores."

"Why didn't you tell me before, Janusz? I would have been happy to put you up, too," Stach said. "I don't think it's a good idea to be beholden to those whiskey men."

"I didn't want you worrying none about me. I ain't been-holding any dern thing. I's being good. Keepin' my britches buttoned, like you said."

Stach studied the man's face, trying to decide if there was some kernel of truth in there or if it was a hundred percent bullshit. Janusz had a way of saying what he thought Stach wanted to hear.

The afternoon sun fell across the old soldier's face, highlighting the groove that zigzagged across his bald skull. The indentation was the width of a finger and nearly as deep. Janusz had come home from the war that way. His brain didn't work quite right, but his manly interests were intact and had a way of getting Janusz in trouble. He didn't know how to control those urges, it seemed.

Stach was concentrating so hard on seeing into Janusz's mixed-up head that he didn't notice Halina coming up the alley behind him—not until she was right there.

She was carrying a jar of weeds, looking like a school girl with a present for the teacher. He had to laugh. One day she was a wise young woman, independent, full of common sense and gumption. Then the next day, well, here she was . . .

"Look what I brought for your newsstand," Halina said.

She set the Mason jar with lilacs and dandelions on the counter, sloshing water over the top and soaking that sad bow tied around the jar.

"Kind of silly, I know. But they were already picked, and why waste them, eh? So, thought I'd bring them with me."

"Well, thank you, Halina. That's darn sweet of you." He set them to the side, out of the way. He could imagine what the mill men who were due soon would think. All he needed now was some doilies and pillows with tassels, maybe some shutters and flowerboxes, just like the cottages at home.

Halina smiled, her dark eyes wide open, with a mischievous glint. She looked halfway pretty when she lit up like that, all giddy and bright, like a carnival on opening night.

"Hey, isn't that bow tied on the jar from your dress? What did you do?" Stach asked.

"Yeah. Got to feeling like a noose, so I took it off." She tilted her head, sticking out her tongue, fake-choking as if she were hanging from an invisible noose.

"Stop that! Now." Stach slapped at her hand that was pretending to hold a rope around her neck. "Don't ever do that again, and *never* let your ma see you do that."

"All right, Mr. Snotty. I was just joking," she said.

Stach knew he had overreacted and felt lousy for it. But, dammit, some things . . . What if Mary had seen her play-acting like that? Well, the girl didn't stay miffed too long.

Halina fussed over Janusz, giving him his own dandelion, telling some made-up nonsense about it being a medal for his bravery. She poked the stem in a buttonhole of the man's coat. Now they both were grinning. These two souls were just muddling along, doing the best they could with the lousy hands that had been dealt them. And he loved them both like family. Stach's throat knotted up. He coughed, trying to make the lump go away.

Stach moved the Mason jar back to the center of the counter where the mill men passing by would be sure to see the weeds, in their wilted, righteous glory, with a droopy bow—a lot like a noose.

Then he put his hands together, rubbing them, ready to stir up . . . something.

"So, who is up for some poker tonight?"

Chapter 8

After her sister had helped her get out of the window, Patcja stormed off, leaving Halina and her know-it-all ways behind. She walked toward town because she had nowhere else to go. She got as far as Camel and Bear's house at the end of the street—one just like all the others, only stained with something dark, something barely visible, but it was there.

She walked around to the familiar back door. She knew it would be unlocked. It was always unlocked, and Camel was always alone during the day. Well, except for his mama, which didn't count for much.

Camel was in his usual spot, and Patcja took her usual spot. There was Camel's tan tweed cap, the one that had earned him his nickname. Because he couldn't be left out, Bear had a cap, too—a brown tweed cap for the boy who was plump like a bear cub and liked to climb trees. Those long-ago days had been so simple. And the simple nicknames, all in fun, now seemed so childish and stupid.

She didn't say much at first, as usual. Then the words spilled out, and she could barely stop them. They tumbled, unpolished.

"Oh, dearie me. Golly, Camel. It was awful, just awful! I don't know *why* I slapped her. But you remember how she gets, don't you? So innocent and cheery. It just irks my spine and makes me want to spit in those black eyes of hers. Creepy things," Patcja said with a theatric shudder. She didn't wait for an answer; knew she wouldn't get one.

"I think it's all this sneaking off I have to do to work at The Corner. It weighs on me, Camel. Something fierce. Can you imagine what Ma would do if she knew I helped serve bootleg whiskey? She'd disown me, for sure. If Pa knew, he'd kill me."

She straightened her dress, suddenly embarrassed at how much coal soot was on the silly thing. Well, Camel wouldn't mind. He loved her no matter what. Always said he'd love her forever, no matter what.

"I'm just going to have to insist that Halina take down that booby trap fastened to the door to our room. Or I will give in and do it myself. No more climbing through windows for me. That was fine when we were kids. Remember that year when Halina was nuts with her nightmares? She kept me awake most of the night, ranting about a face at the window. She was loony. But that was before the war, when everyone was all nervous and twitchy about what would happen to Poland. All the sour faces . . . Remember?"

And as soon as the talk about the Great War slid out of her mouth, she regretted it. Darn, she should be more careful. Some things were better left unsaid. Some wounds, better left un-touched. She ought to know that.

Patcja pulled on the sleeve of her dress, trying to cover her wrist and hand. The scars still looked hideous, even though the fire had been years ago. It had done all the healing it was going to do. She was stuck with this. The mottled pink-and-white skin seemed stretched, paper-thin. The frayed edge of her sleeve prickled at the sensitive skin. She tried to hide it, even from Camel—though he couldn't . . .

"And then stupid Halina called me a . . ." She couldn't bring herself to say those words, either. Was she really a lard ass? All old Polish women were short and wide. It was how they were made.

Was she on her way to being a fat old lady, like Ma? Like Baba? Like the other old women who worked in the church kitchen, always wearing babushkas, bib aprons, and grimaces, as if they had corncobs up their butts?

She'd rather die.

"Oh, what am I going to do, Camel? I'm getting so *old*. Soon, I won't have any choices. I'll end up at a convent, mopping floors, or being a housekeeper for some priest or old widower. I know that working at The Corner isn't much of a job, but it's a job. You're not ashamed of me, are you? There's nothing to worry about. I just help Augie take orders—he owns the place—and I carry jelly jars and coffee mugs with the liquor to tables. Sometimes men leave tips on the tables; sometimes not. I just want to earn enough money for a new dress, a nice hat, some new earrings, maybe. And I'll buy you something, too—those lemon drops you like so much. Would you like that?"

She patted his hand. Dear, sweet Camel deserved a present for listening to her carry on so long. How nice it was for him to listen to her. He was always so kind, a gentle soul who understood what it meant to have hurt in your heart and an ache you couldn't put a name to. She thought of all those afternoons when they were kids, sitting on the half wall of the Patchiecki place after school, pretending to be grown up, pretending to be in love. They were going to run off together when they were old enough.

That idea was gone. *Long* gone.

Patcja thought of Joey. Joey came to The Corner most nights it was open. He seemed sweet on her, at least some. At least *enough*. Patcja couldn't tell Camel about Joey. He wouldn't like that part of her story. She was sure of it.

Suddenly she was out of words, out of time, out of patience and kindness. Her arm itched, and her feet wanted to run as fast as they could. It was some instinct, brutal and self-serving, that took over. She was hungry and needed food, and there was none here, she knew. This sick room, which smelled of old cabbage and urine-soiled sheets, was mostly bare—a bed in the parlor. Another one in the back, in the room with the door. Camel's mama had a spell. She slept most of the day in that back bedroom, not making a sound except some gurgling and grunting. Patcja had to get out while she still could. *Now.*

Joey. She had to find Joey, had to see him. Maybe more sweet-talking . . . Maybe if she told him she loved him . . . Maybe if she promised to be a good wife . . . Maybe if she smiled real nice . . .

A June wedding would be lovely, wouldn't it?

Patcja kissed Camel on the cheek, as usual. Just a peck, but her hair brushed against his sallow cheeks. She opened the door to the back bedroom and waved to the woman who was asleep.

She started to leave but came back. She nudged the bandages over Camel's eyes just a tiny bit to look at his face, his eyes with no eyelids. From mustard gas. He turned his head. She wasn't sure if it was because of the light or if he didn't want her to see what was under the bandages. She knew what that feeling was like, too. She dropped the white gauze, smiling at a man who could barely see, talking to a man who couldn't answer. She couldn't stay another minute.

But wait—

She fished around in her pocketbook. She found a lemon drop at the bottom, sticky. She put it to his lips, until he parted them. She dropped it on his tongue and closed his mouth for him.

"There you go, Camel. Thanks for listening. Bye, my love," she said, choking back more words.

And Patcja hurried out the back door of the house, as usual.

❦ ❦ ❦

She rushed toward the mill, fumbling with her hair and swishing her dress and sweater around, hoping she had aired out the stink from the sick room. She picked some bright-green baby leaves from a budding bush and rubbed them behind her ear, on the back of her neck.

Now I smell like spring! I hope Joey likes spring.

There was much she didn't know about Joey, even though she had been sweet on him for months now. Seriously sweet. *Consumed,* even.

Joey was an apprentice welder. He would come out of the north gate. As she walked, she did the finger-comb thing and tucked her wavy hair behind her ears. She looked more sophisticated like that, she knew, a hint of her neck showing. She pinched her cheeks to make them rosy and bit on her lips to make them pink and puffy. She practiced sucking in her waist and smiling at the same time. It was near impossible.

Men were walking in the opposite direction, coming from the mill, heading home. They walked in bunches, three or four together. No one talked. They looked dead tired; filthy, too. How could they stand to walk around like that? Faces painted with grime, their hands caked.

There! *There!* Was that him, walking by the hedgerow?

"Joey! Hey, Joey, is that you? Joey?"

She caught a flash of a hat that looked like Joey's black felt fedora. She ran into the street to chase him. She had to catch him. She stumbled on a rut in the dirt road, losing her balance. She heard the honk of a Model T and tried to get out of its way.

She spun.

And then there was nothing.

Chapter 9

Halina leaned on the newsstand counter and watched the parade of mill workers file past. First, a few; then, a whole slew, coming and going. First shift ending; second shift starting. Men walked in bunches, some on the sidewalk. Some took up the center of the road, ignoring the mule carts and trucks that had to stop to let them pass. Working men always had the right-of-way in these parts.

"Here they come. The boys are a-coming this way. Look out now," said Janusz, his eyes big and hands clenched in fists, as if he were getting ready to start a fight. Or maybe he was bracing to take a few punches.

"Don't you worry none, now, Janusz," Stach said, placing a firm hand on the man's shoulder. With his free hand, he held up a newspaper.

"News! Get the news! Today's news! Get yer paper right here. Paaaa-per! Paper-paper! Read all about it! Neeewwwsss!"

A few stopped to buy a paper to take home with them. A couple just stopped to look at the picture on the front. Likely, those were ones who couldn't read. Stach read out the headline for them, natural-like, not letting on that he knew their predicament. Stach was like that: a good man, underneath his orneriness.

Halina smiled as she watched. Stach's mustache, full and bushy, twitched around when he was joshing someone for fun. It looked like a small critter dancing a jig. And his hat, pushed back on his head, made him look as if he had just run a race and were still wind-spent. The ratty old thing was probably a right-fine-looking bowler back when Stach was an important university man in Poland, a long time ago. But now it looked as if it had been stepped on, sat on, and chewed on until it was just an inch shy of being fit for nothing more than swatting at flies and wiping the sweat off a horse's rear end.

Stach was darn good at the singsong chant that all newsboys seemed to know. But Stach was no boy. He was old enough to have wrinkles around his eyes and a furrow between his thick eyebrows that never seemed to go away, not even when he was sleeping or roaring drunk. Halina had seen him in both conditions plenty of times—good times *and* bad times. They were friends, after all.

"*Wezmę jeden.* I'll take one of those," a man said, leaving the ranks of the other mill workers to detour to the newsstand. Turned out he didn't have enough money. Stach gave him the paper anyway.

"Take it," Stach said. "Here, no charge."

The man nodded at Stach. That was all. That was enough.

"Why you keep giving away papers, Stach?"

"Don't you worry about it, missy. That one was used anyway. All old news. Janusz and me read all that was good in it. Only the bad news was left," he said, smiling. "Isn't that right, Janusz?"

But Janusz was off the stool, up and taking off, walking at a good trot, as if he were being chased by a bee.

What spooked him now?

Halina craned her neck, trying to see. Some commotion was erupting at the end of the street. The barber, Waldemar, was talking to some fellas, their arms all up in the air and excited about something. And the grocer was selling some pop bottles he pulled out of the barrel, probably that new stuff, Chicago Cola. It was only for men. Halina suspected it wasn't cola at all.

A milk truck was parked at the corner, the driver hanging his head out of the window, waving at some of the mill men as they walked past. The driver kept revving the engine, making noise just for fun—or spite. Who could know about men? Janusz was heading that way, at a run now, his shirttails flapping behind.

"What do you think got into Janusz?" Halina asked, still watching.

"I don't know, missy. But I'm suddenly thirsty for some milk," Stach said. "How about you come back here and mind the news-stand for me?"

Before she could say yes or no, he was gone, down the side-walk, after Janusz and into whatever stupid menfolk commotion was bubbling up.

Milk? *Głupie gadanie.* Bullshit. Cola? More bullshit.

Halina moved the stool back inside the stand. She wanted to look official—the girl in charge of the newsstand. The Young Woman in Charge of the Newsstand. She smoothed her dress, sat up very straight, and fiddled with her hair, trying to make it look presentable. Men walked by. More men walked by. She tried waving a paper. Tried waving a hand. Tried waving both hands.

No one stopped to buy a paper.

Well, that was a fine how-do-you-do. No one would buy a newspaper from a woman? What the hell?

She took a good look around. This was a whole new perspective. She usually stood on the outside of the window, looking in. Stach would never let her in the door. Maybe he was thinking about her reputation. Young ladies didn't go inside newsstands with fellas, he said.

How did he know so much about young women?

Maybe he just didn't want her to see the filth. Spiderwebs hung from the ceiling. Mouse turds filled the corners. An old two-pound coffee can of cigarette butts, ashes, and empty matchbooks was tipped over, spilling on the floor, blowing around, along with scraps of old butcher paper that might have held a sandwich or a chunk of sausage, maybe cheese.

Most of the mill men had passed by now. Just a few stragglers were left, poking along. Halina spotted one man who looked sickly. He walked alone, like a zombie out of a comic book. Creepy eyes stared blank and empty, and one foot dragged a bit, as though it didn't work right. He had no hat, and his hair—what there was of it—was plastered to his skull, wet, greasy, making his head look far too small for his body. And a bulky coat hung on him, like chains weighing him down.

Dadblasted. He was in *bad* shape.

Something stirred in her, some instinct. It was what she imagined mothering ought to be like—a need to take care of someone. Or concern. Whatever. She had no word for it, English *or* Polish. But it was powerful.

"Hey, mister!" Halina stood up and called him over.

He shrugged his shoulders and walked toward the newsstand, slower than any living man ever walked.

Halina could smell him, and he hadn't even reached the curb yet. It was a putrid smell—like sickness, puke and sweat and week-old shit—plus the mill stink of iron ore, something sharp and burnt.

"*Coś nie tak? Czego chcesz?*"

"You're sick. I got something to make you better. Like chamomile tea, but better." Halina put her hand on the matchbox amulet around her neck. She hesitated for half a heartbeat, then untied the twine, opened it, poured the contents into the Mason jar. She took some of the lilacs and rubbed them between her palms, letting the lilac juice drip into the water. Then, the same with some dandelions. She swirled it as fast as she could without the concoction sloshing over the sides.

"Here you go, mister. Have a drink, and take it home. Have your missus make you some tea with it."

"Why you giving me this?" he asked in a thick accent.

"It'll soak the poison outta your gut. You got rotgut poison in you, mister. I couldn't help but see—and *smell*. You stink to high heaven."

"How d'I know you ain't trying to kill me? Poison me?"

"Why would I waste a nice jar on a man I was planning on killing? I want my jar back. When you're better, you can bring it back."

He took the jar with the dingy water, petals clinging to the sides of the jar, ladybug remains floating. He put an eye next to the *a* in *Mason*, as if it were a magic window into a new world where dandelions cured men close to dying. *Could be.*

He left, carrying the jar with two hands. He zigzagged just a little.

Halina crossed herself. "Holy Mary, Mother of Christ, help this man get home so he can die in his bed rather than the street," she whispered over folded hands. "A man dying in the middle of shift change sure would cause a ruckus."

She wondered if her mixture could possibly help or if she was fooling herself and giving false hope to a dying man. If she were a nurse, she would know what to do. A nurse would—How about that? She could hardly believe it. The newspaper in front of her had a picture of a nurse, right there in an advertisement. She'd recognize the distinctive nurse's cap a mile away. And the white uniform—so official looking, so important.

She unfolded the paper to see more of the notice. In the picture, the nurse was talking to another young woman who wore a uniform, too, but one that had a white bib apron over a dress with narrow stripes. Imagine that.

"Become a Candy Stripe Girl for St. Margaret," the notice said in large letters. *"Learn to be a nurse's aide with hands-on training."*

She read the rest of the ad. Twice. Then one more time.

"Bring comfort to the ill. Light up their day with flowers, conversation, and kindness. Learn hands-on nursing skills while also taking practical nursing classes. Ask about our work-for-tuition program. Apply at St. Margaret's Hospital."

How exciting that sounded! She could do that! But she had so many questions: Would they take her? Was she smart enough? Old enough? American enough? She didn't have much schooling. How could she, when she had to help make money? She'd traded book learning for scrubbing sheets and stitching little red poppies on pillowcases and towels. But she knew how to help the sick get well. Well, at least birds and the occasional rabbit, and a stunned chipmunk . . . and now a mill-man with rotgut poisoning—if he lived.

Halina jumped up. She was ready to walk to St. Margaret's now, this minute. Quick, before it was too late. Maybe they would only take a few girls.

Maybe . . .

But I'm supposed to watch the newsstand for Stach. Dadblasted. Now what?

Maybe she could write him a note. Lock up and leave the note on the counter for him to find. It wasn't like anyone was buying a paper from her. Halina opened the cashbox, looking for a pencil and paper so she could leave a note explaining why she had to leave. Stach would understand.

The box was a mess of receipts, notes, and tallies in Stach's handwriting, all wadded up and stuffed inside. She looked for something to write on. Then she saw it—a note written on the back of an empty used envelope. She immediately recognized the tidy penciled letters.

IOU

$3.14

I'm sorry. I'll pay you back soon.

P.S.

Don't tell Halina.

Blasted! The thief had robbed Stach, too?

What . . . ?

She turned the envelope over.

Who is this envelope addressed to?

The name was crossed out, many times, by a pencil pressed hard into the paper. She held it up to the window, rubbing her fingers over the indentations. The afternoon light skimmed over the grooves, making the address legible.

Waldemar Babireck

2939 S 133th St.

Hegewisch, Illinois

What the heck? Waldemar, the barber? His *envelope?* He *wrote the note?*

The barber was stealing money? Why the . . . ?

She shook her head, trying to piece together how that could possibly have any logic. Nope. No possible reason. Nothing made sense anymore. Not a dadblasted thing. Handprints and hotel sheets, notes with her name, hullabaloo over milk bottles, and a barber who stole money from the newsstand . . . The whole town was going crazy.

And what was she going to do about it?

Chapter 10

Patcja blinked her eyes. They were crusty, as though she had been sleeping a long time.

Where am I?

The room was dark and murky, thick with shadows. She blinked again and again, rubbing at her eyes. Her head throbbed.

A dog licked her face, wet and sloppy.

"Stop that, Curly. *Stop.* Go home."

Patcja tried to push the dog away. She tried to sit up. A wave of nausea hit, like a boat rolling on unseen currents. Where was Joey? She remembered looking for Joey, catching a glance of his hat, by the mill.

It was coming back to her. She'd visited Camel, decided she needed to see Joey. The parade of men leaving the mill at shift change—she had looked for Joey. Where was Joey? A man in a hat, crossing the street. The Model T . . .

Where am I? How did I get here?

She blinked again, trying to focus, trying to let her eyes adjust to the dark, make out some of the shapes around her, vague and bulky, ominous in their nothingness. With trembling fingers, she groped at the blanket, the bed, searching for something familiar.

Curly whined, wanting attention, wanting something she didn't have.

Recognition came slowly, drip by drip. It wasn't much of a bed at all—more like a small cot, something that probably folded up, mostly metal and very squeaky. A thin pad sat on top, with buttons that poked into her back. One rusty coil poked at her shoulder. She could smell the rust of the wire, the mildew on the pad, along with mold, sweat, and fumes from a trash bin.

She shuddered, goosebumps on her arms, hair on the back of her neck bristling. The rancid smells made her stomach roil. She pushed the blanket away, then realized it wasn't a blanket at all. Maybe some kind of a dishrag? It smelled like whiskey, the homemade kind.

What's going on? Patcja pushed herself up on her elbows, rubbing her throbbing head, swallowing hard to keep her stomach from lurching. She listened for sounds. Her eyes were adjusting, but that didn't help much. She still couldn't quite place where she was. Maybe a storage room.

Click. Click. Click.

Lights were flicked on in another room. Yellow light crept in from under the door. It was just enough to let Patcja see some details. Shelves lined the opposite wall. Giant jars. Cans. Crates on the floor, straw sticking out, padding for something breakable, probably. Burlap gunny sacks, bushel baskets, three or four broken jars stacked on one another, making an odd sort of ladder to the tin ceiling. The chairs seemed familiar. When she looked up, her throbbing head protested.

She might be sick.

She heard sounds on the other side of the door, where the yellow light originated. Electricity, mysterious and scary, lightning in a glass bulb—who could trust that?

More sounds: feet rushing about, papers shuffling, a thud, something falling, a window opening.

"Hey, who is there? Where am I? How did I get here?" Patcja called out as she stood on wobbly legs.

I must have whacked my head.

No more sounds. No one answered her. Why the heck not?

"*Co tu się dzieje, do diabła?*"

Patcja opened the door, just a crack, trying to see who was there. Curly ran out, glad to be out of that storeroom. The next room was an office, a desk with a single chair behind it. A lightbulb hung over the desk, dangling from the ceiling. She knew the room now: Augie's office.

She had stood in front of that desk many times, trying to explain why she needed a night off, why she was late, or why she didn't give a rat's ass about what kind of fake whiskey he was putting in jars and mugs and sending her out to deliver to tables.

But there was no Augie sitting at the desk. And no neat piles of paperwork, as there usually were. It was a mess, in shambles. A ledger book was open to a page full of lines and squiggles. Someone had been working on accounts, tallying sales and receipts, it looked like. She'd had an accounting class at Henry Clay High and remembered the look of light-green paper with rows and columns.

Henry Clay. Gee, that seemed like a long time ago. And it was. She had only gone one year to the public high school. St. Florian's Elementary on the back of the church only went up to eighth grade, so if you stayed in school, you had to walk a mile to the public school, where everyone spoke English and Polish girls were treated like vermin—or floozies. One year of that had been enough.

I need to get out of here.

Patcja opened the door just enough to slide out. She was quiet, tiptoeing. But why? She didn't know. She just wanted to get out of there and go home.

What time is it, anyway?

There was no window through which to judge daylight. But she was hungry, and she had to pee. She wondered where the crapper was—or even an outhouse.

She hurried past the desk to another doorway. A curtain, brown and plain, faded, hung from a wire suspended across the doorway. She had seen that ugly curtain hundreds of times. This was Augie's tavern, The Corner, where she worked a few nights a week—whenever it was open, whenever Augie had inventory. That's what he called the bottles of illegal whiskey. *Inventory.*

The sign out front used to say "The Corner Tavern," in red painted letters on a hanging yellow board. When Prohibition came, "Tavern" had been painted over with black paint by some do-gooder and the main door had been boarded up. But if you walked around to the side, there was another door that was supposed to be secret. You had to duck under some ivy vines and stoop down a bit to get through the half door that used to be just a window, back when normal was normal.

Patcja was surprised she hadn't recognized she was in Augie's storeroom sooner. But she spent most of her time near the bar, ricocheting from table to table, taking orders, collecting coins, dodging swats on her behind and rude comments from half-drunk idiot men.

How did I get here?

"Augie, are you here? Where are you, Augie? What's going on? Am I supposed to work tonight?"

Patcja went through the curtain and into the main bar, her hand on her hip and her mouth scrunched up into a scowl. She was ready to let someone know what she thought about this.

Until she saw Joey on the floor, with a red stain under him, growing.

Patcja screamed.

Chapter 11

Halina stormed down the sidewalk, bubbling fury pushing her legs. She was more than perturbed, more like mad as hell. It just wasn't right that this lousy thief had struck again, hit Stach for three whole dollars and then said not to tell her.

What the holy heck? Calling out her name in the stupid note might have bothered her more than the actual theft. It was like being mocked, or like some secret joke behind her back.

Oh, I'm going to find who did this.

It was hard to believe it was the barber, though.

He had it in for *her*? She had never done anything to make him mad at her, at least that she could remember. In fact, Halina had always thought Waldemar had a bit of a soft spot for her.

There was that time when she was just a kid and her hair was all chopped up, sticking out every which way, stubble and stray spokes pointing out around her head, like rays around the sun. It hadn't been her fault. A wicked mean streak, a bottle of whiskey, and tinsnips were to blame.

Pa and his temper.

For weeks, while it grew out, she'd had to deal with the funny looks and teasing. She'd tried bobby pins to hold down the worst of the mess, but that hadn't helped much. All of the little crisscrosses had sort of looked like bizarre crucifixes, some Catholic rite gone bad. The rotten boys in her class had sure had a field day, teasing and making jokes. Including Milosz. After one very noisy, messy, snot-dripping bawling incident, Sister Beatrice had given her the old lady's blue straw hat to wear.

Waldemar had fixed it for her. He'd found her staring at her reflection in the window of the barbershop.

"Oh dearie me. Look at you. You might scare away business, little miss. I've never seen hair look quite so bad. You better come in, before someone sees you standing outside my shop."

He had taken her to the back room and evened things out a bit, at least made the stray pieces that were poking out like wheel spokes lie down flat.

That was four years ago.

She couldn't think of a time she had been in the barbershop since then. It wasn't exactly a place for young women. But the men sure liked to congregate there for some reason. And around the back door that faced the alley. Walking by on a Saturday, you could sometimes hear them hooting and hollering, slapping each other on the back over some game. Dice, maybe? Or wagers on something, probably not legal. She hoped it wasn't dog fights or cock fights or . . .

She knew rotten things happened in these streets. Most she would rather not know about.

Now, a bunch of the mill men and some others she didn't recognize were all standing around in the street, talking, pointing, hands waving in some argument, it seemed. Probably some truck and some horse cart had run into each other. Maybe some farmer had spilled baskets of eggs all over the road. Or who knew. Menfolk always seemed to find something to fight about these days.

Damned Prohibition.

Waldemar stood outside his shop, broom in hand, staying back, away from the ruckus.

She could hear yelling coming from the center of the throng, but couldn't make out the words. Her anger was replaced by curiosity. What the heck was going on?

Waldemar didn't see Halina coming, apparently. He jumped when he suddenly realized she was next to him. He almost dropped his broom.

"Hey there, Miss Halina! You shouldn't be here right now. Go on home," he said, trying to turn her around and shove her away. "Go on, get going."

"But why? I want to see what's going on. Why can't I see?"

"You just can't. Now get going," he insisted, taking her arm, steering her back around.

"I can't go home. I got business to tend to. I need to talk to you, Mr. Waldemar. I want to know—"

"Oh, I can't talk to you now, miss. Well, here, go in here, this way. Just go in the shop and stay there. Don't come out." He gave her a good shove into the barbershop.

Halina tried pulling the shade back and looking out the window to see what was happening, but all she could see was Waldemar's back. He was waving his broom in the air, as if he were trying to chase away a fox in the chicken coop.

This is just crazy. What's going on out there?

She sat in the big red leather chair with the fancy metal footrest. If she had been younger, this would have been a thrill. Honestly, it was still exciting. The chair was finely made, its red leather bright against its white trim, with armrests like a throne. She knew the chair would spin—go up and down, too. And for an instant, she wished she were a child again, as if the world could ever be that simple again.

Should she or should she not? Oh, why not?

Halina gave a shove on the floor with her foot and sent the chair spinning, like a ride at the carnival that came through every summer. She stuck out her legs and put her arms up high, a little girl's "*Wheee!*" on her lips.

She caught a glimpse of herself in the mirror and cringed.

She grabbed the counter to make the chair stop. But her mind wouldn't stop. Images whirled.

Young Halina with her hair chopped up. Boys in school, heckling. Men in the alley, tossing dice, while in the back room Waldemar combed and trimmed her hair, fixing Pa's handiwork.

Waldemar had plastered it down with tonic, pausing now and then for business. He'd made notes in a thick book as he took dollars from men mumbling gibberish. *"Sadie's Lady to win in the first."* Later it was, *"The Princely Pauper by a nose."*

It seemed like a long time ago, days clouded in a nostalgic pink haze, like dawn after a rain storm. But had she changed that much? Grown up at all? She still squabbled with her sister, still went running to Stach when she had a problem, still threw tantrums when she was mad, still pretended she didn't know why Pock-Face was following her, looking after her Here and Now.

She heard a noise from the back room. The back door, maybe. The curtain across the doorway fluttered.

"Somebody back there? Who's there?"

No answer, but more rustling sounds.

Halina decided to look.

"Waldemar isn't here. You should come back," she called as she approached the curtain.

She couldn't believe it. Pock-Face Nicky was in the back room, rummaging through papers on a desk. Had she conjured him up by thinking about him?

"You again? You? Why do I keep running into you?" she demanded.

"Ciao ragazza stupida. Fatti gli affari tuoi."

"Well, same to you, fella. Whatever you said."

He kept looking through the desk, didn't even look up. So rude, so infuriating. Maybe she wouldn't want him to come visit her in her new town, after all.

"I think you better leave. You can't go through Waldemar's things. He's outside the front door. I'm going to call him if you don't leave right now."

"I could say the same to you," he answered in a thick accent. "What is a young lady doing in a barbershop—one where the barber is a bookie?"

"Oh, I don't know anything about bookies. I came here looking for money someone stole from me. A clue points to the barber." Halina reached into her pocket and pulled out the note from the Mason jar. "But Waldemar said to wait here for him. There's something going on in the street. Some hullaballoo."

"Hullabaloo, my ass."

"Well, what is it?"

"It was meant to be a distraction, nothing more, so I could waltz in here and find something. But ... well, things have a way ..." He shook his head. "Now be quiet so I can find what I came to find."

"What are you looking for? Did you get a note from a thief, too?"

"You could say that, I suppose. I'm looking for an IOU from a poker game, high stakes. Mr. Salvatore lost something that he wasn't willing to give up so easily. I need the note back, a promissory note. And a deed."

"Is the note like these?" Halina handed him the folded IOUs, the one left for her and the envelope that she'd found in the newsstand.

When he read them, he laughed. Those messy curls tumbled around his eyes. So cute. But then he opened his mouth, and his tone was mocking. "This all you're talking about? A few dollars? You risk getting in the middle of a fight between two rival gangs over a *few dollars*?"

"Well, it's all I had. And there's a principle involved." Halina crossed her arms over her chest, stuck her chin out. "I'm tired of being pushed around. Cheated. Used. What do I look like? The Sears catalog in the outhouse?"

Annoying Mr. Pock-Face sighed. He reached into his pants pocket and took out a crumpled handful of dollars. "How about I pay you back your twenty-some dollars and you go home, don't come back here?"

"Did *you* steal my money?"

"No."

"Then I don't want *your* money."

"You're not going to find *your* money here. Anyone who was in this barbershop for a haircut or shave could have picked up that envelope and used it. *Anyone.* You just need to wait for them to return the money. Be patient. An IOU means they plan to give it back, so wait."

Then she saw it. Thumbtacked to the wall was a note, and it had the same small, neatly penciled letters as were on the IOUs.

Halina took the note down. A chart of dates with times, like a time card, was penciled across the page. "Bear" was printed at the bottom, looking just like the writing on both IOU notes.

Arghhh. Dadblasted Bear!

Halina didn't know whether to be furious or sad. Hurt? *Bear? He'd* written the note, stolen the money? Why didn't he trust her, ask her to borrow money? Why on Earth would Bear need so much money? Maybe it wasn't him, after all.

Biting her lip and twisting her hands, Halina just turned and left Pock-Face, as he continued to rummage through papers, acting crazy, just like all the other whiskey men.

❧ ❧ ❧

The commotion on the street seemed to have run its course. The street was empty. There was no one lingering around, no sign of mill men, no parked motorcars or trucks with drivers honking or gassing the engine. Even the grocer had wheeled his barrel of soda pop back into his store.

And no sign of Waldemar. Everyone had high-tailed it out of there, sudden-like.

Real strange.

Chapter 12

When Stach left Halina in the newsstand, he hurried down the street, trying to catch up to Janusz. He caught a glimpse of him. Janusz was already down the street near the grocers. Stach wasn't sure what the man was up to, but he was sure it wasn't good. Janusz somehow managed to disappear into the huddle of men at the corner.

There was shouting from the center of the throng—Polish, then Italian. Then grunts, jeers.

Stach saw Waldemar in front of the barbershop, holding his broom across his chest as if it were a rifle and he was about to take aim.

"What's going on here, Wald? You see Janusz go by?"

"It's those damned Sicilians, Stach," Waldemar answered, pointing to the milk truck. "The bastards were setting up in front of The Corner, daring mill men to bet on which bottle—both painted white—held the hooch and which one held horse piss. For a dime, they had a fifty-fifty chance of winning a whole bottle of whiskey."

"Aww, shit. Let me guess. The fella had to take a swig to find out if he picked right or not," Stach said, rubbing his chin. He had a good idea of what had happened now. And that sounded like a fool's game Janusz would fall for.

"You got it, all right. And after a couple dumb-asses tried their luck at it, one young fella came up and took a big whiff and figured out both bottles were horse piss."

"That's when the fight started, eh?"

"Yeah. It's moved into the tavern, I think. I can't see much. I'm just standing here, watching my doorway, making sure no fight ends up breaking my new glass window. Know how much a new window costs, Stach? Do you?"

Stach had no idea. Poor ol' Waldemar. He probably replaced that big window two or three times a year. It was his own fault. He wouldn't have to replace a broken window so often if he got out of the business of taking money from habitual losers. Sometimes the sore loser liked to throw a rock or two. Or a brick or two. Plain stupid.

"Yeah, Waldemar, I know. I know," he finally answered, swallowing the lecture that almost slid out of his mouth. Now wasn't the time. Later. Stach wanted to find Janusz. A bad feeling was creeping up his backside, his heart pounding as if he had been running a mile, or debating with God.

The crowd was thinning out. A handful of men lingered outside The Corner's secret entrance, craning their necks to see inside. Two young men with stringy hair hanging out from under their hats leaned on the bumper of the milk truck, apparently guarding it. The old pickup truck had wooden crates in the back with partitions for the bottles. They were padded with straw to keep the bottles from rattling when the truck bounced over railroad tracks and holes in the road. The glass bottles were painted white. At a distance, it might look like the bottles held milk, at least to anyone with only half a brain or greased palms.

Stach knew the men—boys, really.

"Krysztof, haven't you been promoted past babysitting the truck yet? Seems like a pretty lowly job for a smart kid like you."

"I'd say it's a damned important job, Stach. Mind your own

business," the kid sassed back, standing upright, sticking his chest out as if it were bulletproof and he couldn't wait to prove it.

The boy on the opposite bumper, Piotr, stood up, too, sticking his chest out, too. Piotr didn't have many original thoughts.

"Hi, Piotr, how's your mama? She still nursing that bad toe? Did the poultice Baba made for her help?"

"It sure did. I can barely outrun her now when she gets to chasing after me with that big wooden spoon of hers," Piotr answered, rubbing the back of his neck, probably the remainder of a welt from the world's most dreaded weapon—a wooden spoon in the hand of an angry Polish woman.

"Good, good. Now, boys, who is inside the tavern? Who was driving the truck and making up some game that got himself in trouble?"

Neither seemed to want to tell. They hemmed, hawed, and kicked at gravel in the road, fiddling with their hats and lint in their pockets, looking this way and that, as if their heads were on springs wound too tight.

Both Krzysztof and Piotr had gone to school at St. Florian's for a few years. They couldn't be much younger than Halina. Stach saw them around. They still went to Mass on Sundays with their families, were still good boys down deep in their God-fearing hearts, making their mamas happy to have tall boys with them in the pews, for God and everyone to see.

"There's nothing to worry about, fellas. I'm just wondering, not planning to argue with Salvatore or get tangled in his enterprise."

Before either boy could answer, another one of the Sicilian men ran out of the tavern. It was the tall one, Antonio, the lieutenant in Sal's organization. He was in a hurry.

"Hold up there, son. What are you running from in such a hell-bent hurry? See a ghost?"

Stach halfheartedly tried to block the path from the side door to the milk truck, to at least slow Antonio down enough so he could get a good look at his face, his eyes, try to read what was what.

Antonio shoved Stach aside. "Get outta my way, old man! Dumb-ass Polack!"

Stach stepped back out of the direct path, but also stuck his long leg out at the same time. It caught Antonio in the shins. The young man, suddenly all arms and legs, went tumbling down the gravel to the curb. He rolled to a stop in front of the milk truck. His two young pals seemed panicked, unsure whether to help him or pretend they hadn't seen the humiliating spectacle.

But Antonio was up. He glared at Stach and knotted his fists, flexing his fingers.

"Sorry about that, Tony," Stach said, offering him a hand to shake. "No hard feelings?"

Antonio spit in Stach's outstretched hand, then slowly climbed in the milk truck, taking his time, as though he was trying to prove something. Piotr got in the seat next to him, and Krzysztof took a spot in back, next to the wooden crates, his legs hanging over the back, swinging, as if he were sitting on a tree branch on a lovely summer day without a care in the world.

Stach wiped his hand on his pants, then pulled back the ivy vines that were supposed to disguise the side entrance. He ducked under the board that was nailed across the top half of the door. What was going on in here, anyway? Was this the way Janusz ran? Damned fool.

If that fool gets himself beat up again over some woman . . .

Stach hesitated in the doorway, holding the door open so light could come in. He let his eyes adjust to the dimness, gray and muted shadows, thick with tension, stagnant smoke, and . . . The place looked empty. Deserted.

Something was wrong, terribly wrong.

He heard a moan. Or was it a growl?

"Janusz, you in here, my man?"

"Yeah, Stach, I'm here," answered a man's voice—low, muffled, behind something.

"Where? Janusz—that you? You hiding somewhere?" Stach walked farther in, stepping around tables and chairs scattered helter-skelter, some overturned and out of place, like a skeleton with its bones kicked and scattered by hungry dogs.

Then he saw her. Patcja was on the floor, on her knees, her back to Stach. But he recognized the auburn hair, waves perfect, catching a bit of light.

"Patcja, what in the Holy Mother's good name are you doing here in the dark and on the floor?"

He heard whimpers, more like the mews of a sick cat.

Joey was on the floor, eyes closed, limp.

Patcja kneeled in a dark pool, cradling his head on her lap, patting his face, as if he were just taking a nap and needed to wake up. Her hands were wet, dark with his blood. She didn't look up.

"Patcja! What happened? Are you hurt? What happened to Joey?"

Stach stooped down, avoiding the pooled blood. He grabbed Joey's wrist, feeling for a pulse. Next he checked his neck, looking for a pulse there.

Yes! Slight, but Joey was alive.

Her whimpers became tears, then sobs. She put her hands to her face, hiding, smearing red streaks on her cheeks, her chin. She didn't seem to notice.

What got into this girl? Stach tried to focus on the man on the floor. He looked for Joey's wound. Where was the blood coming from?

His shoulder.

"Patcja, Patcja—what happened? Let go, let me see. *Now*," he urged as he pulled Joey from her lap and moved him to the floor. He grabbed his handkerchief from his back pocket and pressed it on the wound. Joey winced at the movement, then winced again at the pressure. Good signs. He might be coming to.

"Patcja, answer me—*now*."

"I don't know. I don't," she finally choked through tears. "I found him like this. I don't know! I woke up in that horrible back room. I came out here and found Joey . . . like this."

"All right now, Patcja. It's not so bad. He's going to be fine," Stach said, still kneeling next to Joey, lifting the handkerchief to check on the wound. "It looks like a knife. Not too deep . . . not too bad. A shoulder is better than a gut wound—or one to the heart."

Stach looked around, getting his bearings. What had happened here? Augustino, the owner of the place, hovered near the doorway to the back room, his office.

"Augie, get over here! What happened here? Did you or your men see what happened here?"

"I saw, Stach! I know what happened," called Janusz from over Augie's shoulder. "I'm here, Stach! Augie made me go in here, in his office. He won't let me come out!"

Augie stepped aside. Janusz ran out of the back office.

"He just wouldn't shut up, Stach. Him yelling and her blub-bering—*crazy!*" Augie growled at Stach, shaking his head, untying the apron from his waist, balling it up, as though he was done and wanted nothing more to do with this place.

"What a mess. What a damn mess this is," Augie said. "Is he dead? The damn idiot, playing brave boy, hero, protecting the little tra—"

"Augie, not now! Not now," Stach interrupted him. Stach knew what Augie thought of Patcja, and he just didn't want to hear it now. At least, he didn't want Patcja to hear it. She was dealing with enough.

"Yeah, yeah, yeah. Whatever you say, Stach. Whatever. We just need to get him out of here. I don't want trouble in here. *You know I can't have trouble,*" Augie hissed in Stach's ear. The old barman was close to panic, it seemed. He wiped his nose on the back of his hand, sniffed and snorted, like a horse annoyed with flies. Then a coughing fit started. Augie wasn't well these days. The fits came more often, it seemed.

"Calm down, Augie. We don't need you passing out, too."

Patcja scooted across the floor, pulling away, retreating, like a fox backing into its hole. But she kept her eyes on Augie, glaring, sending sparks of hatred, then recoiling into fear. Off and on. On and off. Fear and hate. Hate and fear.

"Patcja, stop right there. You can't go anywhere. Don't think about leaving. Look at you, for Christ's sake."

She looked down. Her lap was a large red spot. Her hands were covered in blood, and her arms were spotted, streaked, up to her elbows. She seemed to see it for the first time.

Patcja screamed.

And wouldn't stop.

Chapter 13

Halina was just leaving the barbershop when she heard the scream. It was close. What? Who? The sound was shrill, a noise like a bird being caught. Again and again, until its neck was broken and the sound was gone—mid-breath, silenced.

"Oh, HolyMotherMaryandJoseph," Halina said.

She turned toward the sound.

Was that Patcja screaming?

Halina ran toward the tavern. No one was out front; the main door, boarded up. But she knew there was a side entrance. A few of the mill men were in the doorway, craning their necks to see what was happening.

"Augie's inviting trouble," one man fussed. "He's going to bring trouble on the whole town, all of us. What is he thinking?"

"Never seen such a stupid move. Messing with the Family," the second man mumbled to his pal. "Joey, Augie, Janusz—they'll all be fish food soon. Right in the lake, to the bottom."

Halina heard Joey's name and guessed Patcja might be part of this commotion, whatever it was about. It didn't sound good.

"Move, mister! I need to go in," she said, trying to shove past the two men in the doorway.

They smelled like steel dust, grime, sweat. When she shoved at them, she could feel the dampness of their shirts, the oily grime. Now it was on her hands, too.

"Buster, get out of my way!" she said again as the two blocked her way.

"Ain't no place for the likes of you. Go home, lady."

"I'm not going anywhere—especially not home, mister. Who put you in charge, anyway?"

They didn't budge. They both looked angrier than hell. Over what?

The bigger one grabbed her arms, picking her up.

"Hey! Cut that out, you big oaf! I said *stop*! I'm looking for my sister!" Halina yelled, kicking the man's shins and wriggling to get free.

"Patcja! Paaatryyyycjaaa! Are you around here?"

"Let her go, fellas, will you? C'mon now," a voice from inside the tavern called out. It was Stach.

Thank God, Stach is here!

"We don't need more yelling and attracting attention, do we?" Stach said to the two muscled men holding Halina's arms. They let her go. Halina pushed past them into the tavern.

As soon as she stepped into the half-light of the room, she noticed the overturned chairs and Stach heading back to the center of the room. Something was on the floor. Augustino was carrying a stack of rags.

Her knees went wobbly. Something was wrong. *Very wrong.* She could feel it in the chaos of the dust specks and the tremor of the floor and the nervous slant of light coming from the back room. Janusz was there in the doorway, fiddling with the curtain. He twisted it in his hands, wringing the color out of the faded fabric.

"What's going on in here, Stach?"

Halina paused a few steps in, having second thoughts. Maybe she should leave, after all.

"Have you seen Patcja? I heard someone that sounded like Patcja."

"Halina. She's over there in the back room. She's fine—just scared. I made her go in there and shut up," Stach said, nodding toward the back room.

Halina started that way.

"No, not now. Come, help me."

Halina took another look at Stach crouched on the floor over something in the shadows. A man? Now that her eyes had adjusted to the gloom, she could make out the lump on the floor: two legs, work boots, shoestrings hanging. The man was on his back, his legs curled under him, as though he'd fallen in a heap. He could have been garbage tossed from the roof to the floor. Messy. She remembered the two buffoons in the doorway talking about Augie—and Joey.

"Who is it, Stach? Is he dead? Oh, JesusChristLordandSavior," she said as she recognized Joey on the floor, blood spreading under him.

"No, he's breathing. It's Joey. Doesn't seem to be so deep. Hole from a knife. I don't know why he's not waking up."

"Well, look at this puddle on the floor, growing by the minute! You gotta stop the bleeding, man! Press harder!"

"He moans when I press down. I don't want to hurt him more."

"Are bubbles coming out? Is the lung nicked? Do you hear air sucking out?"

"No, no, I don't think so."

"Well, move over! Let me see," Halina said, elbowing Stach out of her way. She wanted to see for herself how deep the dang hole was. If Patcja's dumb-ass fella died now, Patcja would be hell to live with. Pure hell. No one needed that.

"Joey, damn you! Stop messing around! This ain't your day to die. It's nothing but a scratch. Wimpy ass."

She heard her own voice and wondered who this bossy creature was. What made her think she could tell Stach what to do or act like she knew something about this fool man who was bleeding like a stuck pig? But Stach did as he was told.

And she took over.

She had seen Baba bully and threaten some poor sick fools into getting well many times. Baba often slapped and pinched her patients, calling them nasty names to shock them into responding and get their pulse going. It was one of those Old Country ways. It was something about getting the heart riled up and the juices flowing. Halina didn't understand the science of it, but she knew it worked.

She just had never tried it herself before.

"Joey, you're a bum! This is no way to get out of your responsibilities! *Sit up!*" And she slapped his face a couple of times, still pressing on the shoulder wound. The bleeding was slowing, and the lung seemed fine. Shoulder muscle was jabbed, though. Probably needed some stitching to help it heal and to close up that big hole.

"Someone bring me some towels. And not those rancid rags that have been sitting on the sink for weeks."

She told Stach how to tear the clean towels into strips, then used a lamp to look closer at the gash. Strings from his shirt were down deep. Augie brought her a knife, like she asked, and some whiskey. She doused the knife in the alcohol, then used it to fish out the strings of Joey's shirt and some loose bits of flesh. Joey howled in pain.

"Wasting good whiskey," Augie complained.

"Oh, shut up, man! Just *shut up*!" Stach said.

Augie gagged at the gush of fresh blood and quickly retreated to the backroom office. Patcja and Janusz were still back there, quiet. That was a little suspicious.

I can't worry about them now.

She needed to tend to Joey, fix him up as best she could. Make him right. The baby in Patcja's belly would need a father. Even if it was this bum, Joey.

❖ ❖ ❖

Stach was happy to let Halina take over tending to Joey and his shoulder wound. He didn't know anything about knife wounds. Not a thing. It wasn't often he was at a loss for what to do. He was used to being the one to dish out orders.

Stach walked in circles, on patrol. Then he switched to pacing back and forth, looking out windows, eyeing the door. Listening. His senses were on alert, bristling at every crunch of boots on the gritty wooden floor, every creak of the eaves and the boards nailed across the front door and some of the windows. The wind was picking up, and the place was drafty. Might be in for a spring thunderstorm.

Someone had let that damned stray dog in the tavern. The dog followed him around, nervous, too. They both paced and watched, paced and watched. Stach didn't want anybody slipping in, sneaking up on Halina behind her back. Maybe coming back to finish the job on Joey.

"Curly—go sit. Guard the door."

Stach didn't know who he could trust. A couple of Augie's pals—the kind with whiskey in their veins—were in the back with Augie. He could hear them talking.

"There's going to be hell to pay for this," one said.

"Salvatore's the one we really gotta worry about. He's the one who likes to feed the fish. They say he's got a warehouse called the Butcher Shop—for a good reason."

Then Augie spoke up. "Just git, both of yous. Watch the alley for that tall one—Antonio. Make sure he don't come back," Augie said. "Take this."

Stach didn't have to see what Augie was handing over. He had a good guess. Augie was one of those fools who thought a Winchester could solve most problems.

❦ ❦ ❦

The bleeding was getting under control, it seemed, and Halina was bandaging Joey, yelling at him, the way Polish women liked to do with their patients. Got the adrenaline going, they thought.

Hell, probably just scares the damned fools into thinking they didn't dare die.

Funny. Well, who was he to question Old Country healing? He could tend to other things for now.

"You seem to be all set, little doc. I'm going to check on Patcja and Janusz," he told Halina.

"Fine. Go, go," she mumbled, dismissing him with an absent wave of her hand. Obviously, she needed no help. She sure seemed to have an instinct for medicine. Something she was born with, he supposed.

He heard some scuffling in the back.

"Patcja? Janusz? Are you two back here?" he called as he walked through the faded curtain to the office.

Patcja was sitting at the table, stock-still, staring at her hands, which were folded in front of her on the table. The blood was dry now, a deep color, more brown than red. She could have been digging in a garden or painting a fence, maybe dying a dress, and simply forgotten to wash away the . . .

Janusz was fumbling around, sitting at the table, then getting up, then sitting again. He fidgeted with his hands, folding and flexing his fingers, tugging at his hair and then his ear, then his trousers, then his shirt. He picked and pinched and plucked and twisted at anything his fingers could find for an instant.

"Janusz, stop that! Hold still, now," Stach scolded the man, watching as he plucked at his eyelids, pulling them away from his eyeballs and letting them go, snapping back in place. The *plick* sound made Stach wince.

Stach took the man's big, grimy hands and held them in his own, saying nothing but looking Janusz in the eye. He could see tears welling up. The big oaf looked crazy-scared, like an animal trapped by fire that was closing in.

"I need you to listen, my friend," Stach said, his voice barely more than a whisper, a low monotone that made Janusz lean forward to absorb the words.

Janusz shook his head.

"I can't, Stach! Noises are in my head. Big noises—loud, like guns. Can't you hear them?"

"No, Janny. No, I don't hear those noises. They are far away. You are here with me, and I'm with you. And you are safe. The guns are far away."

"If you say so, Stach. If you say so."

Janusz didn't look convinced. He pulled his hands away and tucked them under his butt on the chair, trying to hold still. He rocked slightly, left to right, as if he were on a rowboat and waves were jostling him.

Stach turned to Patcja.

Now, what do I do with her?

"Patcja. Hey there, honey," he tried in a gentle tone.

She turned his way, curious.

"Come on, now. Joey is going to be fine," Stach added quickly. "He's getting bandaged up. He's coming around. *He's going to be fine.*"

Patcja blinked, as if she were waking up from a nap. She shook her head.

"Joey . . . I need to see him. I have to talk to him about something important," she said, getting up, scraping the chair away from the table.

"There will be time for that. First we need to get you cleaned up."

Stach led her to the small kitchen behind the bar. He sat her down in a chair and set about washing away the mess as best he could. He started with her hands and arms. The soap, cold water, and brisk scrubbing seemed to bring her around. The cleaner she became, the more she returned to the old Patcja: annoyed, then indignant. Then loud. Finally, outraged.

Thank God.

"Stop that this minute, Stach! I am perfectly capable of washing my own face!" Patcja insisted as she grabbed the soapy cloth from his hands and rinsed it in the porcelain dishpan that Stach had been using. She scrubbed her forehead and cheeks, then her chin. Without a mirror, she had no idea if she hit all the spots. She didn't even seem sure of what she was washing away.

"That's good. Your face is fine now," Stach reassured her. "Just your knees left to do."

The blood had soaked through her stockings to her knees when she had fallen to the floor. She looked down, uncertain of what to do.

"Close your eyes," she finally commanded Stach. "Go on! You don't think I'll take off these stockings with you staring at me, do you? I'm not that kind of girl!"

He obliged. He closed his eyes and turned around, relieved to have the familiar Patcja back in her place and giving orders.

"Can you tell me what happened, Patcja? What did you see? Who was here? Did you see who did it? We have to get to the bottom—"

"You can turn back around now," Patcja said as she thrust the stockings into the soapy water. She stood with her bare feet on the cold cement floor, her toes wiggling, little piggies looking for mama sow's teats. She scrubbed the cloth over her knees. The water in the basin became pink, the soap bubbles ebbing away, leaving nothing more than one pathetic white island floating in a pink sea.

"I was walking toward the mill to meet Joey. I stepped off the curb . . . then saw the automobile. Then nothing. Someone must have carried me here—Joey, I suppose. I woke up in the back storeroom."

"Go on. What happened when you woke up?"

"Someone turned on a light in the office. I came out to see who it was, and I saw Joey on the floor. I was so afraid . . ."

"Who else was around?"

"Well, that big dumb lug." She nodded her head in the direction of the office, where they'd left Janusz.

"And then I saw Augie arguing with someone, one of the mill men. And that tall, skinny Sicilian boy who always wears black—Antonio—was by the bar stealing a drink. Over there, by the glasses." She pointed to the shelf behind the bar, where clean glasses were lined up.

"But I just ran to Joey. I was so afraid he was dead . . . ," she said, her voice trailing off as she remembered the terror she'd felt at seeing Joey in a pool of blood.

"I want to see him now," she said, as though she was asking permission of Stach.

Patcja put her bare feet into her shoes. She looked at her dress but didn't even attempt to wash off the mess, mostly dry now, stiff and brittle, like dried mud. She put on a waitress's apron she found on a hook, then tied it around her pudgy waist.

He was suddenly hit with sadness for this girl, this woman. He felt a strong compulsion to put an arm around her shoulder and hug her, to reassure her, but he knew that would hardly help. And she would never allow it.

He led the way back to the tavern's main room, hoping Halina would have good news about the patient.

Joey was propped up with his back against one of the wooden posts. He was slumped sideways, his head drooping. But he was awake. Mostly. Halina looked quite proud of herself, a grin across her face that made her look very young—a strange consideration, since she had just tended to a knife wound and quite possibly saved this man's life.

"Oh, Joey—you're awake! You're better! You're going to be all right!" Patcja ran toward him, dropped to the floor and tried to hug the man, but she seemed unsure of where she should put her arms.

"Oww. Hey. Ouch," Joey winced and moaned, his voice weak,

trying to pull away, trying to protect his left shoulder with his right arm, but the limb seemed too heavy to lift. He shifted, drooping farther downward.

"Whoa, now! Watch out! He's not ready for that, Patcja," Halina said, trying to prop the man back to his sitting position.

"*You?* What are *you* doing with him?" Patcja demanded. "Who are *you* to tell me I can't hug my Joey?"

"*Me?* I saved his sorry life. If it weren't for *me*, he might have bled to death," Halina said.

Patcja simply said, "Oh."

Halina waited, but no other words seemed to be coming. The air crackled with an arc of tension passing from sister to sister.

"Well, here. Hug *your Joey* all you want and all he can endure. Just don't get that shoulder bleeding again," Halina said, standing up, making room for Patcja to sit by Joey on the floor. "I'm going to make some coffee."

"Coffee? Are you sure he needs coffee? Wouldn't a stiff shot be better? A good belt? I've got some real whiskey, not the moonshine kind," said Augie as he came out of the office.

"No, I don't think we want to slow his heart rate. It's already weak and measly. We want to pick it up, get it going. *Coffee*," said Halina, sounding like the authority. She didn't even blink, not a single pause of doubt crossed her face. Her expression and her hands on her hips seemed to dare Patcja to question her.

The artist in Stach tried to memorize the glare, the muscles taut around her mouth, her brow slightly furrowed. He would paint her like this someday. Halina of Hegewisch, warrior woman and healer. He coughed to chase the silly idea away, but he couldn't help smiling, proud of this girl, soft as steel, who suddenly seemed very wise. He sure as hell wouldn't want to cross her when she was like this.

Patcja was on the floor, her hands on Joey's face, kissing his forehead, cooing in his ear little bits of encouragement, thankfulness, vows for eternal devotion, and promises to help him get well.

Maybe the poor man might need that belt, after all. But Stach wasn't about to contradict Halina, the little doctor.

"Hey, Augie? How about you and me go in the office and talk? We got ourselves some figuring to do," Stach said, rubbing his chin, trying to focus on what might have caused all this ruckus. The sun was going down. Revenge happened after dark.

Stach fumbled for his hankie in his pocket, just something to keep his nervous hands busy. Nagging questions nipped at the back of his mind, like mosquitoes on a hot night. He swatted at the air and wiped his neck with the dirty hankie. He tried to see out a window, through the black paint that was brushed on the day Prohibition went into effect.

Any of those Sicilian boys out there? Antonio? Or the Polish boys they recruited, like Krzysztof?

He didn't see anything, but that didn't mean much. Someone wanting to settle a score could get in this place many ways: alley door, cellar, window, roof . . . Hell, the boards on the front door could be pulled off easy enough.

And the Italians, Joey's people, from behind the stinkin' stockyard, Little Italy, and the canals—who knew what those people would think of this? Who knew?

But no way was he going to have Patcja or Halina be in danger over Romeo-Joey and some whiskey deal gone bad. And what in God's name did Janusz have to do with it?

Augie headed toward the office a couple of steps ahead of Stach. He seemed eager to get all this settled and behind him, too. He started coughing again, doubled over. Stach gave him his hankie. Finally, Augie caught his breath, but the cloth was speckled with red. Augie shoved it in his pocket.

Stach stepped into the office, and a bad day suddenly became worse. Now he had a new problem.

"Where the hell did Janusz go?"

Chapter 14

Halina found the coffee pot in the kitchen behind the bar. It obviously wasn't used much, as it was one of the few objects in the greasy, slimy hellhole that were close to clean. The cold griddle was lined with congealed grease that smelled rancid. The counter was littered with used knives and forks, caked with dried mustard. Strings of sauerkraut were hardened, dried on the wooden counter, blending with woodgrain patterns, like raised hieroglyphics.

She knew dirt was bad for wounds but wasn't sure why. She knew old food, old grease, old rags—anything that could turn sour—was bad for wounds, but she wasn't sure why. She just *knew*.

Halina had watched Baba bandage her sister's arm a few years back. Seemed like forever ago. Or yesterday. Halina had been mesmerized by the yelling and slapping and praying and burning of candles, kneeling and singing. Then came the concoctions that were brewed on the stove from mysterious elements in baskets and jars and pouches on the wall of shelves. Baba's kitchen was a strange hospital.

The healing seemed to be about sucking out poisons and applying dressings to keep the wounds protected. But it was also about calming down a hysterical Patcja, making her believe she would heal, and wearing her out so she could be lulled into sleep—despite the pain.

"Don't whimper at me and distract me with your moans. I'm work-ing. God is working. What are you doing to help?" Baba scolded Patcja, pointing at her with her wooden spoon that dripped an olive-colored liquid, thick like molasses.

"I don't know what to do. What can I do to help?" Patcja whined, sniveling, wiping at her nose with her one good hand.

"Pray, stupid girl! On your knees. And while you're there, sing to God—loud enough so he hears you."

Keeping her burned arm on the table, Patcja got down on her knees. Halina did too—why not? Neither could seem to think of a song, though. Finally, Halina found a tune in her head—"Beer Barrel Polka." She hummed, then sang. Then Patcja joined in.

"Louder!" Baba shouted.

The girls sang while Baba pulled back the bandages on Patcja's arm so she could see just how bad the burns were. Patcja hardly winced, she was so focused on the song, the statue of Mother Mary in front of her, and the cold of the cracked linoleum floor on her knees. Halina saw the burns, though. She kept singing; it kept her from gasping—or gagging.

The old woman mumbled, prayed, and chanted strange words the whole time she treated Patcja's arm. Her short, stubby legs and swollen, sausage-like fingers were suddenly nimble, suddenly swift in their fluid motions. But she wouldn't answer Halina's questions.

"Not now. Not now!" she snapped whenever Halina interrupted to ask what leaves she was crumbling up or what powder was in the jar. So Halina just watched.

Of course, now Patcja wasn't happy about the scars, but it could have been much worse. There had been no infection, no gangrene, and no chunks of putrid tissue that had to be carved away. Patcja was lucky she had had Baba to tend to her.

And Joey was lucky he had Halina. He just didn't know it yet. But she would make sure he knew. The way she saw it, the bum now owed her one *great big* favor. And she was going to collect.

First, though, she had to make sure he came through this.

While she waited for the coffee to finish, Halina found a waitress tablet and a pencil. She made a list of what was needed. And then she had second thoughts.

Maybe I should send for Baba. Would she come?

No, of course not. The woman would have nothing to do with bootleg liquor. *"A bad batch will make a man go blind! It will drive a man insane! It will eat away his guts so he dies a slow, miserable death!"* Baba liked to rant when given the chance.

Halina poured Joey some coffee. She took the mug and her list back to the main room. She found some light switches to flip on, too. The few dangling lightbulbs didn't seem to help much, but the yellow light was better than the long shadows that were taking over the place and giving her the creeps. She felt as if she was being watched again, just like when she was under the peach tree.

Spiders were crawling on her arms. Night crawlers were in her boots; ants, in her bloomers. She wiggled, swiping at the crawlies that weren't really there. Drat. She was spooked.

This place had some bad juju. *Really bad.* It floated up from the floor, like those little waves at the end of the road on a hot summer day. She had only been in this tavern once before, back when liquor was legal. That was enough. She'd come to fetch Pa. Then wished she hadn't.

This spot, right here.

She stood on the place where her face had hit the floor that night. The whack of her jaw on the ground had been loud. The whole place had heard. They'd stopped, gotten quiet, turned to look at her. About four beats of her heart—*kathunk, kathunk, kathunk, kathunk*—and then the noise and the movement had resumed, as if it hadn't been interrupted—at all.

That was then. Now, no one was knocking her to the ground without a good fight. Why couldn't she shake the feeling of being watched, though? Maybe she was taking after Ma and her night-time willies.

"Ma, there's nothing to be afraid of. Ma, stop that! It's just dark, that's all. You don't have to light every lantern in the house and a candle every five feet. Ma, that's crazy."

Or maybe she had whacked her head too hard when she was knocked to the floor. Maybe some brains had gotten knocked loose, like Janusz. Maybe she was crazy. Or maybe someone really *was* watching her, waiting for her.

She went to the nearest window, one facing the street. All the glass panes had been painted black, so it was hard to see out. She had to squint between brushstrokes.

What's going on out there?

A group of men stood in a huddle. One had a baseball bat he held behind his back. One had a lantern. He held it up higher, and in a blink, the men's faces turned to goblin faces. No, that wasn't it. They were a lynch mob with a hanging rope. Faces, distorted by the odd shadows and black spaces where nothing but hate grew.

Halina blinked, and they were normal faces again. Just scared, like she was.

She turned away from the window. *Is that the past or the future speaking to me? Or just the crazies?*

She still had the mug of Joey's coffee in her hand. The liquid rippled from her shaking hand. She hummed—"Beer Barrel Polka."

"Here you go, Joey. Are you awake, mister? No more dozing, hear me?"

He was propped up, and his head didn't seem so wobbly now. His face was white, though. His eyelids hung low and heavy, like a man with a hangover who couldn't quite focus. She had seen that look many times.

"Here, Patcja, get him to take some sips of this. Keep talking to him. Make him mad so he wakes up. None of that sweet-talking shit that will make him want to puke. Tell him he needs to wake up 'cause Antonio will be back and might just stab him in the gut and kill him this time. Tell him *that*. That oughtta make him come around so we can move him. He can't stay here—not on this filthy floor."

Patcja's eyes opened wide. Her jaw fell open. Maybe this was the first time her stupid sister realized the idiot Joey might still be in danger and might be putting the rest of them in a heck of a spot, too. How dense could she be?

"I'm awake. I'll be fine. Just give me a minute," said Joey, slightly slurring the few words.

Had he been drinking before he was stabbed? Halina had smelled whiskey but figured it was just a permanent part of the place, ingrained in the wood and bricks. Maybe it was more than that.

"Shut up and drink the damned coffee, Joey!" Halina yelled.

She kicked a chair leg, making it topple over. Some small critter skittered to its hole in the wall. Probably a mouse. Patcja shrieked, of course.

Joey tried to sit up straighter. The movement caused him to wince. Patcja was climbing on a table, as if she had never seen a mouse before.

"I've got a list I need to give to Stach. Where did he go?"

Patcja motioned toward the office, her eyes skirting back and forth from Joey to the place where the mouse had disappeared.

Halina started to pull back the curtain in the doorway to the office, but she paused. Stach was talking. Augie was talking. She tried to hear what they were saying, but they were doing that whisper-sneer-quiet thing—like a confessional kind of talk that men do when they are plotting. She hated that tone—unless she was included in the circle, which was seldom.

She picked up a few phrases. Antonio's name seemed to be in the center of this. And Janusz. And something about the milk truck and bottles of milk. For crying out loud—

She burst through the curtain as if she were busting through a brick wall.

"You know that's not *milk* in those painted bottles, don't you? Even *I* know that! So why don't you call it what it is? *Whiskey.* Rotgut whiskey. Do you really think calling it *milk* is fooling anyone? If you do, you're stupider than—"

"Halina! Be quiet! Of course we know," Stach said. He paused, trying to decide if he wanted to say more or not. He took a breath and went on.

"But it's complicated," he said, sounding like Sister Beatrice trying to explain long division. "We've got two factions both trying to own the whole south side. One sells 'milk' and one sells 'cola tonic,' and it's just easier to call it that rather than saying names. You never know who is listening, and you never know who is loyal to which side. And you never know what deals have been made. So be quiet. *Stay out of it.*"

He looked at her with a question in his eyes. Was she going to go along with it? Was she going to play nice with the big boys and go along with their made-up stupid-shit code words for breaking laws and trying to kill each other over some lousy rotgut?

Hell no.

"I think it is a little late for staying out of it. I'm in the middle of it now, and I have no intention of playing along with your pretend games, Mr. Newsstand Man. I got blood on my hands—just like you do—and that isn't something funny. Not to me *or* to my sister."

"Halina—"

"Here is a list of what we need if we're going to make sure Joey heals up so he can go back to work. The hole in his chest is close to his lung. And I don't think we can send him on his way, back to that hole where he lives, Back of the 'Yards. He'll have rats chewing on the bandages when he sleeps."

Stach looked down at the list.

"Where do you expect me to get these things, missy?"

"How the hell should I know? You're the big man in charge here. Figure it out! I'm just the kid who knows nothing, remember?"

She stomped through the tavern, past Patcja and Joey. Patcja had forgotten about the mouse, it seemed, and was back beside Joey on the floor, brushing the hair off his face with little birdlike flutters.

"COFFEE! Drink the damned coffee!" she growled as she went past.

"Sorry. I forgot," Patcja mumbled. She held the mug up to Joey's lips again, and he took a sip. He shifted so he didn't dribble down his chin. His pants made a clunking sound. Something in the pocket rolled out. A small brown vial of liquid rolled across the floor and landed at Halina's feet.

What the hell?

She quickly picked it up and stashed it in her pocket. No wonder . . .

Did anyone notice?

Chapter 15

Stach had never seen Halina that angry before. And he wasn't quite sure what had set her off, but whatever it was, she sure was fuming and itching for a fight. She sounded just like a good Polish woman, ready to pounce on anything that crossed her path. A protective lot, those Polish women were. Just like a mama bear protecting her cubs: fierce, full of noise and claws, and rearing up tall to come down on you from above. How he loved it!

He thought of his own mama. He would never see her again, he knew. The letters he sent came back unopened. He didn't know why.

He looked at the list again after he left the tavern. It was too dark to read it out here in the night, though. Well, he knew what it said, and he knew he wasn't going to be able to track down the items very easily. He certainly didn't have clean sheets, rubbing alcohol, or a sewing kit in the shanty where he lived. His place was nothing more than a toolshed-sized shack out behind Baba's house. One room held everything he needed: a workbench, the steamer trunk he'd brought on the ship, a table, and a small wood stove. He slept on the dirt floor on a pile of flour sacks and burlap gunnysacks from onions. Suited him just fine. As long as he had a place for the tools. They had belonged to his papa, a clockmaker in the Old Country.

When Stach had first arrived from Poland, he'd done some woodworking. He'd built furniture, scavenging wood scraps from the dump and fixing up junk. He'd given it away to people who didn't have much, just left the items at their doors during the night. Didn't want to embarrass anybody—including himself.

Stach had built the first newsstand for Mr. Skala, the newspaper man back during the war. But the old geezer had gotten a hair up his ass, refused to sell newspapers to the Sicilians. Stach had tried warning him—but hadn't warned him loudly enough, it seemed. One day, Stach had found the newsstand wrecked—all busted up by an ax—and the stacks of paper on fire. Mr. Skala was inside, slumped over his counter, his head bashed in with a sledgehammer. Antonio had stood down the street, watching and grinning.

Stach couldn't do much. Just gave the undertaker his church suit to bury Mr. Skala in. Rebuilt the newsstand. Took over selling papers. He'd had a hungry spot for Antonio since then. Stach had been waiting for a chance to teach him a lesson. The time would come.

Stach wiped a hand over his face, trying to wipe away the memory. He didn't want to think about it tonight. Had enough on his mind.

Focus on the damned list.

He was going to need a woman to help. And not Baba. No use trying to drag her into the mess.

Who else? He could only think of one woman who wouldn't ask questions and give him misery over a mysterious list he couldn't explain. He hoped she would come to the door if he knocked.

He turned down the alley, listening as he went, alert to sounds of that blasted milk truck, the source of all this trouble. But it was a quiet evening, a good spring evening, just a breeze in the air scattering scents of lilac and new grass.

There were the usual smells, too, the ones that never went

away. Gray tufts of ore-stink from the steel mill and acidic runoff from the battery plant were fresh. Then there was the burning coal from the rail switching yard to the south of town. And when a big gust of wind came through, there was the stench of rancid innards from the stockyards.

Ahh, spring on the south side of Chicago.

He paused so he could listen without the crunch of gravel under his boots. Nothing. Just a dog somewhere. Maybe some newspapers tumbling on the wind, getting caught on a fence, the gusting breeze humming over newsprint, making it vibrate and whine.

Stach went on. He didn't want to keep Halina waiting with her mad dog mood smoldering. What had gotten into her? He couldn't imagine what.

Suddenly, apple blossoms were raining on him, a shower of white blooms fluttering down. It was strange, bewildering. Until he remembered the boy.

Stach laughed, shaking his head. Some things never changed. *Thank God.*

"Bear, is that you? You up in that tree again, darn boy?"

Silence. Not even the wind moved; not even the gravel shifted under his boots. He waited, head cocked, looking up to branches and blooms, silhouetted against the orange-black, starless sky.

Then a snicker, familiar and wonderful. Young.

"How'd you know it was me?" Bear asked as he dropped down out of the apple tree with a whoosh of agility that only a teenage boy could muster.

"Well, gotta tell you, Bear, it wasn't hard. Not many fellas other than you like to hang around in apple trees in the dark," Stach said, slapping the boy on the back, brushing a few twigs and scraps of white apple blossoms off his ratty tweed jacket.

"Yeah, I suppose it's only me that's up in the trees these days . . . Who else?"

They both knew he was thinking of Camel, the brother who no longer . . .

"Yep, Bear, quite a talent you have, son. I bet you could cross the entire neighborhood without ever touching the ground, just swinging from branch to branch."

"Shucks," Bear mumbled as he grabbed his hat in a humble gesture. "Ain't really so much of a talent. I just like it up there, that's all."

Stach watched Bear's face. Was this the same boy who used to carry his father's concertina in its leather case everywhere with him? And oh, how he could play! He would break into a polka at the least bit of encouragement.

That was *before* the war.

"C'mon, Bear, play us a tune! We need to cheer up these sad sacks with their lousy mood and talk of war and the Old Country being divided like a scrap of meat among dogs. This is supposed to be a party!"

Stach poured another shot of whiskey and threw it back. "Na zdrowie!" he shouted as he slammed down the overturned shot glass on the table, an old door balanced on cinder blocks.

The whole shanty shook with the noise. The hinges and doorknob on the table rattled. And as Bear took out the concertina and played the first notes of "Beer Barrel Polka," five almost-drunk men crowded around the table, sitting on buckets and wobbly stools and empty apple crates salvaged from the dump.

They cheered, hooted, arms up high in celebration, stirring the haze of cigarette smoke and orange steel dust into cyclones skimming along the ceiling.

Bear played on and on.

That was a different boy. A few inches shorter then, a tad rounder, plump like a bear cub with plenty of good cooking from its mama bear. And he was happy.

Stach wanted to turn away but couldn't. He didn't like seeing the ache that had changed the boy. It was a monster that tugged at him, pulling the boy downward, it seemed. His eyelids, his eyebrows, the circles under his eyes, and the corners of his mouth all drooped downward on their way to somewhere sour.

"In the dark? You hiding from someone, Bear? Or watching someone? Or sneaking up on someone?" Stach wasn't smiling anymore. "You aren't up to no good, are you?"

Bear froze. "Huh? Why you saying that, Stach?"

"Ahh, never mind. I know—"

Before he could finish, Bear was backing away, hopping over the fence, swinging himself back up into the low branches of the blooming apple tree.

"I gotta go, Stach. I have things to do," he called back over his shoulder.

Me, too, Bear. Me, too.

But there was no use in saying it out loud. The boy was out of earshot, long gone, as if he were a spirit that had vanished. Or maybe it was more like a thief who had almost been caught and decided to hightail it down the road while he still could.

Damn that boy. But now isn't the time. Later.

Stach picked up his pace down the alley, annoyed with himself for losing time. Halina would be up to her eyeballs in fury for sure now, spitting red-hot fireballs. For the last minutes of the walk, he could think of nothing else—Halina, Bear, Camel. The melodious notes that used to come from the concertina but no longer did.

No wonder he was all clenched up in worry when he arrived. He went around to the back door. He knew without even checking that the front door would be all locked up by now, sealed tight. But the back door, the one that opened to steps down to the basement, might be open, just in case. Even if it was locked, though, he knew where to knock on the drain pipe that ran down from the eaves. The sound carried to her room two stories up. That was a long way for vibration to travel, but she was a light sleeper—at least, she used to be. It had been years since he'd stood in this place, hand held out, ready to test the doorknob.

Will it turn? Will it be locked?

He felt like a fool, like a silly boy as young as Bear, sneaking around in the dark to meet a girl. But she wasn't just any girl, was she? No—not just any ordinary woman, either.

He tested the knob. Locked.

He found a rock and tapped three times on the downspout pipe. Then he paused and knocked twice more. A pause and three taps. *Three-two-three.* He slid into the shadows to wait. He imagined bare feet sliding into slippers, then racing down the stairs, turning down the long hall, then galloping down the second flight of stairs. They were steep cement steps, he knew.

Be careful.

He almost said it out loud but caught himself. Stach pressed his back against the brick wall of the building, hoping he could feel the vibration of footsteps in the red clay of the bricks and crumbling mortar.

He did. She was coming!

The heavy wooden door opened a few inches, either hesitant or just stiff from rust and weight. A shaft of light from the basement came through, bright against the black sky. She was backlit, making her outline seem to glow. Her hair was covered; her face was obscured in the shadows, but he knew she was frowning. She always frowned at these backdoor meetings, but she always came.

"Hello, Sister," he said.

"Hello, Stach. It had better be important. I have third-graders to teach tomorrow morning. I need my sleep," Sister Beatrice said, her bare foot tapping on the wooden doorsill. She had forgotten the slippers this time.

"I have a list," he said. "And no one else could possibly—"

She held out her hand, a lovely hand, truly. With graceful, elegant lines that looked as delicate as . . . as . . . well, a lady wrestler who was used to winning. She was lovely. But there was nothing timid or delicate about this nun. During the war, she and Stach . . ."Let's get started, then," she said. "We can't take all night about it."

And it was like old times, waging their own battles of resistance.

Against occupation.

Against wrong.

Chapter 16

Patcja was exhausted. Plus, she was dizzy and light-headed. She had been like that recently. More signs. She needed food, something solid in her stomach to stop it from hopscotching around. But she didn't want to move away from Joey. And how would it look for her to be worried about her own stupid stomach growling while poor Joey was . . . was . . .

Oh, he was pale. And his hands were cold yet wet and clammy, like a slimy catfish that had been out of water too long. He had that same kind of panicked look, too, as if he knew he was in trouble, but the more he flopped about, the worse the trouble would be.

Joey was restless. He kept trying to get up, patting his pants pocket, looking for something. He said he had to go take care of business. Patcja tried to explain to him that he had to rest, hold still, just wait. Help was coming. He either didn't hear her or didn't believe her—or maybe he just didn't care what she said.

That last possibility was gnawing at her.

Why was he so horribly headstrong and defiant, always trying to prove he didn't need anyone? No one. He had no mama; no pa, either. Just some cousins who had signed the sponsorship papers so he could come to this country. He hadn't known they had shady connections, he said. He didn't know they were bootleggers, he'd told Patcja, way back when. She believed him. At least, she wanted to. More than anything, she wanted this man to be a good man. She needed that.

"Joey, what can I do to help you? What do you need?"

He just shook his head and groped around with his hands, as though he was looking for something on the floor.

❧ ❧ ❧

She found Augie in the back office.

"Augie, can't we take Joey to the hospital? Major has an automobile—maybe he could drive us. Or one of Joey's pals from his side of town."

Augie stood up. He wobbled, stumbled, and caught himself on the desk, hanging on, knuckles white.

"Patcja, I don't think—"

She heard a tussle at the side door, a scrambling of feet, grunts, bodies slamming bodies, some punches, fists hitting flesh. She ran to see.

It was men she didn't know—couldn't really see their faces, though. Two of them were going at it, swinging at each other, wrestling on the ground. They were both young fellas, skinny and scrappy, like stray dogs. The one on top had blond curls, like an angel in a church painting. But he was no angel. He was using his arms like a sledgehammer, pounding the poor fella on the ground, who hardly seemed to be fighting back. Maybe he was stunned. Patcja saw the face of the fella on the floor. It was all scarred, pocked, like he'd had measles when he a kid. Now his face was red and turning purple. Angel boy jumped on his belly, jamming fists into his side.

Jesus! That had to hurt.

"Hey, you two! Cut that out! Stop it now!" Patcja yelled at them. But she stayed back, clinging to a wall. The guy on top turned to see who was interrupting his concentration. His mouth hung open, gulping air.

She *did* know him! Krzysztof. He used to be an altar boy at St. Florian's. He used to be . . .

"Krzysztof, you big bully! Stop that, this instant! Do you hear me?"

Krzysztof stood up, took a step toward Patcja. He had blood on his knuckles and hair hanging in his eyes, snot dribbling from his nose, pink with blood.

"Who says?"

"*I* do. I know you from school—Sister Beatrice's arithmetic class. You big buffoon! You were dumb then, and from the looks of it, you're even dumber now. Get off that man! Can't you see he's not even fighting back?"

Krzysztof took a step toward Patcja. She looked for something she could swing.

"What would Sister Beatrice say if she saw you now, huh? Have you thought of that?"

She picked up an oil lamp on the table, the only thing she could reach.

"Remember when she put you in the coat closet to teach you a lesson? You had been shooting spitballs. And everyone left at the end of the day, forgot you. Who came back for you, Krzysztof? Who was that? Huh? *Me.* That's who."

Krzysztof stopped. The memory seemed to crawl across his face. He shook it off.

That was all the time the guy on the floor needed. He was up, scrambling to get to his feet; then he was at the door. He looked back once, nodded to Patcja. He limped and held his ribs.

"Tell your sister I was here," he said as he hobbled out. "Tell her she should go home. Can't be here at midnight. Won't be safe.

You, too, I suppose." Then he was gone.

Augie came out of his office, his ledger book in one hand and a shotgun in the other.

"What's going on? Get out of here! We're closed for business tonight! No whiskey tonight. Come back tomorrow."

Krzysztof stood straighter, wiping his bloody knuckles on his pants. "I did you a favor, Augie. Chasing away a do-gooder. One of Sal's boys gone soft. Talking to the law, they say. Making deals. Stupid, eh?"

Augie set the gun down but held on tightly to the ledger, casting a glare at Joey.

"Yeah. Stupid. Damn you, Joey! If your nonsense brings the law on me, you'll be sorry! *I'll* stab you in the gut, I swear! And I won't miss, I tell you." Augie patted the book. "You're costing me business. Your people had better plan on paying."

"Augie, you're worrying about your books at a time like this? How can you? Don't you have *any* heart? Don't you care what happened to Joey?" asked Patcja incredulously.

"I care *plenty*, Patcja, honey," Auggie said. "Right *here* is where I care." He thumped the book, as if he were thumping a melon to see if it was ripe.

"Your Joey—"

Before he could finish the sentence, a coughing fit came on. This one was loud and wet and sounded as though he were going to cough up his innards. He spat half of them—or something—out onto the floor.

"Sit down, Augie," Patcja offered by way of a truce. "Please, before you kill yourself. We got enough dying men . . ." That started the tears. And the room started swirling at high speed. Patcja went to Joey, sat next to him, rested her head on Joey's good shoulder. He didn't push her away, but he didn't say anything, either.

Patcja sighed. She tried to pray, but no words came to her. She pictured herself sitting in the front pew during Mass, Ma on her right, Halina on her left, and the statue of Mary on the altar with her hands outstretched. Her smile was so lovely, kind, and understanding.

"Mary, help me. Forgive me. Show me. How can I be a good . . . m-m-m . . . ?"

Patcja couldn't say the word, couldn't even *think* the word: *mother*. It might make it real. She would rather not think.

She swiped at the snot dripping from her nose, the few tears trailing down her chin. What a mess she was. So tired. Stupid. She realized Joey was no longer thrashing about, agitated. He was still. His breathing seemed calmer, steadier. And then she felt him rest his hand on her hair, brushing back the damp curls from her forehead.

"Joey, that's nice."

Footsteps came in from the kitchen: Halina.

"Oh, jeepers, good God in heaven. I leave you two alone for five minutes, and I come back to find you both all lovey-dovey and mopey-dopey, leaking water like a boat with termites," scolded Halina. She was far louder than she needed to be. And much snippier and ruder than she needed to be, too. Patcja hated that her sister was bossing her around, but at the same time, it was a relief. Someone else was doing the thinking for her.

Fine. Just fine.

Patcja sat up and glanced at Joey's face. His eyes were brimming with tears, about to spill over.

Must be the pain that is getting to him, poor thing.

"We were just resting," Patcja said, patting Joey's arm. Then, in a lower voice meant only for Halina to hear, "I'm not feeling so good, myself," Patcja admitted, with a silly shrug. She didn't think she could hide her dizziness—and her condition—much longer.

That was enough to turn Halina into Big Boss Nurse, which was fine. Let her take over and try to fix everything. Patcja closed her eyes.

❧ ❧ ❧

Halina made Patcja sit at a table and brought her something hot to drink. It was sweet and soothing. Then there was soup—some odd sort of broth made of something strong and slightly bitter, maybe leeks, maybe old cabbage on its way to rancid. And in it something odd was floating, looked like a dandelion flower. What—?

Still, Patcja took sips, then bigger swallows. It wasn't half bad.

Finally, the room stopped spinning. The throbbing in her head eased, too. Patcja looked up and saw that Joey was sitting in a chair. Halina was feeding him some soup, too.

"Hey—" Patcja started to protest. *She* should be doing that. But then again, it felt good just to sit here and drift, letting her sister take charge.

She reached in her pocket and found Pa's tin of toothache pills. She chewed up another tablet. It was the kind that made the world pink and fuzzy, took the pain far, far away.

Then Stach came back.

The flurry that followed seemed to last hours. Or was it just minutes?

Patcja was in a coat pocket. No, it was a cave. No, a dirt burrow lined with rabbit fur. She crawled in when the noise and commotion started. It was safer in her burrow. She could watch if she wanted to or close her eyes and let the soft gray fur cover her and keep her warm. She sank farther down into the softness when the noise started.

People talking and angry voices that she blocked out with hands over her ears . . . and, "Whoopsie!" she said when she tumbled headfirst. Then clean white sheets appeared as if from nowhere for a bed, and they were put on a beddy-bed-bed in the back room. And magically, Joey was moved to the yucky back room and the yucky cot.

Awww, look at him now.

Then the sewing kit came out, and the needle and thread.

Patcja chewed another tablet, then slid deeper into the burrow and went to sleep.

Chapter 17

Halina was out of patience and ready to be done with this Joey nonsense and all the tavern trouble. How did she get sucked into her sister's problem? And Augie's problem? And Joey's? She didn't even like Joey, the big, boastful blowhard.

Halina was tired. Now that Joey was stitched up, bandaged, fed, and sleeping on clean sheets on the cot, she could pause. And the reality of it all was sinking in.

"So, looks like we're not playing poker tonight, eh, Stach?"

"No. Suppose not."

He was at the door, looking out to the street. Was he expecting someone to drop by for a party—or some more trouble? Augie joined him. They did their whispering and arm-waving thing. Halina didn't even bother trying to listen. She was done.

"Well, just as well," she said, mostly to herself. "Since I sure didn't find my poker money." It seemed like a very long time ago when she'd dug up the empty Mason jar and some missing coins were her biggest worry.

It was probably getting close to midnight, maybe a little later. Now she just needed to get her sister home. She couldn't stay here all night, especially under the table.

Hmm. Maybe there were too many mushrooms in the soup. Halina snickered. She would have to remember that recipe. Could come in handy.

"Let's go, sister," she said, trying to rouse Patcja.

But Patcja didn't want to wake up or move. She grumbled.

"Fine, you want me to leave you here? You going to sleep on the floor of a tavern? You really want the whole town talking about you like you're a floozy?" Halina kicked at Patcja's bare feet. "Wake up, now!"

Halina found Patcja's stockings and shoes and prodded her into standing. She still had an apron on, covering the blood on her lap. Good. It was plenty dark out, but she didn't want to risk anyone seeing her sister's dress covered in blood.

"Hey, Stach, we're going. I'm taking Patcja home," Halina said.

"You sure? She can walk all right?"

"Well, *I'm* not carrying her, so she has to walk."

"Go down the sidewalk, not the alley. Watch out for trouble," he warned. "Maybe I should follow you."

"Are you expecting the law or the Sicilians? Or is it the Italians we're supposed to be 'fraid of this week? Who do I need to be watching for?"

"Not the law, for sure. They wouldn't care if we all killed each other. But Antonio might be around. Big bad Salvatore may even take an interest in this little turf skirmish. Who knows?" Stach sneered, as if it were all the game of children—naughty children who ought to know better—and he was tired of playing teacher.

Halina was tired of the games, too. Milk bottles, pop bottles—who did he think he was fooling? She knew it was whiskey. *Everyone* knew it was whiskey. Why couldn't they just say *whiskey*? And why did someone have to stab Romeo-Joey over it? He was no bigshot in this whiskey nonsense, was he?

She tapped her pocket. Yup, the bottle was still there. The small brown bottle was half full.

What is this, anyway? Something so secret that it doesn't have a label? Or is it homemade? Or illegal?

She yanked out the cork and took a whiff. For some reason, she thought of Pa's bench and the smell of habits turned rancid. She choked and jammed the cork back in the bottle as she returned it to her pocket. *I'll think about this later.* She dropped the bottle back in her pocket.

She tugged at Patcja, and her sister followed. She seemed out of oomph. No arguments left in her. *Good.*

"Be careful, Halina," Stach said again, more somber this time. "Take the dog with you."

Curly jumped up from his spot by the door, sensing someone talking about him.

"C'mon, doggie! Doggie-dog-dog, Curly-dog!" Halina called.

Halina and Patcja left, after Patcja gave the sleeping Joey a kiss on the cheek goodbye. They walked toward the barbershop, and Curly followed, smelling at the air. It smelled like rain. Maybe that was what the stray kept sniffing at, his nose up in the air, as if he were catching a whiff of something about to fall on them from the sky.

Dumb dog.

When they reached the corner, they had to pick sidewalk or alley. Alley was faster. Halina chose that route, not caring one darn bit what Stach thought. She just wanted to get home before it rained.

"C'mon, Patcja. Can't you pick up those pretty feet any faster and hurry your butt along? Don't you want to get home?"

Curly led the way. Halina was right behind. Then trailing a few yards back was pokey Patcja, carrying her shoes, running her hand along the top of the fence posts as they walked. She hopped from one patch of grass to the next, avoiding stepping on the gravel.

"Can't you put your shoes on? And hurry!"

Patcja didn't seem to hear. Halina waited, tapping her foot, faster and faster, humming louder and louder.

Then Curly broke out barking. The crazed, fierce, snapping yowls nearly covered the sound of footsteps.

❦ ❦ ❦

Patcja heard boots crunch on gravel. She jumped.

"Hello, Patcja," said Antonio.

And the dog went crazy. Curly growled and barked and jumped, charging at Antonio, teeth bared, nipping.

"Damn dog! No!" Antonio shouted, swiping at Curly with a fist.

"Whoa, dog! Curly! Down, dog! *Enough*," Patcja said, holding back the growling ball of fur and teeth.

Patcja got the dog calmed down. She appreciated the protection, but there was no need to take a leg off stupid Antonio.

Antonio wasn't dangerous. She knew him, his voice. And that face, those arms, and the wonderful way he had of picking you up and twirling you to the sky, as if he could toss you to the clouds if he wanted to. Or just toss you away, like trash, if he wanted to.

"What are you doing here? What do you want?" Halina demanded. "Git outta here and leave us alone."

"I want to talk to Patcja. You can just shut up and keep walking," Antonio answered Halina, keeping his eyes on Patcja.

"Nothing doing." Halina stomped her foot and stood with her arms folded firmly across her chest.

Antonio started to laugh. It was a light, musical laugh—so out of place on the somber face that had become twisted. He used to be cute, handsome in a rough-hewn way, like a chiseled carving that was not quite finished. Now the lines were all slightly askew, broken a few times.

"What do you want, Antonio? I don't really feel much like talking right now," Patcja said. She dropped her shoes and slid her feet into them. Just in case she needed to run. She also tried to tidy up her hair, smooth it down, and tugged at the apron. Did the blood show? Probably not in the dark. *Thank God.*

"I want to know what happened in there. Did that traitor

croak? Bleed out?"

"Joey's no traitor!" Patcja shouted. "And he's going to be fine, just fine."

"What do you care, Mr. Big Shot Antonio? Are you the chicken-shit ass-wipe that stabbed him and ran? I bet you are," Halina sneered. "I bet you have blood on your hands, and your mama told you to come say you're sooorry and beg forgiveness," Halina sneered.

"Hardly, doctor-woman. Hardly," Antonio said, chuckling, as if it were all a joke. Then he stopped abruptly and squinted. He strolled a few steps closer to Patcja, taking a hand out of his pocket with something in it, something shiny . . .

"*RUN!*" Halina shouted.

Halina and Patcja took off down the alley, throwing up gravel in their wake.

Curly lunged at Antonio, barking and growling at full force. Patcja heard Antonio shouting at the dog. Then there was whining; then rustling, tussling in gravel. Thuds. Then rustling in brush. And the sound of the moon sucking on white, exposed bones.

When they got to the corner, Halina and Patcja both slowed down, paused to look back. No one was following. No one was there. Only a dark, empty alley, trashcan lids reflecting bits of moonlight. Various empty crates, overturned barrels, and tall metal buckets filled with trash waiting to be burned lined the alley. Silhouettes, black and sinister, clung to the sides.

Two red eyes close to the ground stared back.

Patcja screamed.

"It's just an ol' opossum," Halina hissed, slapping her hand over Patcja's mouth. "Quiet! You want every other stabbing, stealing dirtbag up to no good in this town to hear us?"

Patcja squirmed away.

"No. One was enough."

They walked the rest of the way home, staying in the shadows, walking carefully to avoid stray junk strewn about, trying to keep the gravel from crunching too loudly.

As they walked, Patcja thought about Antonio. She remembered the first time she told her sister about Antonio.

Halina was in bed, pretending to snore, not wanting to hear about the glorious night.

"Stop pretending. I know you're awake," Patcja said as she lit a candle.

"I'm asleep," Halina grunted.

"I can't possibly go to sleep. Not now. Not ever again. I plan to stay awake always and forever so I don't miss a single moment of this wonderful world," Patcja said, twirling, her arms up high, celebrating.

"That's what you said last week, right before Mikel told you he had enough of you. Then you decided the world was a wretched place. Remember?"

"But this is different. He's different, not a stupid Polish boy. He's tall, with dark hair that falls across his face and a smile that is sweet and just slightly naughty, like he can see right through my dress. He wears his hat—a fedora—pushed back on his head, like he's not afraid of anything. He winked at me, and I wanted to melt. He has a pickup truck. A bit rusty, but it goes so fast! Before I knew it, we were at Wolf Lake. Look, I still have sand in my shoes, and my hair, and my dress." She slid off her dress and shook it. Sand fell, grains catching bits of candlelight as they tumbled. "I think he may be the one . . ."

He might be the one, all right.

He was the one who stabbed Joey. Patcja knew it.

She'd get even.

Chapter 18

Halina woke up slowly. Saturday morning. A very rude shaft of light came through the window and jabbed her in the eye. It was solid and liquid all at once, like an ingot of molten steel. She rolled over and pulled the blanket over her head. The green army-issue blanket was so thin she could see through it.

> *Light through gauze. White light and black shadows.*
> *Limbs flailing in the dark. A bottle flung; shatters on cement.*
> *Ma stands in the doorway. A rolling pin, like a club.*
> *"Get off her! Get out!"*

The scraps of memories came quickly, one after another. She relived the moments she wanted to forget. She was hiding under the blanket, just as she had done as a younger Halina. She saw it all again through the blanket filter.

> *The wall of coal shifts.*
> *The man-shadow, huge, claws his way out*
> *the open eye window, barely fitting.*
> *Coal dust hangs in half-light, orange,*
> *like interrupted fate, misery, and molten steel.*

Halina rubbed the coarse wool across her eyes to make the imag-es stop. *Dadnabbit, holy tarnation!* There was no use in reliving those days, no use in picking at those scabs. But tiny, prickly reminders were scattered everywhere, always catching on her sleeve or tangled hair. Even this lousy blanket, frayed on the edges, made the nightmares come back.

The blanket had many stories to tell. Many nights she hid under it or clutched it to her chest. A corner had been scorched by fire. The top edge was frayed, picked at by nervous fingers afraid to go to sleep because that was when the face showed up in the window.

"US ARMY" was stamped along one edge, the letters ghostly now. The blanket was army issue, stolen during the war. Maybe that was part of the problem. Some bad juju came with it. But in those days, right and wrong were all mixed up. The railyard switching station was so close. Right there. And those boxcars were loaded with so much, and people in Hegewisch had so little. Who could blame Stach for swiping a few crates now and then? And the people never complained when they found packages at their back doors, no note or anything, just a bundle of blankets or a couple of lanterns. Some men got boots and coats. Some families with no beds got fold-up cots. Ma got a case of candles because was she was so afraid of the dark.

They'd had their own Robin Hood. Stach gave up those ways, though. *Probably.* Well, who could say for sure? It wasn't any of her business.

Halina snuggled down deeper, tugging the blanket away from her sister, who slept next to her. She sank in, finding a cool spot on the sheets, letting herself drift in a lazy, tranquil sea of turquoise saints, Latin prayers, and the innocent lilt of jump-rope songs. Thinking of Stach made her feel drowsy, sleepy, safe, as if someone were guarding her, someone even bigger and stronger than those gorilla men who worked the docks. It was a nice feeling.

For a week now, Halina had stayed away from downtown and The Corner, avoiding those kinds of bad-news fellas. She had gone to the funeral for Milosz, just like everyone else in town, done her share of crying and nose-wiping and trying to understand how a good Polish boy had ended up dead on the tavern steps. God wasn't volunteering any answers, and the good priest had been all about sin and warnings about the evil of drink.

Halina already knew that, didn't need to hear any more of it. She even avoided Stach and Baba. As she saw it, her job nursing Joey was done. She'd done what she could to help her sister and because Stach seemed to think brainless Joey was worth saving. Now that it was done, she wanted nothing more to do with Italian hoodlums, Sicilian thugs, and bootlegging nastiness and schemes. Not even Nicky with his curls, the measle scars on his face, and a dog-chewed scrap of niceness that sometimes rattled around in his good-for-nothing head. *Sometimes.* But not nearly enough.

Patcja wasn't too worried about the rotten fella who stabbed Joey coming back around, it seemed. She had been spending several hours a day in the back room of the tavern, looking after Joey, keeping him company while he mended. Halina didn't have a hard time imagining what that meant. But Patcja didn't like to talk about it for some reason, as though she was trying to keep the fool man all to herself. As if Halina cared a cheese curd about whether Joey lived or died.

It seemed, though, that Joey was mending up right fine. He was up walking, Halina heard. And word had it he'd be going back to work soon, if his job was still there. Maybe, after that, when everything seemed normal again, Patcja could get him to think seriously about their future.

Maybe. Her sister ought to do it soon. The church ladies would start talking. And once that began, there was no turning back.

Halina had given up on finding her poker money. And with her money gone, so was her plan of moving on to another town. She couldn't start off on her own with no money. Could she?

So she was back to helping Ma with laundry, sewing pillow-cases, and waiting for the next poker night so she could start saving up again. The torn page from the newspaper was still in her pocket, though, the notice about the candy striper job at the hospital folded into a neat square. She thought about it often. But always, for some reason, she just couldn't make herself go to see about the job. What if they didn't want her? Then there would be nothing left to aim for, only a hole where a notion used to be.

Patcja was snoring—loudly, deep asleep, as if she didn't have a worry in the world. How absurd. She had plenty to worry about. How could that birdbrain numbskull woman sleep? Halina considered nudging her awake. *Get up! Face your troubles, get him to marry you!* But she didn't have the heart. And she really didn't want to have her morning spoiled with Patcja's moaning, groaning, and puking.

Now Halina was certain of Patcja's condition; the symptoms were obvious. She wondered who else knew. Ma? Sister Beatrice? Baba? Patcja seemed to be getting rounder every day. Pretty soon it would be impossible to miss. No bulky sweater could hide the evidence. Then it would be a whole new mess of trouble.

Whew. It was getting hard to breathe with the blanket over her head. Halina threw the rag-thing away and sat up, stretching. Saturday. Chores to do. Halina and Patcja had had a list of chores to do on Saturdays since they were little girls and didn't know enough to be unhappy about it.

Patcja was curled up on her side of the mattress. She was as naked as a jaybird under that sheet, Halina could tell. Ahh, Patcja—always showing off, even when there was no one to notice.

At least Patcja's nauseous spells seemed to be less frequent. Halina looked over to the crate next to Patcja's side of the bed. Good: there were still some bread crusts and a few crackers on a small plate. It helped Patcja to nibble on something in the mornings. But the dishpan was there, too—just in case.

Halina left her to sleep a little longer and got started on the chores.

She decided to start with washing the glass globes of the oil lamps because she hated that job the most. The landlord had put in some electric wires two years ago, but Pa didn't like it, called it devil's work. Ma was sure the place would catch on fire and kill them all. So there was only one dangling lightbulb in the main rooms. They still lit the kerosene lamps every evening. Ma hated the dark. Gave her the willies, she always said. Ma had lots of funny things about her. That wasn't the worst, by far.

Halina found Ma in the kitchen, as usual. She was peeling potatoes at the sink, as Halina had seen her do hundreds of times, maybe thousands. There were many things predictable about Ma. She always wore a dress with a small floral print, something that looked as though it belonged on a quilt. Then, always an apron, usually one of the full-bib kind with ruffles at the sleeves, two big pockets, and embroidered outlines of flowers or vegetables. Silly.

She always wore the same sturdy black shoes with stubby little black heels and tiny buttons that took a hook to pull them through the loops. She wore thick support stockings rolled down to her ankles, black wool ones in the winter. A white muslin babushka was on her head, most days. The red-and-black silk was only for special days, like weddings or funerals.

On Sundays, the stockings weren't rolled down, the apron stayed home, and the bobby pins came out, revealing dozens of tiny curls plastered to her head with some sort of hair cream. Halina had no idea how her mother got her hair to look so ghastly stupid or if she was even aware of the embarrassment she caused her daughters. At least she kept that babushka on most of the time.

Halina and Patcja used to want to be like Ma. They used to play dress-up and pretend to be grown up or some version of that. Patcja had pretended to be a dancer on a stage. Halina was queen of the Gypsies. She hadn't understood when she was little why that term was considered taboo by some, including Baba. When pressed, the old woman insisted she had ridden with the Romani people. In their brightly painted wagons, she had ridden for two years, crisscrossing southern Poland when she was barely seventeen. She learned their secretive ways—how to run from the church and hide from the law. Baba had been sweet on a fella, she would confide sometimes. His *babcia* had been the *chovihano*, the tribe healer. That's how Baba had learned to use plants and herbs to make potions and remedies.

The tin kettle on the stove reflected light from the window. Halina saw in it whirling colors, motions, the images almost real:

> *Patcja toes, cute and pudgy.*
> *Playing dress up.*
> *Bare feet in black stockings: wool, baggy, stretched,*
> *hardly Mary Pickford.*
> *Silk babushka, red and black, slippery like sin.*
> *Then shoes with buttons and heels.*
> *Practice steps wobbling across the floor.*

"What are you staring at, girl? Get busy."

"All right, Ma, all right. What are you cooking so early?"

"Potato soup. I got a ham hock yesterday from town. On sale," she answered, not looking up.

"Was it on sale because it was old and had maggots crawling on it? You know that butcher sells—"

"*Nie, nie.* It's fine, just fine."

"If you say so, but I think I'll skip the stomachache, thank you."

"Fine. You can starve, Miss Skinny. Go ahead. I don't care. Everybody in town thinks I don't feed you enough. They ask me, 'Why is Halina so puny?' and I say, 'She doesn't eat. She wants to worry me to death.'"

"I eat sometimes. I eat enough. Don't worry about me, Ma. I can do my own worrying," Halina insisted.

"Get to work. Stop your talking. Don't let your father hear you."

There was no sign of Pa. His coffee mug had been left on the table, empty. Cigarette smoke still hung in the air over the table. That meant he was probably close. Halina kept one eye on the back door as she collected the lamp globes and got the big tin wash pan out of the pantry.

"So, where is he? Is Pa even here?"

"He's out back. Burning trash, I think. I don't know. What does he ever do? Where does he ever go? I don't know. I don't follow him and keep track," Ma said, shaking her head.

"Well, don't you ever worry? Or at least wonder? Or get mad? Don't you ever want to hit him—like with a wrench?"

"*Nie*. It's none of my business, what he does. Or doesn't. Or yours—none of your business," Ma said, pointing a finger at Halina, scowling at her over the top of her glasses.

Halina noticed the glasses then. The right lens was broken, cracked. A triangular chunk of glass was missing from the corner, the size of a pea. The earpiece was bent slightly, making the glasses sit on the woman's face at an absurdly odd angle. A slight blue bruise was starting to show on her cheek.

"Oh, Ma! What happened? Your face! Your glasses! What happened this time, Ma?"

"I sat on them." Ma shrugged.

"Oh, Ma, you didn't sit on your glasses! I know better than that. How could you sit on your glasses and get a bruise on your face, for crying out loud?"

"I just did."

"*Baloney!*"

Her mother turned her back and walked away, dishing out the most hideous of insults—silence and distrust.

Halina gasped, stung by her mother's cold response. *Why does she shut me out like this? Does she not want my help?* Halina was hurt. She groveled like a child, begging for attention and a hand that would touch her and tell her it was fine. It would be fine soon. They would all be fine soon. She sat on the wooden chair. The seat was still warm from Pa's stupid butt when he'd sat here. She almost jumped up, skittered away like a frightened cat. But that would be giving in. *Spineless.*

She sat. And sat and sat, waiting for Ma to turn back around. But the woman stood at the sink, washing potatoes, as if nothing were wrong. Or was she sniffling?

"Can't you say something, Ma? Can't you at least tell me what he did? If you can't stand up to him, maybe I can. Maybe I can make him stop. But you need to talk to me! Tell me what happened."

Tell me what happened, please! Halina closed her eyes. She asked again: *Tell me what happened!*

But the vision knew no date or time. A random image came:

> *Shadows, fists, limbs flailing in the dark.*
> *A bottle flung; shatters on cement.*
> *Ma stands in the doorway.*
> *A rolling pin, like a club.*
> *"Get off her! Get out!*
> *I killed once; I'll do it again!"*

The violence was so real she could feel the tension and the ache and the anticipation of the whack that was certain to come. She winced and turned her face, buried her head in her arms on the table and cried. For her and her mother. For her sister and her mother. For herself.

The humiliation was raw, too intense and degrading. The will to survive and hunger for revenge reared up. Her bottled-up temper broke free, and foulness poured out. The venom was black and rancid, dipped in sarcasm bitter enough to burn holes in flesh.

"You didn't sit on your glasses, Ma! Maybe they just fell out of your hands, like this?"

Halina dropped a glass chimney on the floor. It shattered into dozens of pieces.

"Is that how it happened, Ma? Huh? Or like *this*?"

Halina picked up the next globe sitting on the table to be washed. She squeezed it in her palms, and it shattered. Broken glass fell to the floor. Shards poked her knuckles, sticking out at strange angles.

"Is that what happened?" she yelled at her mother. "Your glasses fell through your fingers because you're *clumsy*?"

"No! I didn't sit on my glasses! I didn't drop them! And you can't blame your father, either!" Ma shouted.

"What?"

"That's right. So stop it! Stop it right now! You don't know a thing about my problems! And you never will, if I can help it," Ma huffed. Her voice was restrained behind a fat hand with potato peels clinging to her palm. "Do you hear me?" she hissed.

"I hear you, Ma, but I can't listen to your silly lies any longer! I can't stand by and watch you be bashed around and hurt! Why do you cover up for the damned man?"

Halina tried picking at the glass in her hand. She made it worse. Her knuckles were bleeding. She looked at the table where four more sooty globes were lined up, soldiers ready to be sacrificed for the cause.

"That's enough!" Ma said. "Don't you touch another one. You're going to have to pay for each one you break, you foolish thing! What has gotten into you?"

"I don't know, Ma. I just don't know," Halina said, leaning on the table, suddenly very weak. She was out of fury and fumes.

"I don't cover up for him. I cover up to protect *you*," Ma said. "What you don't know can't hurt you."

Halina was confused. She sighed. In the pause, she realized the stupidity of her tantrum. Childish. Why was she like this? Such a damned hothead?

So much like Pa.

Bile rose in her throat, and she gagged on the sour taste.

Halina hurried out the back door, afraid last night's dinner would come up. The blood dripping from her hand left a trail of red dots.

Chapter 19

Patcja eventually woke up. Some crashing noise upstairs did it. Or was it a noise outside? It was hard to say. She tried rolling over and going back to sleep, but she knew that was useless.

Chores.

She nibbled on a cracker to help her queasy stomach and got dressed, putting the oversized sweater on again, buttoning it up.

She went to the kitchen, hoping for hot coffee. She found a mess—glass all over the floor—and a bawling mother. Patcja slowly pieced together what had happened as Ma reluctantly told the story of her insane sister breaking the lamp globes on purpose. It was only half the story, she knew. Patcja guessed at the other half when she saw Ma's face and broken glasses.

Patcja swept up the glass on the floor and wiped up the blood trail as far as the door. By then, Ma was done with her sobbing and shaking and hiccupping. Just like a little kid, the woman had cried herself into a real tizzy. Then, exhausted, she seemed to forget what she was carrying on about. Or why.

Ma wiped her face on her apron and took her place at the sink, back to peeling potatoes.

Patcja watched the woman for a minute, making sure all the hysterics were done and Ma was fine with the knife and the potatoes and whatever excuses and lamebrain hogwash was in her head, making this all be all right and calm and almost normal—for a while. The last thing they needed was Stella showing up. One of *those* spells.

Ma finished another potato and rummaged in the bushel basket at her feet. She pulled out two carrots and started washing and chopping. She added them to the big pot and set the pot on the stove. Her nose was still runny from the crying. Her eyes were puffy, and she tried repositioning her banged-up glasses so she could see better.

"Here, Ma. Let me take those. Let me see if I can get them fixed for you."

Patcja took the glasses, wrapped them in a small towel, and put them in her sweater pocket.

"I'm going out, Ma. I'll finish the chores later." She didn't wait for an answer.

She followed the blood drops as they led down the sidewalk, getting farther and farther apart. Soon, there were few drops. That was all right. She didn't need to follow them at all. She knew where the trail led. That's where she would have gone, too, if she were upset and hurt, mad, needing to get away from the craziness of the house.

She found her sister lying on a waist-high wall of cinder blocks. She was balanced on the blocks—only a few inches wide—like some kind of assistant in a magic act, in a trance. She was on her back, with one arm up in the air, as if she were inviting a dove—part of the act—to land on her palm. The wall had probably once been a basement wall or part of a root cellar. Who could say about the Patchiecki place? It was just a skeleton of bricks, some wood slivers, a fireplace and chimney, some tin here and there, and a round pipe that was probably a vent for the stove. It had been picked clean of anything useful. What was left was just misery and malice, ruins from a fire. And cursed. The whole Patchiecki family had died in the fire.

When Patcja and Halina were young, both still going to St. Florian's, they came here to hide. Or to test God. Would He strike them dead for daring to set foot in this forbidden place that had been declared off limits? Was it forbidden because it was dangerous or because it was unholy ground, where wicked things happened to good girls? They came here when they wanted to prove they were brave, not frightened by the groping shadows or rustling skirmish of critters, the spirits of lingering souls, or the hand of God that might reach down and pluck them from this earth and toss them to hell, where they belonged.

They came here when they were so scared that they couldn't be any more frightened. And fearing rats and ghosts was better than fearing something invisible that lived in their home.

"Hey. Did you get all the glass out?"

Halina opened her eyes but didn't turn her head. "Nope. I need tweezers. Did you bring any?"

"No, but I have a towel. Did the bleeding stop? Do you need it?"

"It's fine."

"Come on, get down from there. You want to tumble off and make things worse, you nut?"

Halina didn't answer.

Patcja snorted and kicked at the nearest cinder block. A big, fat spider scurried out.

"Ooo, look at that! Move over. Darn it—*make room*! There are spiders down here in the grass. Yuck!"

Halina sat up, and Patcja climbed on top of the half wall next to her sister.

They sat, saying nothing, both lost in their own thoughts, legs dangling over the wall, shoes about to drop off. Patcja gave her sister the towel from her pocket, the one that had been wrapped around Ma's broken glasses. She avoided looking at the hand as Halina wrapped it. Patcja didn't want to see any more blood for a long time. Ever. Never, ever again.

Halina started humming some silly tune, something made up. It was her sister's stupid thinking hum, as if her brain were a machine humming away, wheels turning, squeaky cogs and rusty gears. Damn, that was getting annoying. Why did she have to be so childish and naïve one minute and a real know-it-all the next?

Patcja was tired of looking after her. Halina and her stupid temper. Patcja tried to wiggle into a more comfortable spot, but the cement block was pinching at her butt. She had enough. She jumped down, avoiding the spot where the spider had darted.

"Let's go. We can't sit here all day. We're not children anymore. We can't just lollygag around hoping God, or someone, will show up and save us. No one is coming looking for us, worried and acting like they give a crap about us. 'Cause they don't," Patcja said, hand on her hip, watching the grass for more signs of spiders.

"You have Joey."

"Yeah, well, hell's bells. Do you see a ring on my finger? I sure don't. And I'm dangling my hook from the fishing line right in front of his face, waving it around, baited with some pretty promises and mooning and fretting over him, telling him how handsome he is and so brave and the 'blindly devoted, helplessly in love' bit trying to catch a nibble. He ain't biting. Not a tug on the line."

"I think he's already done a lot more than nibble," Halina answered, her eyebrows raised and a smirk on her face.

"What do you mean? I don't know what you mean." Patcja did her best to sound confused. Shocked. Dismayed.

"Patcja. Stop it. *I know.*"

"Know *what*? What on Earth are you talking about?" But she heard her own voice and heard the squeak in it, the shrill sound of panic. She tried to take a deep breath but couldn't.

Her lungs twisted further into a tighter knot; her throat closed. She was being squeezed by giant hands around her chest, trying to squeeze all the air out of her. One of her breathing attacks.

Oh, God, no—not again!

Her mouth opened wide, like a fish out of water, and a sucking sound came out. Wheezy gasps, fluttery sounds: baby birds, wings half-bare, flapping wildly, trying to fly, going nowhere, no air, nowhere. Air . . .

"Hal—"

"Oh, Jesus, Patcja! Stay calm. *Caaalilmmm.* See, like this—*slow* breath in. Calm."

Patcja tried. She tried slowing down the rising panic, controlling the gasps, but they were spasms, fists clutched. Mad fists. Mad. And she was dizzy.

"Listen to me! *Look at me,*" Halina said sternly, grabbing Patcja by the shoulders. "You need to picture blue sky, wind, God. He's here. He's here to help. He's blowing cool spring air in your hair, in your ears, in your mouth. *Open your mouth.* Open your throat, Patcja. Open your chest. God says to breathe. He is filling your lungs with air. It's God, Patcja. You must listen to God. He's breathing for you. He loves you, Patcja. *I love you, Patcja.* You must breathe. Your baby needs you to breathe. *Breathe.* Calmmm, slooww breaths. Like that, just like that. Good, good. More . . ."

Patcja could feel the air come back, slowly, slightly, enough that she knew she wouldn't die, at least not here and now. Tears slid down her face as she cried, grateful.

Halina took her hand and led her out of the overgrown grass and weeds of the Patchiecki house. Patcja let her, not up for arguing. Her breathing was better but still wheezy. The vice compressing her lungs was loosening but still there, a steady grip.

Then she saw where they were heading: Baba's house.

Oh my. The last time she was in Baba's strange, creepy basement kitchen, the old woman had bandaged her burned arm. What an experience that was!

Well, she does know how to make some nice tea. I could use some tea now. And Baba could look at Halina's hand. And maybe she will have some herbal love potion to make Joey love me. Maybe. Oh, how wonderful that would be!

Patcja followed her little sister, still gasping for air and miracles.

Chapter 20

Halina started to knock on Baba's door, but then she heard noises around back, behind the house. The girls followed the dirt path to the backyard. Baba was there, tending to her chickens. Most of the backyard had been fenced off for the noisy birds, an ancient-looking coop in the center. It was in a sorry state, slats missing, leaving conspicuous gaps, like an old man's grin. Twenty-five or maybe thirty white-and-black chickens pecked at the gravel, clucking, strutting, hoity-toity, like church women.

Beyond the coop, near the alley, was Stach's shanty, but there was no sign of him. He didn't have a proper door, just a tarp nailed across the doorway. A brick was holding it down so it didn't flap in the wind. Stach was probably sleeping. He didn't always open the newsstand on weekends. Sometimes he had other work to do on the weekend, he'd say.

For a second, Halina thought about depositing Patcja with Baba and then going to pester Stach. Wake him up. See if there was going to be a poker game tonight. *Later*, she decided.

I wonder if the thief has repaid the IOU to Stach?

Baba was pulling out old straw from the roosting boxes and putting in new. The old was disgusting, matted with chicken shit that stank to high heaven. She was putting the rotten stuff in a wheelbarrow, already piled high. Flies swarmed over it.

"*Witaj*, Baba! *Jak się masz?*" Halina called to her. Patcja hung back, looking as though she might dart away any minute. But her hand was still at her chest. She was still pale, white as a ghost, and there was still a rattle in her chest, as if some gravel had gotten in there and was clogging things up. Damn. That couldn't be good for the baby, could it? If the mama couldn't get air, how could the baby? Halina tried a reassuring smile at her sister and patted her arm.

"C'mon, now," Halina said with a look.

Baba didn't stop her work. Maybe she didn't hear. Her babushka, a heavy muslin, was tied tightly, a knot under her chin. Halina walked closer, unsure how close she wanted to get to all this chicken-shit stink.

"*Witaj*, Baba!"

"*Słyszę cię. Nie krzycz na mnie, młoda damo*," Baba snapped without looking up.

"*Przepraszam.* Sorry. *Nie chciałam krzyczeć.* I didn't mean to shout."

Baba dropped the rotten straw in her hands and looked over the sisters, up and down—first Halina, her hand wrapped in a towel; then Patcja, her hand to her chest, wheezing, mouth open, sucking in gulps of air that seemed to go nowhere.

"*Proszę, pomóż nam!*" Halina said. "*Proszę, moja siostra nie może oddychać.*"

The woman paused, glaring at Halina, staring as if she were trying to drill into her head. The old woman's gray, watery eyes were murky with cataracts—but still fierce. Was she thinking about turning them away? Was she deciding if she could help them—or if she wanted to? Maybe cleaning out the chicken coop was more important to the damn-blasted old woman than helping two stupid, worthless girls who had once again gotten themselves into trouble.

What was the woman thinking? The longer Baba stood stone-still, eyes locked on Halina, the madder Halina became.

"Say something! Help us! Or tell me what to do—I don't know how to fix her breathing. Tell me what to do. *Please!* There's a baby, too. It needs air."

Baba's expression didn't change, but she started toward the house and motioned for the girls to follow her.

As she stepped across the doorway, Halina remembered another time she had visited Baba.

She had been a child. She saw it:

"Good morning, Baba!" young Halina called.

Baba was feeding her chickens.

"Hello, girl," she answered without looking up.

Halina watched for a bit. She climbed on the bottom slat of the fence gate and swung back and forth, anything to stall walking to St. Florian's. She was in fourth grade, studying long division. It might be the death of her.

Baba held the bottom corners of her apron up, making a basket to hold the feed. She wore an old brown knitted sweater over the apron, a handmade one with big, loopy, lopsided stitches that were messy looking. The sleeves were too long for short, stout Baba, making her seem even shorter, dwarf-like, other-worldly. Her sweater was her magic robe, a cloak of ceremony and spirits. Maybe she could vanish if she wanted to. Maybe she could heal wrongs. Maybe she could keep the wrongness away—or at least on the other side of the street.

"Baba?"

"Hmmm, dziewczynka?"

"I was wondering. I mean, maybe . . . well, could you make up a garland for me? Or a poultice or an amulet? Something strong and full of protection, something to keep the heebie-jeebies away?"

The nightmares of a face in the window were so real. Creepy.

Baba studied her for a moment. "There is no color in your cheeks. Pale as a ghost. You need food, not amulet. Come with me."

Baba fed Halina the biggest breakfast she ever had. Fried eggs and potatoes, sausage, oatmeal with raisins and chopped up apples and lots of cinnamon and sugar. Stewed tomatoes from Baba's garden with herbs and twigs of things Halina didn't recognize. And, best of all, there was a hunk of fresh bread with golden crust and lots of salty-sweet butter.

"Jeepers," Halina said many times. She could think of no other words, and she was too busy shoving food in her mouth to talk.

Baba hovered over her, moving back and forth from the table to the stove, bringing more sausages, another scoop of potatoes with crispy onions in them. Then a spoonful of sour cream was plopped on top, sprinkled with butter-crisped breadcrumbs.

Halina was feeling better already. She watched Baba, moving in the background. The woman, still wearing her baggy sweater and babushka on her head, was busy at the stove. Her hands moved in fluid sweeps, like a dancer going through memorized motions. Baba had a wall of shelves with jars and baskets and small bottles of liquids, powders, twigs, and stems. Bundles of cloth were tied at the top with twine. She bumbled around them.

Halina couldn't eat another bite. Her plate was wiped clean, every crumb gone. She wiped her mouth on her arm, then wiped her hands on her dress. Greasy stains smeared the brown cotton.

"Now look what you did! Messy girl."

"What? I ate everything! It was wonderful. Thank you!"

"You made smears on your dress. How do you think you will ever make handsome boy to love you if you look like messy girl?"

Before Halina could answer, Baba attacked with a scalding hot, soapy dishcloth, bubbles from the smelly soap squishing on the cloth and foaming on Halina's face, her arms, her dress, even her knees. She got a good scrubbing, and it wasn't even Saturday yet.

Then Baba gave her an amulet. It was made from an empty matchbox, with secret ingredients inside. Then it was tied with a long scrap of twine so it couldn't spill while she wore it around her neck.

"There! You are all fixed up now. No empty stomach, and no more heebie-jeebies. Amulet will bring luck and protection. It will remind you to be good. It will remind you God loves you. You can shake it and

hear roots and seeds: where you've been, where you're going. Powerful, if you stop to listen."

"Jeepers."

"Amen," said Baba. And she led Halina up the stairs to the back door.

Chapter 21

The sound of voices carried from Baba's yard to his shanty, waking Stach from a sound sleep. Any slight noise in the old woman's yard snapped him to attention. Someone might think he had it rigged with a trip wire to set off an alarm, but no. He just had a sensitive spot for Baba—his aunt, his mother's sister. He owed her, that was for sure. Taking him in when he'd first arrived in America was a kindness he didn't deserve. He had left Poland in such a hurry, a warrant for his arrest hanging over his head—all because of that antiwar sculpture the Germans didn't appreciate. He had shamed the family, but Baba didn't care. She said he could stay in the shanty, make it his own.

Uncle Pawel would be proud of the old woman and the life she'd made for herself here. Too bad he hadn't lived to see it. Stach didn't believe for one minute the stories that he was buried out back under the peach tree. But then again, there wasn't a gravestone with his name on it in St. Florian's cemetery.

He scratched at the stubble on his face and tried to clear his eyes, which were suddenly watery. Must have gotten some dirt in them, or smoke.

He got up to see what the commotion in the yard was about. Who was out there? Probably someone buying eggs, that's all. But with those punks running around, thinking they were in some bad-ass gang and showing off—well, who could say what would happen if Baba took off after someone with a broom, shouting curses and threatening to hex away their man parts or make warts cover them? He shuddered.

He had to wipe away the grime on the window with the sleeve of his long johns so he could see toward Baba's house.

Halina. She was cleaning out the hens' roosts, it looked like. Tossing out old straw, putting in new. Why was she doing that? Odd job for her to do.

Stach put on his boots, then realized he had forgotten his pants.

Oh hell—it wasn't like he didn't have long johns on. And it was just Halina.

"Hey there, missy, what you doing? Some chores for Baba?"

"I'm afraid so," she said, her face showing her disgust. "Some stinky chores. I didn't know chicken shit could smell so bad."

"Well, that sure is nice of you to help the old woman out like that. How did she talk you into it?"

Halina shrugged. "I guess I owe her," she finally said.

He took a handful of muck from Halina and dropped it in the wheelbarrow.

"I'll take out the old. You bring the new. How's that?"

Halina nodded, seeming quite relieved. Beyond words, for once. She brought over a pile of clean straw from the bales stacked behind the coop.

Stach noticed her hand, wrapped in some narrow cotton strips, the ends tied with a neat knot. He recognized it as the handiwork of Baba. So that explained why Halina was there on a Saturday morning. She had come for some doctoring from Baba. Must have been pretty bad if she couldn't tend to it herself.

They worked in silence for a while. Stach decided to wait for her to say what had happened to her hand. He didn't want to pry into business she didn't want to share. Halina kept glancing back toward Baba's house, as though she was waiting for someone to come out.

With the two of them working, the job went quickly. Stach sat down on one of the leftover bales and lit a cigarette, blowing the smoke up high. Halina seemed to notice for the first time that he was wearing only long johns, boots, and his hat. She gasped.

"Oh, Stach, where are your britches? Holy tarnation! Why in heaven's name are you gallivanting around in broad daylight in your skivvies?" She covered her eyes with her hand.

"Kind of late to be in a tizzy about it now. I've 'gallivanted' for right-near twenty minutes, helping you," he said with a self-satisfied grin. He took off his hat and set it ceremoniously on his lap. "Is that better?"

She laughed out loud, for a long time—longer than his little joke deserved, Stach thought. She must have been starved for some humor if she thought that little gesture was hilarious. *Poor kid.*

Finally she stopped, having run out of steam. She sat down on the bale, next to him. Well, it was more like she plopped, certainly not very ladylike. Someone wasn't doing a very good job of teaching the girl some of those ladyfolk manners.

Just as well, he thought. *Town has enough prissy-ninnies with their highfaluting ways.*

He liked Halina just like this. But he didn't like to see her hurt.

"Oh, I have something for you," Stach said. "Funny thing: yesterday, at the newsstand, a fella comes by. Says he is returning something to 'the girl.' I guess he meant you."

Stach went back to the shanty, came out carrying an empty Mason jar.

"So the fella with rotgut poisoning lived! Well, how about that?" she said, tracing the letters on the jar, staring at her own reflection in the murky glass.

"So what's going on, Lina?" he asked as he offered her a puff on his cigarette. She shook her head in refusal.

She sighed, and then the day's bizarre story tumbled out. She told him all of her accumulating worries. First, waking up and seeing through the old blanket a flash of memory about a hulking monster-man in the coal room that was being chased away by her mother. Then, the little fight with her mother over her broken glasses and the shattered lantern globes. Then, Patcja getting all hot and bothered about Joey, and the breathing spell coming on.

"Hmmm," he said, letting her words have time to breathe and settle on the ground, maybe scurry around a little, airing out.

Stach plucked the bandage on her hand, as if he was testing it.

"Looks like Baba performed her usual medical miracles and has you on the road to complete recovery," he said. "And she's treating Patcja now?"

"I hope so. But this time I don't know if some herbal mumbo jumbo is going to be enough. Patcja's breathing problem seems serious—and getting worse," Halina said, fiddling with stray straws of hay.

Stach pulled out some hay from the bale. Tying pieces together, he made a circle the size of a crown and placed it on Halina's head with some ceremonial whistling and fanfare. She let him—for about thirty seconds. Then some cynical thought seemed to settle over her, and her flattered giggle turned gritty, resentful.

"I'm no child, Stach. You can't fix all my problems with a crown of straw, like this is some Old Country fairy tale I'm living," she said. Those dark eyes smoldered. "I'm trying to be serious. Trying to look after my sister, who has got herself in a heap of trouble. And trying to protect my mother, who doesn't seem to mind being battered around. I want to be someone better than all this," she waved her arm, the gesture encompassing the yard, shack, coop, noisy chickens, and wheelbarrow of chicken crap.

"Sorry, Lina. I didn't mean to be dismissive, minimize your troubles, or sound like I was placating—"

"Stach, I don't know what those words mean, but they aren't helping. Just shut up, will you?"

Maybe it would be better to change the subject.

"Going to play poker tonight? The fellas all said they'd come around about eight, as usual."

"Drat. I never got my poker money back," she said. "Don't know how I'm going to play poker with no money to ante up. Hope the damned thief rots in hell."

"Don't say that."

He hated to see such a vengeful side of the young woman. It wasn't pretty at all. How did all those years of Catholic school and Sunday Mass leave a woman without *some* compassion for a friend in need? Maybe she just didn't understand. Maybe she was so focused on her troubles—and her sister's troubles and her mother's—that she missed the other aching people who were also just trying to get by. Could she bear the burden of one more sorrowful tale? Of course. She was a strong Polish woman, full of fight.

"You know, missy, if that fella—someone who says he is a friend—needed that money, you'd let him have it, wouldn't you?"

For some reason, the question seemed to take the girl by surprise. Her face changed expressions a half-dozen times as she worked out the baffling riddle. Maybe he should have explained it better. Stach fumbled for words.

"What I mean is that maybe we should say that we're fine with the fella having the money—for a while. Like letting a hungry cat have some crust from your bread 'cause he's meowing and howling and doing that rubbing-up-against-your-legs thing when it's so hungry it hurts, and we can spare a crust corner. Sort of the good, God-obeying thing to do, eh?"

"But—it was all I had—and I was saving for a train ticket. I just gotta get out of this town, Stach. It's strangling me. Everyone's either stuck in the past or ignoring that all this whiskey business is rotten as hell, sick as hell, and no poultice or string of garlic is going to fix it. And now I need to buy darn lamp globes, and Ma needs new glasses. And what am I going to use for poker tonight? Acorn caps, like when I was ten?"

"Whew. That was a lot. I can't fix it all, but I can see to the poker game. Leave that to me, my little poker queen," he said, already planning how he could get her some money back.

"Really? I suppose I could do some job for you. Empty all your ashtrays . . . or sweep, or wash your window—whatever you want me to do." She blushed and looked down. She drew an arc in the gravel with the toe of her shoe, a familiar old move that he had seen her do a thousand times as a child. She suddenly looked so young. And desperate. How far would she go?

"No. Don't you worry about chores. Just come by for poker. I bet you'll clean up!"

She didn't look convinced.

Neither did Curly. The dang near-dead dog lifted his head, his drowsy brown eyes looking at Halina as though he wanted something from her. But neither of them knew what. The dog had been sleeping at the shanty for a week or so—ever since the encounter with Antonio outside The Corner. Seemed Curly hadn't won the fight that night when he tried to take on Antonio.

Stach had found the dog in some weeds by the alley in pretty bad shape and brought him to Baba, of course.

"Can you work some miracles on this four-legged patient?" he had asked her.

"It will cost you," she'd said.

"How much?"

"Double what a two-legged patient costs you," Baba had said, making room on her kitchen table for the dog, crusty with blood and whining.

"Probably should just put him out of his misery, I'm afraid."

"Where's your faith, man?"

Stach had beaten around on his pockets, patting empty spaces. "I think I left it in my other pants pockets."

But Curly had patched up pretty well. Now he was sprawled on a stack of flour sacks—the patient of honor, a hero, wounded in the line of duty, protecting Patcja and Halina.

Curly didn't look like a hero, though. Or act like one. He chewed on the white bandage wrapped around his leg. It was holding a splint in place and had the same kind of knot that was on Halina's hand, Baba's signature bandage.

"Hey, look, Curly—we match," Halina said to the dog, holding her bandaged hand up for the dog to see.

The dog wasn't impressed. Stupid dog.

Chapter 22

Patcja sat in Baba's kitchen, in a chair by the table. The chair had a gash in its seat and yellowed stuffing poking out, resembling innards falling out of a hog on butchering day—creepy, like everything in this basement. She sat quietly, frozen still, trying to concentrate on breathing while Baba listened to her chest with her eyes shut.

Patcja knew how this healing business worked. She had been here before, so she knew the yelling would start soon. Then the paddling with a wooden spoon. Then the flittering about at the stove, a pinch from a pouch of powder, a twig from a basket, a root from a filthy flour sack stored in the cellar. Then the candles and singing and praying and who knew what other craziness would break out.

I don't like this, not one golly bit.

But she didn't argue. It would do no good. Once you had stepped into the holy sanctity of Baba's kitchen, you relinquished all rights to disagree or question her judgement. But more than that, Patcja desperately needed Baba's healing to work. That last breathing attack had scared the bejeezus out of her. It was one of the worst ever. And she had to think about more than herself now. She had to be careful because ... well, *because.*

Patcja concentrated on the window over the table. A small wooden figurine of the Virgin Mary stood on the sill. She was painted in pastel colors, which were faded and worn from sun and maybe rain. A single cobweb strand spanned from Mary's outstretched hand to the white peeling paint of the sill. The sweet little statue of Mother Mary had been in the same place of honor the last time Patcja was here. The blue of her robe and veil had been brighter then, though; her cheeks rosier.

Since they were in the basement, the window was high on the wall, over her head. Patcja had to bend her neck back to peer up. For some reason, that seemed to help her breathing. She stuck her chest out farther, stretching her neck, as if she were a goose with a long, gracefully curving neck of white feathers.

The thought of white down feathers was soothing. The image of Mary was calming.

Baba placed her ears against Patcja's back so she could listen to the girl's breathing. The warmth of the woman's face and the rustle of the babushka against her back were comforting. Baba's wrinkled hands held her shoulders. They were strong and reassuring. The muscles in Patcja's back and shoulders and arms melted into the sunlight streaming in through the window. She was breathing, in and out.

Innnn and ouuut.

Baba patted her on the shoulder and went to the work counter, where she started mixing ingredients. Her hands moved in swift, fluid motions, tracing paths through the air, well-worn and familiar from years of travel. Soon, a pot of water went on the stove, and Patcja could hear boiling water, its pungent steam filling the room. It was sharp and bitter smelling, like black licorice. She also recognized ginger and maybe honey. Camphor. Patcja wondered if she would be told to drink the liquid, inhale it, or sit in it. She hoped she wouldn't be wearing it around her neck with a string of garlic. There was only so much humiliation a poor girl could suffer.

"What are we going to do with that bubbly stuff brewing, Baba? I'm not very hungry, if you were thinking about a soup."

"Shhh! It's no soup, silly girl!"

Baba hobbled back toward Patcja, spoon in hand. Patcja ducked, on reflex, anticipating the wooden spoon across her back, but the woman just loosened the top buttons on Patcja's dress and pulled her hair to the side. She slid the straps of her camisole and slip down, too, so she could see Patcja's bare back.

Patcja fidgeted in the chair. What was this woman up to now? Patcja eyed the door. How many steps would it take to get up the stairs and out the door? Would she be fast enough to get out before the old woman could catch her? She tried to picture her escape but realized it would never work. Patcja knew she was going nowhere until Baba said she could.

"My back's not where it hurts, Baba. I think I'm doing much better now."

"Yes, *now*. But what about next time? We must fix tomorrow *before* it happens. Understand?"

"No."

"That's why I'm the baba who heals, and *you* are *not*. You are the girl who sits and listens," Baba said. She grabbed the wooden Virgin Mary off the windowsill and set it in front of Patcja with an unholy thud. "You pray. I'll do the rest."

Patcja tried to think of words.

Our Father, who art in heaven, hallowed . . .

Baba drew circles on Patcja's back with something cold and pointy, sharp. It hurt, but just barely. The circles were small, then larger—maybe a spiral.

Patcja tried to imagine the shape on her back. Was it made with a pencil? A fountain pen? Was Baba actually drawing marks that were visible, or just tracing shapes? And how in God's glory was this going to help her breathing?

Trust, she told herself. *Trust*.

She concentrated on praying and breathing, tried to picture the breaths of air flowing from her lungs to the baby's lungs, but she couldn't fathom how that could possibly happen. She just didn't know much about babies and how they developed. One of the mysteries of God's intricate—and sometimes cruel—plans.

Sometimes the plan went wrong. Things happened. Bad things. Maybe something bad would happen to this baby. Maybe it would disappear, just wither away, like grapes on a vine that got no sun. Maybe Baba had medicine on her shelf that did that. Maybe that would be a good thing.

Baba seemed done with drawing on Patcja's back. She fished out a towel that was soaking in the pot on the stove and wrung it out slightly, just enough so it wasn't dripping. The towel was smelly, steaming. Baba draped it on Patcja's back, over those circles.

Eeek. Yikes! Patcja winced and bit her lip to keep from yelping. The circles on Patcja's back sizzled with the sting of medicine in the scratches. Every circle, spiraling to her core, burned like a lit match, then simmered and then was warm and sweet. *Nice.* A warm bath on a cold day.

Then Baba put the steaming pot of brew on the table in front of Patcja and showed her how to lean over it and take deep breaths. Patcja got lost in the waves of scents, steam, and medicine pulsing to her lungs and heart and down through her arms. Her fingers tingled. The hair on the back of her neck stood up; her eyebrows, too; then the hair on her arms. Goosebumps ran down her arms as she shivered. Her head was fuzzy, light, as if it would float away off her shoulders any minute now and she would have to reach up and grab it before it floated out the window.

It was like Pa's toothache pills, but more.

Patcja rode the bubbly current for minutes—or was it hours?—and in her mind, she kept being pulled back to the wall of herbs, spices, and powders, plants and roots, the seemingly simple ingredients and then the ones more sinister looking: the basket of chicken bones, a rat skull, withered hog hooves, a jar of bird beaks, and moth wings with iridescent colors, reflecting bits of light, frozen in imaginary flight.

And so strange: a sealed jar with a cigar in it. The cigar was lit, smoke curling up, hitting the lid, curling down, then back up again in an endless circle.

Patcja floated in front of the wall—no body, no conscience, no fear of God. Which ingredients could smother? Hex and curse? Change God's will and finalize fate, like pinching the flame of a candle? What ingredients would purge her body of the unwanted, undone, tiny form?

Patcja hovered between then and now, deciding.

Did she want to be a mama?

Chapter 23

Halina walked toward downtown, stopping in front of the barbershop. Stach had made her think about the poker money. Maybe he was right. Maybe she should let the thief borrow it and stop being so mad about it. She still wasn't sure who had done it. For a while, his time card in the barbershop had her convinced it was Bear. She'd managed to talk herself out of that horrid thought, thank goodness, but that left no one else to blame.

She stood outside the barber's window and looked in. She could see Waldemar cutting hair and gabbing, as usual. A man she didn't know was in the chair, a white smock around his shoulders. Three other men sat in chairs along the wall, all reading newspapers.

There was Bear! He was near the back of the shop, sweeping.

She went in, the bell over the door ringing. Every face turned to look at her. Bear froze. Waldemar froze, hands midair, as if he had been conducting an orchestra.

"Well, look who is here! It's the girl who sewed up Joey and saved his lousy life," said the man in the chair. "What are you doing here? Looking for more trouble to stir up?"

"Aww, now—leave the poor girl alone! She didn't know what would happen. She was just trying to help," Waldemar said.

"What are you talking about? I didn't cause the trouble," Halina said, getting into her boxer's stance, fists balling up.

"Shhh. Nothing you need to worry about," Waldemar said to her quickly. "But I told you to sit in the chair, didn't I? Why didn't you do that?" Waldemar put down his scissors and comb and took Halina's arm, leading her to the back room.

As soon as they walked through the curtain to the back room, Waldemar let go of her arm but pointed a finger in her face. Bits of black hair clung to his fingernail, jittering like bug antennae.

"What did you want to talk to me about, anyway? What were you nosing around for? Everything was all tossed about, papers tossed around, and something very important was gone when I got back. Did you take it?" he demanded.

"Mr. Waldemar, I am as fed up about this nonsense as I can be! I don't know what you're talking about, but I know someone stole my poker money and left me a note. And left Stach a note, too. The note to Stach was written on an envelope with your name on the front, so I was looking for clues to who stole my money. Yeah, I saw one of the whiskey fellas in here, looking for something, but I don't know what. And I patched up Joey because my stupid sister loves the slimy thing, that's all."

Bear burst through the curtain, broom still in his hands.

"He's here! He's here, like he said! Looking for *you*, Mr. Waldemar. Better come out."

Waldemar grumbled at Halina, huffed at Bear, and stormed back to the main room of the barbershop.

Bear stayed, eyes cast to the ground.

"Bear, what is going on? I wish someone would explain it to me."

"I don't know much, Lina. Seems complicated to me. I just sweep the floor and deliver messages. I just do what I'm told."

"Surely you must hear the fellas talking. What's up about Joey? Is he worse?"

"Nahh. He's coming around right fine, they say. Just about all healed up. But more trouble is brewing. The Italians want to get back at the Sicilians for stabbing Joey."

"Bear, this makes no sense. It's all nonsense, little boys squabbling."

"Nah. It's some powerful, mean-ass, *bad men* squabbling. Antonio, Sal, and Waldemar on one side. And then Augie sided up with the Italians. And Joey, too, because he lives in Back of the 'Yards—you know, the stockyards, in Little Italy. Augie sells that Chicago Cola crap."

Bear looked around to make sure no one was in earshot and lowered his voice. "Close to poison, that stuff. It's got a little funny juice in it, they say. Gets you hooked. Comes in brown vials all the way from China."

"Oh, Bear. You *are* crazy! You're just telling stories now."

"Nope. Cross-my-heart-hope-to-die-stick-a-needle-in-my-eye."

"Bear, stop! Do you know who stabbed Joey or not? Just tell me!"

"Maybe I know. Maybe not. I ain't saying."

Halina looked at Bear as he leaned on his broom and nervously fiddled with his brown tweed cap. Bear looked worried, his forehead knotted and twisted up like an old man's dirty shirt. Bear was no little boy any longer, that was for sure. They were both far beyond those days when they had played together after school and on summer evenings at the Patchiecki place, when Camel and Patcja would go off to be alone while Bear and Halina would sit on the wall, teasing and talking, daring and swearing and double-dog-daring.

Bear fumbled around, looking for words. Finally he said, "Halina, I'm sorry. I took—"

"Bear, don't. You don't gotta say—"

Halina heard a crash, like glass breaking. It came from the barbershop. Then loud voices, lots of them, angry.

Halina and Bear rushed through the curtain to see what had happened. Halina pushed Bear behind her. He was bigger, but she was still older and faster, not about to let Bear get hurt.

A rock had been thrown through the window. A gaping, jagged hole was left in the middle of the window pane. Waldemar was outside the shop, yelling, waving his arm. The men who had been waiting for haircuts were gone. Halina could see the papers they left behind in their chairs—racing forms. Horses.

Then she noticed one man was left in the shop. He was unbothered by the rock through the window, it seemed. She recognized him from pictures in the newspaper—and by his shiny shoes.

Salvatore, the boss, was in the barber chair, leaning back so the cigar in his mouth pointed straight up at the ceiling. He looked as if he were going to a funeral, dressed up in a pinstripe suit with a vest and a watch on a gold chain. Smoke clouds floated up over his bald head, lazily drifting off.

Bear gasped. Halina hushed him, but Sal must have heard them. He sat up, turning to the corner where Halina and Bear huddled. Sal chuckled as he stood up.

"Well, look who we have here! If it's not Florence Nightingale," he said, blowing smoke puffs in Halina's direction.

One encircled her face perfectly before it faded.

"Gotcha," said Sal.

And then a coughing fit came on. He seemed to be choking, suffocating, as if he were in a jar with no air. He tried to break free, but his hands seemed to hit invisible walls.

Halina and Bear ran.

Chapter 24

The afternoon light was about used up. Stach was in his shanty, trying to hurry through the last of the chores he wanted to get done before the poker game tonight. He shuffled junk around on his workbench, looking.

Where is that screwdriver?

He rummaged around, hunting among the hodge-podge clutter of tools and scraps and sketches of ideas and assorted parts—handles, knobs, gears, wheels, hinges, and locks—that he might use in this lifetime or the next.

The workbench was under the west window that faced the outhouse and alley. Afternoon sun streamed in, casting long shadows across the wooden bench and the shelves on the opposite wall. The contrast of glare and shadows wasn't making it easier to find the damn screwdriver. He moved around the sandpaper scraps, an old coffee can of screws and nuts, a pint can of wood stain, paintbrushes stiff with dried varnish, rags smeared with red paint and maple stain.

Where the hell is that screwdriver?

Ahh! Finally! He found the screwdriver under a mound of wood shavings, right where he left it. Or was it?

"Curly, you been messing around with my tools, borrowing them when I'm not around?"

The dog lifted his head when he heard his name, his ears perking up a bit. For just a moment, though; then his shaggy head was back between his front paws, and he was drifting off to sleep.

Maybe Baba gave the animal something to make it drowsy so it would rest and let its leg heal. Maybe. Or maybe the dog's time was close.

Stach heard something outside.

I could hide behind the stove. With her poor eyes, maybe she won't see me. Nah. If I can't face one fierce old woman, what am I?

Stach pulled back the tarp that was across the doorframe.

Fryderyk?

"Well, my man, Fryderyk! What brings you to visit my humble shanty?"

"Uh, well, I'm returning these." He held out a hand with a hammer, planer, and sandpaper. "I, uh, borrowed them. Thought you wouldn't mind, being the halfway decent sort of man that you are."

"No, no, I don't mind. Had yourself some woodworking project, did you?"

"Had to fix the door frame. Got all splintered and busted up. Damned thing had a run-in with an unhappy wrench. Had to fix it. Tried to, anyway."

"Those wild wrenches," Stach said, shaking his head. "Sometimes they get all worked up, in a frenzy. Gotta watch 'em every minute."

"You can say that again," Fryderyk answered.

Stach slapped the man on the back, held his hand out to shake hands.

Fryderyk hesitated, then spoke quietly, in a mumble that was barely audible. "I was just trying to make her speak up, stand up," Fryderyk said, wiping his face with a filthy hanky. "Toughen up, you know? So she could take care of herself, you know? Not let no man scare her into being quiet."

Stach had to guess at what this was about. He had heard some of the story from Halina, but not all the details. Still, it wasn't hard to imagine. "Well, Fryddie, my man, I hear you. I understand, too. I truly do. But that may be the stupidest way of teaching a young woman to find her voice that I ever heard of. Just telling you, man. That was damn stupid. And plenty mean, too."

"Yeah, it was, huh?"

"I'd say so. Go home and tell her you're sorry."

Fryderyk mumbled some nonsense, fumbled around in his pockets. Finally, he turned around and shuffled off, still wiping at his face with that filthy rag.

"Come back any time!" Stach called after him, shaking his head. *What a strange man. Strange, indeed.*

"What do you think, Curly? Any hope for that man?"

The dog didn't lift his head this time. Stach went to check if he was breathing. Yeah, just sleeping. "Well, have a good nap, Curly. I'll bring you back something to eat."

Stach slid the screwdriver into his pants pocket and headed out, checking that Baba wasn't out in the yard before he ducked under the tarp.

It wasn't a long walk to the storage shed. Usually he went at night, though, when he didn't need to worry about being noticed. Today he took a longer route, cutting through the alley, walking along the ditch where the spring grass and weeds were already up to his knees. The ground there was wet and squished as he clomped through. *Maybe this wasn't the best route, after all.* The mud made sucking sounds, trying to pull his boots off his feet.

He came up to the backside of St. Florian's. Beside the grave-yard was a storage building, a garage, with tall weeds growing around it. The door had a padlock, of course. Sister Queen Bea insisted on keeping the key, saying she didn't completely trust him. Well, he didn't completely trust *her*, either. That was what made their alliance work. And he didn't really need the key, not when he had a screwdriver.

Stach fiddled at the lock with the screwdriver. Soon it snapped open. He left the door ajar so he could see inside and find the right crate among the dozen stacked in the garage. They all looked about the same on the outside; all stenciled "US ARMY." He found the one he needed. He took out two gas lamps. The bases were metal, military sturdy, and ugly, but he didn't need those. Just the glass chimneys, and those looked right fine. No one would suspect they were military supply, meant for troops stationed overseas during the Great War. The army never seemed to notice or care that they were reappropriated, so why should anyone else?

While he was in the building, he picked up a few other things he heard people needed. The uniform crate was in the back. He remembered Janusz and his bare ankles. Stach couldn't understand how that fool could lose so many pairs of socks and long johns. He grabbed a couple of pairs—one for Janusz and one for Joey. Joey's bloody long johns had to be burned. Stach picked up some boxes of matches for Mary, Halina's mother, and some candles, too. And from the mess supplies, he grabbed some tin buckets and dishpans. Patcja didn't need to be walking clear out to the outhouse at night these days. Some buckets would come in handy. He put his haul in the bucket, using the socks to pad the glass globes so they didn't rattle and break.

Now to get back to the shanty unnoticed, with no one asking questions they shouldn't ask. Stach relocked the garage and walked toward home, through the brush and down the alley again.

Damn! Krzysztof and Antonio were in the alley, walking his way. Now what?

It was too late to dart over to the next street and avoid them. The two numbskulls obviously noticed Stach. They grinned and took a firm stance, side by side, as if they were trying to stop a herd of rats from crashing through their barricade of brainless brawn and limp dicks.

Well, Stach wasn't about to kiss Antonio's stinking Sicilian ass to get by.

"So, Mr. Stach, Astachio, hello. If it isn't the Saint of Hegewisch, the ringleader of the Godly Polacks, the one who interferes with our plans," said Antonio, flexing his hands into fists.

"*Cześć, chłopaki.* Hello, fellas," Stach said. "Isn't it dinner time? Shouldn't you be home? Mama's probably serving up some spaghetti and meatballs. Some balls, just your size. Itty-bitty balls for a man with itty-bitty balls, eh, Tony-boy?"

And Stach cupped his hands, pretending to juggle two marble-sized balls. He laughed and sauntered past, smiling splendidly like a spoiled cat.

Krzysztof stifled a giggle. Stupid boy.

Stach didn't look back, but he heard the punch and jab, the sounds of Antonio taking his frustration out on the kid.

Well, Krzysztof probably deserved it.

Chapter 25

Baba worked in the garden behind the chicken coop. She planted a mix of vegetables and herbs every year, things to eat, things that cured. She didn't know if she would see this year's seedlings produce, but that would be something else she could leave for the girl.

Today she was hoeing, breaking up the clumps of dirt that had hardened during winter. It was difficult work for a sick woman, but she could take her time, she kept reminding herself, even though she knew time was running out.

She was distracted. From here she had a good view down the alley. She was watching—once again.

She had seen Stach sneak off, stooped over, ducking under the tree limbs to the alley—as if that made him invisible, the fool. It was a good thing he had never been a soldier in the army. He'd be dead for sure. How did her sister raise such a sack full of folly and nonsense notions—always butting in to other people's problems? Mr. Nosy. Do-gooder. If he didn't watch out, he'd be the one she was patching up, a broken bone or bullet hole. He was careless. So she watched, just in case.

The afternoon sun was warm for April. That was good. Buds would open soon, as they should. The wildflowers would all be in bloom in time for the Paschal moon, the first full moon after the spring equinox. It was the moon that determined the date of Easter, so a holy moon, significant for healers—and for the healed.

She had plans for this Paschal moon—special plans.

Baba decided to take a break from gardening. She hobbled toward the back of the lot, behind the shanty, near the alley, under her friend the peach tree. She had not been back there recently, had not been to visit since the weather had turned. Too long. She chastised herself for her neglect. The buried girl deserved to be remembered.

Baba bent over and cleared a fresh crop of dandelions and wild onions away from the stone that marked the grave. It was marshy down there, in a low spot where muck collected. That was why she'd picked the spot. Not likely someone would notice it by chance, move the stone, dig, and disturb the bones.

The stone was not big, about the size of a roosting chicken. It was pretty, though—blue-gray and smooth, probably from Lake Michigan some time ago, another era when Indians lived in this swamp. She suspected it was a stone with some purpose, perhaps used by an Indian healer. It seemed to have heat stored in it, as though maybe it had been in a fire ceremony or had been used in baking or sweating out demons. Now it marked a grave, keeping animals out. That felt right. There was some honor in that.

Baba was relieved to see the stone was untouched. She bent over and patted the rock, as if it were the shoulder of an old friend. She picked some dandelions and set them on the stone along with some mumbled words, most of a prayer, a sign that contained a memory and guilt, fear. The remembered images of blonde hair pasted to a feverish forehead. A child's small hand, cold, limp; blue lips.

Blessed Lydia, rest in peace. Amen.

Baba turned back to the garden, rubbing the chills off her arms. Back to work. Back to watching the alley.

She hoed a few clumps, then stood up, stretched her back, and looked down the gravel alley, which was lined with trash cans and random junk that needed to be hauled to the dump. No crows, no bootleggers, no Stach. She hoed a few more clots, broke those up, earthworms poking out, wiggling, confused about what had happened to their homes. Another glance down the alley.

This time she saw something: that tall, skinny Sicilian boy and Krzysztof—a bad mixture. Bad tempting Good. The struggle was fierce. She could hear it—like claws scratching.

She crossed herself. *Blessed is the Father, Son, and the Holy Ghost. Amen.* Then she spat on her hands, rubbed them together, and kneaded the invisible dough of Gypsy juju with her hands. More and more, then faster, as the Vision and Power melded her disgust into vengeance, a curse of reckoning and judgment.

Let them be judged.

Her fingers tingled with the intensity of righteousness and redemption—holy or not, she wasn't sure. But it sparked, needing air and space for the verdict that would be born, either kindled mercies or misery. Which? And she bounced the lightning, without shape, back and forth from hand to hand, until it was ready.

She saw the two boys take a stand, forming a barricade. There was Stach! He was walking toward the hoodlums, wearing his ornery little-boy smirk. Oh, why couldn't that man be serious for once? Did he not know he was teetering on the edge of Too Late?

Baba's hands started to shake, dripping with conjured justice, mercy, and madness, all mixed up in a stew. She felt the bubbles in her stomach and gagged from the wretched stench coming up her throat. She had held it too long. She needed to send the curse somewhere, to someone, before it ate away at her own bones.

Baba concentrated on the tall, older one. His name was Antonio.

She threw it at him with her eyes, that invisible wad of juju, like a fisherman casting a tangled net into waves crashing on shore.

Did it catch him? She wasn't sure. Time would tell. Time . . .

She watched for a while longer, just to make sure Stach got past the two hoodlums. He did. Just sauntered past on his way.

Baba was tired. She wiped her hands on her apron. Her wrists and fingers ached. The arthritis was acting up. Perhaps she could take a nap. But she had so much to do.

Paschal moon. *Soon.*

She paused, listening. Her arms were being pulled, her heart tugged. Her legs were mush, and the wind was being sucked out of her lungs. She gasped.

She. Couldn't. Catch. Her. Breath.

Just like Lydia had gasped for air, her lungs full of liquid and infection. Pneumonia. Baba had failed her.

The girl's face was calm now, like a lake on a windless day, almost pretty in her sleep. No longer contorted in fear and pain, the fever eating away reason and faith. *God help us.* The basement kitchen was lit only by one candle, next to the wooden figure of Virgin Mary on the windowsill. The warm yellow candlelight made the room glow—mystical, a cloud from heaven. It was the steam in the air. Medicines boiled in the pot on the stove, sending vapors of herbs, roots, and Bible Psalms into the air. The girl deserved so much better. Sold, traded, smuggled, forced . . .

Baba shook away the memory, gasping for air.

Is this my time? Is this how I go? Dropping dead in this dirt? Smothered by a hand I can't see? Lydia, let me go! I'm sorry!

Baba was overwhelmed. Confusion came with the sickness, she knew. That didn't help. She couldn't untangle her guilt from rational reasoning. The guilt toyed with her. She couldn't even fight back or resist. And it wasn't because she hadn't been able to heal Lydia, but because she hadn't given her a proper burial, in God's holy consecrated ground. Why hadn't she done that? Why hadn't she insisted? She had made Stach dig a hole in the marshy ground under the peach tree. They had dumped her in the dirt, wrapped in a sheet. No cross for her grave.

Is it too late?

She rooted around on the ground near the shanty, where Stach threw out ashes and spent wood from his potbelly stove. She found what she needed—a piece of charred wood, gray and sooty. She made her way back down to the peach tree, the mucky spot of ground, the stone marking the spot. The stone the size of grief. Or a Bible, open to Psalms.

With the chunk of charred wood, she drew a cross on the blue stone, a simple cross.

"Find peace. Go home," Baba said. "Go home."

Baba stood in the afternoon sun, feeling ripples over her skin.

"I don't wanna go home. How about that?" a man's voice called out.

Baba jumped, dropped the soot chalk.

"Who's there?"

The voice came from the shanty. A man's deep voice, but muffled, as though it was talking from behind a blanket or pillow.

She saw nothing, no one near.

"Come out! Who is there?"

"No one's home!"

"I *hear* you! Come out, *now*, so I can see you! What are you doing in my yard?"

"No one is home but us chickens," the voice said and then erupted in a squeal of laughter, like a girl being tickled.

Now she knew exactly who it was. Damned simple-minded fool with half a brain.

Baba walked back to the shanty, straight to the doorway, and pulled back the tarp. When would Stach put up a *real* door? One with hinges and a lock. Served him right, having people drop in all the time, just barging in—as drunk as a skunk, too.

She paused to let her eyes adjust for a second. Then she could see him, all right, and just as she expected.

He was a ball of slobber and snickers and flailing arms at the window. He hung on the glass, tasting it with his drunken, stupid mouth, face smashed against the glass, looking absurd yet garish.

Then he slid down to the foot of the workbench, like jelly down the side of a jar. The clumsy oaf spilled a can of paint on the dirt floor. The red puddle oozed toward the door, encircling her shoes.

"Ooopsies . . ."

"Janusz! Get up this instant!"

Janusz clucked back and flapped his chicken wings and shook his chicken tail feathers in Baba's direction. This, apparently, was quite humorous to a man who had just finished a bottle—or two or three—of "milk." The empty glass bottles were at his feet, white paint peeling off. Only the sharp smell of whiskey was left.

"More milk! I'll buy another round," he mumbled, his face implanted in the dirt.

Baba looked around for a broom, something for shooing this drunkard out. She decided to fetch hers from the house. But on the way, she ran straight into Stach.

"Whooaaa there, Nelly!" he said. "Where's the fire?"

Baba pointed to the babbling man cn the floor, just as he got to his knees and started retching.

"It seems your friend had too much *milk* to drink."

"Oh."

Chapter 26

A funny thing happened.

Overnight "someone" left two tin buckets, a dishpan, and two glass lamp globes outside of the coal room window. The lamps were just the kind Halina was supposed to replace. How about that? Too bad there weren't new glasses for Ma or new shoes, also. Or a new blanket that wasn't burnt and threadbare. And maybe a train ticket.

But that would be greedy, to expect more mysterious gifts to appear, wouldn't it?

Be happy with what you have.

Halina didn't know what to do with the buckets, at first. Then she left them by Patcja's side of the bed. As much as the dang woman was puking and peeing, she could use them. Then Halina left the lamp chimneys on the kitchen table for Ma to find. Two problems solved.

The other pains in her side still lingered, nagging. Patcja was still moaning at her about her stack of pie tins, empty cans, and tacks stacked in front of the door, but she just couldn't make herself take it down—not completely. She just couldn't go to sleep knowing someone could sneak up on her. But it was obvious Patcja couldn't go through the window anymore. Roly-poly Patcja, who was going to be a mama.

Halina made a new alarm system, just because, all the time knowing it was crazy. Only a crazy person would be afraid to go to sleep. Maybe Ma's odd ways were . . .

Halina stacked a tower of empty tin cans at each corner of the mattress. They were connected by thread, an almost-invisible outline around the bed. Any creep that tried to bother them at night would cross the string and make the cans tumble, waking her up so she could clobber them with the big stick she hid under her pillow. Should work—the piece of wood had nails sticking out of it. She found it at the Patchiecki house, good and rusty.

So far, Patcja had accidentally set off the tin-can alarm only twice. She'd get used to it.

Next problem: Halina hadn't gotten her poker winnings back yet, and it looked like she might not. Stach tried telling her to be patient. She didn't know how to do that, any more than she knew how to cook or sew—things all good Polish women knew how to do.

She was good at one thing: poker.

And, well, it seemed she had a knack for healing, like Baba. Funny thing, that was. Who would have thought?

She still had the newspaper advertisement about being a nurses' aide in her pocket. She liked to fiddle with it, her fingers tracing the paper in her pocket without taking it out. She imagined the letters and words, all memorized. She imagined what it would be like to work in a *real* hospital, helping people get over their ailments, sicknesses, and wounds—the kind you could see and ones you couldn't. Maybe a pill for Ma and her forgetfulness, one for Pa and his laziness, one for Janusz and his spurts of plain stupidity.

Janusz was the reason poker night was postponed. But even after a day, Halina wasn't convinced Stach had allowed sufficient airing-out time. Janusz stunk up the shanty pretty awful.

She walked over after dinner. Ma made potato soup, and it was gurgling in Halina's gut all funny. She thought a walk and some fresh air might help, but the stink of the shanty almost made the soup retch on up. *Now, that would be embarrassing.*

Janusz, a heap of drunkard foulness, was passed out by the stove, sprawled out on a couple of flour sacks and burlap bags Stach had spread out for him. Stach said to just ignore him, but that wasn't easy to do. The man smelled like he'd pissed his pants and puked on his shirt, and the warmth from the stove was making the stink come alive—resurrected, just like Jesus on holy Easter.

"He just needs to sleep it off," Stach said. "And I want to keep an eye on him, that's all. Might be a bad batch of brew."

"Well, maybe your nose is used to him by now, or you have a stronger stomach than me, Stach, but I'm not sure I can play a hand of poker in this compost pile," Halina said, holding her nose.

"That bad?"

"Yep."

Halina went outside, walked over to the flour-sack bed, where Curly was resting. The dog licked her hand and wagged his tail but didn't stand up, didn't move the bandaged leg.

"The bad leg still hurts, huh, Curly?"

Halina sat down by the dog, put her hand on his back, smoothed the tangled fur. She traced the outline of the leg bone, ever so slightly brushing away fur, trying to see how Baba had positioned the splint.

Fascinating.

Then she sat on the bench by the chicken coop, not sure where else to go. The chickens squawked. A goose waddled over, stretching her neck and hissing, expecting something to eat. Halina checked. Her pocket was empty of bread crumbs. Only the torn bit of newspaper about the hospital job was in her pocket. That wasn't good for much.

They're just words if you don't do something about it.

Stach moseyed out, sat beside her, a cigarette lit. He took his hat off and ran his hand through his curly hair, as though he was looking for something that was itching him. Halina scooted away a bit.

"You got cooties, Stach?"

"No more than usual. No more than most."

He was probably kidding, that silly little-boy humor of his. Part smart-ass and part goofball. She didn't know if she should kick him or hug him, so she did neither. She stayed at her end of the bench.

"Who's coming to play poker tonight?"

He named off a few of the old-timers, frequent players. Waldemar the barber was coming and the grocer, Mr. Marchewka. She hated playing with that one. He had so much hair growing out of his ears that he could hardly hear a thing. You always had to shout if you were raising.

Drat and double-drat.

Stach also said he expected Krzysztof's father, Kacper, who ran the feed-and-grain. And Major, the Polish soldier who had his major's hat permanently attached to his bald head, it seemed. It was from his old glory days, before the Great War, when the Russians first invaded Poland. That's how old he was.

"Stach, you know, you pick some odd old coots to be friends with and play poker with. You know those men got a touch of no-good in them. The barber's taking bets, the grocer's selling something in those Chicago Cola bottles that *ain't* cola, the grain guy has a son who is driving the milk truck for the Family, and Major—well, you *know* what kind of dirty things are always on his mind. Remember Lydia, the girl who disappeared? I still think Major had a hand in—"

"Halina, shut up! We agreed we weren't talking about Lydia and her sickness or the hardware store no more. *Remember?*"

"Yeah, but, Stach, why do you invite these old farts who don't have an ounce of conscience between them?"

He took a long drag on his cigarette, thinking.

"How else am I gonna keep track of what they're up to?" He turned to face her. "How else am I gonna nag at them, pester them to get on the right side of thinking, plant some good seeds in their thick skulls?" He paused. "Understand?"

"Suppose so. So it's like Jesus taking up with the tax collectors and lepers, eh? You think you're Jesus now?" Her voice got a little more screechy and sharp than she meant it to. She just didn't like to be told to forget Lydia. She'd tried to help Lydia. The girl was Halina's age. She had gotten mixed up with some bad business with Major and some roughnecks at the hardware store. Turned up sick— sick as a dog—and then she had disappeared.

And no one cared.

Before Stach could answer, Deaf Marchewka arrived; then Waldemar; then Major and Kacper. Soon, they were all standing at the door of the shanty, telling Stach it stank too bad to go in there. And some of the fellas wanted to know: What was that red stuff all over the dirt floor? Paint, or blood?

No one believed it was paint. Halina knew it wasn't blood. She knew what spilled blood looked like.

Janusz stayed where he was. There was no moving him. They each grabbed their usual seats and took them outside. It was dark and chilly, but Stach started a fire in an old oil drum while the other men brought the table out. The table, nothing more than a wooden door on cinder blocks, was easy to move.

"I sure hope the cards don't blow away in the wind," said Major, always a pessimist. He carried the pickle barrel that was his usual seat. He pulled his army hat down farther on his forehead, as if the stupid thing might fly off. They all knew it was permanently embedded in his skull, and the undertaker would be prying it off with a crowbar—or burying him with it encircling his bald, dead head.

Waldemar carried the tall paint bucket—his seat—and a lantern. "It'll be fine, just fine. Let's just get this show on the road."

The fire helped light their patch of the yard, and as the darkness settled, the orange glow on the horizon to the east seemed to get brighter. The mill was dumping slag, the molten waste that had no use except in making a new shoreline. They dumped it at night, secret-like, not quite legal. But the orange glow looked pretty in an odd sort of way, if you could get past it being the color of hellfire and sin.

Halina sat on the apple crate, next to Stach. They all settled in, adjusting their junkyard seats and shoving the cinder blocks around to get the table steady. Stach poured the first shot—Johnny Walker, the real stuff. He threw it back in one gulp, turned over the empty shot glass and slammed it down on the table. "*Na zdrowie!*"

The hinges and doorknob rattled, as the door wobbled on the cinder blocks. Stach poured another shot and passed it down. One by one, they all had a turn—except Halina, of course.

"*Na zdrowie!*"

"*Na zdrowie!*"

"*Na zdrowie!*"

Mr. Marchewska dealt the first hand, his knotty fingers suddenly nimble. Stach kept the whiskey flowing. Halina picked at the peeling paint on her corner of the door, fidgeting with the little paint turds, while she watched the men drink. They were getting sloppy, silly, stupid. Predictable. She was still prickled about Stach telling her to shut up and forget Lydia. Halina wasn't good at forgetting.

Major won that one.

Stach dealt the next hand, slow, concentrating, counting the cards in Polish, then Russian, then German.

"He's showing off, an educated man, for sure."

The grocer wiped his mouth on his sleeve. "C'mon, deal me sumthin' pretty, you educated cuss."

Waldemar slobbered too, drool at the corners of his mouth. "I'll take three."

"I'll take some of those poutin' pretty women. Some black queens with gold crowns and pink on the inside. Wouldn't that be nice to see?" Major did his hyena-laughing thing, snot coming out his nose as he fell into a fit of laughter.

Stach punched his shoulder. "Behave, Major! Be a gentleman— we got a lady present, so mind your manners."

Stach winked at Halina. He tried to pat her on the head, but she turned just in time to avoid the humiliation.

"I'll see your dime and raise you a quarter."

"What?" asked the grocer.

"I'll see your dime and raise you a quarter!" yelled Waldemar in his ear.

Around and around they went. More shots, more jabs, more jokes and heehaws. They all smoked like chimneys. A couple of coffee cans served as ashtrays, or they threw the butts on the ground. But then the chickens and Goose tried to eat the butts. Halina tried to shoo Goose away. Goose honked and flapped her wings, pissed as hell, charging headfirst into the mess of men.

"Shhh, stupid Goose! You'll wake the dead!"

As the men got drunker, Halina got smarter. She won another hand. And another. Lots of slapping the table as they all took to groaning and hollering over aces that wouldn't appear and deuces that were wild or not wild, depending on Stach's hand—or changing mood. And she snuck a sip here and there.

The cigarette smoke climbed on spirals to the moon. Halina followed the path with her gaze, skating along, wishing on stars, as if they were magic or buttons on God's black velvet vest. And she knew her eyes were the color of night. She threw back a shot and heard ringing in her ears, static, until she focused and concentrated.

Her turn to deal.

Concentrate.

Cards around the circle. The dial on the radio. She tuned into the only radio station broadcasting from the moon. North wind, east sun, west prairie grass, south seas. A circle unending and tonight this was the pivotal point. Right here, right now. She became what she was meant to be.

"Who gave the girl a shot? She's trunk. Thunk. Stunk. Drunk."

"I *ain't*. And I ain't no *girl*, either," Halina insisted.

Major tossed back another shot.

"*Na zdrowie!*"

"Get away, Goose!"

Goose honked.

Halina saw a shooting star.

"Hush, Goose! You're gonna wake the dead, ol' Goose! Hush, I said!"

Halina stole the shot Stach was pouring and threw it back before he could protest.

"*Na zdrowie!*"

"Shhh, stupid Goose! You'll wake the dead!" Halina hissed.

Stach won a hand. Then Major.

And the peach tree by the alley pointed a gnarly finger at Halina. *Your turn to win*, it said.

Halina picked up her cards.

Shadows by the peach tree swirled, roots flexing in the sandy soil. A girl's bones shifted.

Halina peeked at her cards. A full house right from the start—with a pair of kings, three jacks. She kept her face frozen, her eyes still. Only the tongue in her mouth danced in happy circles, from tooth to tooth, tasting a win and moon dust.

"I suppose I'll play these babies," Halina said with a why-not? shrug.

Major whistled as though he had a good hand. Waldemar coughed as if he were dying a painful death. Kacper took two cards.

Goose had settled by Halina's feet, still waiting for some bread crumbs.

"Well, I feel lucky," said Stach. He raised a dollar.

Halina let her eyes go flat, unfocused, unreadable. She called, then raised a nickel, then a dime. Then Stach loaned her another quarter from his pocket. Someone raised. *Again.*

Around the table. And the peach tree cheered.

Major folded. Waldemar folded. Stach folded.

Halina spread her cards on the table and raked in over four dollars in winnings—all coins!

"I won! I won!" She gave Stach his money back and still had plenty! And the night was just getting started!

The men groaned.

Halina jumped up from the apple crate, ready to dance, celebrate, swing from the moon.

She danced with the girl who rose from the peach tree. They twirled like ballerinas, celebrating a brief friendship without barriers. Then, now. Living, dead.

"You know what, little dancer? I have something for you under the workbench in the shanty. Been saving it for you. Why don't you go get it?" said Stach.

"Licorice?"

He nodded, and Halina ran toward—*what?*

She stopped. Froze.

God almighty, no, no, no . . .

There, in the shanty window: a face. *The* face. The face of her nightmares. Here it was again—in Stach's window. Staring at her. Very real. No dream at all. *A real man.*

She couldn't breathe. Her heart thudded so hard it hurt.

The face was flattened, pressed against the glass pane, like in her nightmares. Giant hands, monster-like, were cupped to its eyes. The eyes pressed to the glass, trying to see out—or in. And the mouth— open—tried to talk, but no sounds came out. It just sucked at the glass, tongue on the window, like a slug, clinging to the glass.

A flood of memories. All those nights she had woken up terrified, sure she had seen a face that no one else had. *"Go back to sleep,"* her sister had always said. *"There's nothing there."*

Then recognition hit. It *was* a real man. And she knew him.

Janusz. He had been the one staring in her window all those years. *I'll kill the bastard!*

She looked around for something, anything, to swing. There, in the tree stump by the coop: a hatchet sticking out, its blade catching moon specks.

In one swift, fluid motion, Halina was at the stump, grabbing the hatchet, the wooden handle rough in her sweaty hands, heavy, but she hoisted it over her head easily, her heart racing, pulse thumping.

She charged toward the shanty, screeching, "I'll show you!"

Goose flapped and hissed, got in the way. Wings, three feet long, powerful, got in the way.

Halina tripped. She flew.

So did the hatchet.

Lydia caught them both.

Chapter 27

Patcja walked downtown. The early evening was chilly, the light fading into an unusual orange glow. Wind was picking up, bringing dampness from the swamp and stink from the dump. She pulled her bulky sweater around her neck, clutching it over her chest. She tried pulling the collar over her nose and mouth, as if that could help keep the bad air out. She concentrated on slow, even breaths that matched the rhythm of her feet as she walked.

The breathing spell this morning had scared her. She'd thought she might die. It was that bad. Baba's steam treatment helped, though. And she could still feel the circles on her back, the medicine tingling in the scratches. Baba had painted her back with some ointment goo that had dried, locking in the herbal concoction. It smelled like a big weed field after a rain. Patcja had no idea what was in the mixture, but it felt good—warm, radiating.

Baba told her to rest, stay home, drink the tea she put in a jar for her to take home. But Patcja had to be at work. Saturday evening was *the* big night at The Corner. She needed the money, she needed to see Joey, and she needed to be on the lookout.

Tension was in the air. Revenge was still waiting.

She walked around to the back, to the door off the alley, where deliveries were dropped off—both the secret kind and the not-so-secret.

A parked truck was hogging most of the alley. The back doors were open and two fellas, muscled young men, were unloading crates of bottles padded with straw. They blocked the doorway.

"Can I get through?" Patcja asked.

They ignored her, making her wait as they continued stacking crates onto a dolly, then pushed them inside.

Patcja followed.

Augie was inside, counting the crates, making notes in his ledger.

"Hello, Augie. Stocking up for a big night?"

"It *better* be a big night. I have bills to pay, a business to run," he snapped.

He pointed the man with the handcart toward the bar, showing him where to unload the crates.

"I've counted them. Make sure you unload what I paid for, hear me?"

Patcja squeezed past, not as easily as she used to. Instead of going straight into the tavern, though, she turned down the short hall to the office. One lightbulb hung over a table, and the room was dim—a den, a good place for hiding.

"Joey!" Patcja called out.

He was sitting at the table, smoking, a mug of something steaming on the table in front of him along with a half-empty vial of some dark liquid. Patcja recognized it. Pa sulked around nipping on that kind of vial sometimes, too. The alleys and piers were full of men selling bottled remorse, forgiveness, absolution. If you sucked at that teat enough, you could imagine anything, even that God forgave you. Father Chodniewicz gave sermons about it. Joey's head drooped over the cup, as if he were peering into a deep well.

"Eh, what?" he said, looking up, foggy with sleep—or something else.

"Oh, Joey, you are looking so much better! I'm so glad to see you up, so improved, almost as good as new," Patcja said, hugging the man tentatively, gently, planting kisses on his cheek.

"Yeah, yeah. I'm as right as rain, back to my old self, baby," he said, patting her back, cigarette still in hand. Smoke curled into Patcja's face. She coughed, wheezed.

Joey turned back to staring into his coffee mug, rubbing his head, hands in his hair.

"I need to get my apron and get to work before Augie notices, but I'll come back to check on you when I can take a break, all right?"

"Yeah, sure, baby, why not? Maybe you can manage something to eat, too. I could use a real meal."

"Of course, Joey! Anything for you."

Patcja stopped at the kitchen to grab her apron. She kept the sweater on and put the bib apron on over it, tying it loosely so it hung in a baggy, rumpled mess, a silly clown dress. Or a tent.

She paused in front of the window that looked out to the alley. She turned and twisted, trying to see her reflection in the glass pane. Did she really look as horrid as she imagined? Her reflection wobbled in the watery glass. It was no better than looking in a puddle, ripples distorting, warping the image that was so foreign looking.

"Is that me?"

"Well, who the hell else could it be?"

Patcja whirled around. It was one of the Italian boys with the dolly, chuckling at her, shaking his head like she was crazy. He started unloading a crate of bottles. The labels read, "Dr. Benezzio's Elixir," in fancy red and gold letters. A barrel under the counter had chunks of ice in it. The boy, his black hair hanging in his face, unloaded four bottles at a time from the cart, putting them in the barrel and covering them with ice. He chipped at the ice with an icepick, breaking it apart into smaller chunks, half watching Patcja.

"Mind your own business. No one was talking to you," she sneered.

"Talking to me is better than talking to yourself, honey."

"I'm not talking to myself *or* you. And I'm not a honey."

"No? I thought you was Joey's honey. We were all told you were off-limits, Joey's. Not that any of us Italian boys would stoop as low as to do a Polish 'bushka—not on purpose, anyway." He laughed and made oinking noises at her, still bent over the barrel, arranging bottles in the ice.

Patcja planted a foot firmly on his skinny Italian ass and shoved. He toppled over, off-balance.

"Oh, a feisty 'bushka!" And then he laughed even louder.

"What's going on back here? Do I have to watch you boys every minute? I'm going to count these bottles, I tell you!" shouted Augie, waving his hands and his ledger. "Patcja, I said to get to work!"

"I'm going, I'm *going*," Patcja mumbled, biting her lip, blinking, trying to make the sting of salty tears go away.

The hanging lights in the tavern weren't turned on yet. *Thank God.* That gave her time to get composed in the dimness. Chairs were overturned on the tables, creating giant black shapes, like dead bugs on their backs, legs sticking up. Creepy. Chills ran up her arms. Patcja started pulling the chairs down, setting them upright, bringing the creatures back to life. When she was finished, she flipped on the lights and unlocked the "secret" side door. She propped it open a bit so men would know The Corner was open, ready for business—even if *she* wasn't ready.

Through the propped-open door, she saw men lingering in huddles. Were they waiting to come in or up to no good?

She had a list of other opening chores to tend to, from wiping down tables to setting out ashtrays—cast iron things shaped like a woman on her back, her legs in the air. (Guess where the ashes went and where the men stubbed out their smokes?)

Disgusting. All men. Italian men, especially.

And she thought of Joey. Maybe he would be different. She could *make* him be different, teach him. What other choice did she have?

She could visit Baba. The wall of herbs and roots and mysterious earthly demons in jars and baskets in Baba's kitchen. Nightshade, belladonna, hemlock, Queen Ann's lace . . .

No, no. Of course, no.

Patcja crossed herself. *Forgive me, Mary, Mother of Jesus.* She took several deep breaths, trying to rid her mind of the evil thoughts.

I just need to get busy, work. Get to work.

She found a few ingredients that seemed edible in the icebox. In a basket on the shelf, there were onions, turnips, beets. She started chopping cabbage. She had helped Ma and the church ladies many times in the kitchen at St. Florian's, making goulash so they could feed the bums and hobos and people off the boats and boxcars with nowhere else to go. What would that be like? To have no home?

Girls in the Old Country who had sinned—like her—were cast out, sent away. If Joey didn't marry her, she would have to leave Hegewisch. Maybe a train . . . Maybe that would be better, anyway. But to where? She had read about American cities in school, but had never been farther than Chicago. She knew more about cities in Poland than the ones in this country.

She went outside to the pump for water to boil and realized she wasn't alone.

Someone stood in the shadows between the garbage bins and the empty crates that the elixir came in. The crates, stacked into precarious towers, looked like odd creatures stooping over to hear whispers.

"Who's there?" Patcja called. She reached in the door, groping at the counter for the butcher knife she had been using.

"Hello, Patcja. It's just me," said Antonio, stepping into the shallow light from the kitchen. "Why did you run away the other night? I just wanted to talk to you," he said.

He wore his usual long black coat and the felt hat with the red feather pushed back on his head. He also wore a white shirt and tie under his jacket. All dressed up, fancy, like a waiter at one of the big parties the union men, politicians, and crooks liked to throw. Maybe some of the gangsters from the newspaper, like that Al Capone, would be there. Maybe Antonio knew him. Or worked for him.

"I didn't want to talk to you, Antonio," she said, holding the pail in front of her like a shield. "Some men are saying you are the one who stabbed Joey."

"Eh? I figured they'd try to put the blame on us. Rotten scum. They come to our side of town, shove their way into our business. Plenty of room all over Chicago, and they decide they want the south side to sell their disgusting piss-water hooch, when we sell good whiskey here. Why?"

Did he really expect an answer from her? Patcja couldn't think of what to say. She didn't care about their whiskey wars. So juvenile, silly. She had more important things to worry about.

"Did you do it, Antonio? Did you stab Joey? 'Cause if you did . . ." She raised the butcher knife over her head, her hand shaking. The threat was all spit and air, they both knew.

He laughed. Of course, he laughed that lovely laugh of his, like music. Lyrical and sweet. She remembered the night they had danced on the pier, music coming from somewhere far away—one of the yachts on the lake, some political bigwigs throwing a bash. Some of Sal's men, including Antonio, had been the waiters, wearing white shirts and ties, as he did tonight. Some things never changed.

"No, honey, I didn't. Why would I do that?"

"I don't know. Why do you and your henchmen do anything? Why are you always causing trouble for us? Why can't you leave Hegewisch and the Polish people here alone? Don't you have enough of your own fools to prey on?"

"Because there is nothing easier—and tastier—than a Polish girl, my sweet Patcja," he said, puckering up his mouth in a pretend kiss, mocking her. And he came toward her, arms out, fingers wiggling, as if he were calling a sheepdog.

She raised her hand with the knife higher. This time her hand didn't shake.

"Don't you even think about coming one step closer to me, you slimy—"

Hands came at her from behind. Someone tried to take away the knife. She gripped it tighter.

"Now, now, honey . . ."

It was Joey!

"If anyone is going to scare this annoying prick away, it's going to me," Joey said. "Let me show you how it's done," he said.

What a relief! Patcja gladly released the knife to Joey. He took control of the weapon—if you could call it that—and pushed Patcja behind him.

Joey and Antonio danced left and then right, squaring off, both men bent over, arms out, in a wrestler's stance—each daring the other.

Patcja heard more noise behind her, and a shot rang out. Augie was in the doorway with a shotgun, pointed up to the night sky. He fired again.

"Get out of here, Antonio! We don't want any more trouble. You stick to the hardware store, selling your milk bottles there. Leave us alone!"

"Fine, Augustino. Is that the message you want me to give to Sal?"

"Yes, now go! Tell him that's my decision and it's final," said Augie, waving the shotgun. "*Go.*"

"I'll tell him, but I can tell you, he's not going to like it one bit." Antonio turned, shaking his head, making *tssk*ing sounds, as if he were scolding a puppy who had just shit on his boot.

He walked away, a saunter, as though he wanted to prove that no one was making him leave. No one bothered to watch.

"Whew," Joey said as he led Patcja back into the kitchen, a protective hand on her arm.

"Don't do that no more, baby. You can't take on those crazy hoodlums by yourself. How would that look if I let something happen to you? That would be *my* name being smeared all over town, you know?"

Patcja threw her arms around him. He let the knife drop to the floor and hugged her back with one arm, the other still stiff from the bandaged wound.

"Oh, you *do* love me, Joey! I knew it! I knew you really did love me!"

"Sure, baby, of course I do. Why not?" he said, smirking, giving her a slick grin.

"Can we get married, Joey? *Please?* I'll be a good wife, I *promise.* I'll always take care of you. Do you want me to look after you, take care of you, cook dinner for you? Do *everything* for you?"

Joey was checking his shoulder, eyeing the bandages. A red spot was growing on the white gauze. He cringed. "Sure, baby," he said. "I already said I could use some dinner."

"Really, Joey?"

"Uh, well, what? Yeah, I suppose. Why not, baby?"

"Oh, Joey! I love you! I love you *so* much!" Patcja tightened her hug, nuzzling against his cheek, the wonderful, wonderful man. She was so excited, so relieved. She wanted to cover him with kisses, from head to toe. Patcja laughed, and tears filled her eyes. She let them run down her face.

Joey winced, his face as colorless as the lightbulb dangling from the ceiling. But the bandage was bright red.

Chapter 28

Stach sat in Baba's kitchen, waiting for the breakfast that was promised to him. Baba had wanted some wood chopped and offered eggs and fried potatoes as payment. Now she was over at the stove clanking around, mumbling to herself, creating wickedly enticing smells. But he barely paid attention, more preoccupied with the nagging questions pecking at him from behind his eyes.

It had been two weeks since the poker night incident, but the fiasco still replayed over and over in his head. And still, he didn't understand. And for some reason, he felt responsible.

One minute, the girl was happy as a lark that she had won a hand of poker, skipping off to get licorice from the shanty; and the next, she turned into a wild banshee, purple with rage, sputtering threats and swinging an old ax as if it were a flag in a parade.

Thank God he'd seen it and gotten to her in time.

Crazy girl.

And she hadn't even had a shot of whiskey to get her all riled up. Had she? Maybe she had been helping herself to the bottle or had some of that homemade brew that could eat your brains away? Nah, she was mad, just plain furious. But over what?

She wouldn't explain, either—then *or* now. Once he'd gotten the ax pried out of her hands and had her separated from Janusz,

Stach had tried getting to the bottom of her outburst, but the strange critter was all tight-lipped about it and indignant, mad at Stach for getting in the way.

Well, good thing he did.

And Janusz wasn't saying much, either. He didn't remember doing anything to set her off. He had just been looking out the window, he said. The oaf. He must have done something to provoke her.

Just like during the war. A husband, a French farmer, had caught Janusz in the barn, doing the unholy deed with the man's wife, who might or might not have been a willing participant. Janusz didn't seem to remember that part of the story.

Yes, Janusz was a weird turd, but that didn't mean he needed to be chopped up, did it?

"I am talking to you, bumble-brain!" shouted Baba to get his attention. "Do you want onions in your potatoes?"

"Hmm? Sure, sure. Whatever you have is fine with me."

"Here. Eat this," Baba said, bringing over a heaping plate of food. "Then chop wood for the stove and for a fire outside. Tonight I need a *big* fire, as tall as you, so I need wood—good, hard wood from an oak, not those maple saplings you try to tell me are firewood."

Stach looked at her face, trying to read if this fire would be used for healing or cursing. He had a right to know, didn't he? He didn't want to be pulled into a showdown—Baba against the Family—that ended up with his digging *another* grave.

Maybe it was time to take a stand, take some responsibility. Hegewisch was being sucked into Chicago's black swamp of corruption, crime, vice, gangsters running the show—a cesspool as bad as Sodom and Gomorrah. And he'd let it happen.

Like the time Halina had found Lydia in the churchyard, sick, praying in the dirt in the graveyard because she thought she was too filthy to come inside the building. Halina had fetched Stach to carry the sick girl to Baba, shouting the whole time about words Lydia had mumbled. Sick words. She'd had a fever. Sick deeds, a sick life she had fallen into. The hardware store had been turned into a brothel. Young girls were smuggled in from Poland without the right papers. The Major was likely involved in some way, but Stach had never figured out the particulars—other than that the girls had to work to pay off the debt. But Lydia had come with the Spanish flu.

He remembered it vividly, another time he had simply done as he was told, letting the old woman decide judgement, justice, and how to destroy all evidence of crimes against God. He rubbed his eyes, but the picture was still there:

No matter how many questions Stach asked, he could get no answers from the old woman. For an hour past dusk he worked, digging in the sandy ground behind the shanty, in the scruff of bushes and trees near the alley. Baba supervised, pretending to be deaf or mute or simply a stubborn Polish woman hell-bent on having her way. She chose the location—obviously picking an untraveled, out-of-the-way spot, mostly bog, where no one would walk accidentally. She drew a shape in the ground and told him to start digging.

Stach realized quickly he wasn't just digging a hole; he was digging a grave. He tried to hide his concern and remain calm, like the woman who sat on a bale of straw, watching. As he tossed shovels of the damp sand, he mentally went through the inventory of people he knew, trying to remember when he had last seen each one. His worry turned into anger, jagged and sharp. He couldn't stand not knowing.

"I'm done," Stach said, dropping the shovel. "Unless I get some answers."

He and Baba stared at each other, glaring with the intensity of smoldering embers. It was so absurd, so unreal—yet doused with a desperate reality.

Life. Death. A grave.

Stach stood on one side of the pit; Baba stood on the other side. This horrid void, like a gaping mouth, was between them. What had she been driven to that she couldn't trust him? Why couldn't she confide in him and let him help?

"Oh, Father Almighty," sighed Baba, defeated. She started back to her house and motioned for Stach to follow. Oil lamps were burning in Baba's house, Stach could see as they came up to the back door. Baba led the way down the steps into the kitchen. From the doorway Stach saw the sheet-wrapped bundle on the table. A tidy bundle, small. He could make out the shape, traces of blonde hair.

"Her name was Lydia," Baba said, pulling back a corner of the sheet but motioning for Stach to stay back.

"She had the sickness, the Spanish flu. Probably had it on the ship. She was smuggled past the guards anyway. Some men paid her way. She worked for them. A brave soul rescued her and brought her to me, but I failed her. Now we must bury her and forget her. We won't say her name again."

Stach didn't want to see the girl on the table, but he couldn't turn his eyes away, either. This was the girl from the hardware store's back room, the thinly disguised whorehouse on the edge of town. Halina was the one who had intervened, risked her life to steal away the half-dead girl and bring her to Baba.

Baba whacked the table in front of him with her wooden spoon, jarring him back to the present.

"Wake up! Get busy!" she commanded. "Are you done eating?"

"Yeah, I'm done," he said. "I'm done, all right. Done playing games," he growled, standing up, feeling cranky and irritated, not thrilled at all about helping the woman build a bonfire. For what? What was she up to now? They were playing with dangerous men, living in dangerous times. A little hocus-pocus curse could backfire in times like these.

Tensions between Sal's fellas and Augie's men from Back of the 'Yards were still simmering. Word had it that there was a traitor or two, someone plotting to take over and someone talking to the law. Mostly threats, gossip. He heard it from men stopping by the news-stand. The men gave him what bits they heard. He was supposed to piece it all together.

"What's gonna happen to us?" they would say. "Do something. We need to do something, look out for our own," someone would say. Someone *always* said it—and then looked at him, the man who made green wool socks and army blankets appear out of thin air. But this time, he wasn't sure what he could do.

But he knew it would all blow up before it was over. Blow up *big*.

"Tell me the truth: What is the fire for, old woman?"

"What bug has gotten up your high and mighty ass, *dupchek*?" Baba frowned. She huffed loudly and let out a hissing sound, like a rubber tire with a leak. "How do you dare to question me? I helped bring you into this world, son of my sister, the saintly woman," she added, crossing herself and looking to heaven.

As soon as God and his mother were called into the quarrel, he knew he'd lost. As usual.

"I just don't want any trouble for anyone," Stach said, exasperated now, his frustration bubbling over into something quivering like jelly, hard to hold on to. He knew he shouldn't blame the old woman, but she could make matters worse if she interfered.

"Are you going to tell me or not? What's the big bonfire for?"

"Well, it's the Paschal moon tonight, of course," Baba answered. "You should know that, Your Holy Highness, Stach, the Pope of Hegewisch." She tied her babushka tighter under her chin and went outside.

"I will mark the spot on the ground where I want the wood piled," she shouted back to him, over her shoulder. "And make sure Halina is here by high moon. You bring her."

He looked up to heaven, just as Baba had, and crossed himself—just as she had.

"Yes, ma'am," he mumbled. But she was already gone.

Chapter 29

Halina sat on the half wall at the Patchiecki place, fiddling with the new matchbox amulet she had gotten from Baba. Like the last one she had used for the zombie man with rotgut poisoning, this one rattled with the crumbs of prayers and scraps of nature, symbols, and sacrifices.

And like the last one, Baba hadn't let her see exactly what ingredients were in the matchbox before she'd tied it up. Halina was supposed to imagine and *feel* the power of the elements. That made them powerful, Baba said. That old woman sure had a way about her.

Halina was tempted to untie the twine and look inside, but she resisted. Besides, some knots were next to impossible to untie. This looked like one of those.

She was happy just enjoying the spring day, warm and full of blooms and promises of more. This spot was almost pretty. Cheerful wild daffodils intermingled among the weeds. The apple tree was full of white flowers blushing pink, and a redbud tree, with its lacy shawl of lavender-pink flowers, made one corner of the overgrown yard look perfect, heaven touched. Chipmunks scurried across the branches, teasing, testing to see if she would chase them.

Chip, is that you? Are you all better? I hope so.

She'd come here to think. She had tossed some rocks toward

the tall grass to make sure the rats scurried away. Now that she was perched on this wall, she decided she had no desire to rehash all of her worries, sort them out. It was just nice to absorb the colors and newness of a spring afternoon.

Renewal vibrated, ancient yet new. Green buds returned after the dismal winter, determined to start again. Hope is made of colors—pink and yellow and white, like bridal veils. Beginnings are best—juicy, sweet and tart, exciting.

Like her new job at the hospital. It was a chance to be someone else, someone who wasn't all tied down with crazy Old Country ways. She was so ready to be done with the folk stories, babushkas, and polkas—and the guilt over wanting to be more than an ignorant, displaced immigrant.

Halina let herself fall into a daydream, thinking about the first few days of her job. She had watched young women on the sidewalks in Hammond, near the hospital. They had looked so pretty and perfect in every way, from their snappy T-strap heels and bobbed hair to long beads and smart little cloche hats with feathers and sparkly baubles.

Well, not all of the women were so fancy. Hammond had poor women, too—and even women with black skin and women with brown skin. And there had been the farm women who sold honey and butter and sausages from small carts along the side of the road, children in tow. She had walked past them and wondered what their lives were like.

Where were their menfolk? Working? Up to mischief? Gone?

She had walked past the Hawthorne Hotel, too, whenever she walked to the hospital. Early in the morning, it seemed sealed up, asleep. Blinds on the windows were all down, like eyes shut.

Except one morning, maybe a week ago.

On one of the top floors, the blinds of one window had been pulled to the side, someone looking out. She looked like just a girl.

She can't be more than sixteen, Halina had thought.

They had locked eyes—for a just a second. Then hands had

pulled the girl away from the window. Man hands. The girl in the window had opened her mouth—maybe she was screaming—and a hand had gone over her mouth, pulling her away from the window.

Halina had shivered, had paced the sidewalk in front of the hotel. What should she do? What *could* she do? She had looked back to the window, but had seen nothing. She hadn't even been sure which window it was. They all looked the same: closed tight. Eyes closed tight. She had heard noises from the back of the hotel, clinks and bangs, motors, voices. In the alley, some cooks and maids, along with the busboys and kitchen help, could be seen unloading deliveries, carrying out bins of trash and carts of dirty laundry.

She had paused. Should she tell one of them? *Tell them what?* Someone wasn't being nice to a girl? *Well, that would be good for a laugh, wouldn't it?* She had watched the movement in the alley for a moment longer, wondering if she would see someone she knew, a woman with small hands, just like her mother's, but she hadn't.

There had been no other signs of sheets from the hotel in the laundry she was given to scrub, either. No other bloody handprints. Maybe it hadn't happened at all. Maybe she'd imagined it. She didn't have time to worry about such mysteries that were none of her business.

She was focusing on fitting in with the other young women in the hospital's candy striper program. Eventually, she *would* fit in, she kept telling herself. Sure. It just took time.

The newspaper advertisement had described the program, but it hadn't quite explained that this was a job that didn't pay money. How crazy was that?

It had taken her days to work up enough gumption to first visit the hospital and inquire. Several times, she had started to walk to the hospital but hadn't gotten very far before she'd turned around, her stomach pitching a fit. Eventually, she'd gotten up enough courage to go through the front doors. She'd walked up to the big reception desk and told the nurse she had come for the job—the one to help take care of people and make them happy and get well. The nurse, with her white starched uniform and prim-and-proper fancy, pointy hat, had laughed. "You need training to be a nurse in this country!"

Halina had almost turned around and left right then and there, but she'd had the torn bit of newspaper with her, all folded down into a tidy square. She had shown it to the woman, who had still been chuckling, a little laugh like a tinkle. Eventually, Nurse Snobby had directed Halina to the right supervising nurse, who'd had a clipboard and seemed very important.

This Nurse Clipboard had been a tad nicer, but they'd still had trouble understanding each other. Halina had been sure the woman had the wrong program or was trying to trick her. The nurse had kept saying it was a volunteer position and that meant there was no paycheck. Halina's thought had been that the lady was trying to bamboozle her and keep the paying jobs for girls with nice shoes and nice coats, not girls from Hegewisch. The nurse had seemed rather put-out that Halina doubted her.

"There is only *one* program, and it is the same for everyone—no matter their *shoes*, young lady. Now, sign up or go," she had said with a big, long sigh that was all for show.

Halina had signed up.

She'd had to sit at a small desk and fill out a form. She had been able to read most of it, but there had been a question at the end with several blank lines, a place for references. She hadn't been sure what that meant. A reference was a book, wasn't it? *Książka,* a reference book? She wrote:

I don't have many references. But the ones I have are valuable. The nuns at St. Florian's gave me a book, The Faithful River, *by Żeromski, the famous Polish author. Have you read it? It's very good—about a wounded soldier who is nursed back to health by a young maiden. She was left in charge of the manor house when everyone else fled; and she doctored that soldier to be fine again, just with what she had, herbs and such. I love that book. That is the only reference I have now, but I will get more, I promise.*

It seemed that just having one reference was enough, because they had accepted her to the program.

And she finally got the idea of how this crazy job worked. She did work for them for free, and they let her sit in training classes for free. A trade. If she passed the test at the end of the course in six months, she could be a real nurses' aide and get paid a *real* paycheck. It sounded simple enough. They even gave her a uniform to wear. A lovely thing, white with pink stripes. She was supposed to buy white shoes, but she spent her poker winnings on new glasses for Ma.

Since she didn't have enough money yet for white shoes, she still wore her brown boots. Stach gave her his shoestrings so they wouldn't flap so badly.

And there wouldn't be any more poker games at Stach's shanty for her—not since she had made an ass of herself at the last one—so she wasn't sure how she was going to get shoe money. That's what she had come to the Patchiecki place to think about. She wished she could talk to Stach about it, but he was still mad at her.

Probably. He probably hated her.

Maybe.

Her and her damned temper. She had just exploded when she realized it was Janusz who had been looking in the coal room window when she was a kid. And he had scared her to death. All those nightmares of a man's face in the window, drooling, panting like a dog in heat. When she grabbed the hatchet she had just wanted *him* to see what it was like to be scared to death.

She wasn't going to swing the ax at him. Probably not.

Well, not *hit* him with it. Probably not.

She picked some white apple tree blooms off the ground. *So pretty.*

More flowers fell out of the sky, from branches overhead. Suddenly it was raining flowers!

"Bear, is that you? Where are you?"

He hopped down from a nearby branch, landing in the grass like an acrobat.

"How did you know it was me?" he asked.

"Lucky guess. How long you been up there? You been spying on me?"

"Nope, but I been looking for you. I got a message for you, from Waldemar."

"The barber? What the heck kind of message would the barber have for *me*?"

"I don't know," Bear replied with a shrug. "I'm supposed to fetch you and have you come back with me. Just something important. Must have been. All the men were talking. Major, the grocer, Antonio—they were all hush-hush and shooing me out and writing notes and taking off their hats, waving their arms, silly-like. You know how those Sicilians get when they are excited."

"Yeah, I know. Well, I don't care. I don't want no message from Waldemar. And I'm not going downtown. I am *busy* now. I have a job at the hospital, you know. It's important," Halina insisted. "And I just can't up and walk all the way downtown any ol' time 'cause some dang barber says so. I have homework to do—a book I'm reading. *Supposed* to be reading. I plan to start it tonight."

Halina climbed down from the brick ledge, straightening her dress, brushing away white apple blossoms.

"Can't you *please* come? Do you want me to get in trouble? They said don't come back without you."

"*Phhhht!* What the heck do they think—ordering me around? Tell them I said *no*, and I sounded like I meant it. 'Cause I do."

Bear tried pleading, but Halina wasn't about to give in and follow him. She started to get mad, the more he whined. Why was he still such a little boy? When would he grow up?

"I'm going home, Bear. Get out of my way."

"I can't Halina. I'm your friend. You have to do this for me."

"A *friend*? Like the *friend* who stole my poker money?"

She couldn't keep it bottled up anymore.

"Why did you take my poker money, Bear?"

"I'm sorry, Halina. I just had to borrow some money. I needed it. I will pay you back, *I promise*."

"Well, you better be doing it soon. I need new shoes to go with my uniform. *White* shoes."

"I'll try, Halina. I promise. Just come with me."

"No," Halina shook her head firmly. "Pay up first."

Chapter 30

Halina gave in—sort of.

She agreed to follow Bear to his house. His father would be there, and maybe *he* could repay her. It wasn't a very good plan, but it was better than nothing. She had to have answers, at least—and some idea of when she could have her poker money back.

They were quiet as they walked to Bear's house.

Camel and Bear, Patcja and Halina had walked this way together when they were young. Since they had played together as children, no one thought about insisting they have a chaperone once they were older. That was during the war. All the old notions of properness seemed to lessen some. A war was being fought in the Old Country. Who could think of anything else?

Well, Patcja and Camel sure could.

Thank goodness, Halina and Bear did their best to interfere and keep the two lovebirds from being too involved. At the time, all their hand-holding and eye-gazing seemed disgusting. Now it seemed sweet. Camel would have been so much better for Patcja. He truly loved her.

But about then, Antonio had started nosing around, looking for a Polish girl—all because of the rumors that Polish girls were easy. Patcja took up with Antonio, fell for his false charms. And Camel enlisted. That was that.

Bear took odd little nervous steps, as though he was trying to prolong the walk to his house or something. He kept swallowing hard, as if he had a rock in his throat. *Poor boy.*

❧ ❧ ❧

When they got to the house, Bear insisted on going in first—to see if his father minded if Halina came in to visit.

Why would he mind? She could hear rustling and whispering going on behind the door. *Is that furniture scraping across the floor? What the hell is going on in there?*

She waited. Finally, Bear opened the door and motioned for her to come in.

The house was the same as all the other houses on the street—except the sitting room had a bed, the mechanical kind that could be raised and lowered with a crank. Camel was propped up against the metal headboard, his head tilted as if he were asking a question. His father sat in a chair next to the bed. Then next to Mateusz was Bear's mother, Elinor, sitting in a wheelchair. She drooped sideways, staring into nothing, drool hanging from her chin. A raggedy towel was propped by her neck to catch the slobbers. Mateusz held the hands of both son and wife.

Halina had not seen Camel since the welcome-home parade the town had thrown for him. They had planned it before anyone knew what kind of shape he was in—or that he wouldn't be able to see the parade at all. After he had been carried off the train by some army sergeants and Red Cross ladies, some of the townspeople had cheered for Camel—then they had cried and gone home. What else was there to do?

He had withered since that day at the train station. He was covered with a sheet and an old blanket, but what was under the sheet? A pile of bones—two knees and two elbows protruding at odd angles. They said mustard gas had done it. His face was burned, obviously. The skin seemed pink and near translucent, stretched to cover mutilated features. His eyes were bandaged. White gauze was wrapped around his head, also covering his ears.

Camel moved at the sound of feet coming through the door, bodies jostling for space in the cramped room. He tried to scoot down into the bed, as if he were burrowing.

Mateusz patted the boy's hand. "It's fine, Camel. *Shhh*, Camel," he soothed.

Elinor was propped up in the wheelchair. She was awake, maybe. It was hard to tell. The left side of her face hung flaccid and lifeless. Her left arm, too, hung at an odd angle, as though it had no muscles, nothing connecting it to her body except maybe some wires or string. When Halina came in, she tried to talk, but only drool came out, and muffled sounds, gibberish. Then Mateusz patted her hand, too.

Mateusz looked back and forth, from mother to son, son to mother, seeming unsure of whom to help first, what to do next. Finally he said, "*Shhh, shhh, shhh*," to both patients. Then he turned his eyes to Halina. "Come in, Halina. Welcome. How nice to have a visitor."

"Thanks for having me, sir," she said. She turned toward Camel. "Hello, Camel, it's me—Halina."

Camel turned away, rolling his head toward the wall.

"Bear, why are the bandages on his eyes and over his ears? Can he see or hear?" she asked Bear in a whisper.

"Oh, there ain't nothing wrong with Camel's eyes," Bear said, raising his voice. "Is there, Camel?"

Camel made no sounds, no moves.

If he can see and hear, why the bandages?

Bear explained: mustard gas. It had burned off his eyelids. Without eyelids, he couldn't blink and protect his eyes from light. How horrible that must be.

Mateusz reached for the Bible on the small bedtable behind his wife. It was cluttered—a glass of water, an empty bottle of lilac perfume, a blue barrette, a comb, and a hand mirror. A pink ribbon with some fancy buttons threaded on, made into a necklace, was spread out. And a ladybug ring made of beads.

My things!

They were all Halina's things, the things that had gone missing. Next to all of that was a box of Whitman's candy, a sampler box shaped like a heart.

Bear caught Halina's line of vision. He fumbled, shuffling his feet, twisting his cap.

"She likes to look pretty," Bear finally offered in explanation. "I help her get her hair fixed and put on the ribbon necklace, and she likes a dab of the lilac water. And the Whitman's . . . A sampler box costs an entire three dollars, but sometimes that is all we can get her to eat. It makes her happy. That's why I had to borrow the money."

"I'm glad it makes her happy," Halina said.

The woman blinked and nodded, a frantic look on her distorted features.

"Hello, Mrs. Elinor. It's me, Halina, Bear's friend. And Camel's friend. I came to say hello and to see if you need anything," Halina said loudly, moving closer to the wheelchair, stooping down so her face was close to the woman's face. Eye to eye. Halina smiled. The woman shook her head from to side to side, saying no.

"You're looking very pretty today. Can I help you with your hair?" Halina didn't wait for an answer. She combed the woman's hair, which had been matted to her head with sweat. She pulled droopy bangs to the side and pinned them with the barrette, then held up the little hand mirror for her to see. "There. That's better, isn't it?" she asked.

The woman nodded.

Bear smiled. His father smiled, too, and squeezed his wife's hand.

"Well, how about if I read for you two a bit? Would you like that?"

Camel wiggled, like a caterpillar in a cocoon, side to side. Was he saying no?

Halina took the Bible from the man and motioned for him to move so she could sit in that chair.

"You wanna take a nap or rest? I will stay here a while. I can read."

"No, no. I think I'll go work on tonight's soup," he said, shuffling toward the kitchen.

Halina sat down and flipped the book, the pages well worn, to a random page in the last half of the thick volume.

"Let's try the New Testament, huh? It's a bit cheerier, don't you think?"

She started reading.

Bear sat on the corner of his brother's bed, listening too, drifting on the words of God, the voice of Halina. Camel's tan tweed cap was on one of the bedposts. Bear grabbed it and carefully put it on his brother's head. He patted his arm, then punched it, like a brother would. Camel lifted his mittened hand and jabbed in the air, hunting for Bear. Bear moved in front of the next jab.

"Ahh, you got me," Bear said quietly, so as not to interrupt Halina's words.

Halina kept reading. For the first time, she noticed the words were lyrical, with a rhythm like a heartbeat. So nice.

Bear fell asleep.

And for a few minutes, Halina couldn't imagine being anywhere but there. Those were her people—and they needed her help.

Chapter 31

Halina watched Bear sleep out of the corner of her eye while she read. The bundle in the bed next to him, Camel, was so still that Halina suspected he might be asleep, as well—just two brothers taking a nap before dinner. A sweet thought, but perverse in its twisted contrast of what should be and what was: wicked fate. She winced, repulsed. Then she was disgusted with herself. The lump in her throat seemed to grow bigger, trying to choke her.

Halina paused mid-sentence, listening. Camel's hand moved across the sheet that covered him, as though he was reaching for something, groping.

Halina hesitated, then took the hand, a garish blob of melted, scarred flesh, and held it gingerly between her two hands.

"I'm here, Camel," she said. "Does this hurt? I don't want to hurt you, you know."

He shook his head.

"Good."

Unsure of what else to say, Halina went back to reading. When the soup was ready, she helped Mateusz feed Elinor, dabbing at her chin with a towel when soup dribbled, which was often. Then Halina watched the complicated process of feeding Camel.

Her heart was in her stomach. She was queasy with guilt and

shame and despair. The smell of soup and piss and something else rancid was starting to make her want to puke. She hated herself for that.

"He can swallow," Bear explained. "Just not too much or too fast. We have to be careful he doesn't choke."

She tried to help but realized she was in the way. They had a system figured out and didn't need her interfering, asking questions and trying to suggest different ideas. So she went back in the kitchen to clean up a little instead, but the kitchen was already immaculate; only the pot and utensils used in making the soup were dirty. She washed those up.

Then she was at a loss—out of words, out of answers and places to turn—a rowboat stuck in sand. She decided to leave. The least she could do for Bear was to find out what the dang annoying barber wanted with her. It had better be something important.

From the doorway, Halina waved at Bear. He looked up for a second, but he was busy and didn't wave back, just nodded and smiled an impish little-boy smile. She slipped out the back door, quietly, but sucked in fresh air as though it was lifesaving.

Downtown was busy with people out doing their weekly errands, shopping and gossiping. Both men and women were out and about, seeming to be in a hurry. She knew Saturday was payday at the mills. She had heard plenty of stories of women meeting their men at the clerk's window where pay was handed out. They'd try to get a dollar for groceries before the week's pay was spent on whiskey or cards.

No wonder so many women were against drinking and supported Prohibition. A lot of good it was doing, though.

Halina found the barber trimming some man's crew cut.

Waldemar didn't seem happy to see her.

"I heard you wanted me for something. You sent Bear to fetch me. What is it?" she asked with a scowl.

"Well, that was hours ago. Antonio needs you to come to the hardware store. Now he's mad at you—and at Bear, too, because he failed to fetch you. So he's just ass-kicking mad, and that's never good."

"Bear and I were busy, feeding his brother and his mama. Did you know she was sick, too? She's as bad off as Camel. All saggy on one side."

"Huh? I don't know anything about that. And I don't want to know, either. And I think you better git yourself over to the hardware store before Antonio blows a gasket."

"I know what kind of place that hardware store is—and it has nothing to do with *hardware*. I'm not going out there 'til you tell me what Antonio wants."

"Just a minute, Mo," he said to his customer. "I'll be back." The barber set down his scissors and went to the back room, waiting for Halina to follow. He shut the door and sidled close to her shoulder so he could whisper: "One of his girls is giving his men the clap, and he wants you to figure out which one—understand? And then he wants you to do your healing business to make it go away."

"What? How—?"

"He can't take them to a doc, understand? So you are the next-best thing he's got, seein' how you healed Joey up and all."

Halina gasped, shook her head. She wasn't sure she understood at all, but she couldn't even think of a question to ask, besides the obvious: *What the hell is the clap?*

Since it was clearly something big and important—or it *seemed* to be—she wasn't sure she wanted to let on that she had never heard of it. And if it *was* something that had to be whispered about, it must be something to do with—*that.*

Crud. Now what?

It took a good thirty minutes to walk to the hardware store. It was on the edge of town, on the north side, toward the canal and Back of the 'Yards. So depending on which way the wind was blowing, anyone near the hardware store could catch a whiff of mill stink, canal sludge, or cattle innards. Sometimes all three.

Today canal sludge seemed to dominate, the distinct smell of fishiness and sewage seeming to waft over the sidewalks as she got closer to the hardware store's corner.

Halina had been here before, trying to help Lydia. She had gotten herself in big trouble here before, stuck her nosiness right in a rotten scheme—and she had just been a kid then. She didn't want to think about it. She sure as hell didn't want to be in bad with Sal and Antonio and his boys again, either.

Wait—what if *that* was why they wanted to see her? Maybe they had figured out she was the one who had helped Lydia.

Halina wiped her sweaty hands on her dress and stood in front of the hardware store door a minute to catch her breath before she opened it. She could hear noises inside: voices shouting, chairs scraping across the floor, feet running—toward her.

The door swung open, inches from her face.

Suddenly, Halina was nose to nose with an old woman, her hair in rollers, a cotton robe hanging open over a slip, a cigarette in her painted mouth. The woman was on her way out, it seemed. And in a hurry.

"*You*. Not you again," said the woman, looking as if she had just tasted spoiled milk.

"Hello, Arlene. How you been?" Halina asked.

Antonio came to the door and pulled Halina inside, past Arlene.

"It's about time you got here, little Polack girl," he said. "I've got a job for you."

Chapter 32

Janusz was starting to become a problem, and Stach wasn't sure what to do about it. The man had always been somewhat of a trouble maker, with a tendency to transgress boundaries. But since he came back from the war, the man always seemed to be thinking with his dick. And *that* one-eyed general wasn't too bright.

Stach strolled the streets of downtown Hegewisch among the Saturday shoppers, looking for Janusz and looking for Halina. He figured he might find one or both down here. He just hoped he didn't find them together, a repeat of the scene in the shanty.

Since that night, he had been quizzing Janusz, trying to get to the bottom of what had set off the girl. The story was starting to become clear, and Stach realized he had done Halina a great injustice by not taking her stories of nightmares and a face in the window more seriously. It never occurred to him that it might be a real man, looking in her window, trying to see in—or climb in.

Whether Janusz had ever physically attacked Halina or not was still unclear. Even if he hadn't, though, she had still been scared to death, violated, and he couldn't let that happen again.

But what can I do about it?

For now, he kept his eyes open, watching for the man or signs of him.

Stach stopped by the newsstand and thought about opening for the day, then changed his mind. He'd rather keep walking, looking for the man or the girl. He had promised Baba he would look for the girl, bring her by tonight for that bonfire of hers. He certainly didn't want to get on the bad side of Baba. The old woman was one fierce sister.

He found himself walking toward St. Florian's. He wasn't sure why. Stach usually avoided the church and its rigid walls, so pious and soaked with stained-glass sanctimony.

This time, though, he went in the front door—no banging pipes at the back door, signaling to his secret accomplice. He waltzed in like an ordinary repentant sinner who belonged there, lining up for his turn at the confessional, carrying sins to be dropped off like soiled laundry, piss stained and frayed hems that had been drug through the muck on the outhouse floor.

He stank no more than any of the other men here tonight, too weak to bear the burden of his foibles another day, another week.

When it was his turn, he stepped into the confessional. Stepped into another world, really—like stepping into a tiny tent on a sandy dune in the middle of nowhere. He was alone. The sand desert was sunbaked, scorched, like the scorpions that skittled across his forehead as he lay bound at the feet of a false idol. He had been left here, abandoned on the edge of a garden, waiting for the inevitable news that he had been betrayed by a brother. He heard the coins fall and knew the deed was done.

"Forgive me, Father, for I have sinned," Stach said to the outline of a man on the other side of the flimsy partition. "It has been fifteen years since my last confession."

Stach tossed out a few sins, some nice, juicy ones. *I steal. I drink. I play poker with men I know are more rotten than good. I read the newspaper to an imbecile man who might be a rapist. I buried a dead girl in a shallow grave . . .*

Father C. told him to say five Hail Marys and be on his way. He was absolved.

Funny—he didn't feel absolved.

Stach picked a pew in the back of the church and plopped down, suddenly very tired.

"What are *you* doing here?" hissed a voice next to his ear. The voice was a blend of female and serpent—passion, outrage and hunger, disguised in a penguin suit.

"I came to see you."

"No, you didn't, you fiend. Get out of here! Before you contaminate this holy place with your blasphemies against the Holy Father."

"But I love the *true* Holy Father like a father. It's the *pretend* holy father—all incense and ceremony—that I can't stand."

"Are you drunk?" she demanded.

"No, but we could change that. Come with me, Bea."

"I can't, and you know that. I made my choice. Stop asking me to change my mind." She hesitated, then put a hand on Stach's shoulder. A firm hand, as though she was going to shake him—or shove him all the way to hell. "Are you trying to cause trouble? Why do you keep trying to drag me into your little dramas of children and idiots, uneducated simpletons, and charlatans who try to heal using opiates of hope?" She took a breath. Her hand loosened its grip on his shoulder. There was some ounce of caring still there, after all. "Do you really think I could leave here and spread *gospel* like you do, one whiskey-doused card at a time? *Do you?*" she asked, eyes pleading for some answer she could swallow—believe.

"No." Stach shook his head.

"Then why are you here?"

"I'm looking for Halina. She's been upset. I thought she might come here to pray."

"Oh. Well, why didn't you say so?"

"I thought you knew everything," Stach replied, a smile twitching on his lips.

"Shut up."

"Yes, Sister."

"Why do you need Halina?" Sister Beatrice asked, searching his eyes.

"Well, it's the Paschal moon tonight. Have you heard of it?"

"Of course. It's the date that determines Easter. So what?"

"Well, it seems it is also a good moon for a big-ass fire and naming a new reigning healer."

"Oh, holy mercy."

"Yeah, well, us 'uneducated simpletons and charlatans who try to heal using opiates of hope' have our ways, you know."

"I'm sorry," the nun said quietly.

"Sorry we have a Gypsy healer among us?"

"No, sorry I made fun of it."

"Well, it is a little funny, I suppose. Except, it's also quite . . . well, powerful. The ingredients—fire, herbs, stones, whatnot—all have *some* God in them. Maybe the old woman has just learned how to tap into that?" Stach raised his eyebrows, asking.

"No. I don't see how." She shook her head.

"Well, you can come to the ceremony tonight, if you like, to see for yourself. As long as I find the girl in time. I suppose it will be at midnight. Most of our 'charlatan' ceremonies seem to be at midnight, you know."

"I will be in bed, locked in."

"Alone?"

"I'm never alone."

"Goodnight, Bea."

"Goodnight, Stach."

Chapter 33

Antonio led Halina through the front room, crowded with tables and chairs and a desk. A couple of men, their hats on sideways and eyes just as crooked, sat at a table in the corner playing cards. Or maybe they were just staring, drooling. Hard to say. Empty bottles and shot glasses were scattered around. It looked as though a party had been in full swing—and suddenly interrupted.

Halina had been about sixteen, maybe, when she was here last. She had found Lydia in the churchyard. The girl had mumbled something about the hardware store, not to go there. So, of course, Halina had gone there. She'd thought maybe Lydia's mama worked there or her pa owned the store. Instead, Halina had met Arlene, the woman with the cashbox, who ran the place for the Family.

"Where are we going?" she asked now as she followed close behind Antonio.

"The office."

They walked down a long hallway, rooms on both sides, the doorways covered with hanging curtains. They didn't hide much. She saw shadows in candlelight, men climbing mountains of flesh, heaving and grunting, as if it were hard work. Noises came from behind the curtains, throaty and animal-like. Halina stared forward, at Antonio's back, concentrating on his back.

Don't look at anything else. Don't look.

The office was the smallest room Halina had ever seen. It had likely been meant as a closet or pantry at one time. There was one desk and a chair—nothing else, except an overflowing ashtray and trash piled in one corner, probably a rat's nest. One bare bulb hung over the desk, and it swung from side to side when Antonio walked past it, making the room seem to sway.

Left, right, left, right . . .

Halina's stomach pitched with the rolling of the room. She might be sick. She started to gag, bitter bile rising in her throat. She looked around. There was no trash can, no . . .

"Here's the deal, kid," Antonio said as he sat down on the corner of the desk. He described his problem.

Halina concentrated on the floor tiles, trying to keep her stomach from heaving. She counted the squares, following the lines with her eyes, staring at the intersections at corners. She looked for crosses in the patterns. She made herself breathe in and out.

A few of Antonio's words fell on the lines, breaking her concentration. She studied them, like foreign currency she didn't understand. She had no idea what he was talking about.

He was done, it seemed. He looked at her, then clapped his hands in front of her face.

"Did you hear a word I said? *Stupida bambina con un cervello scoiattolo.*"

"I don't think I can help you. I don't know how to help you," Halina answered.

"You don't know how—or you *don't want* to?"

"Both, I suppose," she said, swallowing a lump in her throat.

"You want girls walking around sick? Spreading their sickness every time they spread their legs? What kind of a healer are you? More like a heathen. All of you Polacks just spread your diseases and no-good stupidity!" Antonio spat.

"I am not *stupid*. And I'm not a heathen. And I'm not a healer.

I'm a girl, *that's all*."

"I've seen you in a nurse's uniform, going into St. Margaret's. And you patched up Joey pretty darn good. He's walking around as big-mouthed and no-good as ever."

"That was easy. I just bandaged a wound and did some stitching. I don't know nothing about what you say these women have. I can't fix that."

"Well, you better figure it out. It's either that or Sal gets rid of this bunch of girls and gets a brand-new bunch. Maybe you and your ditzy, chubby sister would be in the new bunch. What do you think of that?" Antonio's eyes glittered with malice.

"We would never be one of your girls—*never*."

"Yeah? Sal has a way of making girls do what he wants, one way or another. Remember that."

"You can't make me do anything!" Halina hissed.

"We'll see about that."

Antonio grabbed Halina by the hair and tugged.

What the hell? She fought, tried to twist away, but he pulled her down the hall, almost dragging her. That hurt much worse. Too much. In the end, she just walked, following him like he wanted.

Antonio shoved her into one of the rooms off the hall, mostly dark, mostly empty. A girl was lying on a dirty pallet on the ground, a sheet over her. She was curled up in a ball, hugging her knees, her face grimacing in pain.

"Find out what's wrong with her—*and fix it*," Antonio said in a voice that allowed no protest. Then he turned and left. The room was lit by a candle on an overturned fruit crate, the same kind of apple crate—America's Pride—that she sat on in Stach's shanty. She almost laughed, a nervous giggle wanting to come out and make everything better.

"Hello. My name is Halina," she said to the girl. Halina kneeled down on the floor next to the pallet so she could be closer. But not too close.

The girl opened her eyes, blinking, trying to focus. "I'm Margret." Her voice was a whisper. Her face looked pale and feverish, damp with sweat. Her hair stuck to her forehead. It might have been blonde. Now it was something foul, colorless.

"I'm sorry you're sick," Halina said gently.

"Why do you care? I'm not sorry," the girl said, pushing herself up, trying to sit up. "I deserve it," she said, wincing. She grabbed at her belly.

"Well, no one deserves this. I can't think of anything so . . . so . . ."

"So horribly sinful that I would deserve this pain?" Margret finished the sentence for Halina.

"Well, funny thing about sins, see, is that God has this forgiveness stuff going for him. *If* you take him up on the offer, I hear," Halina said.

She regretted the words the minute they were out. They sounded so absolutely stupid and trite. Who was she to offer preaching and Bible talk? She should get Sister Beatrice for that. What could this young woman—this girl, really—have done that was so sinful?

Noises came from the next room. Squeaks of bedsprings and the *thump, thump, thump* of a bed against a wall. Halina knew what was going on. She wasn't *that* naïve.

Margret said nothing. Her eyelids did some fluttering thing, scary-creepy.

"Margret! Margret! Talk to me. What's wrong?"

Margret came back, focused, took a deep breath. She pulled back the sheet. Her nightgown was soiled, yellow with dried pee stains. Margret pulled up the hem of the tattered gown.

The bulge was the size of a squash, off to one side a bit. The skin was dark and bruised, purple or red, hard to tell in the dim light. The bump was too low to be a kidney, too high to be her bowels plugged up. It was low, where her womb would be. That might be the problem. Something had gone wrong with her womanly organs.

"How long has this been here, Margret?"

"Weeks?" she said, unsure. "It'll be over soon."

That made no sense to Halina. How did this girl know? "Over soon? It's getting better?"

"*Nie, nie.* I'm dying. It'll be done," she gasped in a thread-like voice. "It will be done. Soon. I hope."

The girl eased herself back into a ball, tucking her face down into the folds of the sheet she clutched with white hands. She clenched her hands and her eyes. Then she let go, sliding into the blackness of sleep.

"I'll try to help you, Margret. I can try."

Halina shook the girl. She moaned, a sound coming from the other side of somewhere far away.

"Margret, hang on! I can help. I can at least make the pain go away, I think. I know how to make a tea—"

But the girl was unconscious.

Halina checked her wrist to see if she was breathing. Her pulse was weak. The girl was hot, too. A fever. Halina covered Margret's skinny arms and hands with the sheet, tucking it around her. The sheet was frayed at the top, with "HAWTHORNE HOTEL" in blue faded letters.

Asleep like this, the girl looked like a child. How old could she be? Fourteen, fifteen? How long could she live like this?

What can I possibly do to help? What?

Halina wasn't sure. This was so much more complicated than stitching up Joey or making lilac and dandelion juice for a man with a stomachache.

Baba would know what to do, of course. But Halina couldn't imagine bringing Baba here. She would never set foot in this place.

What should I do? What can I do for this girl?

Halina pictured the old woman, drawing her in her mind with the outline of a pencil, filling in colors, adding details, then sounds: chickens in the background, a fire crackling, Goose honking. Baba tended to the fire, poking it, poking, poking it more. Halina closed her eyes tighter. She breathed in smoke and memories and bits of something cold—then hot, passion-touched, hope-kindled.

Halina climbed into the vision. She walked into the fire, because it wasn't really there. But she felt the heat on her back, the embers under her feet, the licks of flames coming out of her mouth. She spoke with fire as words: *"Tell me what to do to save this girl. Her womb is poisoned. Please help me."*

She heard Baba's voice, as clearly as if she stood beside her: *"That place? With wall-to-wall snake-turd grit, cinders, varmints, and rat nests, one splinter will kill you, infected with demons, dog fleas. Devil pawns. Gangrene stink gets under the skin and festers.*

"The dead unborn, once tiny, festers in rotten womb walls; only a knife can remove it. Cut her open or walk away, far away. There's no saving the almost-dead."

"Old woman, I can't stay away! I'm here, up to my knees in dying!" Halina wanted to shout.

Of course, there was no one to hear her rant. Only Margret, and Margret wasn't listening. She was out—for now—hanging on by a string, lost in her own certainty that no one could or would help her.

Halina remembered what it was like to feel abandoned, calling with no one coming.

She remembered calling for help. It had seemed like hours. She was young. She had stepped on a shard of glass at the Patchiecki house. Toes on her right foot had been hanging by threads of skin, tissue, tiny bones that didn't want to let go.

Halina had screamed and screamed for help, but it was Sunday. Only two people in Hegewisch didn't go to church—Pa and Stach. Stach had been off at the railyard, she knew. That had left Pa.

By some miracle, her father had heard the screams and came to see what the fuss was about. He had carried her to Baba's door. He had knocked and banged and hollered for Baba. She wouldn't open the door, had just yelled out the window.

"I'm tending to sickness in here! A girl! Contagious! Go away!

Tend to the foot yourself—you can do that, man! Be a father and grow some balls, for Christ's sake!"

"Evil witch woman, you'll be sorry," Pa had yelled back.

Halina had known it was her new friend Lydia who was in there—very sick.

"Wrap it in clean strips of towel or sheet. Put the foot on a pillow, raised up, so it stops bleeding. Keep mouse shit, fleas from your sorry ass, and coal dust off it. And let her rest. She doesn't need to do any chores for a few days. Feed her. And pray. Now git!"

"That's all?"

"It's enough for now. I'll come by tomorrow. I'll stitch it up then, if it's still bleeding. She won't die from losing a few toes. *Go.*"

Baba had dropped the curtain corner and was gone, clumping away, somewhere into the bowels of her strange house.

Pa had done what he could, then Ma had gotten home from Mass and helped. Halina had been treated like a royal princess for a day. Lydia had vanished a couple of days later. Neither Baba nor Stach would ever say where she went or what happened to her. Maybe they'd sent her back to Poland. Maybe they'd found a real doctor to treat her. They'd told her to never talk about it, forget it. Halina had eventually stopped asking.

Maybe this time, I can help this girl. Maybe it will be different.

Halina marched back to the office. Antonio was sitting at the chair behind the desk, his feet propped up on an open drawer. Two bottles of whiskey—the real kind—were in the drawer, along with a shiny silver switchblade. Nothing else.

"Okay, I'll try to help Margret," Halina said. "But answer me this—how long has she been like this? How did it start?"

"Ask *her!*"

"I can't. She's passed out."

"Then talk to the other girls. Get their list of ailments, too. They all are scaring away business. Josephine! Come here!"

Halina shooed Antonio away from the desk, taking over so she could sit there and interview the girls. One by one, Antonio ushered them all in to talk to Halina. He ordered them to speak up and tell her what was ailing them and what they knew about Margret. Halina took notes.

There were six girls, all young Polish girls with no families. Antonio's family paid for their way there from Poland, arranged it. Now they were expected to work. But they had so many ailments. Halina could never remember them all without some notes. Yet even then, she was overwhelmed and confused about how the girls could be functioning at all, enduring so many pains and symptoms—so private, so embarrassing to put into words.

She knew she blushed. She suspected her face must have looked shocked and horrified at times, too. Because that's how she felt. But she tried to keep a calm poker face.

Pretend I have three aces, a poker hand I've been dealt. Play the cards in my hand.

Antonio left her alone. He stood outside the doorway at times, but as soon as the girls started talking about blood in their piss and oozing sores and heaving green gunk, he would hightail it down the hall. The girls seemed to enjoy making Antonio wince and Halina blush.

They told Halina their stories without much hesitation. It was obvious they didn't care if they shocked this girl-healer or not. And as unlikely as it seemed, there might be some chance that Halina could help. She detected a trace of hope, maybe. Maybe it was just the yellowish light from the lightbulb.

"I'm not a real doctor. I don't know if I can help," she told Josephine. She seemed to be the oldest of the girls, about Patcja's age, maybe. It was hard to say, though, with all the makeup on her face and the cigarette pinched in her mouth. "I will try. I'll come back with some medicines, tea and such, tomorrow."

Josephine told Halina what she knew about Margret's pain. It sounded like a pregnancy that went bad. Perhaps the unborn wasn't expelled; perhaps it didn't start out in the right spot. Maybe the seed was fertilized in the tube, not the womb. That could happen. She had heard women talk in the church basement. While cooking, they shared the stories of the only things they had in common: food, God, and childbirth.

Margret's ailment was different than what the other girls were suffering from. Their pains all seemed to be related to urinating, sores in places they couldn't see, and entertaining men with oversized ambitions and other grossness. None of those seemed life-threatening now. Bad for business, though? Yes. No wonder Antonio wanted her to intervene. Too bad she didn't have the slightest idea how.

Halina was done talking to all the girls. She folded her notes and was going to say goodbye to Margret, tell her she'd be back with supplies. She heard loud voices at the front door. Men's voices.

"Is she here or not?"

Halina knew that voice. *Thank God.*

She ran down the hall to meet him.

Chapter 34

Stach grabbed the back of Halina's collar and marched her toward the door, saying nothing.

Antonio chuckled. Halina squawked. Arlene held the door open for them, waving goodbye.

Stach was furious with Halina. He just wanted to get out of the hardware store as fast as he could, before he decided to take the whole place down. It deserved to be torn down. The rotten place.

It was hard to believe that Halina would come there—he had told her before to stay away. But did she ever listen? *No.* He wished he could paddle her butt, but she was probably too old for that. But damned holy tarnation, why couldn't he get through to her to stay away from these gangster men and their slimy, no-good businesses? What would it take?

He was lucky he found her. He had been walking around town, asking if anyone had seen Halina. The barber was the one who pointed him in this direction. Seemed like Waldemar could have had a little bit more sense, too. How stupid could he be? He knew what kind of filthy business went on there.

And what does he do? Send a girl here—all because Antonio the Ape sends for her.

Stach huffed down the block, still holding tightly to Halina's collar. He walked quickly, with long strides and his hat pulled down over his forehead. He had no intention of talking to her or listening to any of her silly excuses. He resisted looking at her. That sad, sorry face would get to him, he knew.

She seemed to have trouble keeping up. She was making noises. He wasn't sure if they were noises of protest or blubbering, wailing, crying noises. He didn't care. Another block. He pushed on. The same pace, the same silence. Except for his huffs and her mouse noises.

Well, that was damned annoying, too.

"Be quiet," he hissed close to her ear, a half whisper. "Do you want all of the south side of Chicago to hear you and see us walking from the hardware store? Do you not have any smarts in that thick skull of yours? Or do you want every hood and every crook to come out of their hidey holes as we walk by and get funny ideas about what to do with a blubbering blonde girl and a stupid man who is dragging her home? Is that what you want?"

"No."

"Well, if it is, we could stop here, and I could make a big sign with an arrow—'Here she is, Hegewisch's stupidest girl! Come and get her!'" His voice grew louder. "But no one would take you off my hands, because you don't listen to anyone. You follow some wild notions that you can save people from themselves. I've got news for you, sister. You *can't*. You can't save all of Hegewisch."

"*You* do it! Or try to—all the time. How are you better than me?"

Stach threw up his arms and paced in a circle.

"I'm a grown man. I know something. You're a girl. You don't know *anything* about what these men and these girls are doing. I've got a surprise for you. That's no hardware store back there."

"I *know* it's not a hardware store. It's a whorehouse," she said, very matter-of-fact, as if she were telling a story. She stood still, crossing her arms. "Some of the girls have something called the clap. I'm not sure what it is, but everyone says it in a whisper, so it must be really bad. And it feels like you're pissing glass and turpentine. They're giving it to the menfolk customers. It's hurting business for Antonio and Sal because word gets out. Some of the girls have sores on their private parts, too. Men don't like that—they're afraid they'll get sores on their dicks. So Sal is ready to get rid of all the girls and recruit new ones. He'll probably dump the sick ones in the lake. They might be dead when he dumps them, or he'll let them sink, then drown," she said, pausing for a breath—and to see if he was really listening.

"Margret will go first. She is dying," Halina started in again. "She was pregnant, and the baby died, but it's still in her, making her insides rancid. Infection. She'll be dead in a day or two, probably. What else do you think I don't know? What else do you want to explain to me?"

Stach stared at her—mouth open, eyes wide.

Empty seconds passed. He adjusted his hat and kicked a rock. Then he picked one up and threw it. Then another.

"Well, I guess you *do* know something, after all, Lina," he said. "Hmmm. I suppose you do know what's going on in there." He rumpled her hair, then tried to flatten it back down.

Halina slapped at his hand. "Stop that. I'm no child."

"I'm sorry, missy. I know you're not. I shouldn't have carried on like that," he said, taking a deep breath. "But I was mad and worried. And just plain scared. For you. *And* for me. What would I do if something happened to you, huh?"

"Oh. Well, you should worry about Margret, not me."

"Hmmm. Yes, I suppose. We'll see about that. First things first, though."

They walked for another block, both quiet, both watching the shadows and places where hooligans might be hiding, waiting to jump out and charge a toll for passing. It was still early, not yet midnight. The serious troublemakers weren't out yet.

When they got to Avenue O, Stach finally broke the news to her.

"You can't go home yet, Lina. We need to go see Baba. She told me to bring you to her tonight. She wants to talk to you about something important."

"Stach, it's just going to have to wait until tomorrow. I am dead tired. First, it was chores; then I followed Bear to his house and helped feed Camel and Bear's mama. That was plenty right there. But then I went to see what ol' Waldemar wanted, and he sent me to the hardware store. And then I talked to a bunch of sick girls, one after another, all night. I am worn out. My head's numb with hearing about sickness, and I'm feeling right sick about things, myself," she said, yawning and rubbing her temples.

"I think you need to at least stop by and tell her that yourself."

They were getting close to Baba's house. He could see smoke billowing up from behind the house. A bonfire in the backyard was lighting up the sky, its flames licking at the blackness of the night and casting a red glow over the house's roof. He could hear the crackle of wet wood popping from where they stood on the sidewalk.

Halina didn't seem to notice. "Stach, I'm not going to clean out the henhouse for Baba or help her plant herbs or mop up goopy poultice gunk she spilled on the floor—or whatever other chore she has for me. I'm *done* tonight. Tell her I will come by tomorrow after Mass."

"You have to go tonight," Stach insisted.

"Why?"

"Well, missy, because I believe that fire's for *you*." And he pointed toward the bonfire climbing to the night sky.

Chapter 35

This was turning out to be one helluva crazy night. Halina wasn't sure if she wanted to cry or scream at Stach—then Baba. The muscles in her legs ached from walking all over hell's half acre. On top of that, her head felt like it weighed a ton, and she simply couldn't hold it up any longer. Mostly, though, she was just drained—her heart hollow, as if all the blood had been sucked out of her, all the energy and reason siphoned off.

This wasn't making sense.

"Fire? What is that for? Does she aim to roast me alive or what?"

"No, I don't think so. But she was rather vague, I must say."

"Well, she can do her roasting tomorrow. *After* Mass," Halina said.

But her feet kept walking. They just continued, following Stach, as if they had a mind of their own. And as they got closer to the roaring fire, the heat radiating outward, she had to admit it was pretty. And exciting. Scary, too—all at the same time. And she was curious now.

She was suddenly wide awake.

"Hello, Baba. What's going on?" Halina asked.

"Ahh, I was starting to wonder. 'Where is Halina? She wouldn't disappoint me,' I said to myself. And, like I thought, she appears—just like that!"

"Well, it was a long walk. And a long day. I'm pooped—plain ol' drop-dead tired," Halina said.

She tried to look into the woman's eyes. Had she knowingly given Halina the message about Margret? Maybe that was just a dream, a daydream. A *what if* that popped up in her head out of her imagination—or maybe some of Pa's toothache pills or those vials of liquid.

"I have tea for you. It will make you feel better," Baba said.

Halina saw a giant mug of something steaming sitting on the bench. There was only one mug. She wasn't about to drink one of Baba's teas. She was tired, but not *that* tired; and not stupid, either.

"Uh, no thank you on the tea," Halina said, shaking her head. "I'm feeling fine now, I guess."

"Good, good," the old woman said, poking at the fire with a long stick, just like she had been poking at it in Halina's vision. Flames shot higher and sparks flew off, landing just inches from their feet—Stach's shoes, Baba's blue felt slippers, and Halina's boots, with their shoestrings broken and tied in knots.

Halina hopped back. No one else moved.

"Don't be afraid. It's all good, these flames—made from memories, knowledge. The moon fuels the burning. The power of the fire and the moon—it rejuvenates, inspires new stories, new healing. *New healers.*"

"Well, that sure is some fire you got going," Halina said, awed with the intensity, the roar, the crackles and pops.

"Just don't burn anything down, old woman. Hear me? I think it's gotten big enough. Your house is right there. The chicken coop— one spark hits it and *whoosh*! My shanty is right *there*, and I like having a roof over my head when I sleep. I suppose you do, too," Stach said.

"Don't worry. It will die down now. Like all things."

"Aww. Shoot. Can't we keep it going? I think we should keep it going as long as we can. Look how pretty the orange is against the black sky. Like a dragon clawing. And the white glowing wood. Don't let it go out," Halina said, captivated by the flames.

"I thought you were dead tired," Stach said.

"I woke up! Now I'm excited."

"Well, you two fire bugs tend to it."

Stach trudged off to his shanty, sat outside on an overturned bucket. Curly hobbled out to see him, limping on his bandaged leg, looking for an ear scratch. Stach and Curly settled in to watch the fire show. Stach waved at Halina when he caught her watching him.

"Go on, you two do your Transfer of Healer Queen Bee rigmarole ceremony; and I'll be right here, making sure you don't burn down half of Hegewisch—at least, not the half *I* live in."

"*Transfer of healer?* What is he talking about, Baba? What's going on?" Halina asked, confused by Stach's words.

"I am old. I need an apprentice to carry on the ways. I pick you," Baba replied.

Halina gasped. "What? What if I don't *want* to be picked?"

Halina's hands turned to fists. Words came out in huffs and grunts. "Baba, I don't *want* creepy shelves of snake skins and purple powders and roots and weird, spooky shit in my house!" She stomped a foot and crossed her arms. "I don't know what it all means and what to *do* with it! I can't! *I won't!*" Her mouth was a tightly pinched pucker. She closed her eyes into a glare of sparks and fury—directed straight at the old woman. Then at Stach.

Baba did the same, like a mirror. She stomped a foot and took a stubborn stance, arms crossed and a face ready for a fight.

They stared at each other like that, the bonfire still roaring behind them, burning logs toppling, falling into the core of embers and wood with white cracked skins glowing in unfathomable heat.

And Halina noticed a strange, pungent smoke, tinged red, drifting from the large log near her feet. The smoke burned the inside of her nostrils. It was like acid, groping in her lungs to her heart and brain, where it exploded. She saw colors in the fire. They ran along the curling embers, electric caterpillars inching, from hell to mercy, then standing up, soldiers pleading.

Halina saw Camel, his face as it used to be. He was a boy. Long, skinny legs and bony knees stuck out of his knickers. He was clumsy and so intense, always a problem weighing on his shoulders. The war . . .

That day in the shanty . . .

They both waited for Stach. Camel stood by the workbench, fiddling with tools he didn't know how to use. Halina stared at a poster on the wall. Lady Liberty, in a long, flowing robe of blue and white stripes, called for patriots to buy war bonds. She wore a crown of spikes and stars, like the Stature of Liberty. Halina took the bobby pins out of her hair, and her haphazard, choppy wisps stood out like a crown, too.

Pa had chopped her hair with tinsnips, mad because she had poured out a bottle of whiskey.

Halina caught her reflection in the shanty window. She saw Camel was watching her.

"Dadblasted. What are you looking at, Camel? How absurd I look? I don't care!" She threw the bobby pins down.

"No, I don't think that, Halina. I really don't think that—not at all," said Camel, and he scrambled to retrieve the bobby pins from the dirt floor.

They sat on the apple crate. Camel tried to help her arrange the bobby pins. They could see their reflections in the window. Halina watched him, intently trying to fix the mess of her hair. He patted wisps down. Then his hand lingered over her ear for just a second too long, then her neck. It was nice, sweet.

He spat on his hand and tried to smooth down a spike of golden blonde hair.

"Ewww! Camel, did you just spit on me?"

His head dropped. It fell to her shoulder. "I'm so sorry, Halina. I always mess things up."

"No, you don't, Camel. You just try too hard, that's all. I don't mind a little slobber." She licked her lips. And looked at his. "Not really."

Camel kissed her.

Back in the present, Halina saw in the fire Camel's face as it was now, burned in the war, melted into something misshapen, a soap carving, half-finished, caught in the rain. That was what that beautiful, sweet boy had become. He enlisted with a volunteer troop of Polish soldiers just a little over a year after that day in the shanty. He was lost over a noble ideal.

Maybe I can help him. The desire to right that one horrid wrong grew, becoming intense, making her dizzy.

And there was Camel's mother. And Margret. And the girls at the hardware store. And her own sister, who would be having a baby in the fall.

She looked up. Baba was still staring at her, watching, waiting, expecting some words from her new apprentice.

"Well?" the old woman said, her eyebrows raised, hopeful. "Are we just going to stand here all night?" the aged healer asked.

Halina took the long stick from Baba's hands and poked at the fire here and there, nudging outer logs closer to the center, stirring dying embers back to full flame.

Halina looked at the old woman and asked, "What happens now?"

"That's up to *you*," Baba said.

The glow of the fire made red shadows across Baba's face, accentuating the rivers of wrinkles, the puffy puddles under her eyes. She was obviously tired. Without the long stick to lean on, she seemed to wobble a bit, as though her knees might buckle.

Halina led Baba toward the shanty, motioning for Stach to get up and fetch a chair.

"You rest. I'll tend to the fire," Halina said, feeling the shifting weight of the old woman as she moved from Halina's shoulder to Stach's arm.

Baba plopped down on the bench. Her ample size made the legs creak. Stach helped steady the bench—and his aunt. Curly licked her fingers and nuzzled his nose against her knee. She patted the dog's head, closing her eyes, absorbing a moment of absolute devotion from a grateful patient.

"Well, congratulations, you are now successfully out of a job," Stach said to Baba.

"It's just started."

Halina heard their exchange but didn't have time to respond.

The chicken coop was on fire.

Chapter 36

Business was back to normal at The Corner. Men had been strolling in since early evening. The tables were filling up, and the men placing orders had to shout in Patcja's ear so she could hear them.

It was a good thing there weren't many choices: whiskey, gin, highballs, plates of kielbasa and sauerkraut. Nothing else. Not unless some poor slob starting causing trouble, too loud and too sloppy, slinging punches at the air and tripping over himself. Then Augie would tell Patcja to make some coffee. It would be her job to get a couple of cups of black coffee down him before they threw the fool out or he vomited on some shoes other than his own. Cleaning up after the drunks was never easy.

The rest of the job wasn't so bad, especially now that Joey was better. The steel mill hadn't saved his job for him while he healed up. They wouldn't take him back, either, saying they didn't need trouble-makers. So Joey just started helping Augie around the place, a little at a time, doing more every day as he felt better. Augie kept him on, letting him sleep in the back room, too. He seemed to feel obligated, being that Joey had almost died in his tavern.

Tonight, Joey stood at the door, waving some fellas in, turning others away. There must have been some reason behind it, but Patcja sure couldn't tell what made some men good customers and some unwanted. Maybe they were already drunk or were fellas from the mill who stole Joey's job, or they were bad-mouthing some of his Italian pals or guys from Back of the 'Yards. It could be lots of legitimate reasons, she supposed. And she certainly had enough to keep her busy.

Augie was behind the bar, pouring drinks, talking up the men, keeping them buying. He kept tallies of what they owed in his head. After a couple of shots, Augie made them pay up. No one could run a long tab. That was good for Patcja, made things simpler—fewer fights over bills—but it also meant she was carrying money back and forth from tables to Augie's cashbox all night. Her hands smelled like coins and whiskey, no matter how many times she wiped them on her apron.

And the cigarette smoke was thick, making it hard to breathe. Patcja coughed and wheezed but did her best to keep the drinks coming—and the cash flowing.

Finally, there was a lull in the commotion. Patcja was glad for the pause. She could use some air. She made her way to the kitchen, past tables with men shouting at each other and some tables with men playing poker. In the kitchen, two pots were on the stove; one for kielbasa and one for sauerkraut. The sour smells made her stomach lurch.

Patcja ran to the backdoor, afraid she was going to vomit. The cool air hit her face like a slap. She leaned against the doorjamb and let the night wind wash her face, blow back her hair, wipe away the scummy layer of smoke and sweat and harsh, crude words the men had been flinging in her direction. She took some deep breaths. The outside air had its own peculiar smells—mill exhaust and canal slime—but the wind that came from the lake was crisp, as though it blew in from the top of the world where everything was fresh and new and clean. How nice it would be to go someplace like that. *Clean.*

"Oh, I wish . . . ," she sighed, trying to picture what it would be like to live in a place that was white with icicles and fresh snow and a wind that blew across glaciers and mountain tops.

"What do you wish for, Miss Patcja?"

She jumped. Patcja turned to see who had spoken.

Ahhh, just Janusz—big, lumpy, dumpy Janusz.

"You scared me, Janusz. You shouldn't do that, you know."

"I didn't mean to scare you, Miss Patcja. I just heard you wishing for something, but didn't hear what for," he said. "See, if I knew what you wanted, I would get it for you."

"Well, thank you, Janusz. But I don't think you can get what I want."

"Why not? I suppose I'm not good enough—is that it, Miss Patcja?"

In the light from the kitchen, Patcja could see the big man straighten up, his nostrils flaring, like a bull.

Whoa, big boy—take it easy, now.

"No, that's not what I meant, Janusz. I was just wishing for some nice, fresh, clean air, without all this smoke and the stink from the mills. It gets hard for me to breathe."

"Oh, well, if you think this is bad, you should go up to the stockyard. They got it worse, I think."

"Well, no thank you."

Janusz looked confused. He stepped closer.

"You want me to take you somewhere else, though? I would. Anything you want, I would do for you, Miss Patcja."

"Well, no, Janusz. I need to work. I'm going back to work now." Patcja pulled away. "You know ol' Augie. He can get all riled up and mad at me if I don't keep serving the men and keep all the fellas buying drinks."

"That isn't very nice of Augie. He shouldn't treat you like that. That isn't a very good job for a lady as pretty as you, Miss Patcja. I don't think you should be working here."

"Well, Janusz, I need the money," Patcja said, feeling uncomfortable. "I need a job. It's okay. Really." She closed the screen door, putting the mesh between Janusz and her. He pressed his face against the metal screen, and the finely woven wires made a pattern across his nose. He looked absurd.

Augie was calling her. "Patcja! Patcja, where the hell did you go?"

Patcja went back to work. As she walked through the kitchen, she heard Augie and Janusz shouting, fighting over her.

"You need to be nice to Miss Patcja, Augie! I won't let you yell at her no more! *I won't!* I won't let *nobody* hurt her!" Janusz shouted.

"Fine. But you stay outside here, Janusz. I don't think you should come in. Some fellas are talking. I heard some saying you might have been the one who knifed Joey. Now some of Joey's pals have put a price on your head. Do you know what that means, Janusz?"

"I don't have no price tag on my head, Augie," Janusz said, bending down so Augie could get a closer look at his head. "I just have a crack in it, that's all. And no one would want to pay for this cracked old head."

"Right, Janusz, I know. Well, how about you patrol the alley and make sure that Antonio and his boss, Sal, don't come around. How about that?"

"If you say so, Augie. Can I have something to eat if I do that, Augie? And a drink? You know I like a drink or two when I get worried. Okay, Augie?"

Patcja didn't hear an answer. Her head was spinning. Could she believe the rumor Augie had heard? That Janusz was the one who stabbed Joey? He did it? Oh, she would make him sorry.

She heard shouts, impatient men wanting more whiskey. Men from the corner table wanted another round. They were waving her over.

Joey had moved to a station behind the bar, acting as bartender. How wonderful to see him better, back to his usual ways. His smile was back, that slight curl of his upper lip—mysterious, as if he knew her secrets and could see right through her dress—and he liked what he saw. Oh, she did love him. The thought of losing him made her cringe.

Janusz. Damn that oaf.

She wouldn't let anyone or anything hurt her Joey again. She'd protect him. Patcja smiled in his direction as she stepped toward the corner table to get the order.

Joey smiled back and waved the white rag that had been over his shoulder. It looked as though he were waving a flag of surrender.

"Bring us four more highballs, girl!" one of the men shouted from the corner. Patcja made her way over to the bar to place the order with Joey.

He watched her. She could feel his eyes on her, caressing her with his look. He saw her, burns and scars and secrets—and roundness, a bulging belly that was becoming hard to hide—and he still smiled back at her, hungry.

She was just as wanting. She licked her lips, as slowly as possible. Joey liked that. When she finally reached the bar, she was out of breath, excited. She had to stand on her tiptoes and stretch across the wooden bar top so he could hear her. She put her hand on his. Her skin sizzled, as if a jolt of electricity had shot through her.

"Monday, Joey. Let's do it Monday. The JP. I can't wait any longer, Joey. I want to marry you."

"What, Patcja? What do those fellas want?" Joey asked.

"Four highballs."

"Anything else?"

"Yeah, Monday at two o'clock. At the courthouse."

"Sure, baby, sure," Joey said absently. "Why not? Someone need a witness at the courthouse? Just tell me what I'm supposed to say. I'll play along." He pushed four glasses to her on a tray. "And get the money from those bozos," he said. "No one gets nuthin' for free anymore."

Joey turned back to the counter, reaching for more glasses and the gallon jug labelled "Chicago Cola."

Patcja knew Joey had no idea what she was talking about. He probably never intended to marry her, did he? *Why would he?*

Patcja took the men their drinks. She collected their coins. Then an idea hit her.

She told the men around the table to be at the courthouse steps at two o'clock Monday afternoon, for a party, a surprise party. There just might be free drinks.

And as she served the other men the rest of the night, she told them the same thing. The courthouse, Monday at two. *Be there. But not a word to anyone beforehand.* It was a surprise, a big one. Joey couldn't know about it. Or Augie.

Patcja smiled her best smile at all the fellas—even the fat, sloppy ones. She told them how sweet they were, what handsome, good fellas they were. A girl could trust them, she said. They were good, loyal men, she said. She smiled and puckered her lips and smoothed her dress, playing with the buttons at her chest.

"Oh, I know I could count on you, couldn't I, if ever I needed a big, strong man like you to look out for me?"

Some men only grunted. Some didn't hear or care, but a few did. A few smiled back, eager to please the girl with round titties popping out of her dress, when the buttons came undone. Silly buttons.

And feeling quite happy with herself and her ploy, Patcja thought of one more. She knew where some bottles from the bad batch of hooch were stored. Augie wouldn't dump them. He said no one knew for sure it was what had made those men in Whiting blind. Maybe it wasn't, he said. Maybe. Maybe if they were watered down a bit, they would be fine. Or not.

She could only carry four bottles at a time. She left them outside the back door, lined up in a pretty row, like soldiers ready to fight a noble war, protecting the homeland, avenging hideous acts that would never be allowed to happen again.

Janusz, patrolling the alley like Augie had asked, would be back. He'd probably be thirsty. The man who had stabbed her Joey would get what he deserved.

And tomorrow at the courthouse she'd get what she deserved. *No one gets nuthin' for free—anymore.*

Chapter 37

While Baba was at Mass, Stach started clearing out the remnants of the chicken coop, salvaging wood that could be saved and reused. There wasn't much left. The back wall of Baba's house was damaged, too—black and charred. The structural beams seemed intact, though. That was one positive. It could have been much worse. The whole block could have gone up in flames.

He threw two slightly charred planks of siding in the "keep" pile.

Thank God they'd had plenty of buckets and the pumps were working well. Some neighbors had been over right fast, too. Bear and his father, Mateusz, had been there within minutes.

Some small pieces from the window frame went in the trash heap.

They'd had a good-sized crew and managed to get the fire under control fairly quickly. The neighbors seemed rather annoyed with Baba, though. She could have burned down their houses and them, too, asleep in their beds. The neighborhood frustration spilled over onto Stach, as well. Wasn't he supposed to be watching that old woman and her witchy ways? Why did he let it happen? They didn't say anything—not with words, at least—but their glances and glares and the shakes of their heads said plenty.

They were all men with families who had turned to Baba for doctoring, too. Stach thought they ought to be more forgiving. But he saw how it looked—and he *was* partly to blame. He should have watched closer. He tried, but he was no spring chicken anymore, either. His time was coming, he knew. Maybe he needed to be looking for his own apprentice so he could hang up his hat.

That would be a hoot. Who could he recruit to be the neighborhood . . . *what*, exactly? Well, what the heck *was* he? Neighborhood do-gooder? Fixer? Peacekeeper? Sheriff? Guardian angel? *Nah.* There wasn't a good name for what he did.

Sister Beatrice said Baba could stay at St. Florian's until he had her house fixed up. That was nice of Bea, right sisterly. It should be interesting. Baba was a good Roman Catholic, no doubt about that. But she had some extra beliefs, too—ones the good sisters and Father C. might not take so kindly to. He hoped Baba didn't have any more ceremonies lined up soon.

He was almost done sorting wood, except for some boards that needed to be pried off the frame. He could use a helping hand. Mass would be starting soon. All the men who weren't doing a shift at the mill were at Mass.

Except for one. There was only one able-bodied man in Hegewisch—besides him—who didn't go to church.

Stach walked down the street to Halina's house and went to the front door. The girls were at Mass, of course, with their mother, Mary.

"Fryderyk?" Stach banged on the door. "I know you're in there, Fryddo, my man. I need some help. I have a job I need another hand on. Come on, man! *Nie możesz pomóc polskiemu bratu?*"

The door opened. Fryderyk, looking as though he'd just woken up or had never gone to bed, had his good hat on and his wool peacoat, the kind dock workers wore. Fryderyk was ready for work—or something.

"Hey there, brother. Good to see you. How you been? I haven't seen you around much," Stach said, slapping the man on the shoulder.

Fryderyk grunted.

"Well, glad to see you, anyway, man. I could use a hand."

Fryderyk followed Stach, walking a half step behind him, his head down, as if he needed to watch his feet to make sure they were moving in the right direction.

Stach walked slower, but Fryderyk just walked slower, too, keeping a half step back.

They reached the site of the previous night's fire. Fryderyk didn't have much to say there, either. He watched the chickens pecking around the yard, squawking, with no place to roost. Stach thought the man looked sad, as though he was worried about the hens. That seemed odd. Fryderyk was one weird bird, for sure.

"Anybody feed these chickens today? They sound mad, like they missed their breakfast," Fryderyk said, looking around the yard. He found a grain bag of chicken feed and took out a scoopful. He tossed it to the chickens, clicking his tongue, making chicken noises.

"You talk chicken, Fryderyk?"

"You don't?"

"No, can't say I do." Stach shook his head.

"I thought you were smarter than that. A whole bunch smarter than me."

"No, man. I am feeling darn foolish right now. I have a burned-out chicken coop, half an old lady's house charred, and on top of that, I forgot to feed the damned chickens."

"Good thing you came and got me, eh, buster? I guess we better get to work."

Stach laughed, suddenly feeling okay. Maybe Fryderyk was all right after all.

"Yeah, yeah, let's do something about this mess," Stach said. "The pope might want to drop by, and what would he say if he found us with our bloomers all smoldering black and crispy-like?"

"He might wonder why we didn't invite him to the party, I suppose. Popes probably like bonfires, too? Good for roasting little heathen boys who fail their catechism tests, likely," said Fryderyk.

"Likely, indeed. I never knew you were so funny, Fryddo, ol' man."

"I ain't funny. I'm drunk as a skunk," Fryderyk said, still tossing feed to the chickens.

"Oh."

"Yeah, sober I'm just one mean sonnobitch. I wouldn't be helping you if I was sober."

Curly got up from his bed by the stove. Seemed he heard a voice he recognized—and didn't like. The dog stood at Fryderyk's feet and started growling, low and quiet. A warning, maybe.

"Oh, Curly, go back to sleep," Stach said, shooing the dog back toward his spot. "C'mon, Fryddo, let's see how much we can get done before you sober up."

"Oh, we don't have to worry about that. I figure it will be Tuesday before I've sweated off this bottle of hooch. It was a fine one. Chicago Cola. Wicked stuff. White lightning, like nothing else."

That got Stach's attention.

"What is it? A powerful batch or a bad one?" he asked.

"Ain't no such thing as a *bad* batch, but this one is to be feared. Blinded a couple men over in Whiting and another couple from Back of the 'Yards. That's how come the Italians are looking to get rid of it—a little bit here and there. Can kill ya, a little at a time. I can't feel a thing in my feet," Fryderyk said.

And his drunken words turned into a roaring fit of laughter and coughing, spitting and spewing, swearing and scaring the chickens down to the alley and back. Stach watched for a bit, flabbergasted. Then he went back to prying charred wood off the damaged house. And thinking.

Maybe I need to try to round up this bad batch, dump it, before it kills someone.

The bells at St. Florian's sounded.

Fryderyk froze and put his hands over his ears.

"Make it stop! Make it stop!" he moaned.

"What, Fryddo? Have a headache?"

"The noise! Always noise! Noise—like shooting, canons, bombs, grenades . . . so much noise!"

"Shh! No noise! We must reach the ship. Marianna, hush. Shhhh. The soldiers are near! They will hear us. Nie, nie, not now. The baby can't come now. There is no time! They will find us and take the baby. Stop that noise! Stop making noise!"

"Stop your crying, or we'll both be dead."

Fryderyk bent over, groped at the ground, looking for something.

"What did you lose, Fryderyk?" Stach asked. He wanted to help the man but didn't know how.

"Everything. I've lost everything."

Unfortunately, he found Curly. He picked up the dog in one swoop, holding him like a baby—or trying to. Curly wanted none of that. The dog yelped, struggling to get free, and he sank his teeth in Fryderyk's hand.

The man howled in pain. He started to backhand the dog, but his hand froze. He seemed to realize it was only a dog, only a stupid old dog. And there was no one to blame but himself.

Stach took Curly from Fryderyk and put the dog down. The mutt hobbled off, none the worse, only confused.

"It's going to be all right now, Fryddo." Stach patted the man on the shoulder. "Let's go have some coffee together, my man. We can sit a bit, take stock of what's left to do."

Chapter 38

Mary sat as stiff as a board in the church pew, her girls on each side of her as always. But something was wrong, she knew. She wasn't so daft that her motherly instincts were all gone. Both Patcja and Halina were more sullen than usual, sulking over something. And while neither one would say what, she knew without even asking, so she didn't bother. But she watched them out of the corner of her eye during Mass. Patcja continually fiddled with a handkerchief, as though she was nervous. Halina was humming, barely—the hum she did when she was trying to decide something. Both girls were being as annoying as hell.

Mary was trying to listen to the service. She didn't understand the Latin, of course, but she understood the tone of worship and obedience. It was comforting to her frayed nerves.

Ever since she started working for that cigar-fellow, Salvatore, she had been a nervous wreck. Any day, one of his big goons could show up and carry her off to some fate worse than death—all because she didn't clean up some mess well enough or missed a spot. Blood splatters and flecks of flesh and fine bore shards were hard to erase away, and a trace was always left, like a ghost image burned into your eyes. When she closed her eyes, she could see the hotel room where she had met Sal:

Mary stood in the doorway of room 270, clutching her handbag in one hand and her bucket of supplies in the other. She had brought a scrub brush, a bar of borax, a bottle of bleach, and some rags, no idea of what she might really need. When Krzysztof had fetched her, he said it was to do some housecleaning for someone important—someone willing to pay for her services. Mary didn't hesitate to go along. She needed the money. But now, as she stood in that doorway, frozen into a plaster-like pose, she was quite certain she had made a mistake. Krzysztof had made a bigger mistake. His boss should have sent for an undertaker, not a cleaning woman.

Oh, Flora . . .

The woman, naked except for stockings and shoes, was lying in the middle of a big four-poster bed. Her eyes were open, locked in a death stare at the ceiling. It was one of her laundry customers, Flora. And the back of her head seemed to be caved in or missing. With so much blood pooling about, it was hard to say.

"So, the Polack cleaning lady finally arrives," said a squat man with a cigar and a fancy suit, which seemed to reflect the glare of the sun pouring in from the window. "It's about time. I don't have all day, you know. My friend fell out of bed," he said, pointing to the lifeless form. "She made a mess when she hit her head on the floor. The hotel staff doesn't like that. They're peculiar about these things when they happen. So I need you to clean up the mess for Flora. Because she just refuses to do it." He scowled at Flora, shaking his head, making tssking sounds around his cigar.

"How could she do it, when she's dead?" Mary asked.

With three long, quick strides, the man was suddenly in front of Mary. He stooped so he hovered in front of her, eyeball to eyeball.

"Did you just question me?" he hissed as he pulled back his arm and struck Mary's face. Her glasses went flying and skidded across the floor, landing in a puddle of near-black liquid at the foot of the bed. "You won't do that again, will you?"

Mary shook her head. She wanted to run. Instead, she fished her glasses out of the puddle, cleaned them off, wiped her hand on a sheet. And started scrubbing the floor. She also started thinking of excuses. If *her girls asked about her glasses—or her eye, which was throbbing and swelling—she'd just have to let them think Fryderyk had—*

The congregation stood. They kneeled. Patcja was slow to move, lost in some daydream. Halina poked at her sister. Patcja didn't like that and swatted at Halina's hand. Halina swatted back. Right there in a church pew, carrying on like children. Mary pinched both girls on the back of the neck and yelled at them with her eyes.

That got their attention, at least.

Now, if only they could get through the rest of the service with some dignity and God-fearing respect. The last thing she wanted was the other womenfolk talking about her shameful daughters and what a poor mother she was. The church ladies were like that. Always had been.

"The entire village is talking, Marianna. They say bad things, nasty things about you and the soldiers. You help the soldiers, they say. Mari, they talk."

Mary shook her head, trying to clear the jumble of old words and old worries, the wrath of neighbors who could turn on you, betray you, hate you. It was an old worry, a pain that ran deep—for good reason.

Well, that was done. Over. Left behind.

No, it isn't. I'll never be free of those chains.

The choir rose. The congregation stood to sing along. Bodies swayed, unsteady, bowing under the weight of sins, like traitors lined up at the gallows. The girls stood on each side of Mary, both taller than she was. Mary felt shrunken, miniature. The girls looked at each other over her head, whispering back and forth. They were talking about her as if she weren't there. They didn't think she could see them or their disgust for her. They were making plans about her. They were going to march her off, take her somewhere.

"People are talking about you, Mari. They don't approve. They talk. The village talks."

Another hymn. Patcja held the hymnal so Mary could see, too. The words bounced around on the page. Mary took a hanky out of her pocketbook and wiped her forehead. It was suddenly so warm in the church. So many people were there, filling the pews. It was so crowded today. The pews were so close together. Mary looked around to make sure the doors were still there, where they should be. She looked at the faces—neighbors, all good Polish people. Neighbors, the kind who would . . .

The congregation sat, all eyes on the priest as he looked down on them from his pulpit. He looked right at Mary, straight in her eyes, her eyes alone. She flinched, recoiled from the probing stare. She covered her eyes with her hand.

"Mary, you aren't welcome here. We don't want your kind. You're filthy, vile, like the soldiers you lay with in their headquarters."

The girl on her left patted her knee. Why did she do that? Did she know her?

Mary tried to concentrate on what the priest was saying, but something was wrong. She didn't feel well. Suddenly the walls were liquid; the pews were melting. The priest's words were far away, in a tunnel. They sounded like echoes, plunks and thunks on a hollow log. Why was he talking like that? What was wrong with him?

Why didn't the congregation stop him? Why didn't someone stand up and say, *Father, don't talk like that. Don't talk. Don't do this.*

"Don't!"

"Ma, shhh," said the girl on her left. "What are you talking about? The service isn't done," the girl whispered to her, putting a hand on her arm.

Mary looked at the girl. She had auburn hair. That was funny. The soldiers always picked girls with blonde hair. They liked blonde curls. Like her older sister, Stella, had those days. Stella had been so beautiful with her blonde hair, long ringlets. Marianna and Stella had both been barmaids when the Germans came to their village. Stella's pretty hair had saved her. Or cursed her.

"Look at this one, that lovely hair, almost as pretty as a Deutsch fräulein. We'll keep this one. She can keep us company. Maybe the nights won't be so lonely."

"What about the other one? It seems they're sisters, from the way they carry on, hanging on to each other."

"We don't need the ugly one. Get rid of her!"

"We could use someone to clean the toilets, mop the floor, clean the boots."

"Fine, fine, but I don't want to see her. Put her out with the hogs, where filthy Poles belong."

"What happened to your hair, Stella?"

"Ma, shhh! Do we need to leave? Should we leave now? Everyone's looking, Ma."

"I'll leave. I'll go. Just let me pack a satchel."

"C'mon, Ma. Time to go. Give me your arm. C'mon now. It's time to go home," the girl who looked like Stella said. But it wasn't Stella; Mary could see that now. This girl was only pretending to be Stella.

Mary stood up.

"We can't go home. They don't want us anymore," Mary said. She knew father would hate them for what they did.

"Sure we can, Ma. We'll walk home now. We'll go home, and you can take a nice nap."

Church music rang in her ears, with booms of tanks. A choir, far away, sang. Clouds hung from heaven, heavy with incense and Latin. Altar boys walked past, marching in German uniforms. A priest walked past, Bible in his hands, his glasses fogged, steamed from standing too close to hell and damnation.

Two girls, one on each side of her, were up now, standing beside her, mumbling and fussing, squabbling, as children did. It seemed they were arguing over who would accompany her on the walk home. Neither seemed pleased with the chore, as if she were some child who needed supervision. Or perhaps the Germans thought she would run.

Where can I go? I've got nothing, no one. Only Stella. I can't run without her, but they always watch her. She is like a shared pet, adored, never out of sight.

"I can walk to my house by myself, you know. I don't need either of you following me. Let me be!"

"Sure, Ma, sure. It's time to go. I'll walk with you home," said the older girl, the plump one with auburn hair.

The younger one, the puny one with yellow hair, said she had work to do, things to do, places to go and people to talk to—important things to do. She spoke quickly and seemed very worried about it all. Her eyes darted around, unsure of what to look at, where she should turn first.

"Don't fret so much, child. You look like you're carrying the weight of the world on your shoulders. Those shoulders aren't big enough," Mary said, smoothing the girl's hair, pushing wayward bangs away from her solemn face. The girl's face knotted more, lips parted as though they were about to speak but forgot the words.

Mary tried again. "Let it go. Let the Holy Spirit lighten your load. Let the Holy Mary, mother of Christ, carry your worries." Mary motioned toward the statue of the Virgin Mary, so beautiful in her blue gown.

The puny girl followed her gesture with her eyes. Those dark—so very dark—eyes darted away quickly, brimming with tears. The girl wiped at them in quick movements, not wanting anyone to see, poor thing. Mary patted the girl's shoulder. She wished she could help her.

"Have you tried prayer?"

The girl laughed, a silly little-girl laugh, like someone who thought she was being teased and didn't like it.

"Well, yes, but heaven didn't open and drop any miracles down on me," the blonde girl said. She paused, then said, "Maybe I'll light a candle before I go."

"We should all light a candle—one for the baby, too," said Mary. "It'll be born this fall, I think."

The older girl said, "You know?"

"A mother always knows."

The three walked to the altar of candles. Each lit a candle, each with unsteady hands.

After a pause that was too long, they left the sanctuary. The younger girl said goodbye. She said she had to see Baba, who was staying in the room in the church basement while her house was being repaired. The older girl said she would see Mary home. She didn't look happy about it. She didn't look happy at all. Mary hated being a burden. She tried to insist she was fine on her own. No one listened, so she stopped trying.

The heavy double doors of the church were propped open. The sun hit Mary's face. The air was cool, vibrant with spring. In the east, over the lake, the sun was golden streaks breaking through low-hanging clouds. It was bright with promise, hopeful. She felt better instantly. Things were going to be better.

The baby would change everything.

Maybe now Ma and Pa would let her stay, raise the baby in Wrzesnia. *Surely they won't turn me away when I tell them I am bearing a child? It's half Polish. Isn't that enough?*

They walked down Avenue O, toward the old house where she often hid. The soldiers never found her there. The kitchen was off limits to soldiers, just like the pig pens were. Too filthy for the soldiers.

Mary watched for signs of soldiers following them. She saw nothing, but they were there, hiding in bushes, she was sure of it. The girl escorting her started to speak several times, then stopped. Perhaps she wasn't well. Perhaps she was embarrassed to be seen walking with a woman who had sinned, who carried a child as the result. Perhaps this girl knew the whole story and was ashamed to walk alongside her.

"The baby will be a boy, I hope. He'll have blond hair and blue eyes, just like his father," Mary said, letting herself daydream about better days. This was a nice day for a stroll, after all.

"Joey doesn't have blond hair, Ma. You know that. He has black hair, as black as night. You know Joey, Ma. C'mon now. Don't be playing games with me. I don't think it's funny."

"I don't either."

"Well, come along. We're almost there. You can take a nap, and I will make dinner. Halina won't be home for a while, I guess. She's got some doctoring to do for a houseful of sick girls, she says—like that's more important than helping me. She leaves me all alone to tend to you . . . and to get ready for tomorrow, my big day . . ."

"I hope she didn't go far. The streets aren't safe these days, you know. Thugs and thieves and men with no morals or fear of God hide in shadows. Heathens, running from the law, with big talk and little brains. All show. No convictions, no honor."

"I know, Ma, I know," Patcja said dismissively.

"How do you know?"

"I just do. I know some of those types of men. They come in the tavern."

"You stay your distance, then. Do you hear me?" Mary urged.

"Too late for motherly advice, I'm afraid."

"It's never too late to be good." Mary tried to wink at the girl, to let her know she was teasing, trying to be kind to her, cheer her up. She seemed so sad. But Mary's eye started twitching, and the girl didn't notice, anyway.

They walked in silence for the last block. When they reached the house, they went in the back door by the kitchen. Mary lit two oil lamps right away, even though it wouldn't be dark for hours. She just couldn't stand the thought of being in the dark. It snuck up on her sometimes.

A nap would be nice. That stroll was so tiring. The girl still hovered, though. Something was on her mind—her sad, sorry mind. She probably was like everyone else, wanting to know what a German man was like under his uniform, the two-faced idiots.

"Well, out with it. What's bothering you? Curious? Everyone wonders. You, too? Want to hear some details of what happened, what it was like—do you?" Mary scowled at Patcja.

"No, not really, I don't know—"

"Then what?"

"What did you wear on your wedding day, Ma? Do you remember?"

"Ahh, yes." Mary's face softened into a smile, and she sat on the bed, happy to have a new subject—one a little brighter, perhaps, if she told it just right, leaving out . . .

"There wasn't much time," Mary said, adding some suspense to her voice for effect. "We were in such a hurry so we could travel that night in the dark on the backroads, to reach the port. Papa made arrangements with the captain of a merchant ship. After what happened to Stella, he felt he had no choice."

"What happened to Stella? Your papa sent you here, to America?" Patcja's eyebrows knitted together as she tried to follow the story.

"I didn't want to leave," Mary said, shaking her head. "He said I had to go. There were threats. He convinced Fryderyk, too—he was just a boy. Papa said we had to get married. There was no priest who would agree to it, though. Papa said we would have our own ceremony in the barn, the way countryfolk, peasants, did in the olden days when priests stuck to their monasteries and cathedrals. I made a wreath for my hair, and Mama gave me her beautiful red-and-black babushka with long, silky fringe. I wore it around my shoulders. Do you want to see?"

"Can I?"

And Mary went to the chest of drawers where all of her prized possessions were kept. Maybe she would let this girl borrow the babushka, if she promised to be careful with it.

Chapter 39

Halina could barely sit through Mass. Firstly, she was dog-tired because she had been awake far too late last night. Secondly, she was antsy, her legs itching to get up and take off. She had things to do, questions to ask. She knew Baba was downstairs in the guest room, the spare room in the church basement where the sisters put people up when they needed a bed.

When they'd finally put the fire out last night, it was clear Baba was going to need to stay somewhere else for a day or two until Stach could get the back of her house patched. The damage wasn't too bad, but the back wall by the door was a black, charred mess—scorched and crispy, a hole the size of a fat's man's waist burned right through it.

Once the fire was under control, Stach had walked Baba to the church and pounded on the back door for Sister Beatrice to let her in. There was no time to talk to Baba and sort out her crazy talk about passing on her knowledge and Halina being her apprentice. With all the noise of chickens squawking and flames spreading and Stach giving orders and pumping water into buckets and tossing them onto the flames . . . well, it was just chaotic.

Halina was left with her questions. And she had plenty.

The congregation walked out as usual—weary and eager to leave the crowded stuffiness of the sanctuary, yet still far slower than

Halina would have liked. She walked against the mass of people, toward the basement, like swimming upstream. She was pushed and shoved, bodies pressing against her shoulders, faces frowning at her for slowing down the rush outward.

It was a relief to reach the steep stairwell and its quiet emptiness. The basement seemed deserted, too. Often, church ladies congregated in the basement kitchen, cooking or sitting around the large table in the community room, planning the next festival or making Old Country crafts and peasant folk art to sell at the big shops on State Street. But not today. Maybe they had all heard that Baba had moved into the guest room, and no one dared risk the wrath of the cranky old lady who could have burned down Hegewisch with her odd ways.

Halina knocked on the door, her raps urgent. *C'mon, Baba! Hurry up!* She heard shuffling noises behind the door.

"Go away!"

"Baba, it's me, Halina. Open the door! I need to talk to you! *Please!*"

"Well, stop your shouting, noisy girl! I'm not *deaf,* you know."

Baba let her in. The old woman was still wearing last night's dress, stained and stiff with black charcoal and gray from smoke. At least it had dried. The last time Halina had seen her, Baba's dress was wet, clinging to her chubby legs—obscene, comical, and grossly sad, all at the same time. A poor old woman with a wet dress stuck in the crack of her ample ass.

Halina had to remind herself she was annoyed with the woman.

"Baba, I have questions. You didn't answer nuthin' last night. What do you mean, you're passing the duty on to me? What's that mean?" Halina asked impatiently.

"I told you," Baba said, waving a dismissive hand. "I said all the words needed saying. Not my fault you no listen so good."

"Baba, I was a little busy. Trying to help save *your* house, *your* chickens—*and you*—from being burnt up, roasted alive like a pig on a spit! So I might have missed some details." Halina came closer, spoke quieter. "You think I am taking over all your healing and powders and potions and poultice making?"

"See, you have the Vision. You know the truth—it is yours now."

"Jesus, Baba—Holy Mary, Mother of Christ!" Halina gasped. She sat on the edge of the bed, her legs feeling wobbly. Her head was light and fuzzy, as if it might float away.

"Sit. Think. You will understand. Because it is so," Baba told Halina with a stern voice. She didn't seem to appreciate being questioned—or doubted. Her mouth moved as though she was talking to someone, maybe praying, maybe chewing on a string of sauerkraut or a poppy seed she'd found in her rotten teeth. The woman's breath was sour this morning, filling the small room with tainted air.

Halina shuddered. The woman probably had an abscess or an infection. Halina wondered if the witch hazel jar in Baba's kitchen was safe. And the basket of heather. Maybe some bee balm ...

She realized her mind had wandered. Just as Baba wanted, she was thinking about herbs and medicines and the rules of healing. And it made her mad.

"Baba, dadgummit, you can't just tell me I'm supposed to take over for you, then *not* tell me how to do it and what to do! And you didn't even ask if I *want* to take over! Maybe I *don't*!"

Baba shook her head. "You do."

"How do you know? *I* don't know!" Halina's voice seemed to be growing louder with every word. "I'm not sure about this at all—not the least little bit! I don't like being pushed into a corner. You can't assume ... Well, it isn't right! It just isn't!" she finished, her fists balling up in frustration.

"It's rightful *and* righteous, so it's right." Baba shrugged, as if her words alone were enough to make it so.

"Stop talking in nonsense and riddles and mumbo jumbo!"

Baba tightened her lips, crossed her arms in front of her chest, and sat as still as a stone—a statue that couldn't be reached.

Halina jibber-jabbered on with questions and complaints and reasons why she was outraged and confused. Her voice cracked and whined in a shrill tone that was enough to make a dog howl, if one had been around. Baba said nothing. Not as much as a word or a nod to let the girl know she was listening.

"Blast it, Baba! Are you *trying* to make me mad or make me have a heart attack and die right here and now of a busted fuse and an exploded heart? Because I'm saying I *can't* take on any more sickness and people with sickness now! You aren't listening to me! *I can't!*"

"You *can*. You will. You have been picked. This is your fate. Stop your hissy fit and blowing snot out your ass and shit out your nose, and start listening. Are you ready to listen?" Baba fixed her stony gaze on her.

Halina sighed. She swallowed what was left of her indignation and took a deep breath.

Then—at last—Baba talked. For two hours, she talked and explained and convinced and consoled and fortified with reason and practical advice on the changing of the guard and the transfer of knowledge. Her words were simple; her sentences were sharp and concise, but the meaning was complex—flowing metaphors of mystical, vague significance, of double meanings, parables, fables, and subtle nuances of scripture thrown in, adding to the swirl of ideals open to interpretation.

Halina was no surer about what was expected of her than when she first came in the room. But she was much wearier, tired of this talk, tired of the whole thing.

She asked about Margret and the other girls at the hardware store. What was she supposed do for them?

"Maybe you could come with me to see Margret. Maybe you could help me decide what to do. Couldn't you help? It seems serious," Halina said. "I don't know what to do for her."

"It *is* serious. You know what to do," Baba replied with confidence.

Halina jumped up from the bed. "No, I don't know where to

start! Please *tell* me. Please! I don't want Margret to die!"

"Neither do I, but ultimately, it is up to God—not either of us."

"So I shouldn't try to help her?" Halina was confused.

"No—you do your best, but you also ask God and listen to his answers. Don't fight God. Don't try to be God," Baba said.

"What can I do for Margret?"

"When there is something foul, it must be removed—you know that. Remove toxins and counteract poisons. Then purify the blood. Wash wounds and cleanse the spirit. Then energize healing. Continue to fortify and reinforce the righteous. Patch up gaps and holes. Prevent decay and destroy doubts. Celebrate the Holy Spirit and eternal health. There. Simple." Baba shrugged.

Halina laughed.

"*Simple?* Let's go over that one more time—*slower.*"

They spent the afternoon that way, Halina asking for specific details and Baba answering in parables. The girl wavered between being frustrated and inspired, back and forth, back and forth, up and down. Then exhaustion set in.

Halina picked up an old parish bulletin that was on the nightstand, a small booklet produced by some church office, some stupid someone who thought the people who needed more churching could read. It did have one picture of Jesus, though, holding a lamb. He looked kind. And like his toes might get darn dirty, traipsing around in those goofy sandals. She had never seen a man wear sandals in Hegewisch. She ran her hand over the picture and wished she could ask him what to do. She listened, but heard only noises from the kitchen and Baba trying to fix her dress and babushka. No voice from heaven. She tore the picture out of the bulletin, folded it, and tucked it away in her shoe, where it would be safe for now.

Noises from the community room, voices from the kitchen, and telltale cooking smells started to drift into the room. Baba lit an oil lamp that was on the small table. Evening was settling in. The nuns were cooking their Sunday dinner and soup for the line of people who would be waiting at the back door for the five o'clock prayer and meal.

Halina and Baba couldn't resist the delicious smells coming from the kitchen. They followed their noses.

The nuns gave them aprons and put them to work right away. Halina was given a dishpan of potatoes to peel. Baba was asked to chop carrots. The vegetables were left from last summer's garden, pathetic stragglers from the bottom of the vegetable bins in the cold cellar. Supplies were running low. Good thing it would only be a couple of months before gardens would be producing again, Halina thought as she scraped skins off the puny, withered potatoes with eyes sprouting green shoots. The new growth curled, groping for sun and a chance to flourish once again. Renewal. The thought made her heart warm. And her toes. She wiggled the ones resting on the face of Jesus.

She saw Sister Beatrice take Baba aside. Halina could still hear the two women. Sister was offering to wash Baba's dress for her and to loan her a nightgown and some other essentials.

Abruptly, they switched to whispers, as if they were suddenly talking a different language. They stepped back farther into the corner, hands by their mouths, eyes intent on each other, expressions taut, like a clothesline stretched from here to hell.

What are they up to?

Halina tried to hear, curious what they were suddenly all hush-hush about. Maybe Sister Beatrice was giving Baba heck about the fire or something. But the other nuns were jabbering too loudly, their voices bouncing around the block walls and off the cement floor. It could have been a herd of discontent goats, bleating and clamoring over rocks.

Drat. Halina tried to inch closer to them to pick up a few words, at least. But Sister Anna nudged her, shoving more potatoes in her direction, looking pointedly at the clock that hung over the stove.

"Halina, peel faster," said Sister Anna.

Halina forgot about the whispering women and went back to her assignment. She peeled and chopped faster. The rhythm of the big, sharp knife hitting the cutting board was musical, reassuring, calming.

Chop. Thump. Chop. Thump. Chop. Thump.

It had been a difficult day after a long string of difficult days. She still wasn't sure about taking after Baba as a healer. She didn't want to become the wacky witch lady of the neighborhood. She couldn't stand the thought of being laughed at, ridiculed, the non-believers scoffing at her behind her back—until they needed help.

"Halina, enough of that! Now, onions—diced *small.*"

She hated dicing onions. Her eyes watered, and tears poured down her face.

She thought of Margret and the other women in the hardware store who needed help. She thought of Joey and how good it had felt to help fix him up, even if he hadn't once thanked her. She had helped save his life. She did that. And in about six months, her sister would need a midwife. And Camel? Maybe she could help Camel and his mother, too.

And then there was her job at the hospital. What would Nurse Neuberger say? Maybe she would kick her out of the nurses' aide classes. She certainly wouldn't approve.

What should I do? What?

Sister Beatrice and Baba were still hobnobbing at the side of the kitchen like best friends, heads close together.

"What are you looking at, young lady? Mind your own business!" Sister Anna snapped at her.

"Come, Halina," said Baba. "Help an old lady. I want to lay my tired head down before dinner and change my clothes. Come."

Baba made a motion to indicate that she wanted to lean on Halina's arm. Baba moaned. She was weary and aching. As Halina rushed to help her, Baba winked at her—just a quick wink, a conspirator's signal.

Halina helped the woman to her room, even though she suspected some hoax. *What the heck is this old woman up to now? More games? More trickery? More hocus-pocus ceremonies with fire?*

As soon as they got to Baba's room and shut the door, Baba disentangled herself from Halina's helping arm.

"Enough. I don't need help, silly girl! Let go!"

"Well, what was all that moaning and groaning and 'I need help' about? You gone mad, woman?"

"Don't smart-mouth me, young lady! I had to get you out of the kitchen and done with chopping onions. Do you *want* to spend the next two hours chopping onions?"

"No!"

"Well, hush your mouth! We have other business to tend to tonight, more important work. Sister Beatrice has a problem. She wants help."

Baba explained.

Halina wasn't happy about it. She thought Baba had to be joking or that it was a test, trying to see just how far Halina would go.

Eventually she agreed, but she crossed her fingers behind her back while she promised. She wasn't about to let the damned old woman get them both killed, putting them in the middle of whiskey men and their vengeful games. And as she thought about Janusz more and what he had done to her all those years when she was a kid—plastering his face against the basement window and scaring her half to death—an idea came to her. It was half-baked and sticky, like green snot. But maybe he needed to be taught a lesson. Maybe he needed to know what it was like to be tortured with fear.

She waited until the nuns were all out of the kitchen and in the community room. Tonight a dozen men were lined up at the back door waiting for soup. They looked like hobos who had jumped off a train. The sisters made the men wash up at the pump with lye soap before they could come in. Then they had to listen to some preaching and praying before the soup was dished up. They would be busy for over an hour.

Halina slipped back into the kitchen, trying to be nonchalant. She even whistled her I-am-doing-nothing-suspicious-don't-mind-me song. No one looked her way.

She quickly gathered what she needed, carried it in a bushel basket, and made her way down the long back hall, past the supply room, past the broom closet, then to the door to the cold cellar. She had the key, a candle, and matches in her pocket—all supplied by Sister Beatrice. The steps were steep and dark; the candlelight was little help. The air was damp and musty smelling, like wet leaves in the bottom of a ditch.

At the bottom of the stairs she paused, holding the candle up higher to cast its light through the small cellar.

"Hello, Janusz," she said. "I brought you dinner and some blankets and such to make you up a bed. The sister sent me."

The man sat on the floor in the corner. He might have been sleeping. His knees were pulled up to his chest, as though he was cold—or cowering from a monster. His face was busted up, bruised, swollen. He had taken a beating—a good one, from the looks of it. She wondered who had gotten to him. When? Why? He probably deserved it.

This was the man who had terrorized her as a child. And now look at him: he was little more than dribbles of spit and blood.

"Who is there?" he asked, raising his head, holding out his arms, groping through empty air. He tugged at the bandages over his eyes, pulling them off. He stared straight at Halina, blinking, blinking, blinking.

"Who is it? Who's there?"

"It's me, Janusz, your guardian angel. I'm going to help you," Halina said quietly.

"Did you bring me new socks?"

"I sure did. Green ones. How about that?"

"Can I have a blanket that matches?"

"You betcha."

Janusz clapped his hands.

And Halina, who had a butcher knife behind her back, lost her anger for the man-child. She decided that she should forget about the one little plan she had considered. She couldn't threaten this buffoon. And telling him she was going to pickle his testicles and put them in a jar was a stupid thought, anyway. Kind of a waste of a good Mason jar.

"Come on, Janusz, let's get you some dinner. Are you hungry?"

"You betcha."

Chapter 40

Halina needed to be at St. Margaret's Hospital at eight o'clock Monday morning for her class. That meant she had to leave the house at six a.m. to allow for the walk. It was still dark at that time in the morning, making the trek a real pain in the *dupah*, having to sidestep big puddles in the dark and spot piles of steaming horse turds before she stepped in them, worrying about running smack into a dead opossum or live rats after trash.

The dark was deep in stretches of empty road where few houses lined the street and no electric lights cast their eerie yellow glow on the narrow path alongside the road. This was not the kind of walk that was good for daydreaming, strolling along, and collecting pretty rocks. She had to stay alert. Motorcars, trucks, and horses and wagons were on the road, not about to slow down for a girl in their way.

And the troublemakers were still out on the streets, still wrapping up the last of their nighttime shenanigans before they called it quits and went to whatever back rooms they flopped in during the day. The working fellas, the ones from the midnight shifts, were still out, too, ricocheting around, scrounging for food, looking for a place to get a shot of whiskey or coffee.

The sun rose while she walked. Some mornings, it was a pretty sight. On others, the sun could hardly be seen through the overcast clouds and layers of mill exhaust hovering low in the sky. Today was one of those mixed-up days—half-cloudy, bits of sun breaking through with orange streaks. It matched how she felt: gloomy, with bits of hope sprinkled across her eyes.

It was all Baba's fault, talking about taking over for her and then getting her tangled up with Janusz hiding out in the church cellar. Damned creepy weird, that was. Janusz couldn't see much, his eyes all foggy—probably from a bad batch of hooch. Plus, someone had beat him up pretty bad. Some of Joey's pals, it seemed, had gotten the notion that Janusz was the one who had stabbed Joey.

Someone did it. Someone had to pay. That was the way it was.

Halina picked up her pace. She wanted to get there early, talk to some of the nurses, maybe. St. Margaret's was a tall brick building, plain and ugly, with a lot of windows uniformly spaced out, fifteen stories up. It was a big hospital, scary. She had been coming to classes for some time now, but she still got a sinking, twisted feeling in her gut when she came up to the double doors. She was afraid this would be the morning they told her to go away, that she wasn't welcome, wasn't allowed anymore.

But that didn't happen. She walked through the front doors as though she was a young woman on a mission from God and no one was going to interfere. She high-tailed it past the big reception desk, then to the stairway. The class was on the third floor, in a section for education and training and where residents met with the doctors who were in charge. There was a director lady for the volunteer nurses' aides like Halina. She had an office. Then there were some instructors who came and went, teaching on different days, sort of taking turns—as though it was a job no one wanted to do.

There was a break room and a locker room on the floor, too. Halina had her own locker! It had the skinniest metal door she had ever seen, and a combination lock that was built right into the door. She was supposed to change into her uniform when she got there. Most of the other girls changed right in front of their lockers, but

Halina took her uniform to one of the bathroom stalls to change. She didn't want anyone noticing the deplorable state of her under-things—baggy, too-big bloomers and a ratty, torn cotton slip. She didn't have the fancy camisoles with lace and girdles, garters, and stockings like some of the girls had.

That was why she liked to get there early, so she could change before the locker room was full of snooty girls who liked to snicker and giggle, so childish. This morning she must have dawdled too long, worrying over Janusz, because the locker room was noisy with chirping and chattering, girls getting changed into their pretty uni-forms, white with pink stripes, like candy canes.

When she came out of the stall, wadding her regular clothes up in a ball to shove into her locker, a whole bunch of the snooties stopped what they were doing to look at her. They stared as if she were the strangest thing they had ever seen.

"What? Did I put it on backwards or something? Or miss a button?" Halina asked as she looked down at her uniform and felt around for whatever gap or strap was amiss. Maybe it was her shoes. The other girls had pretty, new white nurse's shoes. Halina noticed that her old brown work boots had mud on them from the long walk.

Crud. Mother of . . .

"Ooops. I better not track mud all through the hospital, huh?" She looked around for something to scrape the muck off her shoes with.

No one answered her. They just stifled snickers instead, pivoted on their heels and pretended to not hear.

"Come along, girls, time to get started. Take your seats in the classroom, please," said Nurse Neuberger, one of the big shots who was always hurrying them along, taking roll call, and making notes on a clipboard about who was listening and who was asking dumb questions or daydreaming, staring out the window.

Halina liked to sit in the front row so she could hear every word of the lesson. She took her usual seat, her notebook and pencil ready.

Today the class was about vital signs—a patient's temperature and blood pressure, pulse, the basics like that.

Halina listened, but impatiently. She had so many questions, and this class was interesting and all, but it was taking forever to get around to the good stuff. She wanted to hear what to do about infections, sores on girls' private places, a pregnancy gone bad . . . *something* that might help Margret.

Nurse Neuberger, a not-so-old woman, all proper and pretty, as if she belonged on a label for toilet water, didn't talk about important symptoms, the kind that could kill you. And she *certainly* didn't talk about important medicines, the kind that could save you from misery and make you glad to be alive.

Halina raised her hand.

"When a patient has a temperature, that means an infection, right? And there's something rotten making poison in the body, right? So how do you get rid of the infection?" Halina asked, thinking of Margret, her fever, and the lump under her nightgown hem.

Nurse Neuberger took a deep breath, as if she were sucking up some patience from her knees to her head. "Well, topical iodine, bromine, and mercury-containing compounds are used to treat infected wounds and gangrene and sometimes syphilis. Sulphur powders, too, can be used on open wounds, and there are the rare cases where blood-letting is still appropriate. Some say it reduces the iron in the system, making it harder for the infection to spread."

Gee. All that? Halina furiously made notes: iodine, bromine, mercury, sulphur powder, and—blood-letting?

"How do you know which is right for a girl with a high fever? Like, maybe, let's say a girl who was in a motherly way but isn't anymore. And the death inside her is consuming her. What would work for her?"

"Oh, why *on Earth* would you need to know such—?"

Nurse Neuberger stopped. She looked Halina up and down. The nurse had a curious look on her face. She stepped back a few inches, as if a vapor of stink were coming from Halina.

The class of girls giggled, some whispering to each other, the room buzzing. Halina could feel her face burn, knew she was blushing. *Oh drat.* She certainly couldn't tell the nurse about Margret or the other girls in the hardware store's back rooms. How was she ever going to help them if she couldn't get answers out of this nurse?

Nurse Neuberger dismissed the outburst and tried to carry on.

"That's for the doctor to determine, *not* you. So don't worry about it," she said tightly.

Halina mumbled, mostly to herself, sulking. "I thought we were supposed to *aid* and that we needed to know such things, that's all. No need for a snit."

"Your job is to be a *nurses'* aide. You won't be diagnosing symptoms or prescribing treatment," answered Nurse Neuberger, shaking her head. She clapped her hands, trying to regain control of the class. Her crisp white nurse's cap didn't move one iota. How did she get it to stay so perfect? And why was she frowning and huffing like that over a little question? Halina decided to keep her trap closed.

The nurse resumed her strolling around and lecturing. She talked forever and ever about how to take a person's temperature with a thermometer and record it in the chart. Then she moved on to blood pressure and demonstrated the use of a contraption that wrapped around a patient's arm.

Halina was having a hard time focusing, her ego bruised from the scolding. She didn't deserve that. She thought about Baba and her methods for measuring how the blood was thumping through a fella's veins, racing as if he had just climbed ten stories of steps or were working up to asking a girl for a dance or had spent a night in some back room with a secret door, sucking down twenty-five-cent jars of hard potato mash. Baba also knew what to do about it—coffee for when it needed more oomph and whiskey when you wanted to put on the breaks a bit and slow it down. Then, of course, there was whacking the poor fool with a wooden spoon to get the juices flowing or some yelling and cursing. That worked, too.

"The patient may have some anxiety about the process, influencing the blood pressure reading," Nurse Neuberger went on. "Part of your job is to be reassuring and comforting. Make the patient feel confident that he is in good hands and there is nothing to fear," she said as she strolled back and forth in front of the room, her hands behind her back.

My, she looks so smart, strolling like that.

The nurse asked for examples. "What could you say to make a patient feel comfortable?"

Some of the snooty girls raised their hands and offered ideas.

"Hello, Mr. Smith. Don't worry about a thing, I've done this hundreds of times."

"What's this frown face for, Mr. Jones? Let's turn it upside down now. We are going to have you up and well in no time at all, I am sure."

"How are we feeling today? Let's just have a little look-see so we can get you on the mend, like one, two, three," said one of the girls in a sweet singsong voice that was all honey and horse feathers. To Halina, it sounded more like a jump-rope rhyme than doctoring talk.

Halina couldn't help but laugh a little at the silly patter. Pretty words. Polite words. *Nonsense and bullshit.* Those snooty girls had no ideas what it was like to be face to face with a man deep in misery and close to meeting his maker. That zombie-man with rotgut poisoning on his way home from the mill. Camel, with no eyelids. Janusz, hiding in the church cellar, bumbling in the dark, crazy as a loon, blind as a bat.

And Joey, the man her sister had her heart set on marrying. Halina thought of patching Joey up. Joey, lying on the tavern floor, blood everywhere, his face getting paler and his lips bluer every minute. Hell, Joey didn't want to hear Halina sweet-talking and saying he'd be all better soon! No one wanted pretty lies when they were dying.

Do they?

"You seem to disagree, Halina," said Nurse Neuberger, peering down at Halina. "What would *you* say to give a patience reassurance?"

"Ummm, well, I suppose . . ." Halina hesitated. "Well, I'd say it depends if the patient is just sorta sick or knocking on death's door. I think a fella who is dying doesn't want buttery nonsense. He wants you to be a know-it-all, confident and pushy as hell, so he knows you are serious and aim to fix the problem, one way or another, and that he better cooperate, shut up, do as you say . . . or else."

Apparently, Nurse Neuberger didn't like that answer. Her mouth did a funny gasp thing, as if a wasp had flown in and stung her tongue. It was creepy and funny all at once. Halina didn't laugh, though. She figured she was in enough trouble.

Oh, Mother Mary, Mother of Christ, why do you let me do such blunders?

Halina studied the floor tiles and her shoes, still mud-caked.

"And you don't think that will make the patient *more* fearful? *Hmmm?* I am *aghast* at your answer and *appalling* attitude, miss. We'll talk more after class."

Halina sank in her chair. She patted her pocket, looking for the reassuring lumps of her rosary and those two brass buttons she liked so much, her lucky charms. She wondered what the soldier who had worn them looked like, while she tried to soak up some of his bravery through her fingertips.

Chapter 41

Patcja stood on the steps of the courthouse. It was Monday, just before two o'clock. She was a few minutes early, just to be safe. She wore her black skirt, full and flouncy, with red embroidery around the bottom edge. She left the top three buttons undone. She also wore her best white blouse, leaving it untucked. She had a wreath of lilacs and apple blossoms, honeysuckle vines, and twigs with red ribbons in her hair. She had a matching bouquet of flowers in her hand, tied with a shoestring because she couldn't find another ribbon. She had borrowed her mother's black church heels, too. They were too big and hard to walk in, but they were better than her silly work shoes, which were so brown and ugly. And—best of all—she wore her mother's red-and-black silk babushka around her shoulders.

She hadn't told her mother she had worn the babushka before. Her mother wouldn't like the story.

The shanty was crowded. The usual men were huddled around the table, trying to keep warm. It was fall and cold out. Halina sat on an apple crate in the corner, by the stove. Bear and Camel were there, too. Stach convinced Bear to play his concertina. They all clapped their hands, and Camel danced a little jig in the cramped space. Patcja wanted to dance, too, but there was no room. She climbed on the table, wearing her mother's shoes and her mother's black wool stockings, which drooped down past her knees. Her mother's red-and-black silk babushka—stolen from a drawer of secrets—was draped around her shoulders.

Patcja danced, swishing her dress around her knees, her bare knee showing. She twirled, the skirt flaring out. She clapped, bending over so her hands were near Camel's face, his dropped jaw. She took off the silky babushka that had been covering her neck and shoulders. She twirled it above her head, the red rose pattern glowing in the lantern light. The light passed through the lacy fabric, making the red seem blood red, the roses seem alive, smelling like Poland, although she had never been there. She just knew.

Patcja had felt pretty that night, young and pretty. She hoped she was pretty now. She wanted to be. She tried so hard.

I'm still a little bit pretty, aren't I?

While she stood waiting on the courthouse steps, she twirled small twirls when no one was looking, letting her skirt flare out. *So lovely.* Ma had helped her make it a few years ago for the May Day festival. She had been one of the dancers on the stage. Camel had cheered for her and given her flowers afterwards.

She didn't know Joey back then. Or Antonio.

She waited and waited. People walking past paused and smiled. Some men winked. Some women nodded, understanding just how much effort had gone into the wreath and bouquet and just how important the day was for her. They guessed. It was obvious, wasn't it?

To everyone but Joey.

Patcja was too nervous to smile back. What if Joey didn't show? What if the other men didn't show? What if her trick didn't work?

It must work.

Patcja watched the end of the street, where she thought Joey would come around the corner.

There he was! She waved.

"Joey, Joey!" she called. "I'm here, Joey! Here I am!"

He picked up his gait, even running the last few steps. Until his shoulder seemed to tug at him. He winced and slowed down.

"Hey, baby. Look at you, all dolled up fancy-like. Aren't you a sight for sore eyes!"

He made a move as though he was going to pick her up and whirl her around, but he caught himself, held his sore shoulder instead, and pecked her on the cheek. Patcja threw her arms around him, kissing his cheek back, then finding his lips. It was a long, luscious kiss—sweet yet passionate. Perfect for a wedding day.

"Oh, Joey! Isn't this a beautiful day for a wedding! And you wore your good suit!" Patcja said happily. "You sure are handsome!"

Joey seemed confused. He frowned as he looked her up and down.

Patcja pulled one of the flowers out of her bouquet and poked it in the buttonhole on his lapel.

"There, now you are *perfect*!" she exclaimed.

The flowers, the wreath in her hair, the flower in his jacket. He was starting to understand.

"What's going on, Patcja? I thought I was supposed to be here for some court case. The courthouse, you said. Not the JP. I thought I was here to stand up for some sad-sack loser who needed a fella to be his alibi or witness or something like that."

"Oh, Joey, you are so silly! You *know* we talked about getting married today! You said, 'Sure, baby! Why not?' Remember? So here we are!"

"I did *what*?" Joey's mouth gaped open.

"You asked me to marry you! You did! And I said *yes*. I am so happy, Joey!"

Patcja looked at him, longing, pleading. Her chest closed in, making it hard to breathe. She fumbled in her pocket for her rosary. Her fingers found the beads, the crucifix.

Our Father, Who art in heaven . . .
Breathe. Pray. Breathe slowly.
Oh, Mother Mary, help me.
Breathe.

"Hey there, man!" one of the men from The Corner came up and slapped Joey on the back. Then another; then another. Soon, a cluster of jesting, jabbing, congratulating men was gathered around.

The men from The Corner she had invited for the "surprise" were showing up, one by one. They thought they were coming for a party and free booze. As soon as they saw Patcja and her skirt and flowers, they caught on. It was a wedding!

"Look at you two!"

"Hubba-hubba! Sweeeeeetie!"

"Hey, old man, about time you tied the knot!"

"She finally snagged you, ol' slippery catfish, you! You bit on the hook, and she yanked you in!"

The group was loud, teasing. All cheers and jeers and good-natured jabs. Poles loved a wedding; Italians, too. Who could resist the unbridled joy of young people in love?

Joey was jostled and slapped and shoved along in the throng of cheers up the steps and through the heavy double doors. He hardly said a word. There wasn't time.

Patcja was in the center of the huddle, carried along with him. The men pinched and patted and squeezed and hugged her, as though she was being welcomed into the clan. It was a noisy, rowdy cluster of celebration, and there was no stopping it now.

That had been her plan. It was working. Relief started to warm her hands, her cheeks, her bosom, which was being tickled by the silk of the red-and-black babushka.

"Oh, boys, I'm so glad you came to help us celebrate!" Patcja cooed to the men, squeezing big, muscled arms and blowing puckered smooches toward smiling, ogling men.

"You never know when a bridegroom might get cold feet!" she said, laughing, joking.

"Our big, brave Joey? Not on your life!" one man called out.

"Never, honey, we wouldn't let him!" shouted another.

"Get that ball and chain around his ankle, boys!"

Joey tried to argue, tried to turn, tried to say there would be no wedding. The other men seemed to think he was joshing, playing along, playing the part of a nervous groom.

"No running out now, Joey, old man! You are caught!"

And the throng of men picked Joey up on their shoulders and carried him down the hallway to the door with the brass sign on the door that read, "JUSTICE OF THE PEACE."

The ceremony lasted no more than five minutes. There was no ring, of course. The JP didn't notice or mind. He just left out those words about rings and symbols of eternal circles and such. They signed some papers. There was more back-slapping—and wincing by Joey. Everyone thought it was his shoulder acting up.

"Hey now, boys—watch the groom's shoulder! Now look, he's going to cry, poor bubby-boy!" teased one of the men.

Patcja was teary-eyed, too. She looked around the men, faces she recognized from The Corner, yet people who were still strangers to her. She didn't know the name of a single man—except for one, a man leaning on one of the benches in the courthouse hallway.

It seemed Augie had joined the gaggle without her noticing. He stood at the edge, watching from a step back, perhaps leery of the noise and rough-housing of the men younger than him.

She walked to Augie, kissed his cheek, and hugged him. "Hello, Augie! Glad you came, boss."

"Oh, Patcja, what have you done?" he asked, shaking his head.

"What I had to do, that's all, Augie," Patcja answered. She wiped her lipstick off his cheek. "Don't you worry none. I know my Joey, and I know what I'm doing."

"I hope so, Patcja. I hope so," Augie said.

They exchanged a long look that was reassuring and unsettling all at once. Patcja would figure it out later. There was no time now. She needed to play the part of happy bride. *A bride!* She was married!

"Come along, friends, the bride and groom invite you all back to The Corner to celebrate! Follow me," shouted Augie. "Drinks are on the house!"

Cheers rang off the cement steps of the courthouse, filling the spring afternoon.

Patcja smiled at her groom and locked arms with him as they followed Augie to The Corner.

"I'll make you happy, Joey, I promise. I *will*," Patcja whispered in Joey's ear.

"Sure, baby, sure you will," he said. He smiled, as though he was defeated but impressed by his opponent.

Then he stopped. He blocked her way, stepping closer. She felt his breath on her neck, hot, quick. He adjusted the babushka, pulling it farther down on her shoulders, exposing her throat.

"We'll make sure of that, won't we?" he said, his voice suddenly very different. It sounded strained, taut, like a stretched wire.

Patcja shuddered, the hairs on the back of her neck standing up.

"Yes, Joey."

Chapter 42

They celebrated at The Corner into the night. The first couple of rounds were on Augie. He had some watered-down bottles he didn't mind sharing. But after that, everyone was on their own and paying. As the groom and guest of honor, Joey didn't have to work the bar. Patcja still needed to run drinks, though. There was no one else to do it. Augie couldn't do it; his coughing spells were getting worse. He didn't look so good, either. Patcja was starting to worry.

"Thank you for coming to the wedding, Augie. It was nice to have one person I knew there," she said while she waited for him to mix some highballs. He was moving slowly.

"You're welcome, honey," he said. He patted her hand gently. He had a sad, pitiful look on his face, as if he had just found a stray puppy, one with three legs.

"Why didn't you invite your parents or your sister? They would have come, you know. And they might be darned mad at you for getting married without saying a word to them beforehand."

"I didn't know it would work. I wasn't sure Joey would go through with it. He didn't know why I had him meet me at the courthouse. And I couldn't have my parents or sister be there to see him turn and run, a scared chicken who refused to marry me, even though—"

"—he had an obligation," Augie said, finishing the sentence for her.

"Yes! An obligation. He owes me!" Patcja felt tears stinging her eyes. Oh, but she didn't want to cry—not now. It was over. She'd succeeded. Everything would be all right now. She took a deep breath.

Augie set the drinks on her tray, watching her, then looking out over the tables, to Joey in the place of honor in the center of the crowd, like a king with his subjects gathered around him.

"Where are you two going to live? Back of the 'Yards, with Joey's people, or here in Hegewisch?"

"What? Live with all those noisy, garlic-stinking Italians? I could *never* do that! *Never.*"

Patcja had not thought that far. She had no idea where they would go now, no plans. She suddenly felt weak-kneed.

"I need to sit down, Augie."

She left the tray of drinks on the bar and sat in the nearest chair, while her heart thumped in her hollow chest, empty of air.

Augie managed to deliver the tray of drinks to Joey's table and pass them around, despite his shaky hands. Then he whispered something in Joey's ear. Patcja watched. *Oh no.* Had Augie told Joey she called his people garlic-stinking? *Drat! Drat! Drat!* Why would Augie snitch on her?

Joey wasn't smiling, and he didn't say anything, but he turned and looked at Patcja. He wasn't happy. Maybe this was all too much for him. He was still recovering from the stabbing. Maybe he overdid it today and needed to rest.

Patcja was certainly very tired, exhausted. And it was only eight or nine o'clock. Coffee might help.

The kitchen was a mess, as usual, but it was quieter, a good place to think. Where could she and Joey live? How would she tell Ma? Oh, she hoped Ma wouldn't be too angry. Patcja still had her mother's beautiful red-and-black silk babushka around her shoulders. She rubbed the silk, so soft, against her face, smooth like dove feathers. She let the long black fringe trickle though her fingers, the ends tickling the palm of her hand.

She hid her face in the babushka, as if it were a towel she was using to wash away a day's sweat and steel dust. She pressed the ruby-red roses and dark-green vines to her eyes so she saw only color, intense like a dream.

She heard footsteps.

"Are you all right, Patcja?"

It was Halina. Bear was with her, his concertina over his shoulder. How did he know they were having a party and needed music? How wonderful! But both Bear and Halina looked worried. And Patcja wondered, for a second, if she were transparent, if people could see straight through her skin and flesh and bones to the worry in her heart. And the sins. Could everyone see what a horrid thing she had done—tricking a good man into marrying her when he didn't want to?

"I got married!"

Patcja hugged her sister as hard as she could. Halina hugged her back, squeezing out what little air was left in Patcja's lungs.

The coughing spell lasted several minutes, Patcja wheezing and choking. Bear looked scared to death. Halina sent him to get some whiskey—just a little—and Halina started talking Patcja through the spell.

Breathe in. Slowly. Calm. Easy. Steady. In . . . out . . . Breathe . . .

The episode subsided. Patcja caught her breath, and the coughing settled.

They hugged again, but this time no squeezing, just a careful, light hug. *Careful*. Patcja laughed a little. *Careful?* It was a little late for *careful*, wasn't it? But she didn't say it out loud.

Halina started the questions. She drilled Patcja, one question after another, in rapid fire, like the tommy guns the gangsters used robbing banks.

"Where are you going to live? How is Joey going to support you?"

"We haven't talked about where to live yet. I'm not sure."

"Oh, you can't go to Back of the 'Yards! Please don't! You won't fit in there, Patcja! And your breathing—you need to be careful and stay close to Baba—and me—to help you!" Halina said urgently.

"You would still help?"

"Of course, you dimwit snot-butt. And when the baby comes . . . I want to help. Let me help. I found a book at the hospital, in the residents' library. *Obstetrics and*—well, that means delivering babies."

"They have books on *that*? Do I have to read a book?" Patcja was confused.

"Not *you*, silly! *Me. I'm* reading the book. Don't you worry about it."

Patcja's hands went to her stomach in a protective gesture. She smoothed her blouse, pulling it down as far as it would go.

"Maybe Augie would let you live in the back room here? Or . . . well, maybe you and Joey could live with us, in our house. With Ma and Pa. You could . . . maybe, I don't know—"

"Yes, we could make the downstairs level our apartment! That would be good!" Patcja's face cleared of worry as the idea formed. "And we could save money until we could get our own place. It wouldn't be long, I know."

"Uh, yeah—but where would *I* go?" Halina asked.

"Somewhere! I don't know. How should I know? But you can't live in the same room with me and my husband! *Obviously*," Patcja said. She heard her own voice and knew she sounded shrill—mean, even—but she couldn't help it. She wanted Joey all to herself, with no one else around—especially her sister, always doing the right thing, so holy and good.

For the first time, Patcja noticed Halina carried a large satchel, the one that Pa used to carry junk home from the dump.

"What are you doing with Pa's junk bag? What are you carrying?" Patcja asked.

Halina stuffed the bag behind a trash bin.

"Nothing. I mean, not much. Well, I met someone who is feeling, well, bad in the belly. I got some supplies in the bag here. Might help; might not, but thought I oughtta try."

"So you're learning something in that hospital school, then? Something useful?"

Halina didn't have time to answer. Bear came running into the kitchen, a glass of amber-gold liquid in his hand. And Joey was close behind.

"Patcja, are you all right? What's wrong? Bear said you were choking," Joey said as he grabbed Patcja's arms, as though he might shake her or . . .

"Oh, Joey, don't worry! I'm fine! I just had a frog in my throat, that's all."

She just needed a drink. Patcja took the glass of whiskey from Bear, then hesitated. What if this whiskey was some of the bad batch?

Patcja thought of the four bottles of whiskey she had left in the alley.

"Bear, you didn't get this whiskey from the alley, did you?"

He shook his head.

Thank God. Patcja threw back the liquor in one gulp. She felt the warmth in her throat, all the way down to her belly, the whiskey instantly calming her jitters and jagged breathing.

She tugged on Joey's sleeve, eager to get back to the party.

"How about some music, Bear! Play a song for the bride and groom! Let's dance, Joey!" Patcja said. "Let's dance all night long!"

"Sure, baby," Joey said, taking a deep breath, as if he were about to dive into the lake from Navy Pier. "Why not?"

And Patcja twirled, waving the red babushka in the air, letting it dangle behind her like broken wings.

Chapter 43

For a Monday, The Corner sure was hopping.

Stach had been closing the newsstand for the night when he heard some commotion down at the end of the street. Some fellas where carrying on, arguing politics, it sounded like. Stach decided to see what the ruckus was about. That had been hours ago.

Now he was part of the ruckus, sucked in. He sat on a stool by the bar. He had a good view of the entire place from his spot. He could see the curtain across the doorway to the office, the hallway to the kitchen, the door to the back alley, the door to the cellar. Keeping track of the comings and goings wasn't easy, though, especially after a few shots. Stach was feeling good.

Augie was making deals, it seemed, buying more cases of Chicago Cola from the Italians, still refusing to do business with the Sicilians, Salvatore and Antonio, who sold milk bottles of homemade whiskey.

Joey was cooking his own deal, too, Stach figured. Some of Joey's pals from Back of the 'Yards were showing up, slapping him on the back, congratulating him, shaking his hand, then whispering into his ear—some news from his side of town, probably. Some had envelopes, too, fat ones that they slid over to Joey under the table, hands groping in the dark, unseeing, until they connected and made the handoff.

What was that about? More alliances and payoffs? What the hell now—and what side was the bridegroom on?

Stach watched, as if he were sitting in a movie house, watching the Saturday matinee. Besides the unfolding dramas, he found the faces of these conspirators fascinating, their twitches and crinkled expressions, their furrowed brows and glances left and right, stained hands swiping at their necks with blue handkerchiefs stiff with old snot and mill grime. Stach wished he had a sketchbook and charcoal, some way to record these telling gestures and expressions. How he missed his days as an artist, free to create, free to tell tales with lines and shapes and shades that flowed from his fingertips!

Augie had stepped away from the bar, probably to the back office. Stach strolled behind the bar, looking for some scraps of paper he could use, a pencil—anything to make some quick studies, sketches. He found an old calendar and a wooden pencil, not much more than a stub.

He did a quick sketch of the bride and groom first, the happy couple. Little Patcja was married! And to an Italian! She looked happy. He looked confused. Ah, but weren't most men a little shell-shocked on their wedding day?

Stach's pencil portrait was simple but sweet. He drew Patcja as the dimpled damsel she thought she was and Joey as the handsome prince she deserved. It would be his wedding present to them after he framed it, made it presentable.

Patcja was married! Stach couldn't get over it. She had managed to convince Joey somehow. Stach wondered how she did it. How did that persuasive, plucky thing twist the arm of that Italian Romeo? Maybe Joey wasn't all good in the head, being stabbed and all, still low on blood, coming face to face with mortality and inches away from God's judgment. *Could be.*

Stach helped himself to the open bottle of Cola that was behind the bar and poured two shots—one for him, one for Joey. Stach joined Joey at his table. Patcja was on Joey's knee, perched prettily, like a cat expecting to be petted, her fur stroked.

"Congratulations, Patcja! Congratulations, Joey! Here, let's drink to a long and happy marriage!" said Stach.

Joey tossed back the shot. "*Salute!*"

"*Na zdrowie!*" Stach threw back his own shot and slammed the overturned glass down on the table.

"You didn't bring one for me? I want a shot, too," said Patcja, her bottom lip protruding, a sulking spell threatening to come over her.

"I think you've had enough, Patcja," said Joey, pushing her off his knee. "Get up. Go see where Augie went—he shouldn't have left the bar unattended. Anyone could walk back there and steal some inventory, isn't that right, Stach?"

"That's so true. And did you know bootleg whiskey tastes better when it's been stolen? It's got more of a punch, more flavor, when your pulse is racing, thinking you might get caught."

Joey smacked his lips.

"Yep, I think you are right, Stach—I think so. Seems you Polacks aren't all as stupid as they say. You might have an ounce of smarts in your head, after all."

"Joey! *Stop that!* I don't like it when you talk like that, I told you!" scolded Patcja.

"And *I* told *you* to go find Augie!" Joey snapped.

"All right, Joey—I'm going, I'm going."

Stach stared at this man, this kid. He wore his stupidity like a badge, something he was proud of, something he earned. But really it was just another hand-me-down, like the clothes on his back and the tarnished ambition in his gut.

"So, Joey, do Italian women take to being bossed like that? Groveling at your big Italian shoes and skinny Italian asses?" asked Stach, like a curious student. "'Cause Polish women . . . well, they don't cower, Joey," he said. "They get *even*. They have their ways. And so does their family, their people. So you better start watching your back if you think you're going to talk to our Patcja like that.

Just some fair warning, Joey-boy. Fair warning."

Joey started to stand up, his fists knotting as though he might try to take a swing at Stach. But he was slower than usual, his eyes darting back and forth, having trouble focusing. His knees seemed to wobble. It was hard to say if it was from drink or fear—or God touching the back of his neck with a breath of cold air, a warning.

"Don't bother getting up, Joey," Stach said, pushing the man back into his chair. "I'm going. I'll see about the bar, guard it for Augie. Never know who might try some funny business."

Stach glanced at the bar and saw Bear was there, front and center, his concertina in his hands.

Patcja was urging him on. "Another polka, Bear! One more," the bride pleaded, clapping her hands.

Bear didn't require much encouragement. Chords from "*Gdybym to ja miała skrzydełka jak gąska*" rang out. "If I had wings like a goose," an old Polish folk song.

Chapter 44

Halina remembered another party when Bear had played his concertina. Halina had still been a stupid girl. Patcja had been sixteen, thinking she was all grown up. But she wasn't.

Halina took her usual place in the corner, by the empty apple crates. It was a good place, snug, safe. She could watch, unnoticed. Patcja—obviously—had no intention of fading into the background. She stood next to the wood stove, letting the warm glow from the fire cast a lovely light on her face, like a spotlight shining on the star performer. The red-and-black babushka around Patcja's shoulders, stolen from their mother's room, seemed to glow and give off a heat of its own.

Patcja probably planned the effect. Probably stood just so to make sure she got the best light. Standing in her mother's shoes was obviously a balancing act for Patcja, though. She wobbled, as if she might topple over. Halina was tempted to give her a little nudge just to see her plop on her pretty butt. But she decided to let her be. Why cause trouble for nothing's sake?

Halina watched the thick cigarette smoke climb to the ceiling. The smoke ribbons were almost pretty, mesmerizing, like being lured into a Gypsy trance. Smoke swirled in dragon shapes, fiery breath hovering over the heads of the men gathered for poker and whiskey. The shanty was cramped. The usual men were there—Major, Jocko, Mykel, Warner. Stach had also invited Camel and Bear, Halina and Patcja, too—so Bear could put on a concert.

"Na zdrowie!" *Stach slammed the shot glass down on the table. Stach passed the bottle and shot glass to the next man. "Give us a song, Bear!"*

The boy jumped up. He took the place of honor in front of the window. Bear started in with a Polish folk tune, "Gdybym to ja miała skrzydełka jak gąska." *If I had wings like a goose.*

Everyone sang, the words familiar, comforting, and pensive, like home, the Old Country.

Gdybym to ja miała skrzydełka jak gąska,
Poleciałabym ja za Jaśkiem do śląska.
Lecę ponad gajem, lecę ponad wodą,
Szukać gdzie to Jaśka srogie losy wiodą.

If I had wings like a goose,
I would fly after Jasiek to Silesia.
I'm flying over the woods, I'm flying over the water,
To search where Jasiek is led by the harsh fate.

Camel danced a little jig.

Bear picked a livelier tune, "Beer Barrel Polka." *Patcja started twirling and moving her hips with plenty of sway, lively bursts of motion.*

"Patcja—the real Princess of the Polka!" *Camel cheered, pointing to Patcja, bowing to her as if she were royalty. Patcja danced in place, exaggerating the moves, bouncing and clapping, balancing on shoes with heels, two sizes too big.*

The men cheered.

"Look at Patcja dance!"

Patcja smiled, glowing in the attention, tossing her wavy hair over her shoulder. She paused, just a second, then climbed on the table. The table jostled on the cinder blocks.

"Careful there, missy," Stach said as he steadied the table. Major and Jocko each grabbed a corner of the table, too, steadying the stage for their young—so very young—dancing girl.

Patcja swished the skirt of her school dress, letting the hem tickle her shin, her knee, then higher and more. The black wool stockings—her mother's—were loose, slipping and sliding, the black wool a harsh contrast against her ivory skin. Swish, whisk, ruffle. Swirl.

Glimpses of Patcja's white cotton underthings appeared. The ribbon of lace trim was tattered; torn pieces dangled down like fringe. The fringe fluttered with her dancing, teasing with glimpses of secret places.

The men watched. The polka sped up and Patcja exaggerated the swing of her hips and the bounce of her shoulders, which pulled her dress tight across her chest. Patcja bowed forward, clapping her hands near Camel's nose. The collar of her dress fell open, giving Camel a view of mounding curves, flowing into cleavage, damp with perspiration, so plump and perfect.

Camel's jaw dropped. He blushed bright crimson.

Patcja untied the babushka from her shoulders and waved it in the air, over her head. Halina watched from her corner. She moved closer to the stove, trying to get out of the direct view of her stupid sister. She didn't want to see this.

"Stach, don't you think it is getting late? Maybe it's time for everyone to go home. I'm feeling awfully tired, aren't you?" Halina yawned, her mouth wide open. She stretched, like a mill man home from the midnight shift.

Stach patted Halina on the head, smoothing stray wisps falling in her eyes. "Don't worry," he whispered into Halina's ear. "It's all in fun," he said. "A little fun is good for the soul, no?"

Bear's music ended, the last chords fading.

"Oh, dearie me," sighed Patcja, feigning exhaustion. She fanned her face with her hand and patted the perspiration at her throat with the babushka. Then she tossed it over her shoulder, like a clown tossing candy to children along the parade route. The scarf fluttered past the oil lamp, appearing translucent and magic. The red silk roses glowed for a moment, *then fell to the dirt floor.*

Patcja started down off the table, struggling to climb down with the shoes that were too big on her feet and the black wool stockings that drooped down below her knees. One stocking fell to her ankle. Her bare knee, so pale, was a shocking blend of curves and grace. Patcja struggled to pull the stocking up while keeping her balance.

Major laughed. It was more like a leer. He was drunk. They all were. Except the children.

Camel gasped, reaching out a hand to help Patcja down. Major beat him to it, jumping up from his seat and grabbing Patcja's arm in a clumsy move. As Major stood, his uniform trousers puckered and bulged—strange, as if he were trying to hide a bottle of hair tonic in his skivvies.

And suddenly the bottle leaked. A wet spot spread across his britches. The men roared with laughter, throwing their hats at Major, telling him to hide his filthy business.

Major thought Patcja might want to see it. Stach said no.

Halina turned away. She most certainly didn't want to see what was hiding in Major's trousers, leaking. Maybe he'd just peed a little. Maybe old men peed when they stood up too fast? Halina stared at the ground, shuffling dirt with her shoe. She saw the babushka, where it had fallen and been kicked to the side. The red no longer glowed; it was coated in dust and dirt and shame.

Halina wasn't going to stay in the tavern and watch her sister, the new bride, do her little dance again, putting on a show. There was no doubt that Patcja would be strutting on a table soon enough, showing off her pretty skirt, the embroidered border of bright red flowers and green vines, dainty yet bold, like the Polish flag.

Halina signed.

Patcja, Patcja, Patcja.

What would Ma and Pa say when they found out she was married? And—here was the important part—what would they say about Patcja and Joey taking up house in the coal room? An Italian living under their roof? She couldn't imagine.

Oh my.

And where will I *go?*

Halina had no idea. But she suddenly felt as though sand were shifting under her feet. Her footing seemed uncertain, tenuous. Would she be pushed out? Turned away to make room for Patcja and Joey—and a baby?

What happens to a girl with no place to sleep, no place to call home?

Margret's face came to her. *Margret.* In the excitement of learning about Patcja's marriage, she had briefly put aside thoughts of the girls at the hardware store and the satchel of supplies she had packed.

She remembered the plan with renewed urgency. Why was she wasting time at The Corner with these drunkards and her . . . her . . . her wild sister?

Chapter 45

The walk to the hardware store was long and dreary. Halina's legs felt as if they were carrying the weight of massive stone boulders. Really, it was just loneliness, longing, and worry about what would become of her sister—and herself, now that she would be the only daughter in the house. And there was some other feeling, maybe jealousy. It was just as heavy, but slippier, hard to grasp as it slid from one shoulder to the other.

Will I ever get married? Will any man want me?

She caught herself looking around for the rusty black truck that Nicky drove for the whiskey men. But there was no sign of him.

Halina managed to reach the hardware store without breaking any of the jars in her satchel. One light was on over the front door, barely bright enough to read the painted sign that covered the door and the one handwritten on paper and thumbtacked to the front door at eye level.

"No drunks. No credit. No drink. Lawmen, use back door," it said in Polish, Italian, and English.

Halina decided she'd try the back door, too. There was no light in the alley, though, and the back door seemed locked. Halina put her face to the blacked-out surface of the glass window, barely able to see through brush-stroked lines into the dimly lit hall. As she strained her eyes, she saw movement—shadows, shapes of hulking, slow-moving men and thin girls dressed in scanty robes and silky, bright colors. She couldn't see faces, couldn't see anyone she recognized.

She knocked on the glass pane. Once, then again. And again. And again—louder.

One of the girls, Josephine, finally opened the door.

"We never thought we'd see you again," she said, letting Halina in.

"I came as fast as I could. I had Mass yesterday and a blind oaf who was beat up pretty bad to take care of. And today was my class at the hospital, and then my silly sister got *married*. How is Margret? Is she still holding on?"

"I suppose . . . What you got in that bag? What you up to? You gonna cook some soup?" Josephine asked, casting a suspicious eye at Halina's satchel.

"Nah. I brought medicine. Homemade kind. For Margret first. Then for . . . well, whoever is hurting."

"Hmmm. What's Antonio goin' to say about that?"

"It was Antonio's idea."

"Well, it can't be good, then—can it? Not one bit. You better go see Arlene first. She's up front, at her desk."

After that, Josephine had nothing more to say to Halina.

Halina had no intention of dealing with grouchy Arlene, the fat ol' goose lady, if she didn't have to. She found Margret's room without anyone's help. It was the room that was darkest, the curtain pulled across the doorway gaping open just a few inches, as if someone had been peaking in from time to time.

From the doorway, she could see a lump in the bed—so small, so still that Halina wondered if she were too late.

She tiptoed in, not wanting to disturb the dying—*or the dead.*

She found a candle and some matches on the nightstand and lit them. In the timid light, Halina could see Margret. She was breathing in shallow, wispy breaths, as though the infection had gone to her lungs. Her face was pale and damp, dotted with the sweat of a fever.

She smelled rancid, like old meat writhing with maggots. Halina tried to not gag.

"Hello, Margret. It's me, Halina. I'm back. Remember me? I brought some medicines to try. I'm not sure . . . but maybe . . . maybe, I can try to help," Halina said in a quiet, soothing voice.

Margret opened her eyes slightly, blinking and blinking, seemingly trying to focus or think or remember or understand. Her eyes were cloudy, a film covering her pupils—more signs of infection.

"I remember you," Margret said, recognition briefly flitting across her face. Then it was gone. "Don't bother. There's nothing more for me now. I'm ready."

"Margret, don't say that. There is always hope. We can try a poultice to suck out the infection or—"

"A priest," Margret interrupted. "Can you ask Father to come . . . ?" her voice trailed off as her eyelids drooped shut.

Halina shook the other girl by the shoulders. Shook her again and again.

Margret coughed and gasped, startled awake, sucking in air slowly, cautiously, like someone slurping boiling-hot soup.

"That's it, Margret. Keep breathing. Keep at it," Halina urged.

She thought of what she had said to Nurse Neuberger that morning during class:

"No one wants pretty lies when they are dying. Do they?"

"What would you say to give a patience reassurance?"

"Ummm, well, I suppose . . . well, I'd say it depends if the patient is sorta sick or knocking on death's door. I think a fella who is dying doesn't want buttery nonsense. He wants you to be a know-it-all, confident and pushy as hell, so he knows you are serious and aim to fix the problem, one way or another, and that he better cooperate, shut up, do as you say . . . or else."

Halina figured Margret was knocking on death's door, for sure. But she didn't have the confidence to sound like a know-it-all and promise to fix her. She had no idea where to start.

She thought about trying to fetch Baba or a *real* nurse. Maybe Nurse Neuberger would come. Maybe Sister Beatrice could at least help pray . . . Oh, who could she turn to?

Halina felt helpless—small, unworthy of this responsibility, this life that had been put in her hands.

She lowered herself down to her knees, hands tightly folded in prayer, eyes pinched closed. She tried to find God or Mother Mary. She saw Baba instead.

An old woman, in her babushka, wooden spoon in one hand, Bible in the other. She was standing in her kitchen, Lydia on the table behind her, clinging to life. Baba—the healer who always knew what to do, as if by instinct. Or divine intervention. Or luck.

"Maybe you could come with me to see Margret. Maybe you could help me decide what to do. Couldn't you help? It seems serious," Halina said. "I don't know what to do for her."

"It is serious. You know what to do."

"No, I don't know where to start. Please tell me. Please. I don't want Margret to die."

"Neither do I, but ultimately, it is up to God, not either of us."

"So I shouldn't do anything?"

"No, you do your best, but you also ask God and listen to his answers. Don't fight God. Don't try to be God," Baba said.

"What can I do for Margret?"

"When there is something foul, it must be removed—you know that. Remove toxins and counteract poisons. Then purify the blood. Wash wounds and cleanse the spirit. Then energize healing. Continue to fortify and re-inforce the righteous. Patch up gaps and holes. Prevent decay and destroy doubts. Celebrate the Holy Spirit and eternal health. There. Simple."

Halina stood up—quickly, abruptly. Her satchel of supplies tumbled over, rattling on the floor, making a jarring, horrid noise.

Margret's eyes fluttered open.

Halina clapped her hands, loudly. Time to get serious—loud and confident. Demand that her patient make an effort to get well.

"That's it, lazy girl! Wake up! We've got some healing to brew up," Halina said loudly to Margret. She clapped her hands again to get the sick girl's attention.

Smack, smack, smack.

Halina slapped her hands down on the bed. "C'mon, now. No more of this drooping off and moaning for a priest nonsense. You're my first real patient, and I say you *can't* die. So get that bullshit out of your head!"

She rummaged through her satchel, laying the supplies out in a row to organize them: jars of powders; bromine, like Nurse Neuberger mentioned, milk of magnesia. Magnesium was on Nurse Neuberger's list of ways to fight infection, wasn't it? She had also brought some other ingredients, borrowed from Baba's kitchen apothecary: salts, powders, bark, roots. Garlic, roasted and crushed into a pungent oil; charcoal ashes from charred wood; boiled sorghum; willow leaves made into a mash; turnips, dried then ground into powder; mustard plaster; bee balm; goose grease; raw honey; alfalfa sprouts, steeped into a tea; witch hazel with its sharp smell; and nightshade berries boiled down to a dark red gel.

Something in all that ought to work. It had to.

She just wasn't sure which ingredients to try first. But she would try them all, if she had to. And at the bottom of the satchel was one more powerful medicine. Halina pulled out a crucifix and rosary beads, kissing the figure of Christ on the cross.

Celebrate the Holy Spirit.

Oh, she almost forgot . . . Halina took off her right shoe. The picture she'd torn from the church bulletin, the picture of Jesus, folded into a neat square. She smoothed out the paper, damp from her sweaty foot. The image itself was fine, a little worn on the edge, the ink rubbed off in places. She placed it reverently on the table next to the candle.

"Well, all set. Let's get started," Halina said to herself before turning her attention back to her patient. "Margret! Wake up! We've got some work to do, I said!"

Halina heard a noise at the doorway behind her and turned. Arlene stood there, hands on hips, cigarette in her mouth, its smoke curling around her rat's nest of matted and tangled hair festooned with a red paper flower oddly tucked behind her ear. In the dim light, the red seemed dark, almost the color of blood. Her cotton dress was the same mottled red; so were the beads around her neck, her lipstick, and the open-toed slippers on her feet that showed off toenails that were also painted red.

"Hello, Arlene," Halina said in a voice that was much more confident than she felt. "I'm glad you're here. I need help. We're going to flush the poison out of Margret, and we're going to need lots of hot water and soap. And clean sheets and towels. Do you have *anything* close to clean in this place?"

Arlene took a long look at the parcels spread out on the floor and then looked Halina up and down. She shuffled into the room to the table beside the bed, stepping into the circle of yellow candlelight, and carefully picked up the picture of Jesus, as if picking up an ancient artifact from another age, something sacred.

Halina was flexing her fist, ready to stand up to Arlene if she had a problem with her bringing a picture of Christ into her filthy, stinking house of sin. She was ready to . . .

But Arlene did a strange thing: she caressed the picture, stroking the face with one finger in reverence. She seemed moved, perhaps remembering some past moment of faith or a private miracle. She might have kissed the picture or held it against her heart, her face was so taken, tottering on an emotion that was worshipful, loving.

"Are you going to help me or not?" Halina demanded, breaking the moment.

"Yeah. Yeah, I s'ppose. If that's what Antonio wants," Arlene said. Then she stepped closer to Halina and whispered near her ear, "Having her stinking up the place—half dead, taking up a bed—sure isn't good for business, if you know what I mean."

Halina whipped around to face Arlene, the wicked hyena of a

woman, and slapped her face.

"I *do* know what you mean! And I won't hear that kind of talk! Stop it—*now*! Go boil some water and find clean sheets and towels, woman. *Now*, or I'll tell Antonio what kind of nuisance you are, useless and interfering."

Arlene's nostrils flared. She fumed, sucking in air and holding it as if she was gathering all of her anger.

Josephine appeared in the doorway. "I'll help," she said. "C'mon, Arlene, let's start the kettle of water."

"Thank you," Halina said. "And we need more light, lanterns, and more clean sheets and . . ." Halina realized she was talking to herself. Arlene and Josephine had left, presumably to boil water. She suddenly felt very alone and very . . . well, almost powerful.

"You have been picked. This is your fate."

She was going to help Margret. If God decided it was her time to die, she could at least have less pain and more . . . dignity.

Halina found the wooden spoon in the pile of supplies. She rapped it on the nightstand.

"Time to wake up, Margret! We're going to get your heart a pumping and blood flowing, and we'll wash out the bad—draw out the toxins and purge the poison—and start a fire in your belly to expel the decaying, rotten mass. It's gotta go, Margret. Gotta get the stink out of you."

She beat the bed with her wooden spoon, louder and louder.

Margret opened her eyes wide. Wider and wider. Her cheeks flushed.

"That's it, Margret!" Halina shouted as she started mixing ingredients in a large dishpan. "How about we sing while we work? A polka!"

Arlene and Josephine thought she must be crazed, but they didn't argue much. They just shook their heads and pitched in, following directions as Halina barked them. They made a tea for Margret, and she sipped it dutifully, obeying without question like an old dog.

Halina mixed ingredients for a poultice, picking the same ingredients she had watched Baba use many times. But she added some of her own, as well, not allowing herself time to think, just doing, impulse and instinct guiding her hands, trusting that some power was guiding her. God? Gypsy juju? Years of Knowledge inhaled through bonfire smoke? Science absorbed through the clinging, antiseptic smell of St. Margaret's halls?

Halina hummed "Beer Barrel Polka" while Josephine clapped and Arlene helped tear sheets and soak them in the milky concoction that was supposed to suck the ruined pregnancy out of Margret's rotting womb.

At least, Halina *hoped* it would.

The singing and clapping seemed to be helping raise Margret's pulse. It was also a good distraction as Halina poked on the girl's lower belly, finding the lump off to one side—not in the center as it should have been. That must have been the problem: the baby's water sack wasn't formed right, where it should have been, working the way God intended it to work.

Now what?

Halina tried to think, which wasn't easy with all these damned women looking at her as though she were supposed to pull a miracle out of her ass. Wouldn't Nurse Neuberger think that was funny!

"Your job is a nurses' aide. You won't be diagnosing symptoms or prescribing treatment."

Nurse Neuberger didn't know jack-shit about doctoring poor people who couldn't afford hospitals or risk a run-in with the law—or people who didn't speak English to understand a bit of what an uppity doctor was saying, scaring the bejeebers out of them with their fancy doctor-talk, mile-long words, and names for bones and organs they had learned from a fancy book.

What she wouldn't give for one of those books in the residents' library at the hospital—one with plenty of drawings. That might help. But the next class wasn't until Wednesday.

She didn't think Margret could wait until Wednesday.

"More hot water, Arlene! More singing, Josephine! Margret—more praying!"

Halina heaped more spoonfuls of the warm white paste over Margret's belly and wrapped more bandages tightly in place. She added another layer of insulation—goose grease and willow bark—then another layer of torn sheets. They wrapped her in yet another layer, a cocoon of blankets.

Margret's face was flushed and sweating. Her eyes were open but not focused. Her mouth was agape, panting, her dry tongue hanging out.

"Well, *something's* happening," said Arlene. "I hope you're not killing her. Antonio would really have a fit then."

"Oh, shut up about Antonio!" Halina said, dismissing her in irritation. She was so sick of hearing about damned Antonio, the jerk. She'd deal with him if she had to—one way or another.

"Let's make more tea—lots of honey, corn syrup, sugar, fuel for the—"

Loud banging at the back door interrupted Halina. She remembered the sign: "Lawmen use the back door."

Who else would go to the back? Didn't customers go to the front door?

"Oh, damn. Not tonight!" Arlene said, rushing out, her red slippers flopping on her fat feet.

Halina had no idea who it was or why they were there, but chills ran down her arm. She blew out the candle, Josephine turned down the oil lamp, and they waited in the dark.

Margret's panting and wheezing seemed to echo in the tiny room, the noises bouncing sluggishly from wall to wall. Down the hall somewhere was a man grunting. Some groaning drifted in the distance, too. Voices muffled, muted. Furniture creaked and scooted, metal across wooden floors.

Halina could hear Arlene unlock and open the back door. And

then there were footsteps, boots in the narrow hallway, coming toward Margret's room.

"Shhh, Margret. Shhh," Halina whispered, as if Margret could possibly control her noisy breathing.

Then voices, a low, rumbling mumble. An argument of sorts. Complaining from a disgruntled man. Halina strained to hear the voice. It was familiar, but too muffled to be sure.

"I know who it is! I'll take care of the asshole," Josephine said, darting out into the hall.

"Hey there, Mister Major—my big soldier boy," Josephine purred, like a cat in heat.

"Want Missy Josephine to shine your pistol for you?"

Halina cringed. She wanted to scream *nooo!* to Josephine. Instead, she bit her lip and said nothing.

Chapter 46

A little after midnight, Patcja decided she'd had enough of the dancing and drinking and taking orders from drunken men, a drunken Augie, and a drunken husband. But pulling Joey away wasn't turning out to be easy. He and his pals were deep into some hush-hush conversation that could have involved some petty prank, some stupid money scheme that couldn't possibly work, or something slightly sinister that could land them all in jail or in the lake. Or maybe a meat locker.

Patcja hoped it was just a prank they were plotting. But who could say? She realized she had a lot to learn about Italian men and their ways. Polish men sure didn't conspire like this—at least none of the ones that she knew. It wasn't that the big Polish oafs didn't have brains; they just didn't have any ambitions.

Too bad these Italians had *too* much ambition and not enough brains.

"Joey, let's leave. Let's go to my house. We can sleep in my room, downstairs. We'll tell my parents in the morning about the wedding. *Please.*"

"Can't you see I'm in the middle of something, Patcja? Shut up! If you want to go, *you* go," Joey slurred.

"I can't go without you," she insisted. "Not on our wedding night!"

The men around the table heard that and had a good laugh. They punched and jabbed and slapped the poor man, teasing him about his husbandly duties in the sack. They prodded and laughed and cajoled Joey, practically kicking him out.

Patcja was glad they were leaving, but she didn't like that Joey had to be persuaded. What the heck was wrong with him? A nervous bridegroom? It wasn't like they hadn't been together before. It was a mystery.

They walked to Avenue O, saying nothing. After the noise of The Corner, the street seemed painfully quiet, awkwardly poised in a nothing space, neither here nor there. Joey swayed and stumbled a few times, regaining his balance after leaning on Patcja's shoulder, but said nothing.

Patcja couldn't stand the emptiness and started humming. *If I had wings like a goose. Gdybym to ja miała skrzydełka jak gąska.*

Soon Joey joined in, humming along with her. Then he tried singing. He had heard the Polish folk songs many times, but the Polish words were too much for him. He inserted made-up words and noises—drunken noises.

> *Gdybym to ja miała hmmmm. Hmmm mmmm skrzydełka jak gąska,*
> *Poleciałabym ja za jazjazwowizi doozieski ski ski-olskipolski Jaśkiem do śląska.*
> *Lecę ponad nincompoop Babazabba wabba woo zoobski.*
> *Bagajem, lecę ponad*
> *wodą.*
> *Szukać gdzie to Jaśka srogie losy wiodą.*

At first, Patcja laughed. A giggle slipped out, sounding stupid. Then, his gibberish was annoying. Rude. Mean. This was an important Polish song, and he was making fun of it. She tried to think of an Italian song she could make fun of. Nothing came to her.

"Stop it, Joey! Hush now. That's enough."

He obeyed, but the smirk on his face said he could start up again anytime. He looked like an ornery boy in short britches testing the nun during class.

❦ ❦ ❦

When they reached the house, Patcja followed the sidewalk, out of habit, making her way around to the back of the house and the windows. Yep, one was propped open, as usual.

She took one look at Joey and was sure she wasn't going to get Mr. Know-It-All to climb through a small basement window. *Drunk-assed nincompoop.* Drunk on her wedding night!

Damn him.

The backdoor was unlocked.

Thank you, God, Father Almighty.

As soon as she opened the door, the familiar smells hit her. She flinched, as if the odor were toxic, scalding. Old cabbage, congealed grease, cigarette smoke, unwashed bodies, dust, and shame.

Oh, what will Joey think?

She tugged on his sleeve and hurried him through the dark kitchen to the stairs that led down to the basement, pausing only long enough to light an oil lamp. Long shadows from the lamp pointed the way.

Joey said nothing. His face was blank, un-telling, as Patcja searched for signs of his reaction to her home. Perhaps she could just get him to bed and make him forget, or not notice, how pathetic the house was.

"Just down these stairs," she said quietly. "We turned the coal room into a bedroom. There's not much coal in it now, though—we about used it up this winter—so no one comes down here. Well, not much, anyway. We scrub clothes—well, Halina does—in the furnace room over there. But we can turn this mess into a place that's all ours, Joey. Until we save enough for a place of our own."

He clomped on the steps, clinging to the wall, looking for a railing that wasn't there. But he said nothing.

"C'mon, Joey, sweet dumpling . . . There's a big bed waiting for us, my handsome groom."

Well, that got his attention.

Joey's eyes opened wide, and he licked his lips. He wiped his eyes with a big paw, as though trying to focus, trying to see where he was. He seemed to sway, as if he were on a boat in a storm. Then he started to gag.

Jesus.

"Oh, Christ the Lord, please don't let him puke—not here, *not now,*" Patcja prayed in a whisper.

She hurried to the bedroom door and opened it so she could get the dishpan.

Clatter. Crash.

Tin cans tumbled, banged, rattled to the floor, and rolled. Patcja jumped, startled. The avalanche triggered a string that pulled over a coffee can, pouring out nails. The noise bounced on the cement walls.

Joey jumped in front of her, arms spread out, protective. "What the heck was that?" he asked.

It was the booby trap Halina and Patcja had invented years ago. She had forgotten that Halina had put it back. Why did her lamebrain sister do that?

"Oh, gee! Sorry, Joey. It's just a little trick someone tried to play on us. It's nothing," she stammered.

"Great. Probably woke up the whole damn house," he said, looking over his shoulder.

The door at the top of the stairs opened.

"Everything all right down there?"

"It's just me, Ma!" Patcja called out. "I'm sorry—I ran into something. Go back to bed."

"Bed sounds good to me, baby," Joey said. His protective arms tightened around her, pulling her close to him. He nuzzled her neck, burrowing into the hair on her shoulder, looking for that spot where—

"Not here, Joey. Wait, Joey—"

They picked their way over the cans and nails scattered in the doorway, not bothering to pick them up. They both had other things on their minds. They fell onto the mattress, arms tangled in clothes, fingers groping on buttons.

"Turn off the lamp, Joey," Patcja whispered.

Faint moonlight filtered in from the two windows, an orange glow from the steel mill seeping in. The effect was dreamlike, mystical. Patcja felt like a princess on her wedding night, with her prince, Joey, lavishing her with kisses.

Joey starting humming the folk song. *If I had wings like a goose.*

Patcja giggled. Joey hummed louder, faster.

Suddenly, the door to the coal room opened. Light from a lamp flooded in.

Pa was in the doorway, charging in.

"What's going on here? Who is that? In my house? Get out! *Now!*" shouted Pa, the lamp in his hand held high. "Before I kill you!"

"Pa, stop! We're *married*, Pa—we got married today!" Patcja pulled the blanket up to her chest.

Joey pulled his pants on.

"To an *Italian*? Is this one of those—?"

Pa rushed into the room, hand in a fist, ready to swing. The oil lamp swung. Garish shadows fell across his face, contorted in anger. The image moved in slow motion for Patcja. The furious man, coming at them like a beast, in baggy old skivvies, his chest bare, his feet bare—

"Wait, Pa—Watch out!"

Argrrrrr! He roared in pain and hopped, trying to see what had pierced his foot.

Nails. Two had gone all the way through and were sticking out the top of his foot. Blood dripped, and the man growled, even madder than he had been. He was ready to charge again.

Patcja tore the oil lamp from him, afraid he would drop it.

"Oh, Pa! I'm sorry! But Pa—"

Joey scrambled to the other side of the bed, carrying his shoes.

"Look here, mister—Pappy—don't come swinging at *me*! I done the *right* thing! I *married* the girl—played along! Why not? We're married. *Done.* Legal and official."

Pa paused; the news was starting to sink in, but he obviously didn't like it. He looked back and forth. Patcja. Joey. Joey. Patcja.

"How dare you bring a dirty, filthy criminal into this house! And *marry* one!"

Pa's face was red, the veins on his forehead sticking out, his jaw clenched.

He lunged, then stumbled, the nails in his foot making him wince, trip, and fall to his knees.

"This way, Joey," Patcja said, climbing over the bed to the windows, chunks of coal against the wall creating a makeshift ladder. She had climbed the coal mountain so many times, she knew exactly which chunks to step on. Joey followed. Then he took the lead, pushing open the window, hopping up through the opening. Then he helped Patcja, gently, carefully.

Oh, he was being so nice, so kind—and after such terrible treatment.

How she loved this man! He would take care of her. He would take her away from this . . . this . . . this . . .

And then the tears came.

"C'mon, baby. Let's go back to The Corner. Augie will put us up. We'll sleep in his back room."

That back room . . . so disgusting.

She remembered waking up there and being so frightened. The day Joey was stabbed.

"Whatever you say, Joey," Patcja choked, tears pouring down her face.

She carried her shoes. The red-and-black babushka was still around her neck. She used it to wipe her face.

The scarf smelled just like the house.

The stink followed her.

Chapter 47

Halina stayed the night with Margret, sleeping on the floor next to her bed when she could no longer keep her eyes open. It was a long night.

At first, the noise and comings and goings made Halina worried. She had no idea so many men could come and leave during one evening—and at all hours because of the shiftwork schedule of the mills. Day was night and night was day for some men, the ones who worked the third shift.

By the time that group of customers had filtered out, Halina was getting used to the commotion, the noises coming from behind curtains, the thumps and thuds and groans and shouting. Some men were noisier than others. Some were more rambunctious than others.

Arlene and the girls seemed to know how to handle them, knew how to give them what they wanted and send them on their way—simple enough, with no ruckus. Even Major left in a non-eventful manner. Arlene stayed at the front desk as business picked up. Josephine was busy, too, but poked her head around the curtain a few times to see how Margret was doing. She brought hot water from the stove in the back room, saying that Halina shouldn't be walking around the store. Someone might see her and get the wrong idea. Instead, Josephine made the trips to the kitchen for her.

Halina tried to ignore all the strangeness of being in a whore-house, hoping God would forgive her. She tried to focus on her patient. It wasn't easy.

And she wasn't sure what to try next. She didn't have a thermometer, like Nurse Neuberger had taught the class to use. No blood pressure contraption, either, so Halina was stuck with Baba's tactics for monitoring vitals.

Oh, what would Nurse Neuberger say?

Halina changed the poultice twice during the night, applying more of the thick paste, rewrapping Margret to lock in the heat. The fever went up, climbing as the poultice made a furnace, sucking out the poison. Halina spooned tea into Margret's mouth, too—as hot as she thought Margret could take. The liquid stayed down, which had to be a good sign.

It was a cleansing tea, one that was supposed to flush out toxins and expel . . .

Well, it was a secret recipe the Gypsies carried and would never reveal the ingredients of. It had to be used with care and great forethought and reverence because it was powerful, more caustic than disgrace. Belladonna, nightshade oil, turpentine, white blooms from wild carrot, sometimes called Queen Anne's lace. It was to be used as a last resort to end dishonorable pregnancies that were cursed by sin or demons, violence, rape, or abuse.

Baba told her about the recipe. The woman would bleed for weeks, her insides washed clean. No more baby. *Ever.*

Halina changed the recipe, making it milder—she hoped. Less nightshade, no turpentine. More bicarbonate. More honey. More dandelion root. More Queen Anne's lace. And she added mustard seed because—well, just because it seemed right. Mustard seed was in the Bible. Faith, like a mustard seed, would grow into something mighty.

Sometime just around three or four o'clock in the morning, Halina worried the fever was climbing too high. She started sponging cool water on Margret's forehead, wiping her arms and legs down with water and rubbing alcohol. Margret shivered, her teeth chattering.

"Oh, Margret, I'm so sorry. I'm failing you," she sighed, feeling defeated.

Halina covered Margret with more blankets, tucking them tightly around her. The girl seemed to be asleep or unconscious. What was the difference? How would she tell the difference? One was normal and one was very bad. What kind of healer was she when she couldn't even tell if her patient was asleep, unconscious, or in a coma?

Halina kicked at the damned foot of the stupid bed. Margret didn't move, but some critter scurried into the corner. Probably a mouse. Halina didn't even flinch. Exhaustion was starting to get to her, making her numb and cranky. Mad. Frustrated. Furious at her own ignorance.

So tired.

Halina knelt on the floor by the bed, resting her head on Margret's warm belly, holding Margret's hand, feeling for a pulse.

Yes, there!

Pa-dum . . . pa-dum . . . pa-dum . . .

Steady. She counted the heartbeats but had no watch for telling if the beats per minute were too many or too few. But she counted anyway.

And fell asleep.

She dreamed about riding in a Gypsy wagon, being taught curses by an old woman who smelled like Bibles and incense. And Nicky was in the wagon, too. He had more practical skills to teach.

Chapter 48

There was no class at the hospital on Tuesdays and Thursdays, but the aides-in-training were supposed to put in time volunteering as candy stripers. They were all assigned to different floors and different nurse supervisors. "Hands-on learning experience," it was called. More like free labor, making the girls work their butts off for nothing. But those were the rules.

Halina was assigned to the sixth floor, the trauma ward, where the men with serious injuries were kept. Crushed bones, chopped-off legs, hands burned off from molten steel—that kind of grisly stuff. Halina figured Nurse Neuberger had assigned her to that floor as payback for asking so many questions.

She didn't mind. Those men weren't expecting someone to bring them flowers or talk sweetly to them. They didn't mind a Polish girl with scuffed-up brown boots instead of nice, new white shoes.

Halina arrived Tuesday morning dragging her tail, exhausted, unsure she could put in a full day of emptying bedpans and wiping butts, but her brain itched with questions. Her heart was riddled with holes and the realization that Old Country healing wasn't enough.

Margret wasn't improving—at least, not much. Halina didn't know what else to try. The answers were there, in the hospital—tumbling in the hallways, tucked in the pockets of the nurses, echoing in the coughs of the doctors, whispering from the books on shelves and the stacks of charts filled with patient names and documented procedures—words too long to be swallowed in one gulp.

She had to find them. *Soon.*

Mother Mary of Mercy. Halina ran her fingers through her hair and realized she hadn't even brushed her hair or pinned it back. *Drat.* No wonder she was attracting strange glances and glares already. *A thistle in a garden of roses.*

Well, hell. There isn't much I can do about it now.

Halina reported to Nurse Davies, the nurse in charge of the sixth-floor ward, a no-nonsense woman with a bun of gray hair that was huge and lumpy with hairpins poking out, her nurse's cap sliding and slightly askew. She didn't seem to notice Halina's messy hair—or even to care.

Maybe Nurse Davies would help. Maybe she could explain—

"Girl! Here—take those to 623. Mr. Jenkins soiled his sheets. Change them," Nurse Davies barked with a rushed, strained voice that was worn thin, as though she had been shouting orders to deaf ears all morning. She pointed at a stack of linens on the counter, barely looking up from the chart she was studying.

They had been taught how to change linens with a patient still in bed, but Halina had not had a chance to practice it yet—not with a *real* patient in bed. When she practiced at home with a sack of flour, the whole sack plopped on the floor, busting open and spewing flour all over the place.

Would be a shame to do that to Mr. Jenkins. He deserved better than a tumble to the floor. Room 623 had four beds, all men with orthopedic injuries—broken bones. Their beds were separated by dinky white screens that always seemed to be in the way and didn't offer a whole lot of privacy, anyway. Didn't matter much. All four men in that room were out of their minds in pain and didn't give a hoot about who saw their pale asses or hairy balls.

Jenkins was in the bed at the end, Halina remembered. He

had been there for a week already. His right leg was crushed. Some railcars in the mill had derailed, pinning him. The doctor had tried to save the leg, but that wasn't working out so well. Halina checked the chart at the end of his bed, just to be sure she had the right fella, but the stink from the bed was enough to tell her who had soiled the bed.

"Good morning, Mr. Jenkins. Are you awake?"

He said nothing. No movement, not even an eyelid flutter.

"Don't feel like talking, eh? Well, I don't either, so I guess we'll suit each other right fine."

Cleaning up the man was no easy feat. Apparently, the mess had happened during the night, and he had been wallowing in it for hours, thrashing around. He grimaced and moaned the whole time, hurting badly. A sweat was breaking out on his forehead and upper lip. Halina could tell when she touched his skin that his fever was climbing.

Just like Margret.

Halina rolled Jenkins to the left so she could replace the dirty sheets from one side of the bed, then rolled him to the right to get the other side. As she was tucking in the top corner, leaning over Mr. Jenkins, he suddenly opened his eyes. With one shaking arm, he pulled her closer to him, trying to form words.

"Kill me. Stop the pain. *Please*," the man gasped, his face contorted.

"I'll get Nurse Davies," Halina said before rushing to the nurses' station.

"The next dose isn't due until nine o'clock," Nurse Davies answered. "He just has to wait. I can't give it to him any sooner. There are strict rules around opiates, and I intend to follow them."

"Opiates? You mean opium? I've heard of that—I think," said Halina. She thought of the small brown vial she had taken from Joey the night she patched him up.

"Strong pain killers—morphine, opium. Also *very* addictive, so we can't just hand it out like candy, you know."

"But he's hurting bad. Can't we just—"

"He's going to be hurting worse tomorrow. He's scheduled for surgery tomorrow morning. Going to take that leg off. Doctor decided he couldn't save it. Gangrene is setting in."

"So *that* is the smell?"

"Yep, nothing stinks worse than—" Nurse Davies went on, only to be interrupted.

"Isn't there some way to treat gangrene? Some medicine? *Something* a doctor can do?"

"Sure. Arsphenamine, comes from arsenic. Mercury. Bromine. There are compounds. A few. Works for some, not others," Nurse Davies answered. "Now, go on, stop bothering me with questions! I need to get the nine a.m. medicine ready."

"Can I help? I can help. Just tell me what to do—please," Halina said.

Nurse Davies unlocked a cabinet behind the desk. Halina could see shelves and shelves of bottles of pills and small bottles for injections. So many of them!

The nurse looked Halina over, up and down. For the first time, she met her eyes. Halina wondered what the nurse saw. Could she see that Halina craved answers, that she needed to understand how medicine—*real* medicine—and science could cure someone very ill, someone like Margret?

Or did the nurse just see a foolish and stupid girl, a bumbling Polack?

"Your eyes are almost black," Nurse Davies said. "I had a great aunt with black eyes. From Hungary. She was a witch, cast spells and such. Thought she could raise the dead."

"I'm no witch."

"Well, that's too bad. 'Cause we could use some hocus pocus around here. Might help."

"Might not," Halina shook her head.

"You're right," the nurse said.

"Might just prolong the end—stretch the misery out longer than God intended," Halina said.

"Ah, a cynic, I see," Nurse Davies said, giving her a deeply assessing look. "You're awfully young to be soured on medicine already. That usually doesn't happen until you've lost a few patients."

"I've seen my share of sickness," Halina said.

She told Nurse Davies about Camel and his absence of eyelids and hands that looked melted and his mama who just sat in the chair beside him, not talking, not walking, drooling out mumbled words, gone crazy with grief.

"So, is that why all the questions, why you want to take up nursing?"

"Maybe. I sort of got pushed into it. Didn't have much choice."

Halina thought about telling Nurse Davies about Baba and about being picked to be her apprentice, about the bonfire and Baba's kitchen full of herbs and powders and roots. But she realized she'd be laughed at for sure—maybe even kicked out.

The hoity-toity girls would surely get a chuckle out of that, and she wasn't about to give them that satisfaction.

"My neighborhood needs a healer. They can't afford hospitals and doctors. Don't trust them much, either. They think a poultice is all they need or some tea with dandelions in it."

Nurse Davies laughed and patted Halina's hand.

"Well, folk remedies and homeopathic medicine *do* have some validity and played a role in the history of medicine. But *now*, of course, we know better than to rely on some silly old wives' tales."

"Of course, we do," Halina said, thinking of the mustard seed poultice she had tried using to suck the poison out of Margret's belly. How stupid she had been! She wished she could hide her ignorant face.

"Okay, then. You can help me get the cart of medicine ready—just don't go driving me crazy with too many questions. Hear me?"

Halina nodded eagerly. "Loud and clear."

They went through the patient charts, confirming prescriptions and doctors' orders, then doling out the pills in small cups. And as Nurse Davies counted out pills and prepared hypodermic needs, she explained each of the medicines and what they treated.

"Will you teach me more?" Halina asked, absorbing everything hungrily.

"That's enough, Miss Curious. What do you think this is, nursery school? I'm busy!"

"I was just thinking that the more I know, the more I can help you."

"Well, you go on thinking that. Learn all you want—I'm not stopping you," the nurse said, shaking her head and smiling at the girl's absurdity, as if she had just been told the queen of England was coming for a visit.

Nurse Davies started to push the cart down the hall toward Room 623, motioning for Halina to follow.

Halina hurried alongside her, her old brown boots clunking on the shiny hospital floor.

Chapter 49

Baba was happy to move back to her house. She had had enough of sleeping in the church basement, underfoot of the good sisters and their abundance of holiness. There was only so much praying and blessing and bowing and kneeling and cross-making a person could do in one day.

And she missed her chickens. Stach had built a new coop for them, better than the last. They squawked and cackled their usual commotion when they saw her in the yard. Apparently, they were none the worse from the fire. At least they were still hungry for chicken feed. And Goose was just as feisty, flapping her wings, honking her nonsense threats.

Baba fed the fowl, then went in to take inventory of her doctoring supplies. She hated to think she'd be handing over a poorly stocked cupboard to Halina. The least she could do would be to replace what had burned up in the fire and whatever else had been scorched, damaging the medicinal value.

That could take weeks, though, as some of the ingredients weren't easy to find. And some could only be found in certain seasons, certain places. Some were from the Old Country, and she had been rationing them, using them with care, to stretch them as far as possible. She wasn't sure if they even grew here in this county, all swamp and sandy soil and gritty steel dust in the air that hid the sun, seeming to choke it. How did anything grow in this place?

Bah!

She worked for hours, sorting roots and powders, dried flowers and leaves along with some bones. She tossed the wet or scorched ingredients into a trash barrel. The old wooden barrel was half full, and each time she tossed something else in, she cringed. This task was harder than she'd thought it would be. Her heart ached with the loss—empty jars and empty baskets.

Empty promises.

At least there were enough ingredients left to make the tea for Janusz. It was time for another dose. While she was brewing it, she made a batch of tonic, too—different ingredients, a different jar, marked with twine so she could tell the jars apart.

She packed her doctoring bag, an oversized carpetbag, the kind a traveler getting on a train would use. Baba thought of the big switching yard south of town where seven different railways came together in a hub.

So impressive. So powerful.

She had never ridden on a train. And now, it seemed she never would. Hmmm. She didn't know if she was sad or angry. Maybe she was just tired.

She walked down the street, her carpetbag on her shoulder. It was quiet on the street. No taunting youngsters, no hooligan thugs, no rumbling trucks, no mill hands coming home from the second shift.

Nice. But there was also no sign of Halina, not for days now. Where was she? Or her sister, Patcja—where was *she*?

Baba sighed and loosened her babushka. The day was too lovely for worrying. Spring was in full bloom now. The grass was greening up; the trees blooming, spatterings of color on the branches like powdered sugar sprinkled on *kołaczki*.

She took a good whiff, memorizing the moment.

Baba walked to the Patchiecki lot. She had been here several times in the last few weeks.

That morning when she'd been sweeping and watched Krzysztof unload some milk crates while those two Sicilians supervised seemed like a long time ago. She had put on her boots to retrieve the smoldering cigar. That was when she had found the cellar doors and a cellar full of hooch.

The last time she had been here, the yard was a mess. Now, it had been tidied up, it seemed. Someone had stacked a few bricks into a neat pile. That was odd. There was another stack of bricks on the other side of the path, as well. That was really odd.

The sudden neatness in this overgrown lot was out of place. She looked closer and saw it: a wire was stretched taut across the path, ankle height. The wire trailed off through the grass and weeds, like a snake slithering.

It was a tripwire, a warning device, probably attached to a bell at the end of the wire. She had seen this before, in the Old Country. Soldiers—Russians first, then Germans—marched through, ravaging villages and homes. People buried their valuables in fields, in barns, rigged them with wires and . . .

Baba stepped over the wire and continued down the dirt path, to the cellar door. The double doors in the ground were partially hidden by weeds, thistle bushes, vines, poison oak, and poison sumac, guarding the entrance like gatekeepers. They didn't scare her. She picked her way through, avoiding the oily leaves.

The door creaked when she pulled it open. The steps were steep, moss covered and slippery. She was only on the second step when he showed.

"Hey, who's there? Stop right there," said Janusz, coming out of the shadows. The big man held a lantern, its flame burning low. He squinted from the glare of the sun coming in and flowing down the steps.

"Oh, it's *you*," he said.

"Hello, Janusz. I came to visit, to check on you. How are your eyes? Seeing better?"

"Sun hurts. Shut that door. I don't like the sun," he said, putting his arm across his face to shield it. "You can come in, but I'm not going to let you touch the milk bottles. I'm supposed to protect these bottles. I'm the guard," he said, his chest puffing out proudly, like a little boy who had just learned to tie his shoes.

Baba looked past Janusz. The shelves on the wall of the cellar were lined with bottles painted white. Full. Some held whiskey; some didn't.

She had been coming by the cellar, adjusting inventory. She'd brought Bear, as well. Together, they emptied milk bottles and refilled them with water, a couple dozen every time. Bear carried the crates for her. The boy did as he was told, made four trips back and forth from the cellar to the nearest pump, next door. He fretted the whole time, whining as he went, scared senseless.

But Bear owed her, so he helped her, like a good boy.

So far, their secret seemed safe, as far as their identity was concerned. But someone must have gotten wise to the switch. She wasn't sure who.

Since the curse on Sal, she hadn't seen that one much. But it could have been his lieutenant, the tall one. Anyway, someone had told Janusz he should guard the inventory, and the tripwire was set up. Someone didn't like spilled milk.

Well, blast it. Let the thugs all poison each other with their homemade hooch.

A bad batch was on the streets, she'd heard. Janusz had managed to find a bottle, and it had nearly blinded him. The sisters of St. Florian's had taken him in for a few days, caring for him, feeding him. They'd hid him in their cellar. Father Chodniewicz would never approve of a man who ran with gangsters being housed in their guest room.

"You've got to go. We've done all we can for you," the sister said to Janusz. "Go, before the father finds you."

"I didn't come about the milk bottles, Janusz. I came to see about your eyes—and if you need anything. I brought tea. You like my tea," she said, holding up her carpetbag, letting him see the sealed jars inside.

"Tea?"

"Yes, sir. I'll pour."

She pulled out a china cup, dainty with pink roses. They had a lovely tea, as if they were two very proper old friends sharing an after-noon break. Janusz gulped down the liquid, without suspicion that it was drugged or that his *kutas* would be limp, his *popęd płciowy* would be *kaput*. No more urges to climb through windows scaring girls.

"Your tea is nice," he said. "Nobody is nice to me like you are, Baba."

Baba patted his cheek, wiped the drool from his chin with the hem of her babushka. The man wasn't *all* bad.

"Now, no peeking in windows," she said firmly. "No climbing in open windows, either. You keep your feet on the ground. Hear me?"

He nodded, of course. He always agreed, never argued, with Baba.

She waved goodbye and let the cellar door close with a loud clunk.

Her next stop was at the end of the street. Another house, just like the others. Her carpetbag held two more jars of tonic.

She knocked on the door, its white paint curling like carrot peels. No one answered. She knocked again, knowing no one would answer. They were home, but they never answered. Still, Baba opened the door. It was unlocked, of course.

Camel was in his bed, just as she knew he would be. His mama sat in her wheelchair beside the bed, holding the young man's muti-lated hand. Neither moved much when they heard her come in—*if* they heard. It was hard to say what was happening in their heads, their shared misery, private worlds where no one else was welcomed. Perhaps they were both running in a Polish meadow of poppies, chasing little lambs, rolling with goats.

"Well, hello, my two dear friends! It's Baba. I've come to visit again and check on you. I've brought tonic for Camel and salve for those bed sores. We really must get you moving more. Remember?" Baba said conversationally as she moved closer to them. "And elixir for you, missus. You need your strength so you can take care of this boy. Remember?"

Camel twisted in the bed, kicking his legs, as if he were running in place. His eyes were covered with a bandage, a white cloth tied around his head. It loosened as he writhed, dipping below one eye—wide open, pupil dilated.

Baba tried to fix it, but the boy kicked his legs. She slapped his backside. He froze.

"Don't go kicking at me, soldier boy! Tell me with words, Camel!" she demanded. "If you need something, you need to talk. *Words.* You can do it—ain't nothing wrong with your mouth, boy. You have a tongue in there. I've seen it. Your eyes may have trouble; I'll grant you that. And your hands. But you can still talk. I know it. Tell me what you want—or what you don't want."

Camel's mother dropped the boy's hand and pulled away, squeamish, as though a pack of biting words might charge at her. She turned away from Baba, a crazy woman who spanked her boy.

"My boy sick," she mumbled, the words too fat and slippery, like glass marbles that were difficult to spit out. Her face was lopsided, slack on one side; her arm, too. The woman had suffered some fits. Strokes.

There was a good chance she could recover, if she wanted to. But she didn't, and no one was forcing her to try.

"Well, for heaven's sakes, he's not sick. Just planted peculiar-like, a potted geranium in the wrong kind of flower pot, some old battered-up box, not fit at all for a geranium. It's not fair, not right, but it is what it is," Baba said, looking at the boy, putting her face closer to his. "And so what? You can't get away with keeping quiet and making me do all the talking and guessing what you need. I'm plum tired of it," she whispered close to his ear.

Camel scooted down lower in the bed, as if he were burrowing into dirt.

Baba made the same speech on most of her weekly visits. Different images, different stories, always the same message. But they never got through. That didn't mean she wouldn't keep trying, though.

Still, she wasn't about to wait for a blue moon. Or a miracle. Baba threw back the sheet and blanket, exposing Camel, his boney legs sticking out of a ratty nightshirt that was far too big for the withering man-ghost.

Baba sat down her carpetbag and arranged her supplies. The boy needed a rubdown, oil on his legs, fresh salve on the sores that she lanced and bandaged, and tonic—all before Mateusz came home from the sawmill. Camel's father didn't believe in Baba's kind of healing. An old vision came:

> *Sawdust on the man's shoulders, like fresh snowflakes.*
> *His eyes wide, nostrils flare.*
> *"Out! No gypsy blasphemy in my house! Out with you!"*
> *Spit flies in fury's storm and collects on his chin,*
> *like drool on the boy's face, where lips used to be.*

"Well, looky here. If these aren't the ugliest, skinniest bird legs ever, then I don't know what are," Baba said. "Let's get to exercising them some, soldier Camel. And *Mamkri*, you need to help, too. C'mon, up with you. How about a song? Let's sing."

Then Baba barked more orders and sang, treating both patients, mother and child.

Next time, she would bring the girl. Show her what needed to be done.

Chapter 50

"Stach, I need help," Halina said, plopping down on the apple crate in the corner of the shanty, her usual spot.

"Now what, missy? Are you out of poker money again?"

"Nope. I'm done with poker," Halina said, shaking her head wearily. "Who has time for poker? I'm busy learning how to doctor people—the *right* way. With real medicine and science and pills and prescriptions with doses every four hours, not just any ol' time you want. You have to be precise with medicine, you know."

"Oh, is that so?" Stach raised an eyebrow.

"Yes, indeed." Halina moved to the wood stove, where Curly was sleeping. He had been bandaged up again. A new splint put on, more bandages. But he whined in his sleep.

"See this splint made out of a chunk of wood? That's not very sterile, you know. Not the right way to bandage up a dog's leg, at all," Halina said, shaking her head as though she was weary of such careless veterinary care.

Stach stood at his workbench, painting a small jewelry box. White paint dripped from his brush as he stared at this girl who had suddenly become a medical expert. Apparently, she was learning quite a bit in that course she was taking. Well, good for her. Maybe Baba was right to pick her as an apprentice. She certainly seemed to have an instinct for healing and a notion for helping the sick—like Joey, like the girls at the hardware store. Maybe she could eventually help Camel and his mother. Maybe her own mother, too, keep her from floating in and out of the reality of the present and some strange memories of the past. Maybe Halina could find some magic medicine for making wrongs right. Would it be some of Baba's Old Country healing or new medicine, the kind locked in the cabinets at St. Margaret's? Good for her. But there was something about her know-it-all tone that was prickling—itching and irritating, like little hairs on your back after a haircut.

"Yes, that's how it is at the hospital. They have a rule for *everything*. And people who take those rules very seriously, like they're written by God. The medical commandments, carved in stone," she said.

"Well, what do you need my help with, then? I don't know anything about those commandments and medicine."

"I want you to help me steal something," Halina replied simply.

"Stop right there!" he said, holding up a hand in protest.

But he listened to her plan. And refused.

Then she re-explained it. He still refused her request for help.

The girl was getting mad, he could see. But there was no way he was going to let her get involved in stealing drugs from the hospital so she could treat whores at the hardware store. He just wouldn't do it, not ever, and no amount of pouting and whining could change his mind.

"Halina, *no*. Why don't you just try asking this Nurse Davies or Nurse Neuberger if she will give you some medicine for Margret and the other girls? Maybe one of them will understand and want to help."

"You've never met Nurse Neuberger. That woman—well, there is no way she would break a rule. Ever. And Nurse Davies is almost as bad."

"Oh, those kind, eh?"

"Yep. Sad. Really sad."

Stach laughed. He was never one for rules, especially when they made no sense. During the war, he had helped himself to some army-issue supplies, but only because he'd known people who needed them. Lueke, the guard at the switching yard, had left certain boxcars unlocked after his inspections. He had marked the cars with shoe polish in the shape of a white cross, and then Stach had filled his handmade wheelbarrow with a few parcels and wheeled it back through the marsh, in the pitch black. Then he'd given it all away.

Most of Hegewisch still wore army-green socks and slept in army-green blankets.

Sister Beatrice had been his accomplice, letting him store crates in the church's cellar, helping him pass out supplies to those who needed help the most. She had risked her lovely neck just as much as Stach had. It helped that they had known each other before coming to America, before Sister took her vows, before Stach went to the *uniwersytet*.

He didn't mind breaking rules when it was for a good cause. But hospitals? No. They scared the bejeebers out of him—all that white and all those long hallways and that smell of antiseptic. And those nurses, all straight-laced with their hats with pointy corners that perched on the top of their heads and must have been held in place with thumbtacks. He wouldn't be surprised. They were such an unfeeling lot.

Jocko was a friend. Back in '17, when the Great War was getting started, Jocko had worked in the steel mill and got caught in an explosion, lost most of his hand. Stach had hitched up Moses the horse to Major's wagon and driven it all the way to the hospital, and when he got there . . .

He felt like a bum, a stupid man out of place, a fish on the lake shore, trying to flip and flop to get back to where he belonged. No one understood his Polish. His loud insistence scared the desk people, and he didn't understand their English, but knew the tone. Finally, he found the right desk and the right lady in a white uniform with white shoes and a white cap. He asked for Jocko, and they said Jocko had refused visitors. Just like that: no.

The nurse lady sent him home. She wouldn't even take the package, all wrapped up in butcher paper and tied with twine. It was a crucifix he had carved for Jocko. The lady in white wouldn't give it to him. He carried it home. It still sat in the cart, bundled up and mocking him, with Jesus nailed to the cross, writhing in agony, no one listening.

"What if I came with you? Maybe I could talk to this nurse, use the Stach charm," he asked Halina, hoping he could persuade her to try another way. "Maybe a little sweet-talking and smiles might soften her up. I could tell her who I was, famous Polish artist, until the Germans came along and destroyed my studio. I could say I want to paint her portrait."

Halina didn't look convinced. She did her fretting thing, like usual, trying to make up her mind. Then that humming thing.

Lord help me.

"Stach, if you want to come to St. Margaret's with me, fine. But you're going to have to do one thing first."

"What, Miss Bossy Pants?"

"Take a bath . . . and shave."

"That's *two* things," he said laughing, rubbing a hand over the stubble on his face.

"And one more. Can I borrow some of that white paint? I'm supposed to have white shoes for my candy striper uniform." She held out a foot to display her scuffed old brown work boots.

"You want to paint your shoes?"

"Yep. Why not?"

"I think you mean, 'Why not, baby?'—don't you?" Stach asked in an Italian accent, a perfect impression of Joey.

It was funny, in a bittersweet sort of way.

Chapter 51

Patcja combed her hair, trying to see her reflection in a small, cracked mirror she'd found in the storeroom. She was going through ordinary motions, trying to make sense of her new life and line up the odd-shaped thoughts in a neat row. So much had happened, so suddenly.

Augie had put them up, just as Joey said he would. They'd turned the back storeroom into their apartment. Joey had even found a bed for them from somewhere. He wouldn't say where, though. Everything else they needed was already there—the kitchen, tables, chairs.

Augie moved his cot into the office. It was that old stinking thing Joey had slept on when he was recovering from his knife wound, and traces of Joey's blood were still visible. Every time Patcja went past it, she cringed. It was a daily reminder of how lucky she was—and how dangerous this place could be.

Augie said he didn't mind sleeping in the office, letting them have the back room. He seemed happy to let Joey work as bartender as payment for room and board. They got the apartment; Augie got a new bartender. The Corner could use some fresh blood, Augie said. Patcja had almost gagged at the mention of blood. She hoped there would be no more bloodshed here. She had had enough.

She was still feeling queasy these days. All the commotion with Pa walking in on them in the coal room hadn't helped, either. She'd had a breathing attack that was bad, scary. She had gotten dizzy and had to stay in bed. Joey told her to rest, that she would be fine. She was trying. She looked rather pale, though, from what she could see in the mirror. She pinched her cheeks for some color and bit her lips for more color. Maybe Joey would notice.

It was a weeknight, a night The Corner wasn't usually open. Augie was out somewhere; no one seemed to know where. Patcja had asked about him several times. No one had seen him for days. Word was, he had a woman in Back of the 'Yards who was kindly to him, took up with him even though Augie was older than dirt and had that loud, honking cough. Joey said Augie's honey was young—not much more than a girl. She was Italian and sassy, but she hated liquor.

One of the damned fool abolitionists. Believed in Prohibition, so they said.

This morning, Patcja had overheard some fellas talking. She had been trying to nap, but the men were too loud. Sounded like half a dozen of Joey's old friends from the mill and some from the stockyard, too, were in the next room, Augie's office. Sounded like they were all making themselves at home, like they owned the place, like they weren't afraid of Augie coming in and having a conniption fit. One of the fellas had said Augie's sweetie had joined the Temperance League and that she'd learned what *temper* meant. They had laughed as if it were the best joke in the world.

Patcja didn't like those snooty temperance women, either. Did Augie's woman have a banner and a sign on a stick? Did she march in parades and protests, on white horses and in carriages with ribbons dangling? Did she buddy up with the highfalutin' ladies, all of them demanding the right to vote and the end to drink?

Two crazy notions.

Maybe that was why Augie didn't bring his sweetie around to

The Corner. Maybe she thought she was too good for them? She probably was.

It was late morning, quiet in the place. Patcja made the bed, pulling up the old blanket—army green—and smoothing it out. She wished she could do the same for her worries, just wave a hand, wipe away the wrinkles, make everything smooth, like ice on a lake.

Joey sat at a table in the main room. As soon as he saw her coming in, he jammed something in his pocket. Something small. A glass vial, it looked like. *What the heck?* She thought of Pa and his toothache pills.

Elixirs for the weak; false courage for the cowardly.

Joey was writing notes in a ledger book he had starting keeping in his coat pocket. This was something new. But he never left that dumb little book out of reach, as if the pages were made of gold or held the recipe for turning tin to silver.

One window was open, letting in some light and some fresh air. The place could use a good airing out.

"Can I open more windows, Joey? Let some air in, shoo out some of this old cigarette stink?" Patcja asked.

"Sure, baby," he said absently, obviously paying more attention to the scribblings he was making in his book than to the words she said.

The fresh spring air and the breeze felt good, energizing. It would be a good day for accomplishments, first steps in her new life as a married woman.

Maybe she could talk to Ma. Maybe get a few things from the house: her nightgown, her hairbrush, her Bible—the little white one Sister Beatrice had given her on her First Communion. She had carried it with her to Mass every Sunday for many years. She hating leaving it behind.

But the thought of running into Pa made her nauseous. Maybe it would be better to not go, just ask her sister to bring her some things. *Maybe.*

Patcja went to the kitchen to make coffee and do some cleaning. If this was going to be her home, she would have to spruce it up, get rid of the pigsty filth that was layers deep. She looked around. It seemed like a daunting task.

She pictured her mother, continually in the kitchen scrubbing something—or telling her and Halina to scrub it. She looked old and tired in the image, confused. Patcja shuddered, chills running up her arm. Would she become like her mother?

Patcja closed her eyes, prayed. Took a deep breath.

She took a cup of hot coffee to Joey, carrying one for herself, as well.

"Can I sit with you, Joey? What are you busy with? Something important?"

"Yeah, you can sit down for a while," he said dismissively. "Yeah, it's important. Of course it's important. It's the map to our future, our fortune, baby. I have plans. *Big* plans." He turned the book so she could see small sketches. "I'll put a stage in the corner. And room for a piano, maybe. Add a menu for food. Can you cook, baby? Sing? I know you can dance."

"Oh, Joey, You're so funny! I can't dance! Or sing," she said, laughing.

"Well, we'll see about that. You have to help, you know. We're a team now, baby. You can be the star of our stage. Show off those lovely knees and lovely—"

"If you say so," Patcja agreed eagerly. "I'll help, Joey. I'm proud of you. Proud to be your wife."

"Just keep thinking that, 'cause I'm gonna make us a fortune, baby. Right here. Turn this piss-poor rat trap into something. Better than the drinking joints in Gary or Whiting. Better than Hammond or East Chicago. You know why?"

She shook her head.

"It's simple: there is no law here. Chicago coppers have no interest here—too far up the shit-creek, out in the swamp and the sticks, and not enough joints to pitch in for payoff. Indiana has no jurisdiction here. The G-men won't waste their time in a town with only one liquor joint, a couple of copper stills, and a hardware store for laughs. No mayor of its own for making speeches about the evils of whiskey," he said, holding up his coffee cup as if he were making a toast.

Patcja chuckled. How she loved to see him excited!

But he wasn't done with his speech.

"It's too far of a ride for Big Bill Thompson and his goons in blue. Besides, everyone knows the Chicago mayor is on the take. His office has more dirt than a hole to China used to have. And, hell, Governor Lowden, he's never even heard of Hegewisch, doesn't care nothing about a bunch of Polish immigrants who don't even speak English and can't write his name on a ballot. See, Patcja, it's invisible! Hegewisch is the *perfect* invisible stew pot," he said as he took her shoulders and looked in her eyes. "Good for cooking up whatever we want."

"*Anything?*"

"Well, almost," he answered, and kissed her on the nose, twisting some of her amber curls around his fingers and tugging.

"What about Augie? Doesn't he have some say?" she asked. "Isn't it up to him what happens with The Corner?"

Joey's smile disappeared, turning into something dark and secretive.

He pulled harder on the curl wrapped around his fingers.

"How about you go cook up some lunch for us, baby?" he said, not answering the question she had just asked.

Patcja found some sausage in the icebox, potatoes in a basket under the sink, cabbage, onions—all the Polish staples. What else could they need? Maybe Joey would give her some money so she could go to the grocers, stock up on some canned goods. At least until she could put in her own garden.

She heard sounds outside the kitchen door, in the alley. *Now what?*

It was Antonio. He stood in the alley, hat pushed back on his head, his long arms dangling and swinging, as though he was ready to dance; he just needed a partner and music. He had a silly, boyish smile on his face, as if he had just stolen a cookie from the pope's cookie jar.

"Hello, Patcja. Dear, sweet Patcja. A married lady now, I hear."

"Leave, Antonio. You have no business here. Leave us alone."

"Well, you see, that's why I'm here. That's the problem, Patcja—no business. Your Corner Tavern doesn't do business with the right suppliers," he said, staggering. "You don't sell our milk bottles here. Did you know that? My uncle Sal is pretty annoyed about it, too. Did you know that, Patcja?"

She could smell whiskey on him. And sweat, as though he had been working hard at something. Or running in circles.

"Antonio, I don't give a rat's ass about what your uncle Sal thinks or where Augie gets his whiskey from. Just leave us alone, will you, please? *Please*."

"Patcja, Patcja. You *should* care. That's what I'm here to warn you." Antonio pointed a finger at Patcja. He put his thumb up, cocking his fingers at her like a gun.

Patcja pushed his hand away.

"*Warn me?* What the hell do you mean? I'm married to Joey now. You don't scare me!"

"Not *me*, Patcja. *Sal.* And he has some other boys who work for him, ones who don't question his orders. Big Janusz. No sense in that fat skull of his. Those are the kinds you need to watch for, Patcja."

"Why are you telling me this? I don't believe you. You're just being mean."

Antonio stepped closer and whispered, "There's going to be a fire, Patcja."

"*What?*"

"A fire. And all the doors might be locked. Blocked. Then what?"

"Antonio, stop it! Tell your uncle to stop—Joey has nothing to do with how Augie runs the business. Joey's just the bartender."

"That's not what we hear, Patcja, honey."

"You're wrong," she insisted.

"Ask Joey where Augie is. See what he says. Then watch his right eye. I've played poker with that buffoon. His right eye twitches when he bluffs. It's his tell."

"What do you mean? Where is Augie? What do you know?" Patcja demanded.

"I wonder if dead Polacks sink or float when they're tossed into the lake?"

"Get out of here! Now, before I scream!"

"Bye, Patcja. I just wanted to warn you because I always liked you, Patcja. You and your sweet—" Antonio stepped through the alley door, into the kitchen. He grabbed Patcja's shoulders and pulled him to her. She pounded his chest with her fists, but it didn't stop him, only made him smirk. He kissed her hard, and she twisted away, repulsed.

"Hey—what's taking so long with that lunch, baby?"

Patcja turned, trying to break free from Antonio's grasp.

Joey came around the corner, into the kitchen. He stood in the doorway, confused, aghast. A long fuse lit.

And somewhere in the next room, glass shattered.

Chapter 52

Mary knocked on Baba's door. She didn't know where else to turn. The old woman had to be home. Had to be. Had to be.

C'mon, open the door, old woman!

She knocked again.

The wind had turned chilly. Even though the afternoon sun was out, the spring wind had a bite in it, coming across the lake. It reminded her of Lodz, of leaving Poland that night. The worst night of her life. It was spring then, too—with a harsh wind, just like this. She was frightened then, too.

Mary pulled her babushka down over her forehead. The wind nagged and needled. Annoying. Maybe she should go home. No, she couldn't. She needed help. The not knowing was making her crazy. She needed answers. *Where is Patcja?*

Finally, she heard footsteps behind the door. It creaked open.

"*Cześć, panienko, przyjaciółko.*"

"*Cześć.*"

The old woman held the door open so Mary could come in. They went to the kitchen, and Baba started the kettle without a word. Mary paced. She looked over the wall of medicine, half-full. A barrel of trashed ingredients stood in the middle of the floor, and the smell of smoke and charred spices and roots hung in the air. She noticed the patched walls. They still needed paint. They looked so out of place in this old shack. Too new, too clean, uppity and bragging. Mary didn't like their attitude, but she said nothing.

Baba moved slowly, it seemed, prolonging the kitchen tasks, preparing something.

Coffee? Tea? Arsenic? Redemption?

Mary bit her lip, then her thumbnail, trying to be patient. Hopeful.

Baba poured hot water into two mugs and spooned in something dark and rich. She added heaping spoons of sugar. Three spoons for Mary. Baba knew she had a sweet tooth. Baba knew her well—perhaps *too* well. Mary had confided in her so many times, come to her so many times when her girls were babies. And, of course, Baba had delivered the babies—at least, the last two, both such difficult births with complications. Baba knew why.

"Sit, Mary. Here. We will drink. Then, we talk. I will listen. *We* will listen." Baba moved the small statue of the Madonna to the center of the table and lit a small white candle.

Baba whispered, "Holy Mother of God, touch us with your blessings and guide us. Bind us together as sisters, drawing strength from each other. Give us vision, compassion. Heal us of our pains; forgive us our sins."

The drink was warm and sweet. Mary felt lighter already. Her ears rang with a song she could barely hear.

"I had a fire," Baba said, breaking the silence. "Small one, not too bad. I lost many of my supplies, though. A shame."

"I heard. I saw it, too. The flames climbed over your roof. I was asleep but woke up from the commotion. I looked out—"

"Chickens went crazy. Coop went up first. It was gone in minutes."

"And your house, it could have burned down completely! Then the rest of the block," Mary added with an arched eyebrow.

"Ah! *Nie, nie.* A tame fire. Trained to behave. Sometimes you need to purge the old. Make room for the new, some fresh wood, fresh paint, fresh blood. Halina was here. She helped put out the fire," Baba said.

"Oh? Did she have some hand in starting it, too? That girl—so careless with a lamp! Or was it a candle? I've told her a hundred times—"

"No, no. Hardly. I managed to start it all by myself. Stach cut the wood and piled it, but the rest was all me. Quite a feat, but I did it," Baba answered proudly.

Mary was confused. This woman sounded as though she had started the fire on purpose. Perhaps she was daft, like people said. A senile old witch.

Baba was focused on the candle, her face unmoving. Soon she seemed transfixed by the hypnotic dance of flame, like a sleepwalker, unseeing.

Mary watched the old woman, uncertain what to do. Again she thought about leaving. Mary could see the candle flame reflected in the old woman's glassy eyes. She watched the mirror image. It was mesmerizing.

The kitchen seemed hot. Mary wiped her sweaty hands on her dress, and the ringing in her ears grew louder. She heard the crackle of fire. She saw flames—not a candle flame, but giant flames climbing in the black sky, wood hissing and popping. She saw embers fly away, like electric bugs.

Mary shook her head, and the image was gone; so were the sounds. Baba was talking, but the words had no volume. Mary couldn't hear, as if her head were dunked under water. Baba's mouth moved; her hands gestured. Out of her fingertips came colors—magnificent, vibrant, unearthly.

Mary could smell the colors:

> *Green, like new grass.*
> *Red, like fresh blood.*
> *White, like the mucus film on a baby's face, in his nose, across his eyes.*

Something was wrong, very wrong. She didn't like floating, didn't like it at all. She was mad, and the rising anger cleared her mind. The old woman had drugged her!

Blasted tarnation!

Mary tried to land, to plant her feet firmly on the kitchen floor. She pushed her coffee cup away. She should have known better than to drink something brewed by the old woman.

"Ready for more coffee?" Baba asked.

"No, no." Mary shook her head. She grabbed hold of her purpose for coming. She hung on tightly. She focused.

"I don't need your coffee with potions, Baba. I need *answers*. I think you may have them. I came about Patcja. I'm worried. Where is she? Do you know? I saw you talking to her a few days ago. Why? What did she need? Is it her breathing fits? Did you give her medicine?"

Baba nodded. "I gave her a poultice to warm her lungs and an amulet to protect her—and sprinkled her with something for Joey, something little to make him hurry his affections. Patcja wanted to get married to the man, so I helped. Just a little."

"You *what*? How could—But where did they go? Where is she now?"

Baba shook her head, unsure. She took a pinch of sugar from the bowl and sprinkled it on the candle flame. The wick sizzled orange, then blue. Smoke danced toward the ceiling, curling wisps, ribbons, telling.

> *Glass shatters. A flaming rag ball hits the ground, rolls on the wooden floor;*
> *a vapor trail of gasoline fumes. Smolders, brooding, like a spoiled child, insistent. Flames crawl. More smoke.*
> *Girl runs to the pump. Pump. Pump.*

The smoke made Baba cough. She coughed louder, choking. She gasped. Mary tried patting her on the back, but it didn't help. The old woman's face was red and growing redder.

Mary went to the pump at the sink. She ran her hands under the flowing water.

Pump. Pump.

More water. She saw her daughter's hands in the water. She felt her daughter inhale deep breaths of acid-like, smoke-filled air. Patcja choked as Baba choked, as if they were in the same room; and Mary was looking in, the watcher.

Mary gave Baba the full glass. Their hands touched, passing the water from one to the other, sizzling like a smoldering current. Baba drank the water and was better. Mary hoped Patcja was better, too.

Patcja, Patcja.

"Is she all right? Is she safe? Where is the fire?" Mary pleaded of Baba.

"Patcja and Joey are at the tavern, The Corner. I see hands joined as one. They are married now. Joey is a big man now, taking over for Augie, buying bottles and bottles of tonic. And brown vials of poppy oil, devil's tears, he mixes with the whiskey. There is a blackness where Augie used to be, a deep hole filled with water and molten metal. And mystery. Now enemies play with fire," Baba said.

Mary tried to absorb the news. "Married? To Joey? *Why?* Why couldn't she marry a nice Polish boy?"

"Joey will make a good papa, she thinks."

"Oh, I see," said Mary. "I understand now."

Envelope, fat with bills, money for the ship and secrets,
Papa thrusts to the boy, innocent, young, Fryddie, so weak
with grief.
"Take it. Take her," the old man insists, shame burdened,
fearing a soldier's revenge.
A captain haunts, his heart pierced by a pitchfork red with

German blood.
One daughter, with golden curls, hangs, self-condemned,
from barn rafters,
her swinging shadow, back and forth, like the clapper of a
bell tolling,
begging for mercy that didn't come.
Another daughter must run. Run. Run, before she is
arrested, shamed,
or the soldier's child is born.
Fryddie takes the envelope, sells his soul.
Marianna washes dried blood from her hands and packs.

Baba nodded.

They sat a while. Neither spoke, wallowing in their own silences and mourning the innocent who were lost—then and now. It was so quiet they could hear the flame of the candle nibbling on the wick, wax melting, dripping.

Finally Mary spoke. "What should I do?"

"Pray. Then send her somewhere. Away—where fire doesn't reach."

Chapter 53

Halina checked on Margret and found she was about the same: weak, in pain, unable to eat much. The fever had gone down, and her breathing and pulse were improved, but there was still a large bulge in her lower abdomen that hurt to touch. Sitting up was unbearably painful, as her ribs pressed against the swollen area.

Halina had hoped that putting pressure on the mass might make it rupture so it would drain. Or maybe it could be expelled—one way or another. But that wasn't happening on its own. She was either going to have to cut it out with a knife; stab it and drain it through a tube; or reach inside Margret's *piczka* to poke the infection, soak it up, and pull out the lumpy thing—whatever it was. None of those ideas sounded fun—for her *or* for Margret.

Halina went to class as usual the next day. She arrived early and went straight to the residents' library, where the fat books were stored. No one stopped her. No one even seemed to notice. Maybe it would be her lucky day.

But the shelves held hundreds of books. Where to start? She ran her fingers over the spines, scanning titles as she walked, hoping one would stand out. Since Margret's pain had started after a pregnancy, Halina was fairly certain that the problem was related to her womb. That was all she knew.

It didn't take long to find the books on female anatomy, gyne-cology, and obstetrics, thanks to illustrations on the covers. They all showed line drawings, a cross-section of a woman with an unborn baby inside her, upside down. The illustrations never showed a face, never the agony or elation that was in the woman's heart because of the child that would soon change her life—for better or worse.

Halina chose the book that showed the most wear, its pages dog-eared and its spine cracked, consulted many times by residents. She took it to the corner table and tried to make sense of it.

She might as well have been trying to read a book written in Greek. The long words and medical terms seemed like gibberish. She felt as if she were trying to crack an impossible code.

Soon, she gave up on the words and concentrated on the illustrations. Some were intricate line drawings; others were simple outlines, with numbers and corresponding labels. All of them were a surprise. She'd had no idea there were things called the uterus, ovaries, and fallopian tubes that connected them. Amazing.

She wished she had more time to study the pictures, but it was time for class. She looked around. Two young men in white coats sat at tables across the room. They both had their heads down, focused on books they were reading. Good.

Halina slid the book on obstetrics into the satchel at her feet and hurried out, the big carpetbag on her shoulder weighing her down. She almost regretted taking it, but not enough to make her turn around and put it back. She hurried to class.

Today's topic was anesthesia and pain control. It was hard to concentrate. The images from the obstetrics book kept bouncing around in her head, shifting old ideas, rippling and cascading.

And not only did the pictures apply to Margret; they applied to her, too. Halina had those parts inside of her! Her own body had been hiding secrets she knew nothing about. She put a hand on her side, where she thought an ovary might be. She pressed hard, harder, but she felt nothing. Maybe the book was wrong, or maybe there was something wrong with her. Maybe her ovaries hadn't come in yet.

Halina tried to focus on the class. Nurse Neuberger stood at the front of the room talking about ether and how to administer it. She was holding up a thing with a handle and net that looked like a strainer or flour sifter—might be good at separating an egg yolk from the whites, too. A nice, handy little thing. But apparently, it went over the patient's nose with a cloth in it, and the nurse was supposed to drip ether into the mask-cup-mesh thingy. She didn't explain if it should be big, fat drips or little prissy, puny drips, but Halina was afraid to ask, not wanting to call attention to herself or the satchel under her chair.

Nurse Neuberger moved on to chloroform and its effects and then morphine and opium administered to reduce pain. Halina took detailed notes, even though she had to guess at how to spell the words that were so important.

"Unfortunately, morphine and other opium derivatives can be obtained illegally on the black market in many cities, allowing these powerful drugs to be abused by unsavory characters lacking in moral convictions. Criminals and low-class burdens on society often turn to opiates to ease their guilty consciences and hide in a false sense of wellness," the nurse said. She looked straight at Halina.

Nurse Neuberger went on, saying, "Charlatans are also known to include small doses of the drugs in their tonics and witch-doctor elixirs, fooling patients into mistaking a drugged euphoria for health and wellness, until the patient eventually becomes addicted."

Halina had a spark of realization. It was suddenly so clear. Pa's toothache pills were like that. How interesting. And now Pa was addicted. Did that mean he couldn't stop even if he wanted to?

"Now I will demonstrate," Nurse Neuberger said. She pulled a giant doll from the cabinet at the back of the room. The doll was used to show students proper techniques when she couldn't get a volunteer. It was life-sized but didn't look much like a real person, its yarn hair unraveling and its muslin body losing stuffing here and there, limbs coming loose from repeated bandaging and tourniquet demonstrations, button eyes hanging by strings.

It reminded her of the scarecrow in the garden, face stitched into burlap with weather-worn yarn. She remembered hiding behind the stuffed plaid shirt, afraid of Pa as he tended to his trash fire. Now, that seemed so absurd.

Afraid? What was I afraid of? That old man, sick, tangled in the grip of poppy-colored chains?

Halina took pages of notes and even drew a little picture in her notebook of how the net was to be positioned over the patient's face to cover the nose and mouth completely. She tried to picture Margret's face, calm, feeling no pain, asleep.

If she only had some ether . . .

After class Halina went to the sixth-floor orthopedics ward to check in with Nurse Davies and start her shift.

The nurse, sitting at the floor desk, chuckled when Halina came up to the counter.

"I see you finally got white shoes. Paint—a nice touch," Nurse Davies said.

"Like 'em?"

"Well, they are a creative solution to a problem—I'll give you that."

That was all the small talk Nurse Davies had time for today. She sent Halina to make rounds. That meant bedpans. Nurse Davies returned to her paperwork—files for each patient, records of medicines administered, inventory of supplies. Glass cabinets were along the back wall of the nurses' station—some locked, some not. Keys were on a circular metal keyring. It jingled like bells on a sleigh horse when Nurse Davies tossed it in the top drawer of her desk. Halina watched, noticing where the keys fell in the shallow drawer. Far to the right, behind a tin of thumbtacks.

Two other nurses were on duty today, too. Nurse Bug Eyes worked on one half of the ward. On the other side, it was the skinny-ass one, Nurse No Butt, who looked as though she would blow away in a strong wind. Both nurses were all serious, all rules, all antiseptic and silence. They could be in a competition to see who was the grouchiest. Nurse No Butt would probably win. She was small but fierce.

Nurse Bug Eyes—with her thick, round glasses—could be caught smiling at patients when she couldn't help herself. Her smiles were worse than her frowns, though, revealing pointy little teeth that were yellow and stained with cigarette smoke and coffee. That woman loved her coffee. She kept a thermos and a big coffee mug close by, no matter where she worked or what she did. Today Nurse Bug Eyes was assigned the right side of the ward, the serious cases. She was making her rounds, checking vitals, making notes on the clipboards at the end of the beds, pen in one hand, coffee mug in the other.

Halina tried to keep her distance. She pushed her cart stacked with bedpans—both clean and dirty—down the hall, starting at the end with room 623. Mr. Jenkins, the man with the crushed leg who had been in so much pain, was still there in the last bed. He seemed asleep. His face was almost as white as the sheets that were pulled up to his chin. His bad leg was still propped up on a pillow. It was under a sheet, but from the mound, she could tell it was chopped off at about the knee. Some blood seemed to be seeping through the bandages, through to the sheet. A wet spot, dark like fresh blood, was showing through, the size of a quarter. That couldn't be good. Wasn't he supposed to be all sewn up, the stump of his leg patched over with some skin stretched over the bone and muscles? She wondered what they had done with the part they chopped off. Had it been thrown into the trash? Tossed in the dump with rusted fenders and moldy rags, where rats could chew on it?

She shuddered, chills running up her arms.

As she came closer, Halina could see the man's breaths were shallow and slow, as if his tired brain had to ponder each one. He didn't seem long for this world. Only a few days ago, he had begged her to help. And what had she done? She'd run to Nurse Davies.

No more morphine yet, the nurse had said. *He must wait. We have rules*, she had said. *Too bad*, she had said.

Damn the rules.

Halina crept closer to the man's bed.

"Hey there, Mr. Jenkins. You awake? You need the bedpan? I got my cart. I can help you."

He tried to open his eyes, but his eyelids were crusty with yellow gunk. He rolled his head, left to right, saying no. His lips parted, but no sound came out. Too weak, drifting off to the hereafter, like floating down a lazy river, taking his time, meandering off to meet God.

Maybe it would be best. Maybe not.

She wondered if a priest had heard his confession and performed last rites. It wouldn't be good to have him floating off to heaven without his sins forgiven. Halina took her rosary out of her pocket, kissed the crucifix that was warm with her body heat, and put it in the man's hand. His fingers moved, ever so slightly. She wished she could think of something else to do.

She knew what Baba would do: Coffee. And yelling. And some whacks on the bed with a wooden spoon. And some singing. That's what this man needed. Some noise. Get the heart pumping and fearing and the scared-of-dying juices flowing. He needed some riling and wailing, some commotion to get him kicking in that lazy river and turned around, back to the living. One leg or not, he ought to have some good fight left in him, at least enough, shouldn't he?

Halina put her mouth close to the man's ear. He smelled like antiseptic soap.

"Mr. Jenkins, you need to wake up," she whispered to him. "And come back to the living."

His eyes fluttered.

She repeated it, this time louder. "Mr. Jenkins, you need to wake up and come back to the living!"

His eyes fluttered open further, focused. Then he shut them tightly.

Halina pulled back one eyelid with her thumb. "I see you in there. No more hiding. *Enough!* Time to quit this lazy-ass drifting to heaven *bzdury* you think you can get away with. Time to do some kicking upstream in that pity river you are floating in!" She stomped her foot and whacked the foot of his bed with her hand. "Hear me?"

"What's going on in here?"

Halina turned around. It was Nurse Bug Eyes in the doorway.

"Ah—nothing! I mean, Mr. Jenkins asked for some water. I said I would get it for him."

The nurse hesitated, skeptical. Then she came in.

"So you are finally awake, Mr. Jenkins? Then let's just see how you are doing, shall we?"

The nurse bustled around the man, taking his pulse, temperature, and blood pressure, then making notes in his chart before leaving to get supplies for changing the dressing and the afternoon medicine.

"Sorry I yelled at you," Halina whispered in the man's ear when the nurse was gone. "And I'm sorry I lied about you wanting water. I just had to—"

"Water . . . ," the man groaned. "Water . . ."

Halina poured some water for him and tried holding the cup to his lips. She lifted his head to make it easier. He sipped. First small sips, then more. And more.

"Well, look at you, Mr. Jenkins! Good for you," Halina said. "I knew you could do it."

Nurse Bug Eyes was back. She frowned, shooing Halina out of the way.

"Aren't you supposed to be tending to bedpans?"

The nurse brought a metal tray of supplies—fresh bandaging, gauze, funny-shaped scissors, and small, clear bottles of medicine. And her coffee mug. The nurse set them all on the bedside table. Halina tried to read the labels on the bottles but couldn't quite make out what they said.

She had to know.

She intentionally knocked over an empty bedpan. It made an awful clatter, but as she bent to retrieve it, she got a closer look at the bottles, one long enough to read the labels. *Morphine*. And she also got a whiff of the nurse's coffee. It wasn't plain coffee. Smelled just like Pa's coffee.

Useful information, indeed.

"Oh, look—your mug is almost empty," Halina said to the nurse, as innocently as possible. "Why don't you finish this last couple of swallows, and I'll fetch your thermos for you? Go ahead."

Nurse Bug Eyes shrugged and gulped down half a mug of whiskey-laced coffee. Halina ran to the nurses' station and was back with the thermos just as Nurse Bug Eyes was pulling back the sheet to look at Mr. Jenkins's bandaged leg stump.

With some persistent urging, the nurse took a few more swallows before she started removing the bandages. Then some more before she started cleaning away the blood that had seeped from the black stitches.

"Look how well you are healing, Mr. Jenkins!" the woman squealed. She sounded almost giddy over the way the leg was mending. She hummed, then whistled a tune.

Halina started worrying she had primed the nurse with *too* much coffee. She didn't want her dancing in the hallways and swinging from the IV poles.

Egads, woman! Can't you hold you liquor?

But she didn't say it aloud. Instead, Halina hovered near the tray, hand on the table, fingers crawling toward the bottles. Three of them. She recognized the name on only one but figured that if they were good for Mr. Jenkins, they might help Margret, too. They certainly couldn't hurt, could they?

This was her chance. Halina grabbed the bottles in one swoop and shoved them in her uniform pocket. She felt as if she was being watched. Hairs on the back of her neck stood up. Halina looked around. The other men in the ward were all staring at the ceiling or sleeping. The nurse was dabbing at the leg, along the stitches, with iodine-soaked gauze. Halina noticed Mr. Jenkins. His eyes were open, staring at her. He looked at her bulging pocket, then back at her eyes, then back to her pocket.

He knew.

He winced as though pain was shooting into his brain. He held out his hand with her rosary.

"Take it," he whispered. "I don't want anything from you."

Nurse Bug Eyes didn't notice.

Suddenly, raised voices rang down the hallway. Halina heard an argument—stern voices, some kind of fuss. The sounds came from the direction of the nurses' station.

Could it be? No. Surely not!

Halina put her hand in her pocket to keep the medicine bottles from rattling as she ran to the doorway. What was all the commotion about? Was that a voice she recognized? The man's voice—

Holy Mary, Mother of God.

It *was* him—Stach. He was at the nurses' station. What was he doing there? Yesterday he had said he wouldn't help her steal medicine. He had been all high and mighty about it, too, wanting nothing to do with her idea. Had he changed his mind?

Or did he come to stop me?

Chapter 54

Glass shattered. Patcja ran toward the sound, leaving Antonio and Joey in the kitchen to glare and fume at each other. As she entered the tavern's main room, a flaming ball streaked through a shattered window. It landed and rolled across the floor. From the smell of it, it was made of fabric strips soaked in gasoline.

Patcja screamed, "Joey, help!"

A line of flames smoldered in the ball's wake, biting into the wooden floor. The fireball stopped under a table, flames taking hold.

Patcja stomped on the line of flames, trying to put them out. Smoke swirled around her feet, under her skirt, making the thin fabric billow like a cloud. The line, running from the window to the table, was just smoldering embers now, but the fireball under the table was growing.

Panic crawled up her spine. She remembered the agony of fire eating her arm.

"Joey! Joey! Come quick!"

She ran back to the kitchen, passing Joey as he stumbled into the room. She rushed to the pump at the sink and started filling a bucket.

Pump. Pump. Pump.

She pumped the red lever as quickly as she could. Joey grabbed the half-full bucket and ran with it.

Splash. Sizzle.

Patcja found a washbasin and started filling it. Joey came back to the kitchen and traded with her, taking the basin, giving her the bucket to refill. They did this five times, maybe six. Each time, Joey took the bucket or basin; then Patcja would hear the splash and hiss of water on flames. With each toss of water, the sizzle was less. The fire was out, but the smoke remained, hovering in the air, wet and heavy. The smell was bitter.

Patcja couldn't breathe. She felt as if fingers were clawing at her throat, a rope around her neck, strangling her.

"*Help*, Joey!" But her voice was weak.

Patcja stumbled out the kitchen door to the alley, wheezing. The fresh air hit her face, slapped her cheeks, made her gasp. She forced herself to take longer, slower breaths. Deep breaths.

Inhale slowwwwwlllly. Exhale slowwwwwllly.

She had the spell under control. She had stopped it in time.

"Thank you, Jesus," she said, crossing herself, grateful the fire was contained and that her breathing spell was minor, not too serious—this time.

Joey came to the alley door. His pant legs and shoes were wet; his sleeves, too. His face was red, a blue vein bulging on his forehead.

"Why are you out here?" he shouted. "Are you okay? Are you hurt?"

"I'm fine, Joey. Is the fire out?" Patcja pulled her sleeve down over the scars on her arm. "Are you okay, Joey?" she asked.

"Yes, it's out. I'm *fine*—no thanks to you, baby." His voice had changed. His eyes were dark and squinting, drilling holes into her.

"What? *Me?* What do you mean?"

"Why was Antonio here, Patcja? Did you invite him to come by? You two have something going on?"

"Joey! Of course not! That bum?"

"Yeah, that no-good, slimy, Sicilian bum. Why was he here?" he demanded again.

"He said he came to warn me. There would be fire, he said. His uncle was angry at you. We should be careful, he told me."

"He came to tell *you*? *You*? You!" Joey shouted. Then he slapped her face.

Patcja fell back to the wall.

"*He's* worried about *you*? Concerned about *you*?" He slapped her again. "Why would that be, Patcja? Tell me!" He grabbed her arm and twisted it, pulling her closer.

"No, Joey! It's not like that!" She grabbed a broom with her free hand and held it between them. It became her shield, a worthless protection made of stick and straw.

"No, Patcja? Then, how is it? You and Antonio have plans, a future planned out?"

"No. He said there will be more fires. His uncle—"

Joey let go of her arm, shoved her away.

"Salvatore thinks he can scare us away," he said. "Is that it? *Hmmm?*"

"He wants you to sell *his* whiskey, the milk bottles. And—and he says something happened to Augie. Where is Augie, Joey? What are *you* hiding, Joey?"

"Sell *his* whiskey? Not on your life." Joey turned to walk away, rolling up his wet sleeves as he went.

"That's what I'm afraid of, Joey. I'm afraid." Patcja rubbed her cheek. Maybe she had deserved that slap. Maybe not.

She stood up taller. Then she took a deep breath and asked again—louder this time, "What happened to Augie?"

"Augie? He decided to leave town. Don't worry about it. It's done. He won't be back. It's for the better."

Patcja wanted to believe that, but she looked at Joey and saw his right eye twitch. Just as Antonio said it would. Joey was lying.

Patcja was crushed. She wanted to be happy and safe. With Joey and the baby. She wanted it all. She needed it, deserved it.

What had Joey done to Augie? Could she be next?

It was this tavern. All this whiskey.

"Maybe we should leave town, too, Joey—you and me. Get away from here, away from Sal and Antonio and his boys. Janusz and Krzysztof are always sneaking around. They give me the creeps, Joey." Patcja shuddered. "And my pa, Joey—he'll never be right with me marrying you. Nothing seems right in this stupid town anymore."

"Leave? *Run?* Never! The tavern is *mine* now. I've got what I want. I'm not giving up a thing. That means you, too, baby."

"I'm afraid of fire, Joey. I can't help it." She held out her arm, showing him the scars, as if that would explain her intense fear. "I was burned once, really bad. Look."

He looked at her scars. He had seen them before. He had touched her arm before, even kissed the scars before, in the dark, his lips on the uneven patches, the puckered and rippled skin.

"Fire? There are plenty of things worse than fire, baby," he said. "Stop worrying. I've got it covered."

She wanted to believe him. Patcja leaned into Joey, resting her head on his shoulder. She sighed. It would be so nice to trust him, to let him take care of her. She rubbed her cheek, still feeling the sting of his slap.

"Enough," he said pushing her away. "You mop up this mess. I'll see to the window," Joey said.

Patcja looked past Joey's shoulder, down the alley. Movement caught her eye. It was big, old Janusz, stupid Janusz, strolling down the alley toward a waiting milk truck. Grinning like a little boy with a sack of penny candy. Swaying, unbalanced. Carrying a gasoline can—red and yellow, the color of flames and agony.

Patcja could hear the gas slosh in the can as Janusz ambled away.

He'd be back, she knew.

She couldn't stay. She knew that, too.

Chapter 55

Stach was at the nurses' station, making a commotion, shouting and waving his arms as if he were trying to wake the dead—or at least half of the ward. Nurse Davies was facing off with him, insisting that he hush. She had a clipboard in her hand and looked as though she might swing it at him. Her face was all scrunched up in that look that meant she was thoroughly disgusted and beyond annoyed. She was angry and not about to let some strange visitor disturb the order on *her* floor while she was in charge.

Halina rushed down the hallway toward Stach. What was he up to? And why had he shown up there after he had said he wanted nothing to do with her plan? Perhaps he had changed his mind. Perhaps if he carried on long enough, loud enough, Halina could get her hands on those keys in the drawer and open the medicine cabinets.

As she came closer, she could hear Stach's odd ranting. *What an act!*

"I tell you, nurse, I simply must see my dear brother right now—visiting hours or not! I *must* see him—*now*! I demand it. Or, with the Holy Mother Mary as my witness, I swear, these hallowed halls just may come tumbling down with the wrath of God." Stach pointed upward as he ranted, his voice booming like a traveling tent preacher's.

Oh, how wonderful of him!

For a second, Halina was overwhelmed with relief and appreciation. He had come through after all. Stach was a gallant man, beautiful in his unkempt passion, his curly hair hanging about his ears. He was elegant in his brutal, bare simplicity. Passion. Conviction. Halina knew he was there for one reason: to help her.

"I am sorry. You *must* keep your voice down, though, sir. And, I repeat, there will be *no* visitors on my floor unless it is during official visiting hours," Nurse Davies answered, her voice rising into something shrill and grating.

"But my reason is most urgent. Lives depend on it! My brother's life, *my* life!"

Halina came up behind Nurse Davies as quietly as possible, still not sure what Stach had in mind. Did he have a plan? Or was this odd riot act of yelling and waving his hat and pointing at God his idea of a plan? If so, it was kind of a lousy plan. Well, maybe she could still get the keys.

She nodded at Stach. He winked ever so slightly and then started in again, moving down the hall, away from the nurses' desk, as though he was going to find his imaginary brother, come hell or high water.

"Nurse, I have been called here by God. My brother is . . . is . . . is . . ." Stach faltered, seeming to run out of story. He groped for the string's end—and found it. "He is on the brink of despair, dying! And I must give him the message that our dear, sickly mother forgives him. She forgives him! Glory to God! He should hear it before, before—"

"Sir, I don't care what your message is . . ."

Stach and Nurse Davies carried on, back and forth. Halina tuned them out and focused on the desk drawer. The keys were there! She grabbed them and hurried to the medicine cabinet. She found the bottles she wanted and had the cabinet relocked and the keys returned to the desk before Stach had exhausted his excuses for distracting Nurse Davies.

Halina, with two pockets full of medicine bottles and a hypodermic needle, ran down the stairs to the third floor where her locker was located. The glass bottles clinked as she ran. The needle poked at her. Thank goodness the floor seemed empty. The classes for the day were over; residents were on their rounds; the other candy stripers were on their assigned floors. She shoved the loot in her satchel, already fat with the obstetrics book, and slammed the locker with no problems. She was home free.

Until she ran into Nurse Neuberger. The nurse was reading while she walked, concentrating on the top paper in a stack of papers, folders, and—of course—the clipboard.

Halina was looking behind her as she walked, not ahead.

They collided, and Nurse Neuberger screamed, startled.

"Holy Mother Mary!" exclaimed Halina, falling back on her butt. Papers went flying.

"You! Look where you are walking, please!" scolded the nurse, as if she were talking to a mischievous child.

Halina apologized repeatedly as she knelt on the floor, hastily scooping up papers and stacking them.

Wait! They were evaluation reports—one for each student. Her name popped out at her.

Should she look?

No! Yes!

She scanned the page as quickly as possible. Checkmarks, checkmarks, checkmarks.

At the bottom, scrawled handwriting in red pencil . . . The words seemed to scream from the page: *Unorthodox. Interrupts class with inappropriate questions. Lack of respect for proper procedures. Needs self-discipline* . . .

Halina gasped, all the air sucked out of her lungs. She was crushed, afraid to read more, yet she couldn't stop herself.

. . . but shows innate understanding of patient care. Exhibits desire to learn. Strong potential, despite her questionable upbringing.

Nurse Neuberger snatched the papers from Halina's shaking hands and rushed off down the long, empty hall, her white shoes squeaking on the polished floor.

Halina returned to the sixth floor to finish her shift.

Chapter 56

Mary had never been in The Corner Tavern before. She had no business there. If she had been younger or more interested in keeping up the pretense of her marriage, she might have gone there looking for Fryderyk a few times. But she had no soap-bubble delusions that made her try to fuss about the man and follow him around, hoping to make him something he wasn't. That would have been stupid, she knew, and she wasn't stupid on most days.

She also knew that her girls didn't need to suffer from the man's foul temper and meanness simply because his real love, Stella, had been lost to him during the war.

Stella—if only she had left with the Gypsy caravan as Papa had wanted. Stella was so headstrong, so, so, so . . .

Mary's walk up the three steps to The Corner's double door seemed monumental, as difficult as climbing a mountain. Still, she made herself do it, one foot after another. She was out of breath. It was not from some big physical exertion, just her heart pounding, scared for Patcja and what Patcja would say or *not* say. It was hard to guess about that girl. Keeping a serious thought in her head was never one of Patcja's strengths. Poor thing. Mary wanted to do right for her.

Patcja was married?

She vaguely remembered giving the girl a wreath for her hair and her prized red-and-black silk babushka.

"What did you wear on your wedding day, Ma?"

"There wasn't much time. . . . in such a hurry so we could travel that night . . . the backroads. Papa made arrangements . . . a merchant ship.

"Papa said we must get married. But dear Fryddie loved Stella, not me.

"No, Papa! No, Papa!

"Stella ran to the barn. She found a rope.

"I made a wreath for my hair, and Mama gave me her beautiful red-and-black babushka with long, silky fringe.

"There's no saving Stella. She's gone."

Mary heard the words in her head, but the images felt like a dream or maybe a play she had watched from the side of the stage, behind the curtain. Mary wondered what had become of her babushka. She loved the red silk and black fringe—so elegant, colorful, heart-throbbing and dangerous, like dancing near fire.

There. Her mind went wandering again, her heart skipping beats.

What is wrong with me?

Something was wrong with her mind, she knew. She had tried confessing her sins, as if that might help. Father Chodniewicz had said God forgave her, but the good father couldn't possibly know, couldn't possibly understand what had happened during those last days in Poland.

Baba knew.

Mary, when she was a young bride having just arrived in America, had confessed to the old woman, had told her sad story over magic tea that loosened the lips. Mary had talked, reliving the ordeal.

"I fell to the ground, muddy, beside the river, among the tall grass. At first it felt like cramps. Then the pain was overwhelming, consuming. It ate through me. 'Za wcześnie! Jeszcze nie! Nie!' Too early! Too soon!

Fryderyk put his hand over my mouth. 'Shut up!' he said. 'They'll hear us,' he said. He was so frightened.

"We could hear soldiers nearby. We heard the hollow sound of boots on the wooden bridge. 'Achtung!' Halt! 'Wo gehen sie?' We didn't know if they were talking to us or not.

"The moon came out from behind a cloud, and in the sudden moonlight, my white apron over my dress seemed to glow. I was horrified, tried burying myself. Fryderyk fell across me, hiding me. His black coat and gray trousers blended in better, but his weight added to my agony. I could feel the warm gushes of blood. And I could see past Fryddie to see the trickling stream of red though the dirt, to the bank of the river. Blood pooled in footprints, and I kept thinking, that is from me, that's me.

"The soldiers walked on paths along the river's edge. We were farther back in the farm field. It had been harvested already, and only brown empty stalks were left.

"The baby arrived silent. So small. Months too early. He fit in Fryddie's palm, bloody, blue cord attached. The baby was covered in white mucus film and blood. Fryddie wiped the baby's face with his handkerchief and put the baby in his hat. It was a cradle and casket. He handed the hat to me. It weighed nothing, like nothing was there. Fryddie started clawing at the dirt, his face like stone that was crumbling. He dug a grave, small, shallow, not nearly deep enough, but we needed to hide the baby from the soldiers—and the animals.

"I touched the tiny hand, kissed the fingers. They were see-through, like bug wings. Then I got on my knees and pawed at the earth, too, even as I dripped blood. We both knew it was futile. Wolves that come down from the hills in packs would eventually find him. That tiny, fragile body, the tiny hand . . .

"We had to get to the ship before it left the port. The captain already had been paid all our money. It was still hours away. The ship would leave at dawn—with or without us."

Mary made up her mind: she had to help Patcja so she could have her baby in a safe place. She had also made inquiries and plans.

It hadn't been as hard as she'd thought it would be. Women talked; they gossiped about such things. It had been easy to steer conversations toward such unsavory topics, asking about that girl, years back, who had lived in the neighborhood, then left mysteriously for a few months. Someone had known the name of the place where she had gone, a convent in Indiana—south. St. Mary's of the Woods. It took in girls.

Mary had the name of the town and the convent—even bus fare, a few dollars she had been saving from her laundry money. Now she needed to convince Patcja it was the right thing to do.

She remembered what Baba had told her:

"She must leave. Patcja isn't safe here. The baby is in danger," Baba said with an urgent tone, certain of the future she was predicting. "There will be more fires and smoke. She won't be able to breathe in the smoke. She'll be afraid, and her breathing spells will get worse. Patcja is so afraid of fire, you know."

"What can I do?"

"Make her go away until the baby is born. Then she can be brave and fight the beasties that breathe fire."

The light was shallow, early evening. No man was standing watch at The Corner's door, deciding who could come in or who would be sent away. Mary had been practicing what she would say to the door guard, but it was a relief to not have to be approved to enter. She just strolled in as if she belonged there. Confident, even though her knees were weak and her hands were sweaty. She pulled her sweater tighter across her chest, fiddled with the buttons, preached to herself.

Jesus loves you. God provides.

Now what? Where was Patcja?

Mary walked farther in, looked around. Golden rays of light slipped in through brushstroke gaps and places where the black paint curled away from the glass panes of the windows. Dust hung in the air, the gritty red steel dust from the mill. She could smell smoke from a fire and wet wood, wet grease, old beer, whiskey, and piss and cigarettes. It was familiar and yet strange.

The beer hall in Wrzesnia had smelled of beer, but not this kind of filth. The Jakubowski family had owned that fine hall in the village, had run it for generations. Mary and Stella had worked there, sweeping, mopping, helping at the counter, helping in the kitchen, serving good, hard-working men. It had been an honorable job.

Until the soldiers came.

Do as we say, and you won't be hurt. This is our headquarters now. You will tend to it and to the men. Cook; bring them food, drink, whatever they want. There will be patrols. They will need directions. You will be their guides, help them find the Polish cowards who hide in barns and sheds, shirking their duty to serve alongside our troops.

"Patcja! Patcja, where are you? I've come to talk to Patcja," Mary called out.

The curtain across the doorway moved. Mary held her breath.

Patcja peeked out of the doorway. Mary waved, relieved to see her.

"Mama!"

Patcja rushed to her mother and hugged her, stooping down so she could put her head on her mother's shoulder. How nice of her—a good girl, a dear girl.

Mary smoothed Patcja's hair, her fingers fluttering over the tangled curls.

"Why is your hair in such a mess, Patcja? Haven't I always told you—?"

"What are you doing here, Ma?"

"Patcja—we must talk. Where can we talk?" Mary asked her daughter, looking around.

Patcja led her mother to the corner table, near a window that had been boarded up. Pieces of glass were still on the floor.

How careless. Someone could be hurt.

"Who made this mess, Patcja? They should clean it up."

"I know, Ma. I know. I was—I will finish after a while, though. I was tired. I had to lie down . . ."

Mary held her daughter's hand. A lovely hand. Five fingers, healthy, lovely. And she turned the hand over and saw the burns up her arm. Mary traced the lines and shuddered. She patted the hand and kissed it, swallowing the guilt the scars always stirred in her. The burns were her fault. She had known that night Fryderyk was drunk, angry. She had known he was stumbling around with a whiskey bottle in one hand and a lantern in the other. She hadn't stopped him. Even when she heard him clump down the stairs to the coal room, Mary hadn't stopped him, hadn't warned Patcja. She had done nothing. Even when she heard Patcja's screams, she had done nothing, paralyzed with fear of the dark, seeing German soldiers in the shadows, fearing another visit from Hans, the one who had held her down in the dark of the pigsty. His uniform buttons—trophies—were hidden in a cigar box in her dresser drawer, a continuous reminder of her sins.

What a pathetic mother she had been. Well, this time she could be better. She could help Patcja, send her away, where she would be safe.

Patcja pulled her arm away. She pulled her sleeve down over her wrist and held it tight.

"It's a little late to be sorry, Ma," Patcja said. She sounded angry. She sounded sad, defeated.

"I know, Patcja," Mary said, shaking her head sadly. "But it's not too late for you. You need to leave now."

"How can I leave, Ma? Joey and I are married now. Where would I go? Why?"

"I found a convent. Sisters who will take in girls—girls in trouble. I have bus fare for you. I've been saving from the laundry money. Quite a wad I have hidden in a coffee can, buried by the back door. You're not safe here, Patcja," Mary urged.

"How do you know?" Patcja looked hard at her mother, wondering what she had heard.

"Baba knows. She *sees*."

"*Pffft!* That old woman!" said Patcja, starting to get up. Then she hesitated. "What does she know? What does she see?"

"Fire," said Mary.

Patcja gasped, her fear of fire showing in her anguished face.

Joey came out of the back room. He looked more surprised to see Mary than Patcja had been. Mary hadn't planned to see Joey, the bum. She wished she had some place to hide, some way of slipping out unnoticed.

Too late.

"Well, hello, *Madre* Mary!" said Joey, opening his arms wide. "Welcome to The Corner! Just in time—we could use someone to clean up this mess for us, eh, Patcja? Why don't you get your mama the broom?"

"Joey, no. Don't talk to Ma like that," Patcja said, standing up, moving in front of her mother.

Mary froze.

Jesus loves me. God provides. Jesus loves me. Holy Mother Mary . . .

"What? She brought her own broom? Good," Joey sneered in Patcja's face, pointing at her mother. "'Cause I wouldn't give the old woman a broom to sweep with or a pot to piss in."

"Joey! Stop that! Don't talk like that!"

He laughed.

"I'm just kidding, baby! Just a joke, baby!"

He picked up the broom that was leaning against the wall and handed it to Mary with a formal gesture and a malicious wink.

"Clean up all you want, Madre. *All you want*. But the shift change is at four. The ol' factory boys will be coming around for their drinks. Be sure to be done by then—we need to be open for business."

Joey went back to the office, chuckling. He pulled a small brown vial out of his pocket and tossed it in the air, as if it were a lucky coin.

Mary started sweeping. Why not? It would help her daughter, and there was no point in making more trouble. She had already seen enough. Working for Sal as his special cleaning lady meant she saw what happened to women—or men—who made trouble. At first, it was only once a month or so that she was summoned. Then, more and more. There would be puddles or stains to try to wash away. Splatters were the worst. And getting the mess on her hands—where to wipe them? She thought of the bloody handprint on the sheet that Halina had found.

Mary's handprint, outlined in Flora's blood.

Flora had become sassy. Sal didn't like sassy women, she had been warned. She cleaned up after that disagreement. So much blood. Staring, open eyes. Dear Flora . . .

Patcja took the broom from her mother and hugged her, holding her tight.

"I'm sorry, Ma. I'm so sorry."

"Hush. Don't fret now. Go home and pack—take that old leather valise. It's under my bed," said Mary, taking charge, snapping orders in a whisper so Joey couldn't hear. It was as if she were assigning a secret mission to a soldier. "Take the shawl hanging by the door. Get my church-going dress, too. You'll need something bigger soon; you can wear that. Take my wool stockings. And your Bible. Don't forget your hair ribbons, either—you want the sisters to see how pretty you are."

"Are you sure?"

"Of course, Stella. Of course. *Now go.*"

Chapter 57

Halina almost managed to finish her shift on the sixth floor without more excitement.

At first everything was just fine, peachy.

Stach had left with an abrupt change of heart that was sort of silly. Suddenly, he had put his hands in his pocket as he faced his sparring partner and said, "Okay, fine. Bye-bye." Then he had turned and ambled his way down the hall. Nurse Davies had looked baffled but relieved. She had been victorious!

Halina had given her a congratulatory smile and nod. "Who was that weird guy? What a dumb snot!" Halina had said, pointing at the departing figure as if she had never seen him before.

Jeepers, she was heaping on the sins today: lying, stealing, lying some more. The worst part was that she was getting good at it and had no qualms at all about her deviousness. Well, *almost* none.

She'd had to make the rounds to a couple of rooms before her heart slid out of her throat and back to her chest and starting thumping right and her knees stopped being all jiggly, like pudding on the stove. But all in all, she was proud of herself. She had managed to get the medicine that would help Margret. At least, she hoped it would. She would worry about that later.

She was making her way down the hall, pushing her cart of

bedpans and minding her own business, trying to concentrate on not spilling any piss on the floor, when she heard more ruckus—shouting and fast-talking. Slamming, too. Well, that put an end to any chance of her heart beating normal-like.

Holy Jesus Christ, now what?

She looked around, making sure the shouting wasn't aimed at her. No, no one was pointing or giving her the evil eye.

Thank you, Jesus.

But Nurse Bug Eyes looked to be in a deep heap of trouble.

She was staggering around the nurses' station, side-stepping clumsily, as if she were dancing in sand. Ah, it seemed Nurse Bug Eyes had been nipping at her coffee mug some more—*a lot more.* And Nurse Davies wasn't happy about it. The head nurse was doing an "I'm disappointed in you" kind of speech, with her pointed finger sharply wagging up and down.

Halina crept closer, curious.

As Nurse Davies carried on, Halina started to pick up more of the words. It was more than a scolding about sipping whiskey-laced coffee.

"And on top of your disgraceful behavior spilling dinner trays all over the ward, I have completed the inventory and discovered that several dosages were not recorded correctly! The supply cabinet and the medicine log do not agree, and I am afraid your sloppiness and carelessness must be to blame!" Nurse Davies said sharply.

Oh no! Nurse Bug Eyes was being blamed for the missing medicine bottles. *Damn.* Halina hadn't wanted someone else to get in trouble.

Nurse Bug Eyes didn't have a response to the accusation. Her mouth gaped open, but no words tumbled out.

Halina walked away, not wanting to hear more.

Halina's guilt was like a heavy box that was slippery and hard to carry. She tried not to think of Nurse Bug Eyes during the rest of the shift and all the way home. The walk back to Hegewisch seemed to take forever.

Halina tried to focus on the good—helping Margret. She tried to plan the course of treatment, but she needed to read the book first—well, at least look at the pictures. Maybe scan the parts about fever and pregnancies that got started but abruptly ended. Halina didn't even know what to call that—not in Polish or in English.

How dumb she was! How could she possibly do this?

She decided to ask Baba for help.

❧ ❧ ❧

She didn't even have to knock on the door. Baba opened it.

"Hello, girl. Come in, come in! I was expecting you. So, on with it. What do you need? Tell me."

Halina sat in the woman's kitchen and spilled the story as quickly as she could. She left out the part about Stach and Nurse Bug Eyes. No need to cast a bad light on either of them. Then she brought out the book, placing it on the table with reverence, as if it were the Holy Grail. She showed Baba the medicines, too, and explained how they were being used for Mr. Jenkins, a man with a fever, infection, and the same kind of stink that Margret had, the same kind of rotting smell. Maybe gangrene?

Baba listened intently, nodding, making faces; sometimes her eyebrows arched; sometimes her mouth puckered in thought, like a philosopher pondering a riddle.

"I see," Baba said. "I see . . ."

"Will you help me? Will you come with me to the hardware store, please?"

"No, I will not. I will not touch the sickness of these men who try to turn our town into their Sodom and Gomorrah with their evil ways. Their blasphemy is too dangerous."

"Ah, so you're scared. Is that it?" Halina asked in surprise.

"Yes, and you should be, too."

"That's a lousy excuse, Baba. Not good enough, not good enough at all."

"How about this? Is this *good enough*? I have a grave in my yard, marked only by a small stone. We buried a girl there—*Lydia*. That was the last time I tried to help a girl caught in the net of whoring and sinning. I treated her here at this table for a week, and I have lived with her death every day since."

"What? *Lydia?* She died? She's buried in your yard? Why did you lie to me? You lied to me!" Halina exclaimed. *"How could you? Does Stach know? Did he lie, too?"*

"We thought it would be easier for you. We didn't want you to grieve. You were so young, so worried. We were afraid your temper would set you off, and you'd try to get revenge. Payback. We didn't want that, so we lied. Both of us. We meant well."

"How dare you!" Halina fumed, glaring at the old woman.

"I didn't want you to live with the guilt of failure."

"*I* didn't fail her! *You* did!"

"You're right. I failed. In many ways," Baba sighed.

"Now *I* will live with the death of Margret every day—unless I can help her. Unless *you* help me."

Baba opened the book.

Halina and Baba looked at the pictures. Baba lit an oil lamp as the sun started to go down, and the lamp cast an other-worldly yellow glow on the text. Halina felt as though they were reading some holy document, a scroll that explained the meaning of God's plan. It was fascinating.

Baba was mostly quiet, sometimes an *hmmm* punctuating her absorption.

They didn't even try to read the paragraphs. Most of the words were too long to understand, too confusing—Latin sounding, like Mass.

Each uterine tube is approximately 10 cm in length and 1 cm in diameter and is situated within the mesosalpinx. The mesosalpinx is a fold in the broad ligament. The distal portion of the uterine tube ends in an orientation encircling the ovary. The primary function of the uterine tubes is to transport sperm toward the egg, which is released by the ovary, and to then allow passage of the fertilized egg back to the uterus for im- plantation.

Fortunately, there were many diagrams, and they were labeled. There were detailed line drawings of organs and how they were connected. Baba ran her fingers over the ink on the page, as if she could absorb the meaning through her fingertips. Maybe she was memorizing the line drawings, the shape of hoses connecting the egg bags with the womb-vase where the baby's sack would grow.

The focus of the book was on pregnancy and its stages. Then, several chapters on birthing. Then, finally, a section on things that went wrong. *Miscarriages*—that was the word.

Ectopic pregnancy: The first successful surgical management of a ruptured tubal pregnancy occurred in April 1883, when the British surgeon Robert Lawson Tait performed a laparotomy and ligated the ruptured tube and the broad ligament.

The diagram illustrated a fertilized egg implanted in the tube, growing in the wrong spot, then rupturing. As she studied at the pic- ture, Halina become convinced that was Margret's issue. No wonder the girl hurt so bad. No wonder she had a fever.

But the words describing treatment offered little encourage- ment. Poison? Electrical current? Surgery? Infection?

... puncturing the cyst and injecting poisonous fluids into the mass or passing through it an electrical current, to kill the fetus and cause ... flush itself of the toxins. Techniques spare the patient the high risks of surgery ... yet high mortality rates due to infection.

Halina felt more discouraged than she had before. She had a name for Margret's ailment and even pictures, but still no hope for what she could do without a hospital. She couldn't perform surgery! Could she?

"Baba, if you won't come with, at least tell me what to do. *Please.*"

"You'll need a sharp knife, but smaller than my butcher knife. Small, sharp . . ."

"Like a switchblade," suggested Halina.

Baba nodded. "Yes, and I know exactly where to find one."

Baba told Halina where to find Janusz; maybe Krysztof, too. One of them would certainly have a switchblade, she said.

Halina started for the door, taking one of Baba's oil lanterns with her. She hoped it wouldn't take long to find one of those two idiots. It was dark now, and in the dark, the prospect of cutting open a half-dead girl seemed downright creepy. Cold, uncaring. How could she do it?

She looked behind her and saw that Baba was putting a big pot on the stove, then selecting some roots from the baskets on the medicine wall.

"What are you doing?"

"I will brew some medicine—*my* medicine—to mix with those bottles you brought from the hospital. It will be ready when you come back with a knife. And find your sister—you will need an assistant."

"Yes, ma'am." Halina said.

Chapter 58

Patcja found the old leather valise. It was under Ma's bed, where she had said it would be. She took the shawl and one of the dresses from her closet, too, as she had been told. And the stockings and hair ribbons.

Patcja was down in the coal room collecting a few things she wanted to take. Her Bible went into the satchel along with the few clothes she had. She looked around the room. There were a few good memories here, but mostly pain. It was the room where she had been burned when Pa had dropped a whiskey bottle on a lit candle.

It was also the place where she'd woken up and seen a face at the window looking in. Some peeping *dupek*. She'd thrown a shoe at the window to make him leave, and she'd tried to keep an empty flour sack tacked up at the window like a curtain, but it was always falling when she and Halina climbed in and out of the window. That was pretty dumb, for sure. But they had just been two kids who didn't know much of anything past chores, the Bible, and trying to stay clear of people who had a snootful.

Maybe they should have told Ma that Pa liked to come in and watch them sleep. Sometimes he would pet their heads, stroke their hair—especially Halina's blonde hair. And sometimes he would pet their arms while they pretended to be asleep, the way a man would pet a collie. He would leave soon enough, though; he never stayed long.

Sometimes he cried. Sometimes he mumbled, talking to Stella. Always stupid Stella. Halina, with her blonde hair, looked like stupid Stella, it seemed.

Patcja was so sick of stupid Stella. And her stupid mother. And her stupid father. And her annoying-as-hell stupid sister.

Who suddenly appeared in the window.

Damned Halina! What is she doing here? Now?

Patcja opened the window for her.

"I thought we agreed to use the door, not the window, numb-sk—" Patcja started to call her sister numbskull out of habit. But that seemed so childish now. Halina had helped her so many times with her breathing spells. She might even miss her while she was away at this nunnery Ma had found for her. She didn't know how she would tell her sister she was leaving town. She wasn't sure which was more shameful—staying or leaving.

Patcja hid the valise behind her, not wanting to explain the big, long, sad story. She might cry and didn't want that. Halina would surely laugh at how stupid Patcja had been—falling for Joey, marrying him, and finding out what he was really like.

"Well, I went to the back door but heard Pa banging around, slamming pots, grumbling about no supper being ready for him." Halina paused and made a face. "So, being chicken, I decided to avoid the whole yelling nonsense and came in the window. I'm kind of in a hurry, so it's good that I found you so fast. Baba said to fetch you."

"*Me?* Why on Earth do you–or Baba—need *me?* Is that a switch-blade in your hand?"

"Um, yes, it is. And a dandy one, too, don't you think? Look at this. You click this little doohickey and the blade pops out, magic-like." She demonstrated three times, exclaiming in surprise each time.

"But what's it for?" Patcja asked. "Why do *you* have it? Don't cut yourself, silly—" Again, a name had almost slipped out. Being nice to her sister was hard. Especially when she was flashing a switchblade like a fool.

"Well, it's a long story, but here's what you need to know. Margret, one of the girls at the hardware store—which really isn't a hardware store, you know—had a pregnancy go bad. I borrowed medicine from the hospital and a book. The book says she needs surgery," Halina spilled out in a rush of words.

Then she flicked out the knife. "Ta-da!"

"*What?*" Patcja gasped.

"Yep. Baba won't go there to help me, though, being so against the damn Sicilians and their bootleg. Plus, well, it would be darn far for the old lady to walk. She's been ailing, you know. But she says I need an assistant, and that's why I'm looking for *you*. Simple."

"Simple? I don't think so!" Patcja shouted. "You are nuts! *Crazy!* What do *you* know about doing surgery? You will kill her for sure!"

Halina went into a long-winded explanation of why her stupid idea was logical and the best choice. Patcja tuned her out after the second or third reason. It seemed her sister had learned enough working at that hospital that she thought she was an expert. *How absurd.* But then again, she had taken care of Joey and patched him up pretty well. And she *had* helped Patcja with her breathing spells. And she always watched what Baba was cooking up. Who else would help that sick girl?

"Why don't you take her to the hospital? That would be better, I think," Patcja insisted.

Halina had reasons why that wouldn't work, either. Antonio was number one. Plus, the lack of an automobile or any other way to get the sick girl there seemed to be a problem, too—a big one.

Patcja thought of Krzysztof driving the milk truck. Maybe he would drive the girl . . . But he was one of Antonio's boys, and if Antonio refused to move her, well, then . . .

She tried to think of other people with vehicles. *Major.* But just the thought made her shudder. No.

Patcja sat on the bed, a lumpy old mattress on the floor. There was a green blanket on top with "US ARMY" stamped along the top edge. Lots of people in Hegewisch had the same blankets, supplied by Stach, stolen from an army train. Stach looked out for people. So did Baba, Bear and his father, Sister Beatrice, Father Chodniewicz . . .

It was a community that stuck together.

She was going to miss these people. Suddenly, she was feeling rather nostalgic, and she hadn't even stepped on the bus yet.

Maybe that was why she agreed to help her sister perform surgery in a whore house with only stolen medicine, a text book, and a switchblade to aid them. How crazy. But Patcja said she would help.

She would walk to the bus stop after helping her sister. How long could surgery take? A few minutes? She finished packing the valise. She wouldn't tell Halina why she was packing, though—even though her persistent sister kept grilling her.

"None of your business!" she snapped, shutting the latch on the bag. "Let's go, before I change my mind."

Halina collected some supplies—clean sheets and towels and sewing thread—then started to climb up the coal pile to go out the window.

"No," said Patcja. "We're going out the door—like normal, civilized, grown-up people do."

They climbed the stairs to the kitchen. Pa was there, sitting in a chair at the table, asleep. A plate of half-eaten fried potatoes sat in front of him along with a mug of coffee that smelled like whiskey. He must have fixed himself some dinner. He was snoring now, clearly having had too much coffee to drink. The tin of toothache pills was on the table, too. She thought about borrowing some, then decided not to.

Patcja just paused beside the sleeping man, watching him breathe. He was so pathetic. She was filled with mixed-up fury and confusion about whom to blame. Why must someone always be blamed? Patcja realized she didn't blame her father anymore for her burned arm.

"I forgive you, Pa," Patcja whispered and patted the sleeping man's shoulder lightly. "Bye, Pa."

They went out the door, shutting it behind them as quietly as they could. They walked down the sidewalk to Baba's house to pick up the supplies, the book, the medicine from the hospital, and that medicine Baba was brewing up.

It was a short stop. Baba had everything bundled up, easy to carry. She and Halina talked doctoring for a bit, but not long. Halina asked a few questions, but Baba's answers sounded like mumbo-jumbo nonsense to Patcja, so she didn't listen. She waited in the doorway, thinking of all the times she had been in that kitchen, getting treatments from a Gypsy healer who liked to wallop patients with a wooden spoon and make them sing.

The old woman had probably saved her arm from being much worse than it was. A few scars weren't so bad.

Then they were on their way to the hardware store. They walked quietly for a couple of blocks, both lost in her own thoughts. They passed The Corner without even slowing down. Lights were on inside, but Patcja could only make out silhouettes of people through the painted windows. Was Ma still in there, sweeping or cooking? Patcja wanted to go in and say goodbye to Ma, but she couldn't risk seeing Joey. He couldn't see her with a packed valise. So the two girls walked by on the opposite side of the street. Both carried bundles that were heavy, slowing them down. On the edge of downtown, they paused to rest. They sat on a curb, rubbing their shoulders and arms, sore from carrying their loads.

Halina checked her pocket for the switchblade. She fiddled with the button that opened it a few times.

"So where did you get that knife? Did you steal it or get it from Stach?" Patcja asked.

"No. Janusz let me borrow it—just had to persuade him. Found him at the Patchiecki place. He's hiding out there." Halina stood up and started walking as she talked. Not having to look at her sister made it easier to be honest. "The Sicilian boys found the cellar behind the fireplace, and they're storing crates of milk bottles there. They even have a wire rigged up that warns them if someone is coming. Pretty smart for stupid Sicilians. But someone keeps sneaking in and dumping their whiskey, refilling the bottles with water, so now Janusz is on guard," Halina explained. "Anyway, I told him I needed to borrow his knife."

"I can't believe he just gave it to you," Patcja murmured.

"Oh, I had to convince him. Told him I'd tell his little secret if he didn't let me borrow it."

"You mean the secret that he likes to peek in windows and scare women half to death?" Patcja asked.

"No, not that one" Halina shook her head. "Who would care about that? But lots of people might care if I told his other secret."

"What secret is that?"

"Janusz was the one who knifed Joey."

Chapter 59

Halina wasn't sure why she told Patcja that Janusz had knifed Joey. Just seemed like she had the right to know, that's all. She should know the score, right? She should know whom to trust and whom not to—especially since she was planning on running away somewhere.

Patcja wouldn't admit it, but that packed valise said *plenty*. Where did Patcja think she could go? And why now, so suddenly?

Halina had her suspicions, but she couldn't deal with that now. She had to focus on helping Margret. Performing surgery in this place wouldn't be easy, at all.

They went around to the back door, and Arlene let them in. The woman was cranky, as usual.

"We wondered when you would be back—leaving us to do all the work of sponging down sickly Margret and trying to get her to drink that soup you left."

"Sorry. I got back as soon as I could. I got supplies, medicine from the hospital—and a book. I even have a name for what ails her: ectopic pregnancy, tubal. Says so in the book. We need to cut it out—that's the only way to help her now."

"Cut it out? Are you *nuts*?" Arlene roared.

Halina pulled the switchblade from her pocket and flicked it open for Arlene to see. The woman was not impressed, probably had seen plenty of switchblades in her time. Maybe she even had one of her own.

"Yep, apparently I am. But I brought an assistant—my sister, Patcja."

Arlene grumbled some more, putting up weak objections and fussing about customers, whining about interrupting business, that kind of thing. Halina didn't listen, though. Instead, she went straight to Margret's room. Patcja followed, her face white and eyes wide with shock.

Josephine was in the room with Margret, sitting by her bed and sponging her face with water.

"How is she doing?" Halina asked her.

"About the same, but the fever seems better. The poultice seems to be drawing out the infection, like you said it would. But she still has pain, there in her side where the big lump is. She won't let me touch it."

"Good, don't. We don't want it to rupture. We're going to cut it out."

Halina gave quick introductions to Josephine, Arlene, and Patcja. There was some glaring between the two sides, warning looks that passed between the women and the newcomer with her air of judgement.

"We all need to work together," Halina told them.

The women nodded, somber. They looked scared as hell. Halina knew the feeling, but she wasn't going to let them see that she was worried, too.

Confident!—she had to be confident and show them she was sure about this. They had to trust her and listen to her. And above all, they had to believe. They all had to believe that Margret would live.

Margret will live.

Halina unpacked her supplies. Josephine brought a small table from her room so that there would be a place to set the medicine and the supplies, the knife, the needle and thread. She emptied her pockets, too. That string of twine from the Mason jar, her rosary, and two old brass German uniform buttons, pretty but useless, she set aside. With so many people in the small room, the space was cramped. Arlene stayed out of the way in the doorway, like a guard.

"First, we need to sterilize as much as we can with boiling water or alcohol. Everything that touches Margret needs to be clean—really, *really* clean. That's how they do it at St. Margaret's." For the first time, she realized Margret's name was like St. Margaret's. Maybe that was a good sign.

"There's no way we will ever make this filthy hellhole clean like a hospital," Patcja whispered in Halina's ear. "I've never seen a place so disgusting."

"We need to do the best we can and leave the rest to God," Halina answered. She heard herself and was surprised at her own matter-of-fact tone. She sounded a little like Sister Beatrice. That might be a good thing—or not.

Patcja looked for a minute or two as if she might make a run for it. She was eyeing the grime in the corners, the sawdust and mud tracked in by men's boots, the mouse droppings along the wall. And the sour smell of a woman who had been sick in bed for more than a week, close to death for days, was nearly unbearable.

"Go on, Patcja, Josephine will show you where the kitchen is. You can boil water in there. Then we need a table in the brightest room with the best light—a lightbulb, though, not lamplight. I'll find the room. Arlene, you stay with Margret. Wash her with soap, clean her up, as best as you can. Get all the piss and shit off her. I can't believe you couldn't even keep her clean, help her to the toilet or a pot. What were you women thinking, leaving her in her own waste, like a dog in a cage?"

Arlene started to argue. She started to move, lash out, maybe slap Halina's face, or perhaps punch her with a fist. Her hand was clenched, getting ready, but she paused and seemed to change her mind.

This time it was Patcja who intervened in the face-off and offered some reassuring words.

"Come here, ladies," she said. "Arlene, Josephine, Halina . . . In a circle and take hands. We're going to pray," Patcja said in a voice that sounded very grown-up, a voice Halina had never heard from her before. Halina was flabbergasted but took one of Margret's hands to include her in the circle. The girl was groggy, barely conscious, and making small mewing sounds, words that had no shape. Patcja took the girl's other hand.

Josephine and Arlene seemed unsure. Perhaps it had been a long time since these women had prayed, but Josephine pulled a rosary out of her pocket. Arlene dropped her cigarette on the floor and ground it out, coughing.

"Our Heavenly Father, we come to you with a humble request. Please guide us, help us care for Margret. Show us how to serve her and care for her, as she is one of your children, a lost sheep, just as we are. Help us, Holy Father. Amen."

They all started on their assignments.

Halina quickly decided that the kitchen was the best place to work. A lightbulb hung over the table, fairly bright—at least better than a lamp or candle. Halina brought in every lamp she could find, too, setting them around the room in a circle. She set up the supplies, sterilized the switchblade, tongs, a soup ladle, a fork and spoon, a needle and thread, scissors . . . and the small statue of the Madonna that Baba had placed in the bundle among her jars of paste and poultice goop.

How Halina wished the old woman were here. Well—in a way. She also cringed at the thought of all the shouting and spoon-banging and singing polkas that would be so wrong now. Margret's condition was far too serious. Life. Death. The responsibility felt heavy.

Halina thought her knees might buckle. How had she ever thought that Baba's silly Old Country folklore could save a seriously ill woman on the edge of eternity? Such a faint, fragile veil floated between Margret and God.

Above all, she wanted to move with respect, working so closely to where God had touched, with someone he had whispered to and invited to join him in heaven. She smoothed down her dress, finger-combed her hair, pulled up her stockings to make sure her knees were covered. God must surely be watching. She could almost feel his breath on the back of her neck. The small hairs stood on end and goosebumps ran up her arms.

Hello, God. I'm Halina. I'm trying. I am. I'll listen. You tell me what to do, and I'll listen—I promise.

Suddenly she felt as though she was interfering. How dare she step in and offer a detour around the direct route to God's paradise? Why would Margret ever want to take the tenuous, rocky journey offered by medicine? Maybe she should just let Margret slide into God's outstretched hand.

"Something wrong?" Patcja asked, draping a clean sheet over the table to make a place for Margret.

"*Nie.* No, everything's fine. I was just wondering if a stiff belt might be good for Margret—or me. But I don't think so. I'll just go check on Arlene, see if she has our patient all cleaned up and ready."

Patcja nudged Halina to the corner so no one would hear. She put her face close, eye to eye.

"You don't have to do this, you know. There's still time to say there's nothing you can do. Or maybe just throw a fit, insist that Antonio drive her to the hospital. Maybe?"

"You think I'll blunder it, is that it? Totally botch everything?"

"No, that's not it," Patcja said, a hand on her sister's arm. "It's . . . I think she's close to dying, and if God decides to take her, you'll feel awfully bad. It won't be your fault, though. Just—well, God always wins."

"I know. But maybe he hasn't made up his mind yet. Maybe if he sees someone is willing to fight for her, that she's worth saving . . . And now, there's four of us. Four of us tugging at her, hanging on. You know? That might be enough."

"Yeah. Yeah," Patcja said softly. "That might be enough."

Halina turned to go check on Arlene.

Patcja called after her, "You won't botch it, Lina. I know."

"Yeah? Well, you're a dumb-butt," Halina said, with a reluctant smirk. Then she stuck out her tongue.

"You're a numbskull," countered Patcja, making a face, using fingers for horns, sliding into giggles.

"No, you are!"

Arlene came in and heard the two girls acting as if they were six years old, teasing, then falling into a hug, at first awkward, then sincere.

"Let's get going. Time is money," Arlene growled. "And you better hope Antonio doesn't drop in on your little medical experiment."

Chapter 60

"What am I going to do with you, Janusz?" Stach asked. "You stink worse than horse *gówno* in August, and I'm tired of trying to keep you out of trouble. You're a pain in my side, do you know that?"

"Where?"

"Brother, you're paining me, right *here*," said Stach, pointing to his side. "And *here*," he added, pointing to his backside.

"Well, I don't know why. I didn't punch you there, Stach. Not you. Not there *or* there," Janusz said, pointing with both hands.

The two men were in the vegetable cellar in the back of the Patchieckis' empty lot, arguing over Janusz's new job babysitting shelves and shelves of whiskey-filled milk bottles. He had a fold-up cot and a blanket. Apparently, this was a twenty-four-hour job and he was living down here. One oil lamp was lit and burning on low, but even the dim orange-yellow light that was little more than the glow on the end of a cigar made Janusz squint and shade his eyes with his hand.

Someone had given the big lug some bad hooch, nearly blinding him. Stach didn't know whether to be furious with the idiot or feel sorry for him, but something had to be done. A man couldn't just get away with something like that.

Stach knew Janusz was the one who had stabbed Joey. It wasn't that hard to figure out. Antonio had put him up to it, of course. This clash between the two gangs, all over selling whiskey, was getting out of hand. Why the hell did those fancy-hat goons care so much about who claimed Hegewisch as their territory? Not like the local men were big drinkers or big spenders. Were they?

It reminded him of the Great War. Russia, Austria-Hungary, and Germany—all fighting over Poland. All three powerful nations fighting over Poland. Why did they want it so badly? The port. Gdnask was a major port for shipping, freighters . . .

Finally Stach got it. These wise guys wanted to control Hegewisch because it stood between Chicago and the rest of the region, from the south side of Chicago to northwest Indiana—Lakeshore, the steel mills, Gary, Inland Steel, US Steel, Bethlehem Steel, Youngtown Steel's Harbor Works. Then there was the railroad switching yard and the canal that had been promised to the town since old man Hegewisch had first opened his two-bit steel mill and built rows of workers' shacks to house the Old Country misfits. If the canal were finally finished, Hegewisch could be something. A doorway.

That was what the Italians and Sicilians were betting on. And the damn Poles were in the way.

Stach hummed, thinking. He rocked back on his boot heels. *Now* he got it. But what to do about it and that other thing—the Janusz dilemma?

Janusz sat on an overturned apple crate, looking oddly too big, like an ogre on a toadstool in a children's storybook. How was that crate holding up this boar, with his stink and stupidity and knack for finding trouble? Peeking in windows, rubbing up against anything with two legs and a bosom, waving that damn switchblade, taking orders from Antonio in trade for a little poisoned moonshine that was probably laced with opium.

Stach had caught glimpses of the brown bottles with no labels, had seen Joey dribble some into the whiskey he served up. A nasty trick for creating addicts—customers that would keep coming back. No wonder the battle between the two whiskey gangs was heating up.

And Janusz had gotten himself in the middle of it. Antonio had told Janusz to stab Joey, Stach was sure of it. But how could he prove it? And how would he keep Janusz from following fatal directions again? Janusz could do as he was told, just not decide right or wrong for himself. Hell, weren't most men like that?

Stach was out of patience. He paced around the cramped cellar, watching Janusz's face as he rubbed a green blanket against his whiskered cheek, seeming to get comfort from it. Or was it exciting him? Who knew? This man seemed to have the brain of a ten year-old. No, more like a thirteen-year-old who had just discovered his willy had another purpose. Stach laughed at the thought. Camel, Bear, Krzysztof—all young men who had been hounded by Sister Beatrice when they wanted only to stare at the girls wearing sweaters they had outgrown and white cotton anklets that fell around their ankles. He'd heard so many stories. *Nice* stories, when Sister Beatrice told them.

Beatrice was a good woman. Their mama would be proud—too bad she didn't live to know her children were safe in America. Austachio, or Stach, was a magnate in the publishing and newspaper business; and his little sister, Izzie, was a nun in the St. Florian church, Sister Beatrice now—a saint in the making.

"Janusz, my man, have you thought about getting yourself an education?"

"Nah. Can't say that I have. Not sure what I would do with it."

"Well, man, it isn't so much what you would do as what you *wouldn't* do anymore. You got some bad habits need purging, a damn good purging," Stach said. "*Discipline*—you hear of that word before?"

"Sounds like something you feed a dog, or a snot-nose kid."

"Sure does, sure does, all right," answered Stach, slapping Janusz on the back. "But we won't let that bother us. Will we?"

"Whatever you say, Stach. I trust you."

Stach was happy to hear that. That was all he needed to hear, some words of faith from the man—busted-up brain or not. But he was about to test the man's loyalty. What would Janusz think when he found out what happened to this whiskey cellar? It was probably nice and safe and quiet down here for Janusz. Not to mention the low light and the steady supply of drink.

Well, he would adjust. They all had to keep adjusting. Cotton skivvies or wool skivvies, depending on the season; prominent artist in Poland one day, selling newspapers and living in a shanty the next. Adjustments, all of them.

"Janusz, grab your things. Today is moving day for you."

"Aw, why I gotta move? I like it down here," Janusz whined.

"Can't stay here, my friend. Things are going to heat up fast."

Stach broke a milk bottle, letting some whiskey pool on a shelf. He set his lit cigarette hanging over the edge, the smoke curling up, the red end glowing in the dim light. As the cigarette burned, the ash grew longer and the red dot of fire drew closer to the whiskey.

Stach hurried up the cellar's cement steps. Janusz followed without question, as always. He carried his cot and blanket, along with a pillow and a pair of clean socks—still new—the ones Stach had brought him a while back.

They were halfway to St. Florian's when they heard the explosion. It wasn't very loud, especially considering that it was cases of moonshine going up in a fireball. The dirt walls and dirt ceiling had probably fallen in, collapsing the cellar and smothering the flames. The fire would die out safely enough, Stach was confident.

"What was that?" Janusz asked.

"One doorway closed, that's all. Don't you worry about it, Janusz. You stick with me now. And Sister Beatrice. You'll be safe. You're part of the family now. And I'm sending you to school—St. Florian's Elementary. I'm thinking third grade ought to be right."

Chapter 61

Baba made herself some hot tea. Nothing too strong. Just enough so she could see around corners, past silk babushkas and long johns, through bottled time. She had people to watch over. She had patients. In this world and in other worlds, past and future.

She sat on the bench in her backyard, watching the small, lazy fire she'd made in the firepit. It was nothing like the bonfire Stach had helped make on the night of the Paschal moon, but it was enough. She saw the explosion in the vegetable cellar at the Patchiecki place before she heard it. By the time the vibrations reached her, she knew exactly what had happened and why. She saw it clearly in the flames.

> *Cigarette ash on dirt floor marks time.*
> *Orange fangs of flames nibble on the pine shelf.*
> *Liquid gold fuels, sizzle, steam-hiss, consume.*
> *Open doorway to hell.*
> *Explosion collapses the cellar.*
> *Done.*

She was relieved. Crates of bad liquor were gone, just like that. Stach was a pretty smart fella. He would take care of Janusz, she knew.

They had argued about him years ago.

Stach shouted, "I tell you, he's dangerous!"

Baba hit the table with her wooden spoon. "I tell you, he's not!"

"Have you seen that girl? She looks like she hasn't slept in months. She's afraid to close her eyes to go to sleep," Stach said.

"She's afraid of the boogieman, like all kids," Baba said with a shrug.

"Halina keeps talking about a monster-man pressing his face at their window. Could it be Janusz?"

"He still thinks he's at war. He sees those wool blankets, green army blankets, and he's in France, at war," Baba said.

"So it's my fault? The blankets I passed out? It's all my fault?"

"US Army issue, you stole. You brought war and death and dying here. You're not innocent in this, Stach."

"No one is." He shook his head.

"Janny is. He has half a brain, for crying out loud."

"Think of the girl!" he shouted.

"I'll watch him," she said.

"Can you heal him?"

"No, but I'll treat him," she vowed.

The spring night was turning chilly, the wind picking up and blowing embers around. She stepped on the fire specks, no bigger than lightning bugs, that landed outside of the fire ring. Baba stretched her back. Oh, how it ached. The pain was growing in her bones. She could feel it crawling through her wrinkled old body. Her blood was a river, spreading the sickness from one shore to another, one bank to another. Like Wrzesnia to Hegewisch.

She had traveled so far. The Romani people she learned to love. The red wagon. The boy, so lovely with his long black hair. Long, moonless nights of fire and magic. Loocng nights. The rhythm of the wagon came back to her. Images bobbled up and down, like the waves, like the ship that had carried her to America years ago. With a husband who died too soon. That was half a lifetime ago.

Her head swayed on a tired neck. Her sickness was making past and present jumbled. The fire conjured dreams; memories turned into a picture-show. She let the images wash over her, soothing. A trance, death-like, lured her with sweet old images:

> *Young hands, Gypsy lace.*
> *"You're so beautiful."*
> *Dancing by the fire. Bare toes. Tambourine with ribbons trailing, red.*
> *Caravan of painted wagons,*
> *like a snake, crawls over borders.*
> *Men pay for a whirl. Twirl. Potions in bottles.*
> *Curses. Visons. For sale.*
> *"Will you teach me the cures?" she asks.*
> *The old woman nods.*
> *Bonfire on the Easter moon. In a farm field in Romania*
> *One doorway opens. One closes.*
> *Closes. Closes. Closes.*

Baba's eyelids were heavy, but she still had questions. Not yet! She wanted to see how the surgery had gone. That was why she had built the fire. How was Halina faring with Margret? She should have gone to help. Baba wished now that she had followed the girl and tried to help, but she also realized she knew nothing of hospital medicine. It was foreign to her. Strange, frightening. That was Halina's garden to hoe.

She pulled the bench closer to the fire so she could warm her hands, warm her heart. She had been cold in this life many times, she knew. Cruel witch, some called her.

Baba thought of that mama and the boy with the hand mangled in some potato mash machine. The mama had begged her to look at the hand again, and what did she do? She had pretended to grab the hatchet. The boy ran. The mama ran after him. Now neither would come back. The boy would lose the hand for sure now. *For sure.* Unless she went and found him, tracked him down.

Maybe Halina could give him some of the hospital medicine. Maybe. Maybe that would work.

Baba looked up, sensing movement above her, around her.

A crow circled and circled and circled. Birds that were roosting in the trees by the alley flew away, over Lydia's grave. Baba's sickness made visions, flashes of color and light, like lyrics to songs. She heard the song, melancholy:

> *Winged silhouettes, black against moon orb gold light,*
> *speckled, gritty with steel dust from smokestacks.*
> *Clouding the memory-vision. Swallows? Angels?*
> *No, bats from the other world. Taunting of mistakes in*
> *this world.*
> *A grave under the peach tree, marked by a stone. But no*
> *name.*
> *Lydia, the wind says. Lydia, the night says.*
> *Lydia, the stone should say.*

Baba shook her head. She tried to stay in this world.

She had tried her hardest for Lydia.

It wasn't enough. I failed.

She had done her best for Camel, too, when everyone else had forgotten him. Except, of course, Mateusz, his father, and his addled, grief-paralyzed mother. Baba had done what she could for them: tonics, oils to rub down bony limbs, recipes for teas—she would need to give that to Halina.

She had a recipe for Fryderyk, too, to mellow out that temper. Sometimes she sprinkled it on his pipe tobacco, just a bit of mushroom dust and dried poppy petals. That seemed to ease some of the man's temper—and his sorrow. But the ache in him was powerful, eating at his gut, driving him to drink as he tried to forget. How could a man forget such horrors? Baba had seen the grief Mary and Fryddie endured.

> *"They'll find us. They're coming. Hurry, Marianne.*
> *We must hurry.*
> *We must make it to the ship. Shhh. Here."*
> *Thistle bush. Shadows and boot steps.*
> *Black leather boots within sight.*
> *Hand over Mary's mouth. Blood flows from her; a river,*
> *red, flowing to the bank, pools under soldier boots.*
> *The solder turns; he walks away, leaving crimson footprints,*
> *made of her blood.*
> *Will he look down and notice?*

All that soldier on patrol had had to do was look down, and he would have seen a rivulet of blood flowing to the bank of the river. If he had traced the flow, he would have found a young girl giving birth in the stubble of a farm field. No wonder Mary needed medicine, too, to calm her nerves, to keep her from hearing voices and thinking she saw the ghost of her sister, Stella.

Mary needs her medicine.

Mary shouldn't go without her tea. She had fought bravely against those guards at the beer hall, with a butcher knife. In the mud of the pig pen, fighting off a soldier. Who would blame her? The hell at the beer house was only the beginning. When they had finally gotten away, the villagers had accused the girls of being traitors. Stella couldn't face the shame. She had hanged herself. Mary had found her.

> *Mary calls, "Stella, where are you?"*
> *She tries the barn. Stella is there, noose around her neck,*
> *feet dangling over a toppled hay bale.*
> *Her shadow sways.*

Should Halina know that truth? Maybe it would help her understand her parents' misery. Or maybe it would be another noose, a frayed rope tying her to a horrid past.

There was so much for Halina to learn. Would the girl be able to pick it up, carry on, continue down the path Baba had started?

Nie. She can forge a new one.

"Fire, tell me," Baba said out loud. She was surprised by the weakness of her own voice. She tried again. "Where is she, the new one?"

Baba stirred the dying embers with the long stick. New flames leapt, flared from the red-glowing log. Bright. The new vision came:

> *Girl sleeps on the table; arm hangs over edge;*
> *blue vein pulses, faint. Ether mask hides her face.*
> *Woman, garish with face paint, hovers, drips ether as*
> *needed. Switchblade makes a line, and red seeps. They all*
> *stare, shocked at mysteries under the skin. God's creation.*
> *Gone wrong. Wound oozes poison.*
> *Fist-size mass, black like night and death and agony*
> *unleashed.*
> *Unborn baby bones, like toothpicks, poke out, filament thin.*
> *Oh, Jesus, look at that. Almost a hand! Webbed, unfinished.*
> *Gasps, gags. Wonder and horror at once.*
> *Hospital medicine. Clear liquid. Science-brewed.*
> *They cut, scoop, tidy up.*
> *Then sew.*
> *A darning needle and white cotton thread from Woolworth's*
> *five-and-dime,*
> *boiled clean.*
> *White paste over stitches, layer of poultice in cheesecloth,*
> *then sheets, torn in strips.*
> *Done.*

Baba sighed. She would have done nothing differently. Well, except for the hospital medicine and the ether. She had no idea how those worked. Opium, though, she knew. She hoped they had plenty of opium for the girl when she woke up. Or tea. She could make some tea.

I'll leave that to the girl. She will know what to do.

Baba kicked dirt on the fire to put it out, satisfied that she had seen everything she needed to know—and then some. She could go to bed now. Sleep sounded nice.

Tomorrow—*if* tomorrow came for her—she would check on Halina and Margret. And Janusz ... Camel, Mary, Fryderyk ... and, of course, Patcja—carrying new life in her womb.

The fire sizzled, popped, ashes smoldering, almost done.

A candle flame dances, orange-yellow, gentle. Halina sighs.
She pats Margret's hand. The girl stirs, waking.
Groggy. Groping for a handhold this side of heaven.

The old woman kicked dirt on the fire, putting it out. She went inside her house.

She got as far as the kitchen.

Chapter 62

Mary started sweeping the broken glass into a pile. Dust, dirt, horse dung that had been caked on the wooden floor came, too. The cloud of dust made her cough, but no one heard. She was alone, thank goodness. She could do what needed to be done and leave. No one would suspect.

Joey was in the office. A couple of his cronies were at the side door making sure undesirables—whoever that might be—didn't come into the tavern. She heard the young men—no more than boys, really—throwing dice against the curb for some game she didn't understand.

Apparently, it involved betting and equal shares of obscenities and threats. In Italian, naturally. She didn't understand the words, but she knew the tone well.

They paid no attention to the Polish woman inside cleaning up the mess on the floor. She was just another woman tidying up after all the posturing, noise, and mayhem were done. There was always someone left to sweep up.

It had been the same in Wrzesnia. The first soldiers had come at noon. At first, only ten or so. They were polite and spoke Polish. No one thought to shout or shoot or run. No one thought to say, "No, you're not welcome."

They had simply wanted to set up a communication post for their officers, a place for a few men to sleep overnight. They would appreciate lodging. The beer hall would do nicely, they said.

The tanks had come after midnight. Then, more soldiers—hundreds of them. They had circled the village, posted troops at every bridge, every ferry crossing, every road to the mountains and coast. By dawn, Wrzesnia had belonged to Germany.

Mary and Stella had been put to work.

The smells of this tavern—The Corner—were so familiar. Some things never changed, despite the years or the distance. She could smell the spilled whiskey, the old beer, the rotting wood floors, the layers of old cigarette smoke, and the sweat of men who wanted to drink to forget or to bolster some courage. Booze made even cowardly men stupid. Then, fights broke out. Blood soaked into the porous floor and left oily stains no mop could wash away.

Mary—Marianne then—had been the girl with the mop, the one to clean up. Stella had poured the beers, served the men, giggled when they pulled her braids. Stella had smiled prettily. Marianne had grimaced at the jokes, the slaps, the groping.

Hans had taken pity on her. He had been kind, had brought food out to the pigsty where she was forced to sleep. Stella had had the bed of an officer, with goose down pillows and a brick warmed on the hearth and wrapped in flannel to keep the bed and her naked butt warm. Marianne had hated Stella for going willingly, for being warm, for being fed when she was so cold and hungry and filthy with pig-stinking muck. And left in the dark—endless nights of dark, so black she couldn't see the hands that grabbed her, beat her, held her down in the straw. She had wanted to die.

Hans had kept Marianne alive.

For what? So I could clean up after them, empty chamber pots and mop up the puke and piss from the floor after their drunken—

She shook her head. There was no point in thinking about it now. Nothing good could come of it. Except for one thing. Mary *knew* she could do it—what had to be done.

She went to the kitchen looking for a dustpan, something to pick up the broken glass. She heard footsteps behind her. Clumsy, heavy feet, shuffling and staggering. Her eyes went to the chopping block and the butcher knife next to it, just out of reach. She took two steps toward it, stretched—

"What are you doing here, woman? You should be home! This is no place for you."

"Fryderyk, you scared me," Mary said, relieved. She turned and saw her husband, a man who was spent and used up, worn out a long time ago. What was he doing here?

Why did he hang on? Why didn't he go to Stella? She would be waiting for him. They were the ones meant to be together all along.

Fryddie had never loved Mary. Maybe he would have if he had only tried. Maybe a little.

"I'm helping Patcja," Mary answered, even though she knew that must sound stupid. "There was a broken window, and I said I would sweep up for her. And why are *you* here? You have no business here either, foolish old man."

"I heard an explosion at the Patchiecki house. Moonshine went up in a ball of flames. I know the girls go there to . . . Well, who knows what the devil they do there or why." He rubbed his scruffy face, unshaven for days. He hit the wall with a big hand, his shoulders heaving in a pathetic shudder—or perhaps it was a sob, a heavy burden he couldn't carry for another moment.

"So, where are they, Mary? Where are the girls? Were they at that dump of a house? I can't find them, woman!"

"They're fine, Fryddie. They're—"

"Well, isn't this a fine surprise! Both in-laws came to visit me." Joey stood in the doorway to the kitchen. He had Augie's shotgun. "Here for some kind of family reunion? Maybe welcome the groom to the family?" Joey raised his eyebrows, a strange smirk on his face. "Even though I seem to remember you weren't fond of Patcja marrying an *Italian* man." He said the word *Italian* with the same disgust that Fryderyk had used that horrid night when he found Patcja and Joey in the coal room.

"Nuthin's changed. Still not likin' it. Still not going to have the likes of your kind in my family," Fryddie said. He stood up, planted both feet firmly on the floor, as if he were bracing for a big wind. He suddenly seemed taller. "Sleazy criminals, all of yous. Italian henchmen . . . bribing and plotting, doing deals, passing money under the table. Who can trust you?"

Mary stepped between the two men, her hand groping on the counter behind her, trying to remember where the knife was. Another inch . . . There!

"Just go, Fryddie. Let's go," she said, pointing Fryderyk toward the door to the alley with her one empty hand. The other hand gripped the wooden handle of the knife close to her back. She felt the blade tip poke through her dangling apron ties.

"We're going, Joey. Just don't mind us no more. Never mind us." She backed toward the door, keeping the knife hidden. She wasn't about to put it down.

Fryderyk pushed his wife aside.

"Maybe we're going. Maybe not. Maybe I don't wanna leave without Patcja—my firstborn. Where is she?" Fryddie's voice was low and gruff, dry. The man sounded sober.

What has gotten into him? He's going to get us both killed, the fool.

Joey stepped closer to them. Mary, still standing between the men, could smell them both—hot breath, cigarettes, coffee, rotting teeth. Rotten men. She wasn't sure which one she hated more.

Until Joey raised the shotgun, the stock on his shoulder, taking aim at Fryddie's head. The old man's white hair fell across a wrinkled forehead. That old hat . . . worn, stained . . . The hat where Fryddie had placed the baby that night while they hid, when she had given birth to a son who had been dead before he arrived. Fryddie had cut the umbilical cord with a pocket knife. Blood. Pain. Soldiers.

Fryddie had carried her five hours that night to the merchant ship.

She knew what she had to do. Like the night she had killed Hans for raping her sister.

Joey squinted. He'd made his decision. Cold. He would do it. He squeezed—

Mary raised her arm and drew the butcher knife across his throat.

Joey fell to the floor, gasping, hand to his throat, his artery gushing, squirting blood like a fountain. He gurgled once, twice, a third, sad time.

Barely. No more.

And for the second time that spring, Joey was sprawled on the floor with a dark puddle spreading underneath him. But this time he didn't move. This time, there was no Polish girl to patch him up.

Fryderyk and Mary stared at the boy, and the sudden silence was immense, thick and woolen.

Mary had no tears. No words. No regrets.

Fryderyk finally spoke.

"Go home, Mary. *Marianne.* Lock yourself in the house. I'll get my shovel. I'll do my part. I know how to dig a hole, shovel dirt, compost the stinkin' garbage."

"Don't let the soldiers see you. Don't let them find us, Fryddie."

"Have I ever?"

"No, Fryddie. You've always protected me."

"So, go now. Hurry."

Chapter 63

The hardware store was quiet. Arlene had put up a sign on the door that said simply, "Come back in an hour." That gave them some time to perform the surgery and move Margret back to her bed without being hassled by drunken, noisy fools who would ogle and ask questions.

Halina was happy it was over. Such a relief. Only the waiting was left. A few hours, maybe a day or two should reveal plenty. Margret should start improving quickly now that the infected mass had been removed.

"Remove toxins and counteract poisons. Wash wounds and cleanse the spirit. Then energize healing. Fortify and reinforce the righteous. Patch up gaps and holes. Prevent decay and destroy doubts. There. Simple."

Halina was surprised at how easy it had been. Maybe it was all luck? She had been right in her diagnosis. The fertilized egg, the beginning of a baby, hadn't implanted in the right place, where it could thrive. Instead, infection had set in, making a downright mess of Margret's insides. It was fascinating and scary all at the same time.

It was as though those drawings in the obstetrics book had come to life with depth, dimension, and color, blood and breath—life—like magic. And, like magic, Halina had seemed to know what to do. Instinct had kicked in, or God had been whispering in her ear, or she had seen Margret through borrowed vision, through the eyes of a real surgeon. There was no logic for what had happened.

Margret was back in her bed. Patcja was cleaning up the kitchen, putting supplies back in the bag, washing blood off the switchblade, collecting the bloody towels that were scattered on the floor. They had made a mess. Arlene was answering questions from the other girls, reassuring them that all was well and Margret would get well soon. Arlene seemed to believe it. That was good. Hope, confidence, faith—they were all good. That had to help.

There was still a lot that could go wrong, though. They had to be cautious, keep the incision clean, change the poultice and bandages. Maybe give her a few more doses of the hospital medicines, just small doses in the hypodermic needle, as she had seen Nurse Davies do.

Then "*energize healing. Fortify and reinforce the righteous.*" That meant some hearty, healthy meals would be good for Margret. Some leeks in soup, maybe some beef shanks in a stew.

Margret stirred, waking up from the ether, eyelids fluttering, eyes unfocused. Halina patted her hand.

"Hello, Margret. It's over. You were the perfect patient."

Margret blinked, focusing. Her eyes asked questions, but her mouth couldn't find words.

"I think you are going to be fine now, Margret. I think we fixed it. I think you'll get well now, but you gotta work at it, keep fighting."

Margret focused. She managed some words, a whisper Halina had to come close to hear. "I watched you. From the ceiling. I floated there, deciding."

"Deciding what?"

"To stick around."

Halina gently hugged the girl—the young woman.

"I'm sure glad, Margret. 'Cause I could use a friend. And help. Once you get all well, maybe you could move in with my family, take my sister's side of the bed . . ."

But Margret had drifted back to sleep. That was okay. There would be plenty of time for making new plans, for helping Margret—and the other girls.

Halina stared into the candle flame, watching the light flicker and dance, seeing all she needed to know. Maybe some of the future should stay a surprise. She blew out the candle.

Sleep, Margret. Sleep.

She had one more job to do tonight before walking home and going to sleep herself. She was dead tired, felt like a walking spirit, a half-gone goblin Baba might have conjured up from under the peach tree.

Halina chuckled at the thought of being afraid of the peach tree and those gnarly roots. She had been close to Death tonight, her nose in its stink, her hands in its gore, and she hadn't been afraid. So she wasn't going to be frightened of any creepy-trying tree. Not ever again.

In the kitchen, Patcja was almost done cleaning up.

"Thanks, Patcja. You were a big help. I'm so glad you stayed tonight to help me," Halina said.

"You're welcome, snot-brain," Patcja said, smiling. She looked tired, too.

They discussed the bus ride, the home for girls, the convent across the state line.

Patcja decided to stay there, at the hardware store, for what was left of the night. She'd sleep on the floor by Margret. She'd walk to the bus stop in Hammond in the morning, she said. Or maybe Stach could borrow Major's mule and give her a ride in that wagon of his. That would be nice. She wasn't feeling up to walking all the way to Hammond on her own.

"We'll figure it out together. In the morning," Halina said. "Maybe you don't have to go all the way to St. Mary's. Maybe you could stay at St. Florian's for a while, until all the hullaballoo settles down."

"Maybe . . . ," Patcja answered. "I'm going to have to confront Joey some time, though. Settle things with him eventually, I suppose."

"Maybe it'll all just work out . . . somehow, baby." Halina smiled at her sister. She smoothed some of the auburn curls on her sister's shoulder and tucked some stray strands behind Patcja's ear.

"That's the last time someone calls me 'baby'—the last."

"I know. It *is* the last time, the very last."

"How do you—"

"I just know, that's all."

Halina looked around the kitchen, found the bowl with a towel draped over it. She hesitated from looking inside.

"What do we do with that?" Patcja asked, her nose wrinkled.

"I'll take care of it."

Halina went out back, down the path past the outhouse, then farther to the alley.

Funny timing. The milk truck pulled up and stopped next to her. She wasn't afraid. She could see it was Nicky driving.

"Hey, what you doing here? How come I keep running into you?" she asked.

"How come you keep needing me to give you a ride home?" he replied.

"I dunno. I guess I'm that kinda girl."

"Yep, guessin' so," he answered. His eyes did a funny sleepy-dreamy thing, like Patcja used to do when she talked about . . .

"I can't help it, you know. Not going to change, either," Halina said.

"Any fool would know that. Get in. I'll take you home, make sure you get there all right."

"Hold on a bit. I have some things to take care of first," she said. She smiled. It was nice to have someone worrying about her. Very nice.

Maybe he likes me.

She walked a bit farther, waving at Nicky to wait there.

Nicky. That's a nice name.

Halina focused on her task. This was serious. She found a sandy patch of soil by the alley fence, out of the way. She'd forgotten to bring a digging spoon, so she just clawed at the damp earth with her hands, digging and digging. She wanted the hole to be deep so it would be safe from critters, rats, dogs . . .

She started to pour the contents of the bowl into the hole, but that seemed too callous, too cold. This was a baby that almost was. She picked up the bloody pouch. The sac was torn away, the tiny thing showing. It was hard to call it a baby. That would be too tragic. And, honestly, the barely formed infant looked more like a pollywog or baby bird—minus the beak—than a human.

Had it been a boy? Maybe. She wasn't sure, so much mucus and filmy yuck. Infection. But she could see hands and fingers, tiny, partially webbed, not done. Bones, supple, like veins in a leaf. The fragile body, the tiny hand that would never grip his mother's finger . . .

> *And he wipes the baby boy's face,*
> *white mucus, film and blood, with his handkerchief.*
> *His hat is a cradle and casket.*
> *He claws at the dirt, stoic, digging a grave, hidden from*
> *soldiers and animals.*
> *She touches the tiny hand, kisses the fingers, see–through, like*
> *bug wings.*
> *She kneels, paws at the earth, too. Futile motions.*
> *She knows. Wolves will eventually find him.*
> *This fragile body, the tiny hand that will never grip his*
> *mother's finger.*

She got it. Finally. Halina saw the images from another time and place and understood the agony and loss. The history of her family clicked into focus. Her parents had buried a stillborn infant. They were never whole again. Yet instinct for survival had kept them living, breathing, walking this world, mourning in a never-ending arc of grief.

Halina kissed the tiny hand of the almost-baby she held in a towel. A string of bloody mucus clung to her lip. She brushed it away, wrapped up the bundle, and placed it in the grave.

She replaced the soil and patted it down, then made a tiny cross—matchbox sized—out of tree twigs. She patted her pockets, looking for that piece of twine from her Mason jar, the frayed scrap she had been carrying around for weeks now, in case she found her poker money. How ridiculous that seemed now. Well, she must have lost it—along with those stupid ideas of leaving town.

Halina looked around for some other stretch of thread or string. Saw nothing. Except . . .

From the tattered hem of her dress, a string dangled. She pulled it and pulled. It seemed fitting that she take something of hers—a part of her—and use that to make the cross and mark the grave. She felt as though she had already given part of herself. She was different, she knew.

She tied the twigs with the string, around and around again. Safe, sturdy. Well, as sturdy as twigs and string could be. And that was enough.

> One grave is marked by a cross of twigs.
> One grave is marked by a stone.
> And a grave, somewhere near a coast in Poland, is marked only by time.

I better check on my patient before I head home.

Tomorrow she'd check in on Camel and his mama, too. Maybe get them up, out into some spring air. That would be good for them.

Spring, the season of miracles.

They would like to get out, probably. Well, if they argued, she'd just take after them with a wooden spoon. She was going to have to get one of those. A nice, big wooden spoon.

I have so much to do.

If you enjoyed *Tied with Twine*,
continue reading for a preview of
the next enchanting novel by Pam Records:

Trapped in Glass

Hegewisch, Illinois 1929

Halina hesitated, hand on the doorknob, listening for the banging upstairs. Had it stopped? She slipped off her shoes so she could run if she needed to. She could never tell about the attic. One minute it'd be all fine and dandy; the next minute creepy-crawlies would be running up and down her arms and she'd be hightailing it down the steps, spitting blasphemies and hexes over her shoulder. Well, half hexes. She didn't remember any whole ones. Halina was in no mood for any of that nonsense tonight. It was late and she was tired. The storm already had her nerves on edge. The whole house was rocking and wheezing and sighing. Damned wind. She took a deep breath and opened the attic door, holding the oil lamp high so she could see the stairs.

Whack. Whack.

The banging started in again, sounded like an elephant waltzing up there—a drunk one. It was probably a loose shutter, that's all. Or the dang raccoons were back, knocking over the jars and baskets, wasting what was left of the nightshade, bee balm, willow root . . .

She'd show them! She'd shoo them out this time. She grabbed a broom from the kitchen, carried the lamp in her other hand, then ran up the stairs, taking them two at a time. The stairway opened to a room as wide as the house, almost as deep. She stooped slightly, her head touching the dusty rafters, gray and chewed by age. She held up the lantern and looked around, listening. Nothing. No sign of any four-legged critters—except for some dried-up droppings, too big to be from a mouse—or rat.

To the left and right the ceiling sloped downward at sharp angles. In the corners, trash had collected over the years: old, dried leaves that had blown in from the window, crumpled newspapers, some empty cans, and stained rags. The makings of a cozy nest for some—

She stopped. Froze. *What the hell is this?*

Just beyond the pile of trash, a blanket was spread out on the floor, like a bed. The green, standard army-issue type of blanket was stretched out, neat and tidy. Was someone sleeping up here? Who the . . . ?

Halina's eyes adjusted and she looked closer, bowing lower to keep from hitting her head. She was right about the blanket. "US ARMY" was stenciled along the edge. Half of Hegewisch slept under that kind of blanket, all "borrowed" from a troop supply train that paused at the switching yard back during the Great War. Everyone knew Stach had appropriated them. No one minded much, except Father Chodniewicz. Halina and her sister, Patcja, had one as kids. The old thing was threadbare now, little more than a rag. This one in the attic seemed new, hardly used, as though it had been preserved in a vault all this time. Halina shook her head, and those heebie-jeebies started crawling up her arm. *This is just so freakishly weird.*

"I'm not running this time," she declared loudly, trying to sound emphatic and sure of herself. But she heard her own voice and the telltale squeak, as if she were still a child, naïve, superstitious and talking to ghosts named Lydia and Stella. Not to mention Baba's husband, buried in the roots of the peach tree. HolyMotherMary-andJoseph, I won't get tangled up again in God-knows-what kind of hullabaloo and high jinks. I won't. I swear." And she made the sign of the cross, in the name of—

Whack. Whack. Whack.

She jumped and yelped, then realized it was just the shutter on the window. The attic's single window looked out to the street, overlooking the front porch below. And one dadblasted shutter was loose, banging on the house, swinging on hinges all rusted, as old as sin. Rain pelted the window pane, hitting hard, making a roar. She crept closer to the window, and she could see a jagged crack in the glass, rain coming in, streaming down the wall, and forming a puddle on the floor.

Could she fix it, either the glass or the shutter? With the next gust, rain sprayed her face. The puddled water was cold on her bare toes. She cringed and ducked as the shutter flung toward her, as if it had a mind of its own and was throwing a conniption. "Oh, stop this, house. Be quiet," she mumbled. She looked around for something she could put across the window for tonight, and any more signs that someone had been up here.

The rickety, cluttered work table was to the left of the window; the shelves to the right. Nothing looked out of place; nothing new; nothing missing. When was the last time she was up here, though? She couldn't remember. Her brain was doing that hopscotch-jumping thing, nervous and fidgety, a cat scratching at a locked door afraid of being trapped. Forgotten. Alone.

Her imagination flared. She saw images, dipped in red and orange colors:

> *The knife wound in Joey's shoulder,*
> *red like the cellar explosion, like the bonfire ceremony*
> *on the night of the paschal moon.*
> *Then, in the orange glow of dawn,*

from the frayed hem of her dress, thread dangling,
unraveling, she pulls it, twists it,
tying two twigs into a cross, matchbox size, marking a
grave.

Halina wiped the rainwater out of her eyes with the palm of her hand, trying to get rid of the vision. She pulled up the hem of her dress and dried her face with it, smearing around the cold, the dread, and old pictures she had been trying to forget for nearly a decade. She gulped some air. Some more.

"I'm not running," she said. "I'm not."

Concentrate. Think. She remembered how she used to talk her sister through her asthma spells. She'd help her slow her breathing and open the clenched airways with words as her only medicine. Silly. But what else did she have?

She calmed herself down. Breathe. In. Out.

What should she do first? She couldn't allow these ingredients to get wet. Why waste them? Plus, hard to say what rainwater might do to some of these old powders, crumbled petals, and crushed roots. Some of the Mason jars and old bottles held powders back from Baba's days with the Romani, traveling in southern Poland, long before the war. Halina couldn't name all the roots now, let alone recall their uses. But she kept them, in case.

Thinking of the old woman made Halina's throat tighten up, a lump of regret growing. Why hadn't she written down more of Baba's lessons when she had a chance? Made notes when the lessons were fresh in her mind. Why didn't she take it seriously then? Why wasn't she more careful?

She had been a reluctant apprentice in those days, when the old woman tapped her to take over as the town's healer. She couldn't be expected to remember every root, every herb, and every flower petal, could she? So she had a few failed tries.

Looking over the shelves, now half empty, she felt emptiness well up in her, too, a hollowness that no medicine on these shelves could fix. Not even the hospital medicines could fix what she had done. No amount of scolding herself over her stupidity was going to do any good either.

Halina tugged at the necklace around her neck, patted it out of habit, looking for comfort. A small glass marble hung on a chain. Inside the glass was a seed, suspended in the orb.

The necklace, on a shelf in the kitchen, caught a bit of sunlight—and a little girl's attention.

"Baba, what in tarnation is that in there? A dead bug? A bird's brain? An eyeball from some disgusting creepy-crawling thing?" Halina asked as she wrinkled her nose and tried scooting the apple crate she was standing on so she could reach the counter. But her Mary Janes slid and she plopped on the linoleum floor.

The woman glared, her eyes throwing sparks from under the shield of her oversized babushka. She reached for the wooden spoon she had used all morning as she had stirred and stirred the foul-smelling concoction in the brass pot over the fire.

Halina winced and ducked instinctively, knowing that all Polish women consider a wooden spoon to be part cooking aid, part educational aid, part weapon against the dull and stupid. She felt rather dull and stupid this morning, realizing she was asking far too many questions, making the old woman snort and sigh like Major's old mare.

Baba didn't raise the spoon toward her, though. Instead, she held up a spoonful of soup from the pot, flecks and stems floating, seeds suspended in the thickness. The seeds looked like the one in the necklace.

"Mustard seed," said Baba, "which a man took and put in his own garden. It grew and became a large tree, and the birds of the sky lodged . . ."

"You want me to grow mustard in a garden?"

Baba shook her head, obviously disappointed. "Nie. Have faith! Foolish girl, have faith and it will grow like a weed."

The glass marble in her hand seemed warm. It must have

collected heat from her body, magnified it. Thinking of those old days brought out a warm feeling in her, too, one that seemed sweet on the surface, deceptively innocent. She was so young when Baba started filling her head with folk stories from the Old Country about healing herbs and natural ingredients, words that had sacred meanings, and curses that could make the living miserable and near dead.

Halina scoffed, irritated. That damned rain was still coming down. She still needed something to cover the window. She still needed to move these ingredients to somewhere safer, away from the rain. And she still had a blanket spread out in her attic as though someone was planning on sleeping here, in her house.

This was turning out to be one hell of a night. And she still had to change into her uniform and take the trolley to the hospital for her shift, which would start in about two hours—if she could stay awake. Being the night shift nurse wasn't easy, but it had its advantages. She needed to get moving.

She had an idea. Not seeing anything else to use, she gathered up the mysterious blanket and held it up over the broken window. She tucked the corners in around the window, jamming it in the gaps between the window frame and the two-by-fours framing the walls. It seemed to hold. It at least blocked the wind and kept the rain from spraying all over. Good enough for tonight.

Then she tugged on the table, trying to scoot it farther away from the window. Just a few inches should be enough. The bottles rattled, clanking against each other. *Oh crud.*

She saw a blue-green Mason jar wobble, start to topple. She reached for it. The jar was almost empty, holding only a half-smoked cigar, one end chewed. And—strangely—the other end looked lit. Smoke seemed to be coming from it as if the cigar had just been dropped in the jar, the lid sealed, minutes ago. Of course, that couldn't be true. But then again, this had been Baba's house. These were her supplies. Strange things had happened in those days when the bootleggers first arrived in town and the old woman was flinging curses left and right, crazy-like. Who could say?

Halina's hand wasn't fast enough; her arm not long enough. The jar tipped, rolled, fell from the table. It hit the floor and shattered, shards of glass flying. The crash was loud and shrill, more like a bird squawking than a jar breaking. Halina ducked, expecting a bird to fly at her, but only the cigar rolled across the floor and came to a stop at Halina's bare toes. The red ember glowed, swelling, as if someone had taken a big puff on the chewed end. Gray ashes grew. Smoke, alive, swirled in spirals, climbing to the attic ceiling, then slipped out.

That was enough. Time to go—*now*. Halina rushed down the attic stairs, forgetting the broom but carrying the lantern so she could see her way. With her free hand, she tried to swipe away the creepy-crawlies running up and down her arms and across her neck, down her back, but there was no getting rid of the feeling that trouble was coming. As she looked back over her shoulder, words came out of her mouth in a jumble, not a single thought making sense. Blasphemies, threats and hexes, Polish scripture, Latin Mass, confessions and vows . . . She mumbled until she was back in the kitchen. Safe.

And Baba had nothing else to say.